PRAISE FOR
BEFORE I WAKE

"Tragedies and supernatural miracles are expertly layered with ordinary domestic life. . . . *Before I Wake* is a classic thriller: creepy in all the right places and deliciously suspenseful. . . . He is a gifted storyteller who has graced the Canadian literary landscape with a unique, spellbinding and ultimately uplifting gem."
The Globe and Mail

"Robert Wiersema . . . has written an accomplished first novel, the sort of book veteran novelists might well envy."
National Post

"I wept over this book as I read it, and I'm still haunted by it. Wiersema's compassion for us all shines through in writing that is vivid and very often disturbingly powerful. He is a beautiful writer, and this is a beautiful book."
Gail Anderson-Dargatz, author of *The Cure for Death by Lightning*, *A Recipe for Bees* and *A Rhinestone Button*

"This is a wonder to behold. A deft fusion of intimate family story, suspense and religious exploration, *Before I Wake* is one of those books you just don't put down until you've read the last page. . . . The climax is a strange and wondrous moment, not quite believable. But then very little of this story is, and somehow that's not just acceptable, it's magnificent."
Edmonton Journal

"It's a daring book that falls into the can't-put-it-down category."
Times Colonist (Victoria)

BEFORE I WAKE

ROBERT J WIERSEMA

Vintage Canada

VINTAGE CANADA EDITION, 2007

Published in Canada by Vintage Canada, a division of Random House of
Canada Limited, Toronto, in 2007. Originally published in hardcover in
Canada by Random House Canada, a division of Random House of Canada
Limited, Toronto, in 2006. Distributed by Random House of Canada
Limited, Toronto.

Vintage Canada and colophon are registered trademarks of Random House of
Canada Limited.

www.randomhouse.ca

LIBRARY AND ARCHIVES CANADA CATALOGUING IN PUBLICATION

Wiersema, Robert J.
Before I wake / Robert J. Wiersema.

ISBN 978-0-679-31374-8

I. Title.
PS8645.I33B43 2007   C813'.6   C2006-907034-2

Book design by Kelly Hill

Printed and bound in Canada

6 8 9 7

For Cori
Such is the principle of magic,
drinking from the same cup

*Miracles are not contrary to nature,
but only contrary to what we know about nature.*
—*St. Augustine*

BEFORE I WAKE

I only looked away for a moment.

That one phrase haunts a parent when something tragic happens to their child. It echoes in the mind like an accusation. Or a curse.

"I only turned my back for a second, but somehow he managed to reach the handle of the frying pan . . ."

"I just went inside to answer the phone. I thought the gate to the pool was locked . . ."

It's a cry for understanding, a challenge to the universe. I hear the guilt, the recrimination, and I understand: *If only I had been paying attention . . .*

He wouldn't be burned.

She wouldn't have drowned.

I didn't look away.

We believe that vigilance can prevent tragedy, that if we pay attention, we will be strong enough, wise enough, fortunate enough to counter fate.

"If I had been watching . . ."

It's a lie.

It's a trick that the universe plays, a way of increasing the guilt and despair while seeming to explain it away.

I didn't look away. I wish I had.

Sometimes we can only watch, mute witnesses as our lives change in a moment, in a heartbeat, in the time it takes a three-year-old girl to take a single step from our side.

I let go of her hand.

I *didn't* look away.

And my baby is gone.

ONE

April 1996

"Jubilee, this is A32. We have two, repeat two, en route. Hit and run. ETA four minutes. Clear."

"Copy, A32. Please advise condition. Clear."

"Copy, Jubilee. Advise one adult female. Some bleeding. Shock. Holding stable. Clear."

"Copy, A32. Advise."

"Copy, Jubilee. Advise one female child, three years. Severe head trauma with decreased level of consciousness and spontaneous respirations. Severe bleeding from cranium. Clear."

"Copy, A32. Trauma One will meet you at the gate. Clear."

KAREN BARRETT

Sherry and I were walking to the mall, holding hands.

Hillside Shopping Centre is only a few blocks from the house, and every Wednesday morning in the food court clowns and jugglers and musicians perform for the kids. I had dressed Sherry in her little blue dress, the one with Winnie the Pooh on the front. She had chosen it herself: "my sky-blue dress, because it matches the sky." I zipped up the back carefully, so as not to catch any of her wispy hair between the metal teeth. I tickled her gently under the arms as I finished.

Was that the last time I heard her laugh?

Sherry loved the clowns, and the noise of all the other children packed into the food court was like a wall of pure joy. We usually had a snack, a muffin or some french fries, before we walked home, and by the time we got back it would be nap time for both of us.

It was a beautiful spring day. The sky was a clear, cold blue, but there was no chill to the air. In fact, the air was heavy with warmth and growth and green and flowers as we walked through our neighborhood. We stopped to pet familiar cats, to smell the lilacs just in flower, to pick up stones that weighed down my pockets.

I checked both ways before we stepped into the crosswalk on Hillside. I always do. The street is too wide to take any risks: three lanes in each direction with a concrete median, and the cars and buses just roar through. There's no light at the crosswalk, so I'm always careful to check. Better that we wait a few seconds than take any chances.

We waited for a station wagon to pass from the left and I saw a truck a good distance away on the right, but it was perfectly safe. I took her small hand in mine.

Perfectly safe.

We walked quickly. Six lanes is pretty far for a three-year-old, but we'd done it plenty of times.

We should have waited at the median.

The next time I looked up, the truck was right there, maybe 100 yards away. It was old and beat up, red with white fenders. And it was roaring toward us.

I felt her fingers slip from mine. Felt her moving.

"Sherry," I called as she skipped away. We were in the same lane as the truck, so all we had to do was get to the next lane. It wasn't far. No more than a couple of feet.

I should have picked her up. I don't know why I didn't pick her up.

She turned to look at me.

"Sherry!"

I watched her pudgy white legs scamper across the pavement, her little white shoes, her little blue dress.

Her sky-blue dress.

When I turned to check, I could almost see the face of the driver in the truck. He had shifted lanes to go wide around us, weaving into the next lane, the lane in front of us, the lane that Sherry had just quickstepped into. The roar of his engine blocked out all other noise.

I reached for her, my fingers just brushing her blond hair before the truck pulled her away from me.

I could hear, over the roar of the engine, the sound of her body hitting the bumper as the truck took her beyond my reach.

I could feel the wake of the truck as it sped past me, as I threw myself toward her. Tried to reach her.

There was a squealing of tires. A scream.

And the next thing I saw was the ceiling of a hospital emergency room.

"9-1-1 Operator. How should I direct your call?"

"I just killed a little girl . . ."

"Sir—"

"I swerved . . . I swerved around her . . ."

"Sir, where are you?"

"I'm at the Hillside Mall . . ."

"Where are you at Hillside Mall, sir?"

"I only looked away for a minute. I checked my mirror. I changed lanes. I swerved, but she . . ."

"Sir, where are you calling from?"

"I just killed a little girl . . ."

"Sir . . . Sir? Sir?"

SIMON BARRETT

10:53.

I checked the clock on my desk as the two City of Victoria police officers opened the door to my office. Sheila followed them closely, her face tight.

"Mr. Barrett?" asked one of the officers.

A lawyer doesn't usually get unannounced visits from uniformed police, but it does happen, especially when you're handling accidents and personal injury cases. I would have been more concerned had I been a stockbroker.

I rose from my chair. "How can I help you gentlemen?"

"I wanted to buzz you," Sheila started.

"That's fine, Sheila. Mary . . ."

She was sitting at my work table with the Anderson file.

"We'll finish this up later."

Mary rose to her feet, her eyes darting between the officers and myself. I shook my head slightly. She followed Sheila out the door.

10:54.

I came around from behind my desk and offered my hand to the officer nearest me. I have learned, from observation and experience, that one person's body position in relation to another is the key to determining seniority. The senior or more significant partner will usually stand just slightly forward from the other or the group. Perhaps just a half step, but enough to be noticeable. Enough to be significant.

The officer whose badge read "Clement" took my hand and shook it. Not much of a grip. His hand was cool and soft in mine.

"What can I help you with?" I asked again.

The officer glanced at his partner, whose badge I couldn't read. That glance unsettled me. If police officers are uncomfortable, it usually means that they are not in complete control of the situation. That lack of control makes the situation much more difficult to play.

"Mr. Simon Barrett? Of 2718 Shakespeare?" the second officer asked.

"Yes. What is it?"

"I'm sorry to tell you—"

"Yes?"

"Sir, there's been an accident . . ."

"Sherry? Is it Sherry?" I felt for the desk behind me and leaned my weight against it.

"Your wife and daughter were involved in an accident this morning near the Hillside Shopping Centre," Officer Clement continued. "If you'd like to gather your things we'll take you down to the hospital. We can explain in the car."

"Is there . . . ?" I fumbled for the words, but I pulled myself together. "I'll have Sheila cancel my appointments."

As I pressed the intercom button and instructed Sheila, the clock read 10:56. Grabbing only my jacket, I followed the officers through the reception area.

Mary was waiting just outside my office door. I didn't make eye contact with her as we passed.

In the shadow of a fast-food sign, the man in the black coat watched as the truck hit the child, as the mother fell away from the wheels. He watched, without moving, as cars squealed to a halt, as people rushed to crowd around the two fallen bodies. He didn't move as the mother screamed, as the sirens grew in intensity, as the crowd parted to allow the medics through to the victims. When they stood up from kneeling beside the girl, their knees were wet with her blood.

He clenched his Bible in one hand and worried a silver coin with the other. As the ambulance screamed away, lights flashing, the stranger turned and began walking toward the hospital.

KAREN

At first, I had no idea where I was.

Everything was white, too bright and out of focus. All I could hear was confusion, a blur of voices and echoes. When I tried to rub my eyes clear, my hand tugged and flashed with a sharp pain. An IV line disappeared into my wrist, held with tape that pinched my skin.

The emergency room. Sherry.

I was covered with a green sheet but still dressed. There was a tightness around my head that, when I touched it, felt like bandages. My vision was slow coming into focus.

Green curtains matching the sheet enclosed the bed. Simon was standing just across the steel rail.

"Simon?"

"The police came for me. At work."

"Sherry?"

I tried to struggle to a sitting position but found myself swooning, tangled in the IV tubing, in the green sheet.

"Don't sit up yet. Lie back." His voice was calm and deliberate, the way it gets when he's upset and trying not to show it.

"Where's Sherry?"

"The doctors just want to be sure . . . Are you okay? They said you struck your head when you fell."

His use of the word *struck*—so clinical, so precise. Distancing himself, trying not to worry me with whatever is worrying him.

"No. Not me. Sherry. There was a truck . . ."

He shook his head, and I realized that no part of him was touching me. I wanted him to reach out, to touch my hand, my face.

"There was a second car . . . The driver saw everything . . . She called the ambulance from her cell phone."

"Where's Sherry?"

He took a deep breath, and in the pause between my question and his answer I could feel tears forming in my eyes, burning.

SIMON

Our miracle . . .

That's what Karen has always called Sherry.

Our miracle.

Karen and I spent the first years of our life together struggling not to have children. It was a game for me to remind her to take her pill every evening as we went to bed, as if our continued happiness depended upon us remaining childless. I suppose it did.

We lived through some close calls. Missed pills, missed periods. Midnight talks about what we do if . . . The month in Thailand when we forgot the pills altogether.

Only after I was established with Bradford & Howe did we begin trying to have a child.

I guess we'd always wanted a family—children. It was just a matter of when. We both wanted to be ready, for everything to be perfect. Not when we were both students. Not when her job with the paper was barely putting me through law school and keeping us in tiny apartments.

It was almost a checklist: house bought, car paid for, trips to Europe and Southeast Asia and the Caribbean behind us.

Perfect conditions.

When we started trying, we thought it would just happen, that there would be no complications. Instead, we tried without success for three years.

Thirty-nine periods we didn't want.

Thirty-nine cycles of rising hopes and sudden disappointments, her blood haunting us, black in the blue toilet water.

We both went to the doctor. We were worried that we were getting too old, that our years of putting it off had cost us our only chance to be parents. He examined us, performed a battery of tests.

Nothing seemed to be physically wrong with either of us.

Karen took up yoga. We changed our diets. I gave up coffee and saturated fat. I started running again. We both started swimming.

And after three years of trying, it finally worked.

Karen collapsed midway through the seventh month, while covering a story for the paper. Ironically, the story was about a nursery school. The doctor ordered her to bed: high blood pressure and anemia. Continued activity posed a substantial risk to the growing fetus. Child.

Sherilyn was born thirty-three days premature, tiny enough to fit into my cupped hands.

She spent the first seventy-two hours of her life in an incubator. Our only contact was during feedings, or momentary caresses of her tiny, soft belly, her silky legs, through the access holes of the Plexiglas box.

Our miracle.

I pushed the memories away.

"She's in surgery. The doctor said that there was severe trauma to her head. There's internal bleeding." I stopped talking.

Karen seemed smaller than I had ever seen her, face blanched white, almost the same color as the gauze wound around her head. Her blond curls were matted with blood.

"Is she going to be okay?"

I leaned forward, wanting to touch and reassure her, but unsure of where it would be safe to do so.

"They don't know. They'll tell us as soon as they know anything. As soon as she's out of surgery."

Twin tears fell from her eyes, trickled into the green pillow on either side of her face. Her pupils were wide and black, leaving only a sliver of green around the rim.

My cell phone vibrated gently against my ribs. I knew that I wasn't supposed to use the phone in the hospital, but I couldn't turn it off. I couldn't be cut off. I stepped away from Karen's bed to answer it, checking my watch. 11:42.

"Barrett."

"Simon, it's me."

I held my hand up to Karen, turned through the green curtains and into the chaos of the emergency room itself.

"Mary, why are you—?"

"Is everything okay?"

I tucked myself into a pay-phone cubicle on the wall, my

back to the noise and the bustle, my voice dropping. "There's been an accident. Sherry was hit by a car."

"Oh God, Simon. Is she all right?"

"They don't know yet. She's still in surgery. Karen—Karen's hurt too. She's okay. She fell. Hit her head. She's okay."

"How are you holding up?"

I shrugged, then realized she couldn't see me. "I'm fine."

"I was worried."

For some reason, the idea surprised me. "Why?"

"It's not every day you get taken away by the police before lunch." She laughed a little, awkwardly. "When will you know more?"

I could feel my shoulders tighten as I realized that I had no idea, that things were completely out of my control. "I don't know. Sherry's still in surgery. We won't hear anything until after that. Even then it will probably be too early to tell."

"But she'll be all right, right?"

"I don't know."

"Are you okay?" Her voice was nearly a whisper.

"I'm okay."

"Let me know if I can do anything, okay? I'll be here, or on my cell."

"I know. Listen, work up Berkman and . . . check the records on Radinger, then call it a day. I'll contact you later."

"You can—"

A hand fell onto my shoulder, gripping it tightly. I jumped and turned in a single motion.

Karen had climbed out of bed, wheeled her IV stand into the emergency lobby and found me. She was still pale, but her cheeks were red from the exertion. She mouthed, "Who?"

"The office," I mouthed back. Then, into the phone, "No, nothing that won't keep."

"Is Karen there?" Mary asked.

"I'll be in later to check on things. I left my briefcase—"

"Will I see you? Will you call me?"

"Right. Later then. Thanks."

Karen was shaking her head. "Not a moment's peace. Not even now."

"They're all just worried. They saw me leaving with the police. Should you be up?"

"I'm fine," she said. "Who was it?"

"Sheila," I lied, taking her shoulder and guiding her to one of the orange plastic chairs.

MARY EDWARDS

Simon had been distant with me, but that wasn't anything new.

Sometimes I feel like I am the only one who really knows him. And sometimes he's a complete stranger. Like in court, when he cross-examines a witness or makes a summation, sometimes I don't even recognize him. The speech might be everything that we had talked about, everything that we had planned, but he'd make it fresh, like he was making it up as he went along. It was amazing how he could be a completely different person at different times.

Or at this past year's Christmas party, when Sheila brought me over to where they were standing and introduced me to his wife. It didn't even seem to faze him. "Oh, yes, this is Mary. She's been a big help to me. You two should get to know each other. You've got so much in common . . ."

I just about dropped my punch cup when he said that, as if we hadn't spent the afternoon in my apartment.

I moved stuff around on my desk. I opened up the Berkman and Radinger files. I told Sheila that Mr. Barrett had phoned to explain what was happening. She must have known that I was lying—all incoming phone calls go through her desk—but she didn't let on. I'm sure she knew about Simon and me, what had been going on for months.

I had noticed the way she had started to look at me. I'm sure she had seen it all before.

I'm not a home-wrecker or anything. I'm not one of those little twenty-year-olds that come to the Christmas party and are introduced as "My wife, Tiffany," all dressed up in Armani or Versace, when it's perfectly obvious that not so very long ago Tiffany was going to school with her current husband's daughter.

I wasn't interested in marrying him. Not really. I just liked what we had, those times when we were together, at work and alone.

I'm a lawyer. His junior, but he really listens to my opinions. Respects my thoughts. I like the way he looks at me, the way he nods and kind of smiles when I say something that he is not expecting. We respect one another. That is the main thing.

But just once I wanted to be able to watch him sleep. Our afternoons were too short, so cramped by the time and excuses for being out of the office that we had never had time to relax, to really let go.

Instead, I would watch him as he dressed, his tight butt and legs, his narrow chest with its light dusting of dark hair. And after he disappeared into the bathroom I would dress hurriedly, ensuring that my clothes were right, that my makeup was perfect by the time he returned.

I wanted to watch him sleep, watch his face as he drifted away, as the mask loosened and disappeared. To watch his face soften, just to see what it was really like, to see if I really knew him as well as I thought I did.

SIMON

I think time passes so slowly in hospital waiting rooms because there are so many ways to keep track of it. The rhythmic beeping of machinery, the patterns of security guards and orderlies with carts, the Muzak, the grating laugh tracks from the television mounted on the wall, the ongoing misery of the other people waiting. Time is an almost physical presence.

Nevertheless, I kept checking my watch until Karen put her hand over mine to stop me.

"Sorry."

Every time a doctor or nurse emerged from behind the desk we both half-rose, and every time we were disappointed.

Karen paced. She sat. She called her mother in Winnipeg. She paced more. She waved away the offers of more painkillers. She finally allowed a nurse to guide her back to the curtained bed just so that the IV could be removed from her arm.

I bought us each a cup of coffee from the vending machine near the nurses' station. The paper cups sat on the table in front of me, mine black, hers with a little cream. Piled alongside them were several packages of sugar.

"I thought we should try to keep your blood sugar up," I explained. "Not being on the IV anymore . . ."

She laid her hand on my thigh and squeezed it gently.

"Mr. and Mrs. Barrett?"

The doctor, a vague shadow in green scrubs, was reading from a metal clipboard. We both stood before he finished saying our names.

"How is she? Is she going to be all right?" Karen asked. "Will she be okay?"

I watched his face—his mouth and his eyes—as he spoke.

"Mr. and Mrs. Barrett, let's sit down." Karen grasped my hand as we sat back down, and he took the chair opposite us.

"I'm Dr. McKinley. I'm on call today." He didn't extend his hand. "I performed the surgery on your daughter."

"How is she?" I asked, watching.

"I wish I had better news for you . . ."

I took a deep breath. "Is she . . . ?"

The doctor shook his head. "We had to open her skull," he said. "There was a lot of bleeding. A lot of pressure that we had to let off. We managed to stop the bleeding and we removed some debris that could have caused some problems. The surgery went very well."

"Oh my God," Karen cried, tears streaming down her cheeks. "Oh my God."

"Then she's going to recover?" I asked.

"In situations like this there is quite often a lot of damage that we can't see, at least in these early stages." He took a deep breath. "I'm sorry. Your daughter is in a coma. It's too early to tell . . ."

We waited for anything that might sound like reassurance.

"It's important to remember that the coma is a resting state, a chance for the body to heal itself in the places that we can't get to. In cases like this, quite often the patient will spontaneously pull themselves out. That's the way we're treating this. Your daughter is having some problems breathing so we have her on a respirator, and right now it's just a matter of waiting."

Karen leaned toward me, whispering. I draped my arm around her.

"I'm sorry," the doctor said, leaning forward to hear better. "I didn't hear what you said."

"Sherry," I said. "She was telling you that our daughter's name is Sherry."

The doctor flinched. "I know."

"Our miracle," she whispered. I don't think the doctor heard.

HENRY DENTON

I didn't kill that little girl. She just floated away.

I turned away for a second, that's all. I saw her and her mother in the crosswalk, and I changed lanes to go around them. I checked my mirrors as I changed lanes, and when I looked back . . .

She rose up into the air.

She floated away.

I didn't stop. I couldn't stop. I just watched her as she floated away. I watched her mother scream, but I couldn't hear it over the Tragically Hip tape and the sound of the engine. She was reaching out for her child.

I cut back around the block and parked the truck in my usual slot by the air and I called 9-1-1 from the pay phone at the gas station. My hands shook as I punched in the numbers. I wanted to try to explain, but I couldn't find the words. As I hung up the phone I couldn't help myself—I threw up all over the wall of the phone booth, the concrete floor. I managed to miss my pant legs and shoes. I kept heaving until nothing else came out, until I could see these patches of light and dark with my eyes closed. My head felt like it was going to split open. I wanted to scream.

I kept seeing her, floating up, hanging in the sky just above me, watching me. Watching me.

I stumbled out of the phone booth, dropping my keys on the ground beside it. I felt like I was going to be sick again.

One of the day-shift guys called after me, but I heard him the way you sometimes imagine hearing your name in a crowd. I don't think I could have answered even if I had tried. Instead, I turned toward Hillside, stumbling across the intersection. I followed the walk lights wherever they guided me, and everything behind me fell away.

KAREN

On television, hospitals always seem so clean, so new, so carefully organized and arranged. Even on *ER* the chaos is rendered attractive. Television did nothing to prepare me for the reality of this place. Crumbling plaster, leaking ceilings, gray floors that didn't even look swept, let alone waxed. I was expecting nurses who would be able to tell us what was going on, to help us. Instead, they treated us like children, doling out information in careful measures. I was expecting technology, a glassed-in room where doctors would fight for Sherry's life as we stood outside the window looking on. Instead, we were able to stand by her bed in the critical ward, no barrier between us and her profound silence.

Her head was bandaged tightly, a tracery of pink along the edge of the dressing. Her blood. Tubes entered her nostrils and her mouth, taped down to the soft skin of her cheeks. They ran to the respirator at the side of the bed, its accordion bag rhythmically inhaling and exhaling, filling and shrinking, Sherry's chest rising, falling, rising, falling. An IV line ran into her arm, and under the covers she was catheterized, cloudy urine collecting in a bag at the edge of the bed.

But she was still my daughter. Still my Sherry, so tiny in the full-sized bed. So fragile that she needed all of these tubes, these adhesives, these machines to keep her together. I gently rubbed the inside of her left arm, the only place I could, telling her that she would be okay, that Mommy and Daddy were here, that everything was going to be all right.

At the beginning we had spent so much time in the hospital with our Sherry. The first few weeks of her life we spent huddled around the incubator, our arms around each other, our faces pressed to the clear plastic. Those days brought us closer than we had ever been before. Parents. Together.

And now another hospital. Another bed.

Simon stood perfectly straight, fingers tight around the cold steel rail. The set of his jaw, the tightness of his shoulders, frightened me.

I lightly touched the back of his hand. "It's gonna be okay," I whispered, willing him to turn toward me. "She's gonna be all right."

He slowly faced me. "I know," he said, after too long a pause.

"She is," I urged him. I could feel the heat of tears on my cheeks. "She really is."

He rubbed away the tears on my face with his thumb, nodding in agreement.

"She seems so small, lying there." My words were too loud in the small room.

Simon took a deep breath and checked his watch. "I have to go into the office for a couple of hours. I need to clear some stuff from my calendar, move some stuff around."

"Really? Can't you—?"

He continued to speak, directing his words to the air above Sherry's head. "If you need me, call me on my cell. I won't be long."

I wanted to argue with him, to tell him how much we needed him here, how much *I* needed him here, but I just stared at him.

"I can clear my schedule for tomorrow. That way I don't have to worry about it."

I pulled him close. "Don't be too long," I whispered into the wool of his jacket.

His hand came up to cradle the back of my head. "I won't be. A few hours." He kissed me fleetingly on the forehead. "I'll be back soon."

He looked at me from the doorway, and I could see the worry stretching his face, but he was already reaching for his cell phone.

Already gone.

MARY

I went to him the instant he came through the door. I had been sitting on the couch with a Diet Coke, pretending to read A. S. Byatt. He had called me from the hospital to let me know that he was on his way to my place, that his daughter was in a coma.

He looked terrible. His skin was gray, his hair unkempt, his tie askew.

"Are you okay?" I asked.

His eyes met mine before he could answer, and his expression seemed to break open. "Oh God, Mary," he said. "Oh God."

I gathered him into my arms. I could feel his back start to shake as I stroked it.

"She's so small. Oh God, Mary, she's so small. And all the tubes, there are all these tubes—"

"Shh," I soothed. "Shh." He buried his face in my shoulder and I could feel the heat of his tears through my shirt.

I let him cry. I held him until he went silent; his life, his pain, filling my arms almost to bursting. Then I asked, "Do you want to go anywhere?"

"What?" He raised his red eyes to mine. "No."

"I thought—it's a beautiful day. Maybe a walk would help clear your head." I knew it wasn't going to happen, but I wanted to offer. We never take walks. It's one of the rules of being the other woman—the wife has custody of public spaces—but I felt like he might need the fresh air and shouldn't be on his own.

"No . . ." He shook his head, looking away. "I have to go back to the hospital soon. I think I'd like to just stay here."

I nodded. "Of course."

Our eyes met. Without warning, he pressed his mouth to mine. His lips were cold, hard, his breath a hot rush.

"I'm sorry," he muttered as he was kissing me, his voice cracking again. "I need . . ." His arms tightened around me, drawing me into him. "I need . . ."

"It's okay," I said. "It's okay."

I wanted to blanket the pain he had brought with him from the hospital.

He pulled my clothes off as we stood in my living room. He popped a button from my shirt, and looked down at it for a long moment, as if shocked that such a thing could happen. That something so small could be broken so easily.

After I was naked, he undressed himself quickly, his eyes never leaving me. He pushed the coffee table to one side and pulled me down onto the couch. He made love to me desperately, as if trying to hide within me. He controlled everything, his hands on my hips setting the rhythm, his mouth at my breasts, my lips.

After he came, he didn't release me like he usually did. Instead, he pulled me closer, laying his head against my breasts.

I could feel the rough tug of his whiskery face, and the heat of his tears, as he softened within me.

SIMON

I hated myself for being there, for being so weak I had to run to her. Hated myself for lying there, watching Mary as she stood up, her high, small breasts, the dark, narrow line of her sex.

I tried to rise, but she touched me gently on the chest with the palm of her hand, pressing me backward with an even pressure. "No, you stay here."

"I have to—"

"You can sit for a minute. There's time." The tone of her voice brooked no argument, but it wasn't her court voice. It was smoother, warmer, like honey in tea.

I glanced at my watch. 6:42. There was still time to stay, to sit. I had left the hospital at 5:32, caught a cab from the emergency room door, arrived here at . . .

MARY

What was that expression? That little lift in his lips as he slept.

Was it satisfaction? Relief? Comfort?

Comfort . . .

Could I really settle for comfort? Probably not. But for now, I'd settle for the thought that I could help take his pain away for a little while.

I curled myself into the sofa between him and the picture of my parents on the end table. He slept with one arm at his side, palm up, the other hand draped across his belly, rising and falling gently as he breathed.

His sandy hair was just beginning to hint at gray. I knew that he would comb it fastidiously before he left—he always did, no matter the weather, no matter if he'd have to comb it again once he got to wherever he was going. He never went out in public unless he was absolutely perfect.

If he were younger it would have annoyed the shit out of me. "The great tragedy of middle age," my best friend Brian had once said about the carefully coiffed men who were always trying to pick him up, "is watching these guys trying so desperately to hold on to a youthful beauty they only imagine they had."

But Simon was beautiful. He hadn't let himself go. His belly was flat, his chest tight, his face barely touched by wrinkles at the corners of his mouth and eyes.

I liked that he wasn't young. He was old enough to be sure of himself, to be confident, to be powerful. He could change the mood of a room with a single glance, a curled lip or a doubting lift of his eyebrow. His stare could make you feel like you were on trial, or that you were the most adored person in the world.

I should wake him up and send him back to his daughter. He shouldn't be gone too long.

I pulled the quilt up over my shoulders. Leaning my head back against the cushions, I watched him sleep, the flickering of his eyelashes, the tiny tremors within. I'd let him sleep just a little longer.

Locking the door behind him, the stranger turned the hot-water faucet as far as it would go. Steam began to fill the small bathroom, and the rushing water drowned out the sounds of the emergency room next door. The stranger slipped out of his coat, hanging it on the hook on the back of the door with his satchel.

Plunging his hands into the scalding water, he began to scrub the dirt of the road from his nails, from the creases of his knuckles. He couldn't remember the last time he had been properly clean. The dirt of a continent stained the water brown.

With red and swollen hands, he set his wire-framed glasses on the back of the toilet tank before dunking his head into the steam. He splashed handfuls of water over his face and his closely shorn head. It burned, but he scrubbed at his cheeks, rubbed at his skin until it squeaked.

Shaking his hands, he tore off a strip of paper towel and dried his face and head.

From the hanging satchel, the stranger withdrew the cool, stiff white circle of a collar, which he laid on the back of the toilet, next to his glasses.

It took him a moment to button the top of his black shirt, closing the fabric over the scarred loop of russet, twisted flesh around his throat.

The careful placement of the collar hid the evidence of his shame.

If they could see him now, he thought, all those who had come to him so willingly—who would come again, he knew—would turn away, repulsed by the sudden realization of his transgressions. But when they saw his collar, they saw their own chance at redemption, the promise of the glory, the rightness of the path. Who better to show them the way than a man of God?

KAREN

The steady rhythm of the respirator was lulling, its cool, measured pace encouraging sleep. But it was impossible to ignore the reason for that rhythm, the ebb and flow my daughter's breath. It was impossible to close my eyes knowing that.

The doctor had come in on his rounds about half an hour after Simon had left. If he was surprised that my husband was gone, he didn't show it.

"How are you holding up, Mrs. Barrett?" he asked. I was relieved to see he didn't have to check the file for my name.

"You can call me Karen," I said, as if this were the most normal situation in the world, just a couple of people getting to know one another while a machine breathed for my daughter.

"Karen, then. Are you doing all right?"

"I'm fine."

"Have you had something to eat? You're recuperating too."

My fingers strayed to the bandage on my head.

"I'll get them to bring you a dinner," he said, making a note in the file. "And later on I'll see to it that they wheel in a cot. These chairs are a pretty uncomfortable way to spend the night."

"Thank you." I was on the verge of tears again.

He waved it away. "It's too bad this room isn't a little bigger. There's only enough room for one cot, so someone's going to have to spend the night in the chair." He winked at me. "You'll have to draw straws."

I tried to smile.

"So how's our other patient?" He leaned over the rail, taking Sherry's narrow wrist between his thumb and forefinger, timing her pulse with his wristwatch. Untucking the stethoscope from his pocket, he gently folded back the bedclothes and raised the gown she was wearing.

I stepped back a little, tasting bile. Her body seemed to be a mess of bruises, mottled black and purple, bandaged in places.

He noticed me staring. "It's not as bad as it looks. Just bruises, from the impact of the truck and from the fall."

I nodded.

"We've bandaged up the worst of the contusions. They'll clear up pretty quickly. Nothing to worry about there . . ." He snapped the stethoscope in his ears and leaned over her, placing the cold metal disc just under Sherry's left nipple. He stared out into the middle distance as he listened, moved the stethoscope and stared into the distance again.

He nodded slowly as he straightened up, lowering Sherry's gown and tucking her back in.

Then he carefully lifted her eyelid with his thumb, moving the forefinger of his other hand slowly across her line of vision before taking a small light from his pocket and following the path of his finger with it.

He slid the light back into his pocket and made his notations in her file before he spoke. "Well, all of her vital signs are stable. Her heartbeat is a little slow and her temperature is a bit high, but that's to be expected."

"Will she . . ." The words were out of my mouth before I realized it, and I wished immediately that I could take them back.

"Will she be all right?" he asked.

I nodded.

He took the briefest of moments before he spoke.

"It's still too early to say, one way or another. We just don't know." He shrugged. "But we are going to do everything in our power to ensure Sherilyn's full recovery. Everything we can do."

I smiled wanly at him.

"Okay?"

I nodded. "Okay."

"Good. Now I'm going to get you some dinner and we'll see to it that you get a cot in here." He turned toward the door but then stopped. "I want you to take care of yourself, okay?"

I nodded again.

File of Barrett, Sherilyn Amber
4/24 18:25
Notes: bp 90/60, P 54. Pupils sluggishly reactive.
Glasgow Coma Scale 6. Low grade fever. Bibasilar
rales and increasing oxygen requirements. Possible early ventilator associated pneumonia. Start
ceftriaxone and gatifloxacin now.

S. McKinley

KAREN

I pulled the chair to the foot of Sherry's bed and angled it so that I would be able to see when Simon returned. I looked up every time someone passed the open doorway. Nurses would stop and glance in, ask me if I wanted anything. An orderly brought dinner, covered with a plastic lid, and left it on the table without a word.

I waited for my husband, listening to the machine breathe for my daughter.

"Mrs. Barrett?" The man in the doorway was a dark shadow against the bright lights from the corridor.

"Yes?"

He took several steps into the room, a tall stranger in a black coat, clutching a battered brown book to his chest. The light from above Sherry's bed reflected off the smoothness of his head, from the wire rims of his glasses and from the white of his clerical collar.

"Mrs. Barrett, I'm—"

"No." I shook my head. "No. We don't need you here."

He let the hand holding his Bible fall to his side. "Mrs. Barrett—"

"I'm no longer in the Church," I said.

He nodded. "I understand. But faith can be a comfort and a source of guidance in these times."

I shook my head. "Did my mother call you? Did she?" Calling a priest to come to the hospital was exactly the sort of thing my mother would do.

"No, I was making my rounds."

"Please . . . I don't need you. We don't need you."

He nodded as if he had heard that response before. "There's a chapel here, if you change your mind."

He stood there for a long moment, staring at me as if waiting for me to speak.

I turned my attention wholly to Sherry. Eventually I heard his footsteps receding down the corridor.

The Church. That was the last thing I needed.

"Karen?"

I glanced up again, barely recognizing the woman who stood there.

"Jamie?"

When she threw her arms around me and hugged me, I tried to remember how long it had been since I'd last seen her.

"How is she?" she whispered.

"I don't . . . The doctors don't know. They say she could wake up at any time."

"Oh, Karen." She kept an arm around me as I turned back to the bed.

We both looked down at Sherry as her chest rose and fell, rose and fell.

"It's been a long time, Jamie," I said.

"Couple of years."

"I sort of dropped off the map."

"You had a new baby. It was natural to want to stay at home."

"Is that really how long it's been?"

She nodded. "I think the last time we really spent any time was at the baby shower."

Jamie had been my closest friend at the paper, my only confidante. "I'm sorry."

"It was as much my fault as anything," she said, gently squeezing my shoulder. "Water under the bridge."

"How did you hear about Sherry?"

"Someone at City picked up the 9-1-1 call on their scanner this morning. Did all the usual follow-up, and when it came back that Karen Barrett had been involved . . . Everybody's hearts are with you, Kar."

"Thanks."

"Are you okay?"

My hand went to the bandage. "Bumps and bruises. Nothing that won't heal."

"And Simon?"

"What?"

"Is Simon around?"

"Oh, he'll be back. He had to go in to the office, clear his calendar."

"How's he taking it?"

"Well, you know Simon."

She didn't. Not really.

"Can I get you anything?"

I tried to smile. "No, I'm okay. But thanks."

"No big deal."

"No, I mean, thanks for coming. You didn't have to."

"Aw, hon, I got here as soon as I could."

SIMON

The cabbie took the corner sharply onto the Johnson Street Bridge, changing lanes and cutting off an Audi next to us.

Mary had awakened me with a kiss to my temple. So beautiful, the sight of her face as I opened my eyes. I was naked under an old comforter that had probably been on her bed as a teenager, that had accompanied her to university, to law school and now into her apartment overlooking the Inner Harbour. Her apartment.

I jerked up. "I have to . . . How long have I been asleep?"

She glanced over at the clock on the VCR. "An hour or so."

"Shit." I dumped the comforter onto the floor as I stood. "Why did you—?"

"I thought you could use the sleep," she said. "I'm sorry."

I shook my head. "No, it's my fault. I should have known better. I shouldn't have—" The look on her face stopped me from finishing the sentence.

The cabbie leaned on the horn, cursing under his breath at a cyclist who dared to ride in the same lane.

"Hey," I said. "You want to ease off a bit, maybe get me to the hospital alive?"

He responded with a grumble, turning up the radio.

The taxi slammed to a stop at a light on lower Johnson Street, throwing me forward. Glancing up, I made eye contact with the cabbie in the rearview mirror.

Mary had wanted to drive me to the hospital, but I had shaken my head.

"You're right, that'd be stupid," she said.

"No, it's not that. I think I just need a little time to myself."

"Okay. Just call me when you can, all right?"

I nodded. "Oh, and listen . . ."

I guess she heard the work tone in my voice, because she interrupted me, smiling, to say, "Sheila cleared your calendar for the next couple of days. Tom's going to argue for a postponement on Kitteridge. Bob Arnold was a little pissed, but everyone understands." She shrugged. "Won't be a problem."

As soon as the light changed, the cab squealed into motion, slamming into the right turn lane, passing the sedan we had been behind, jerking back in front of it. I lurched from side to side. "Jesus Christ," I muttered, my voice rising as I found my balance. "What the hell are you doing?"

"You wanna shut up, pal, or should I drop you off right here?" He half-turned in his seat to face me.

"Just watch your driving."

He pulled over to the curb and hit the brakes, jarring to a halt in a cloud of natural-gas exhaust.

"You wanna get the fuck—" He started as he turned to face me again. I lunged forward and punched him in the nose. There was a popping noise as the cartilage shattered and blood poured onto his shirt front in a gush.

"What the fuck?" he sputtered, frantically holding his nose, spraying blood with every breath. "I'm gonna call a cop."

"Go ahead, Mr."—I glanced at the license for his name—"Fredericks. Go ahead. You can explain your driving, your recklessness. They'll probably take your license. Go ahead." I opened the door and extended one leg to step out.

"I'm gonna call my lawyer," he called after me.

Leaning in, I dropped a five-dollar bill on his seat along with one of my business cards. "Please do."

I slammed the door behind me.

So I was walking to the hospital, where my daughter lay dying.

Make no mistake—I knew what was going on. I knew how much the doctor was leaving out. "She could wake up any-time . . . it's too early to tell . . ."

Downtown was deserted except for the prostitutes, the street kids with their dogs and drums, the drug dealers and the junkies. The prostitutes stood brazenly at the curbsides in miniskirts and tank tops, or trench coats that flashed the nakedness underneath. I was subject to close study as I walked past, avoiding eye contact.

The doctor hadn't come out and said that Sherry was dying, that she would never wake up, that the damage was too great and there was nothing anyone could do. But I knew. For Karen's sake, I was grateful for the dissembling. It gave her the time she needed, a chance to adjust, to accept, to say good-bye in her own way.

Good-bye.

Oh Christ, what sort of a world . . . what sort of a person . . .

No.

I choked back the rage I felt building, and the tears. I'd had my time for weakness. I still couldn't believe that I had run to Mary, leaving Sherry in that bed, leaving Karen hurt—and hurting. That was enough self-pity and weakness for one night.

The walk to the hospital passed in a blur. I steeled myself before walking through the emergency-room doors, checking my watch. 9:20. I prayed that Karen wouldn't be too angry. That she wouldn't ask too many questions.

She was where I had left her all those hours before, leaning over the bed in a pool of harsh yellow light. She looked up as she heard me come into the room.

"Jamie was here," she said.

"Jamie?"

"From the paper? You remember."

"Of course."

"Where have you been?"

I set my briefcase on the floor beside the bed. "At the office." I leaned over the bed rail. "How is she?"

"I tried calling."

"You know how hard it is to get a call through once the switchboard closes. Did you try my cell?"

"I needed you." She was biting her lip, and I could see that she had been crying.

"I know. I'm here now."

"Did you get everything done that you needed to?"

"I think so. I might have to go in for a bit tomorrow, but it should be all right." Such a bastard.

She nodded. I slipped my arm around her back, shifting as she snuggled into me. "How is she?"

"The doctor came in just after you left, checked her, said that everything was stable. They'll do some more tests in the morning. Have you had anything to eat?" She gestured at an untouched hospital tray.

Mary had made me a couple of slices of toast and a poached egg. The smell of the hospital room was making the food congeal in my belly. "I'm fine."

"They'll be bringing a cot up soon, so one of us can sleep here. I don't want to go home tonight. I don't want to leave."

"Of course not."

"One of us has to sleep in the chair, though." She gestured at the molded plastic furniture and grimaced.

"I'll take the chair."

"No, you take the cot. I probably won't sleep anyway."

In the end, neither of us slept. The cot stayed folded up where the orderly left it. We stood at the bedside all night, not speaking, watching our daughter dying before our eyes, though only one of us knew it.

HENRY

I walked downtown from Hillside Centre, through James Bay, then along the water and back into downtown. I needed to keep moving. I kept checking behind me, half-expecting the police or the mother of that little girl to be following me, but no one seemed to notice me. There was no eye contact with anyone, no strange looks.

But everywhere I went I could feel her with me. I could feel the little girl I had hit in the crosswalk hovering over me. I could almost see her.

It felt like I was drifting, but I wasn't surprised when I found myself outside the hospital. It was where I had been heading all along, without even realizing it.

The little girl's mother was sitting in the waiting room, a bandage around her head. A man sat on the vinyl bench next to her. They each held a coffee cup, and they both looked up when I came into the waiting room. I took a step back, but she had no way of recognizing me.

They both turned away. I was completely alone, a ghost, a spirit haunting their lives.

A doctor brushed past me, and the two of them stood up as he came over to them.

I didn't hear too much of what he said. Coma. Accident. Their names.

Simon. Karen. Sherry.

Sherry was the little girl's name.

It was late in the afternoon before I even thought of Arlene and the kids. Would the police have come to the apartment looking for me? Arlene must be worried sick. For a moment I thought about going home, or at least calling to let them know I was all right.

But I didn't.

I wasn't.

Victoria New Sentinel
Thursday, April 25, 1996
Hit-and-Run
Girl, 3, comatose following accident
Police Seek Driver
~ City Desk ~

The family of three-year-old Sherilyn Barrett
waited anxiously last night for a change in their
daughter's condition following a hit-and-run accident on Hillside Avenue yesterday morning. The
girl has been in a coma since being struck by a
vehicle while crossing at a marked crosswalk
near Hillside Centre with her mother, Karen
Barrett.

"It's really too early to tell," said a hospital
spokesperson yesterday afternoon. "We're optimistic."

Police are requesting that anyone who may
have seen the accident please contact their local
detachment to assist in the investigation. Police
are also seeking Henry Denton, 24, for questioning.

KAREN

"Can I take a look at that file?" Simon asked, gesturing to the
folder that Dr. McKinley was holding loosely at his side. The
doctor was looking freshly pressed in clean greens. It seemed
we were his first stop of the morning.

He hesitated just a beat before handing it over. "Let me
know if there's anything in there you can't read, or would like
me to explain."

"Simon does a lot of personal injury work," I explained.
"He's good with charts."

The doctor glanced at me, then busied himself checking
Sherry's breathing.

Simon rustled through the pages, taking it all in, nodding fractionally as he moved from point to point.

"What do you think?" I asked, lowering my voice as if the doctor couldn't or shouldn't hear us.

"Just what he said. Too early to tell." He closed the file.

The doctor looked up from where he leaned over the bed, listening through his stethoscope. He held up one finger, holding our attention and our silence for the few seconds it took him to finish. Then he folded the stethoscope and tucked it into a pocket.

"I'm a little concerned with Sherilyn's lungs," he said.

A new sense of dread took hold.

"Her breathing seems a little . . . moist. I'm worried that she might be at risk for pneumonia."

Simon and the doctor exchanged a look.

"What's going on?" I asked. "What aren't you telling us?"

"It's the pneumonia we're most concerned with right now. If she gets it . . . there's really nothing we can do."

I started to speak, but he held out his hand to stop me. "I'm increasing her antibiotics. We'll do everything we can to stave it off, but while she's on the respirator she's at risk for opportunistic infection."

"Then take her off the respirator."

I could feel Simon's hand at the small of my back. That frightened me more than the doctor.

"We can't," Dr. McKinley replied.

"What? Why not?"

"They can't," Simon said. "They think—"

I turned my head away.

The doctor started to speak, but Simon cut him off with his courtroom voice. "The trouble with the respirator is that with all the bacteria and viruses in the environment, what happens is that the patient is more susceptible. If she catches pneumonia . . ." He shook his head.

I took a step backward. "Why are you saying this?"

"But they can't take her off the respirator because she can't breathe on her own," Simon finished, so logically.

"Is that true?" I asked the doctor, ignoring Simon altogether. He hesitated a moment, then nodded.

"So what do we do?" I asked the room, Simon, the doctor, Sherry. "What do we do?"

"We just have to wait and see," the doctor answered.

SIMON

After the doctor left, Karen turned on me.

"How can you be so calm? How can you be so cold? Sherry is dying. Don't you care?" She was shaking with anger.

"Of course I care," I said. But somebody needed to be strong, to be able to think things through. I didn't say that. I couldn't.

"You don't. You don't care at all!"

"Karen—"

"Get out," she said. "Get the hell out of here."

She didn't mean it. I was sure she didn't mean it.

"Get out!" she shouted.

I picked my briefcase up and turned toward the door. "I'm going to go home and get us both a change of clothes, okay? I'll be back in a little while. Is there anything else I can bring you?"

"You're going?" She called after me. "How can you just leave? How can you just leave us again?"

I could hear her sobbing as the elevator doors closed.

KAREN

"Are you okay?"

I jumped. I hadn't seen the doctor come in.

"What?"

"I saw your husband leaving and I just wanted to check . . ."

I nodded. "I'm okay."

"Listen."

I turned to face him. I was amazed at the depth of concern on his face.

"Why don't we sit down," he said

Using just the slightest pressure on my upper arm he guided me to a plastic chair and sat next to me.

"I'm sorry about your husband," he said

I found myself shaking my head defensively, not entirely sure why. "That's just . . . Simon's got a different way . . ."

"No, it's not that. You shouldn't have had to find out . . ."

"Find out?"

"Karen," he stumbled a little on my name. "I would have given it more time." He sighed.

"What do you mean?"

"There have been some developments."

"Developments?"

"I didn't have a chance to update Sherilyn's file before your husband read it. Your daughter's already started to exhibit the symptoms of pneumonia. We upped the antibiotics last night . . ."

"Then?"

I will not cry I will not cry I will not cry I will not cry . . .

"Listen, Karen, we're going to take her for some tests this morning. CAT scans, MRI, neurological responsiveness, that sort of thing. We're gonna be gone for a few hours. Why don't you go home, get something to eat, try to get a little sleep. I know that you . . . that neither of you got any sleep last night."

More than anything the doctor recommended, I needed to talk to Simon.

SIMON

It was strange: coming home didn't feel like coming home. Something was wrong. Different. The house itself was unchanged, almost everything the way it had been when I left for work the day before. There was a small pile of laundry in the middle of the living room, a basket of unmatched socks and underwear in front of the couch, a half-empty cup of coffee on the side table. A pair of Sherry's shoes next to the laundry basket.

Karen had done the breakfast dishes. The cloth hung sloppily over the neck of the faucet. A pool of water edged a chicken she had left to thaw on the counter. I picked it up and threw it into the garbage under the sink, washing my hands in hot water after, straightening the cloth over the faucet.

The bathroom light was still on upstairs, a towel in a wet ball in the corner. I turned off the light.

Sherry's door was open, her floor littered with stuffed animals and brightly colored toys, a little undershirt on the unmade bed, another pair of shoes on the blue carpet nearby.

It was only as I set my briefcase down on the floor of our bedroom that I realized what I had been feeling since coming through the front door. This wasn't home anymore.

This house was where I lived, where my family lived. This was where we had brought Sherry from the hospital, where we had planned and laughed and fought and cried and made love, struggling to conceive. This bed, these clothes, the office just off the bedroom, all of this was mine, ours. Or had been.

My life had changed in a moment, a dividing line between before and after. The house was before: unfamiliar to me now in its strange silence, like a garment belonging to someone else. Fundamentally alien despite its near-perfect fit.

Leaning over the bed, I pressed the Play button on the answering machine to stop the red light flashing.

"Karen honey, it's Mom. I just got your message . . .
oh my . . . it's 1:30, Wednesday afternoon. I'm calling the airline right now. I'll call you right back . . .
I love you both . . . I'm praying for you."

"Karen, it's Jamie . . . from the paper. Todd just
pulled something in on the scanner . . . is everything . . . listen, I'll try later . . . I hope . . . I'll see you
soon."

"Mr. or Mrs. Barrett, it's Kent Lutz calling from
CFAX Radio, Victoria's News Authority. I was wondering if I could speak to either of you, or both of
you, about what happened this morning. You can
reach me at . . ."

"Karen, it's Todd Herbert from the *Sentinel*. I really
hate to be calling at a time like this . . ."

"Karen, it's Mom. I hope everything is okay . . . the
earliest flight I can get is Friday morning . . . I'll be
flying Air Canada . . . I'll take a cab from the airport
into town. Call me, honey. I'm praying for you all."

"It's Tonya Hopper calling from CHEK-TV. I was
hoping I could have a word . . ."

"Simon, Karen, it's Sheila from the office. I just
wanted to let you know how terrible everyone is
feeling. We're all praying for you . . ."

"Oh my God, Karen, I just saw the paper. Is Sherry
gonna be okay? Are you okay? Should I . . . I'll . . . I'll
call you back . . ."

SIMON

I sat on the edge of the bed, listening to voices I didn't know, or couldn't remember. I couldn't move. Literally could not even shift my weight. Paralyzed.

The telephone rang, but the sudden noise didn't startle me. I could easily have picked it up; I didn't.

Looking at myself in the mirror on the closet door I noticed the awkwardness of the position I was sitting in, weight shifted to one side, one leg balancing the body, a teetering support that could, at any moment, fall away.

The telephone rang.

I felt suspended, outside of time, separated from everything I loved, everything I had worked so hard for, as if within a plastic bubble.

Untouchable.

On the fourth ring my voice clicked in, distorted by the answering-machine tape. "You've reached the Barretts. Please leave a message . . ." My voice was cut off by a beep, and suddenly Karen was in the room with me.

"Simon? Simon? Are you there?" In the lengthy pause that followed I watched the red recording light on the face of the machine. "I thought you were going home . . ."

The connection broke with a click, followed by a shrill beep as the machine reset itself.

The room was now vibrant with Karen's presence. I could see her dressing, curled in sleep around a pillow, nursing Sherry in the chair by the window. Everywhere I looked I saw my wife, and everywhere I saw her, she was smiling.

My cell phone vibrated against me. I answered it before the second ring. "Simon Barrett."

"It's me."

"Hey."

"I tried you at home."

"I'm almost there. Just turning onto Shakespeare now."

"I spoke to the doctor. We need to talk."

I found myself nodding. "Okay, I'll come—"

"No. Could we meet somewhere? I should probably eat something."

"Anywhere you have in mind?"

"Maybe John's Place?"

"Fifteen minutes?"

"I'll see you there."

The silence that followed was a pale shadow of our early days together, when neither of us could figure out how we wanted any given telephone conversation to go, or how it should end.

"I love you," she finally said.

"I love you too. I'll see you soon."

Karen clicked off.

After I locked the front door behind me, I lingered on the front step for a moment before walking to the minivan. It seemed bewildering that the air was heavy with spring blossoms.

Karen was seated at a table in the window by the time I got to John's Place. I waved to her as I opened the door, but she stared down into the dark depths of her coffee cup. She looked broken. I'm used to that look on people. I see it all the time in clients, the red eyes, the shaking hands, the pale skin. People weak from fighting battles they were unable to win on their own. It was shocking to see it on Karen. Her blond hair so dull, the pallor eating away her usual vividness.

"I'm here with someone," I said to the waiter as I moved around the few people lined up for tables to slip into the chair across from Karen.

She looked up.

"It took a little longer than I thought," I found myself explaining to her, unable to just sit in the silence. "I checked the answering machine." I pulled the folded piece of paper from my pocket. "Mostly newspapers, TV, radio. Jamie called. Your mom called a couple of times."

Her face brightened slightly.

"She can't get a flight out until tomorrow."

"Damn."

"My mother called us back too."

"You still need to call your dad, though."

I didn't say anything.

"Before he reads about it in the newspaper."

"He doesn't read the paper."

"Still, he is her grandfather. Even if they've never met."

I reached across the table and laid my hand over hers, trying to change the subject. "How are you holding up?"

"I talked to Dr. McKinley after you left. That's what I want to talk to you about."

I gently squeezed her hand. "Karen . . ." I waited until she met my eyes. "How are *you* doing?"

She pulled her hand away.

"Fine, fine," she said. "I need a shower, and some food, and some sleep—"

The waiter materialized next to us. "Have you had a chance to look at the menu?"

I hadn't even noticed it lying on the place mat in front of me. I gestured toward Karen.

"Just toast, I think. Brown."

She seemed drained, weakened.

"I'll have the same. And a coffee."

He scooped the menus up and disappeared back into the kitchen.

Karen sighed heavily, took a sip of her coffee. "I talked to Dr. McKinley after you . . . after."

I nodded.

"He said . . ."

Both of her hands were wrapped tightly around her coffee cup where I couldn't reach them.

"He, uh, they . . ." She sniffed and ran the back of one hand over her nose. "They're taking her in for some tests. Scans. They—"

"MRI?" I asked.

"I think so."

"Another one."

"What?" She asked, confused.

"They took her for one yesterday. Before the surgery. If they're taking her in for another one . . ."

We both stopped as the waiter arrived with my coffee, setting the cup heavily on the scarred tabletop, dropping a handful of creamers next to it. "There you go," and to Karen, "I'll come around in a second to warm yours up."

Her face was tightly drawn in, straining, as she nodded to him.

"He said you were right. She already has pneumonia. That she . . ." Tears ran down her cheeks.

KAREN

He reached over and lifted my hand away from the coffee cup and held it between both of his. He was shaking his head, his eyes soft.

"Let's not talk about this right now," he said.

"Simon . . ." I couldn't form a coherent thought, and I was embarrassed to be visibly crying in a restaurant.

"No, listen," he said, squeezing my hand. "We don't have to talk about this right now—"

"I don't want her to die, Simon."

He shushed me and squeezed my hand again. "Don't even think about that right now. Just let it be."

"Simon—"

"Just let it be. We'll eat breakfast, get you home, get you showered. It's going to be okay."

I nodded, trying to smile a little.

"I love you," he said in a near-whisper. "I'm here for you."

I could only nod again.

SIMON

I checked the time as I answered my cell phone. 12:48. Karen was in the shower, and had been for more than seventeen minutes. She had called her mother when we got home from the restaurant, hung up crying and retreated into the bathroom with her robe over her shoulder.

"Barrett," I answered.

"Mr. Barrett? It's Dr. McKinley calling from the hospital. I tried a couple of times to get through on your home line and it was busy."

We had turned the ringer off after Karen had spoken with her mother. While we had been out for breakfast another half-dozen messages, all from journalists, had been left on the machine. "No problem. It's probably easiest to get through to us on my cell."

"I'll make a note."

"How is she?"

"Well, I know I told Karen that she should try to get some sleep, but I think you two should probably come back as soon as you can. Sherry's running quite a high fever, and there is a lot of fluid present in her lungs. As well, we've run some tests . . ."

"And?"

"And I'd like to talk to both of you about the results."

I closed my eyes before answering. "We'll be right back. Where will we find you?"

"Have them page me."

He hung up without saying good-bye. I sat for a moment in the silence, the only sound my breath, a quaver noticeable with every inhalation.

Karen had turned off the shower and a moment later the bathroom door opened with a burst of light and steamy warmth redolent of raspberry shower foam. She was wrapped in her blue robe, and gently drying her hair with a towel. She stopped when she saw me on the bed, telephone in hand. "Is it . . ."

I nodded. "We need to go back to the hospital."

She retreated into the bathroom, closing the door behind her.

KAREN

We were holding hands when we got back to Sherry's room. I don't think I would have been able to get through the door without Simon holding on to me.

Dr. McKinley was staring at her chart. "I just took Sherry's temperature."

"How bad is it?" Simon asked.

"Forty degrees," he said, double-checking his note.

"Oh Jesus," I whispered, my knuckles white around Simon's hand as we stood by Sherry's bed. *Deathbed.*

"Is that—"

"Is that why I called? No. The tests we ran this morning— CT, neurological scans, I jumped the line for the MRI again . . ."

We waited.

"Since the surgery, there's been considerable swelling, and some bleeding. I don't know if we missed it, or . . ." He paused, suddenly unable to meet our eyes. "Unfortunately—"

I fumbled for the bed rail with my free hand.

"We failed to detect any trace of brain activity." He turned his gaze on Sherry, lying as if suspended within the institutional sheets. "I'm sorry," he said.

"Brain-dead?" I whispered.

"We don't . . ." He stammered as he caught Simon's look. "That's not what we call it anymore."

"Are you saying she's never going to wake up?"

I wanted him to argue, or to reassure me, but the doctor didn't say anything.

"So what do we do now?" Simon asked.

"I want to say that we should wait. That there might be some change . . . But I can't." The doctor lifted his eyes to ours.

"She's never going to wake up," I repeated, watching her chest rise and fall.

This time he shook his head. "No. No, she won't. There's just too much damage . . . I'm sorry."

"Is she in pain?"

He seemed surprised by the question, and it took him a moment to answer. "No. No, she's not feeling anything."

Not feeling anything.

"I know that this sounds terribly sudden, but we should probably discuss the possibility of organ donation."

"Yes."

"There are a number of children—"

Not feeling anything.

"Sherry could help a lot of—"

"No," I said, the firmness of my voice hiding the confusion I was feeling. I wanted to scream. I wanted to tear things into pieces. I wanted to push these men away from my daughter and take her in my arms and not let her go. Instead, I repeated myself. "No."

"I'm sorry?" The doctor turned toward me.

"Karen, it's for—"

"I can't. I just can't, Simon." I shook my head. "It's all moving too fast. It's all just . . . Yesterday I was holding my daughter's hand as we walked down the street, and today—today you're asking me to decide, to decide if she should live or die. And I can't. It's all too fast. It's all too—"

"I'm not—"

Simon glanced at the doctor.

"There's still some time—"

"She's not in any pain?" I asked again.

The doctor shook his head.

"Then I'd like to wait. I'd like to wait and I'd like to get a second opinion. Maybe the tests were wrong. Maybe he's wrong, Simon."

"Of course," Dr. McKinley said. "Of course. I'll leave you alone."

Simon shuffled out of my way as I sat down in the chair at Sherry's bedside. I took her hand and held it in mine, its warmth burning into me.

Not feeling anything.

SIMON

It began to rain shortly after three that afternoon. At first, I only noticed because I was standing at the window, but the wind quickly picked up and started to drive the drops against the glass.

Karen had not looked away from our daughter since the doctor left, rubbing her thumb in a slow circle on the back of Sherry's hand as she held it.

I had tried talking with her, but she hadn't responded. I couldn't tell if she hadn't heard me, or if she was ignoring me.

So I stood at the window, watching the water run in dirty rivulets down the glass, across my reflection.

In the gray light, the room could have been a painting. Everything was still, shadowy, except where the bedside lamp cast a pool of golden light on Sherry's face, a warm circle over my daughter and her mother in a world of cold darkness.

I walked over to the bed.

"I'm going for a walk," I said in a whisper, not wanting to startle her. She didn't move. "Do you want me to bring you anything?"

I waited a moment for a response—a word, a gesture, something—but there was nothing. It was like I wasn't even there.

KAREN

Will I ever have this moment, this time, again? Will I ever be able to sit with my daughter, just sit with her and watch her sleep? Watch the rise and fall of her breath, trace the curve of her cheeks?

No. Never.

The machine breathes for her, and when it stops . . . No amount of wishing will make her whole. No amount of watching will bring her back.

How do you hold a moment, knowing that it is the last? How do you take in enough to endure a lifetime of absence? How do you remember enough to see you through?

How do you know what will last?

Will I be surprised someday to realize I've forgotten the color of her lips, barely pinker than her face? Or the way the corners of her mouth lift naturally to hint at a smile? Will I need photographs to remind me of the way her hair falls? The way her smile bursts open in pure joy?

What of my daughter will I take with me from this room? Nothing. Nothing if I can help it. I don't want to remember her like this—broken and bleeding, the sound of the machine that presses air into her tiny lungs, the IV line and the bag of urine collecting under the bedsheets, the way the edges of the bandages around her head are stained with blood.

I don't want to remember this room, the sound of the rain and the sight of her here. I want to remember yesterday, the way she laughed and ran, the way she looked at the flowers and rocks, the way she was so alive, so filled with joy. I want to hold the stones in my pocket—the three stones she picked up on the way to the mall—as a reminder of Sherry growing and learning, smiling and running.

But I know that I can't choose. I know that I'll remember this room as much as those mornings with the three of us in the big bed, snuggling and tickling and refusing to face the day. I know that I'll remember these bloodstained bandages as much as I'll remember last Christmas, her look of wonder as Simon read her the note that Santa Claus left her, thanking her for the cookies and the carrots for the reindeer. I know that I'll remember the moment I choose to let her go, the moment I feel her last breath, as vividly as I remember that gush of blood and love I felt as I heard her first cry, as I first saw her, tiny and twisted and perfect, wailing to raise the moon.

Ashes to ashes. Blood to blood. Cries to silence.

SIMON

It was cold outside the emergency-room doors but sheltered from the wind and the rain. A small crowd had gathered around the garbage can, and the air was thick with smoke.

"Can I buy a cigarette from someone?" I asked the group in general. "A cigarette and a light?"

A kid near me, no more than sixteen or seventeen, wearing a plaid flannel coat, fumbled for his pack. "Here," he said, handing me the du Mauriers, waving away the dollar I held out to him. "Take a couple." It was only when he turned to share the flame from his lighter that I saw that his face was a mess of blood, most of it coming from a jagged wound near his hairline. His right eye was swollen shut, his cheek scraped raw and bloody.

"Thanks," I said, inhaling the first lungful of smoke, handing him back the cigarettes.

"No sweat." He seemed remarkably composed for someone whose shirt was crisp with dried blood. Shock, probably.

The girl with him, a pretty blond in tight jeans and a denim jacket, looked more concerned.

"Are you all right?" I asked him, the nicotine rushing through me.

He seemed puzzled by the question. "Oh yeah. Just a little spill off my bike." He lit a cigarette for himself and offered the pack to the girl, who waved it away. "What about you?"

I shook my head. "Not me. It's my daughter. She got hit by a car. A truck, actually."

"The one on the news?" the girl asked.

I nodded. "Sherry."

"Oh shit, man, that's"—she shook her head—"I don't know."

"I know."

"Did the police get the guy?" She was wearing glittery silver lip gloss, and her cheeks were pink.

"What guy?" the boy asked, looking between us.

"I told you inside," the girl said. "The guy who hit his— who hit Sherry. He just took off. The police are looking for him and everything."

The boy stared at me and took another drag off his cigarette. "Oh wow, man. If it were me I'd fuckin' kill that guy. That's just, I mean, she's just a little kid."

"Three," I said. "She's three."

"That's sick, man. I tell ya, I'd kill him. And there's not a jury that would convict me."

"Yeah," I said.

My cell phone rang as I was taking another drag. I didn't need to check the number to know who it was.

KAREN

Simon came back just before nightfall. No sunset tonight, no warm orange glow, just a slow darkening of the rain, the sky, the room.

"How are you?" he asked when he saw me looking at him.

I shrugged.

"I brought food." He set the bags on the swing table next to the bed. "And coffee."

I tried to smile. "Thank you."

He leaned over the bed and smoothed back Sherry's hair, careful to avoid the bandages.

"You missed the doctor," I said.

"What did he have to say?" he asked without looking up.

"Not Dr. McKinley. Dr. Tompkins. A specialist."

He straightened up. "And?"

I couldn't do any more than shake my head before bursting into tears. Simon came around the bed and held me until I stopped crying.

"So nothing has changed," he said, as he stepped away from me.

I nodded.

He busied himself with the food on the table.

"It's not much."

"What?"

"The food. It's not much. Just doughnuts." He shrugged, and I tried to think of where he might have found a doughnut shop nearby. "I thought we could get something from the cafeteria a little later."

Eating was the last thing on my mind. I couldn't bear to watch as he picked up a jelly doughnut and bit into it, the sugar sticking to his lips. He washed it down with a mouthful of coffee.

"I talked to your mother," he said, his voice thick as he chewed. "She called my cell. She could have got out earlier, but she didn't want to fly standby. She'll be here around one."

I couldn't imagine my mother flying standby. "That's fine."

"She sounded like she really wanted to be here."

I nodded. "I know. It just makes everything so much harder. She'll have a priest in here, she'll be praying—"

"It's a comfort to her."

"I know. But it's not a comfort to me. It makes everything so much harder."

I could imagine trying to tell my mother that there was nothing we could do, that there was no hope for Sherry to recover.

"Of course there's hope," she would say. "There's always hope." Staring up at her God.

I wouldn't want to fight with her; I never do. But that's how we relate, I guess. She puts all of her faith in a God who either doesn't exist or who takes a particular delight in testing her very limits. The Lord will provide? The Lord will save my daughter? Where was your Lord when Dad was dying? What good was your faith when he was wasting away before our eyes?

Where was your God yesterday morning when a truck hit my little girl?

"One o'clock?"

Simon nodded. "She'll take a cab in from the airport so we don't have to worry about picking her up."

One o'clock. It would all be over before then.

It would all be over.

HENRY

I couldn't do it anymore.

The day of the accident, I walked until I couldn't walk any farther, and then I collapsed in a small park, on the grass next to a cedar tree. I could barely feel my legs, and I thought I'd fall asleep right away. But I didn't. Every time I closed my eyes, I could see her, Sherry, hanging in the air in front of me, her eyes locked to mine, the sound of the engine drowning out her scream.

I wanted her to go away, but she didn't, and I lay there all night, not sleeping. By morning I was wet with dew.

I had nowhere to go, nowhere to turn. I had tried to go home, had stood in the hallway listening to the sound of my family, but I couldn't bring myself to open the door. What would I tell Arlene? That I had hit a little girl with my truck, and then run away? How could I face my boys, knowing that?

I kept replaying the accident in my mind, seeing her appear in front of the truck, spinning skyward. I couldn't shake the image. I couldn't turn it off.

I walked back to the hospital, in the pouring rain, trying to reassure myself, *She's still alive. She has to be.*

If she made it through the first night, she'll make it. Isn't that how it's supposed to work? She would make it. I knew she would.

I saw Mr. Barrett just outside the emergency room. He was leaning against a wall with his eyes closed, a cigarette burned to a column of ash between his fingers.

It took me a few minutes to find her room, just around the corner from the nurses' station on the fifth floor. I was standing outside the door when the specialist examined Sherry. I couldn't hear what he said, but the way Mrs. Barrett looked after he left—the way she fell against the bed, sobbing with her face buried in the blankets—told me all I needed to know.

She had made it through the first night, but she wasn't going to make it.

I had killed her. I killed that little girl.

The little girl I could still see, hanging in the air in front of me, as I fled the hospital.

I couldn't do it anymore. I couldn't keep seeing her, seeing the accident, over and over in my head.

I needed to make it stop. I needed to make her go away.

SIMON

I fell asleep in the chair. I wouldn't have thought it possible; I don't think I've ever been less comfortable. But I guess it all catches up with you.

The dark window reflected the room, the half-drawn curtain, the bed. I checked my watch: midnight.

My back seized a little as I straightened up.

Karen was still at the side of the bed, her hands tight around the steel rail.

"Hey," I said quietly.

"You fell asleep," she said, not looking at me. Her voice was flat.

"Yeah." I stood up and stretched. "Sorry."

"You probably needed it."

When I reached over to rub her back she flinched, and I drew my hand away. She finally turned to look at me. Her eyes were deep-set in gray pockets, her face lined and tight and pale. She looked like she had been beaten up, like she was barely able to stand of her own volition.

"How is she?" I asked, resting my hand on Sherry's knee.

"The same," she whispered.

I looked away from Karen, down at my daughter, at the mechanical rhythm of her chest under the sheet. "Right."

"Dr. McKinley said we could call him. Anytime."

I lifted my eyes to meet hers.

"I think we should call him," she said.

KAREN

I don't think I breathed as Dr. McKinley laid the stethoscope on the pale skin of Sherry's chest.

You can talk and talk and talk. You can make it all make sense in your head. You can lay it out and cry and plan and think and accept . . .

He lifted her eyelids and shone a light into her wide pupils.

Accept the inevitable.

He laid his fingertips against the warm inside of her wrist.

But when it comes down to it, it doesn't make sense. You haven't really accepted anything. I mean, how can you let your child die? How can you make that make sense?

He added his notes to her file, all without saying a word.

"Well?" Simon finally asked.

Dr. McKinley took a deep breath. His face was ashen, and there were dark circles around his eyes too. "There's very little change from earlier this evening. Her temperature is dangerously high. She's non-responsive. And I'm hearing a lot of fluid in her lungs. I've ordered an increase in her IV antibiotics, but—"

"All right," I said, not lifting my eyes from my daughter.

"The trouble is that, with the pneumonia—"

"I think that we should disconnect the life support," I said.

"Are you—"

I looked up at Dr. McKinley. "I want you to disconnect my daughter from the life support."

"Well, usually we—"

"You what?" I asked. "You treat her? You bring her temperature down, clear up all the symptoms, keep feeding her antibiotics, knowing that she's not going to wake up?"

"Can we discuss—"

I shook my head. "I can't. I'm sorry, but the idea of organ donation, right now, it's more than I can bear."

The doctor nodded. "I understand," he said. "It's just that you'd be helping so many people."

"I know. I know we would. I know we should, but I just can't."

"We both have organ donor cards in our wallets," Simon said, as if that might make up for this selfishness.

The doctor was silent for a moment. "Do you need more time?"

"We know this isn't a decision that you can make, or that you can counsel us to make," Simon said, looking down at our daughter. "You'll want us to sign a waiver," he added.

I don't know how I had spoken the words, how I was able to keep from screaming, let alone crying, as we stood around her bed, knowing that Sherry was going to die. Was dead already.

Our miracle.

HENRY

Off Dallas Road, the wind whipped from the ocean, and the trees leaned away from the cold. The air was thick and damp with spray, and the moon and stars were bright and full over my head. It smelled of salt and rotting seaweed.

I walked the concrete path toward the cliff's edge with my hands in my pockets, shivering but focused on the lights of Port Angeles across the strait. There were a few other people out, bundled against the cold, but I brushed past them and nobody seemed to notice me.

We used to bring the kids here for the afternoon to play catch on the lawn. Arlene always warned them away from the drop down to the rocks and the beach below. The boys and I would tease her—see how close we could get to the edge before she'd yell at us. Then we'd take one of the narrow paths down to the beach and walk along the water. Connor would shriek when his legs got drenched by a wave, and we would all laugh.

I would never be able to tell Connor what I had done. How do you tell your son that his father is a murderer, that he had killed a little girl the very same age as him?

How could I ever look Dylan in the eye?

And Arlene.

When I reached the end of the sidewalk, I stood facing the black water at the edge of the grass. The beacon down the shore turned and flashed, but the light was cold and far away. The surf boomed against the rocks and sand.

I didn't deserve to have a family—not when I had stolen one away.

I didn't deserve a normal life.

The lights across the strait shimmered orange on the dark water. I stood on the edge of the world, in the black and the cold, and even the stars seemed to have gone out.

I had been trying to get home as fast as I could after my shift.

I had only looked away for a moment, but that was enough. When I turned back I saw her fly into the air. I didn't even have time to touch the brakes.

I killed that little girl. Sherry. She would never wake up. She would always be with me.

I'm sorry, I said to her. *It was a mistake. I didn't mean to . . .*

A gust of wind buffeted me, and I nearly lost my footing on the edge of the cliff. My heart raced with the fear of falling.

It was so ridiculous I almost laughed.

I couldn't think of anything else to do, anywhere else to turn. And if I was going to do it, it was important to do it right, to hit the rocks headfirst, to end it quickly. Not to struggle as the water dragged me away from the shore. What a coward, worrying about suffering while that little girl was dying.

Drawing a breath, I raised my arms above my head. Leaning over, I bent my knees—

I'm sorry, Arlene.

—and pushed off into the night sky.

I love you, Dylan.

My feet left the ground.

I love you, Connor.

I angled down, headfirst, toward the surf and rocks below me.

I'm sorry, Sherry.

The black water looked like asphalt after rain.

I'm sorry . . .

Without warning, I was wrenched backward. The wind caught in my shirt, my hair. It felt as if a hand had grasped my shoulder and pulled me back toward the cliff. I landed heavily on my side on the wet grass. The force of the impact left me breathless, and I struggled to sit up.

"What the hell . . . ?"

The beacon light flashed, and the shadows of the trees danced in the wind, but there was no one else there. No one else who could have pulled me to safety.

I was completely alone.

But I could feel the pressure of the hand, of the fingers, on my shoulder. By morning I'd be bruised, the handprint clearly visible on my pale skin.

SIMON

Dr. McKinley summoned a night nurse from the station down the corridor to witness Sherry's death. Once she was in the room, he closed the door. The sound of the medical equipment was overwhelming.

"Mr. Barrett, could you please make your request one more time?"

I cleared my throat. "Knowing that the damage to her . . . Knowing that there is no chance that my daughter will ever wake up, I would like you to remove her from the life support equipment."

The doctor glanced at the nurse to make sure that she had heard. When she nodded, he turned to Karen. "Mrs. Barrett?"

She had moved to the head of the bed and was tracing her fingers along Sherry's face. Tears were running steadily down her cheeks, and she was biting her lower lip.

"Mrs. Barrett?" he asked again.

She nodded, unable to speak.

"I'm very sorry," he said, stepping forward and reaching for the control panel.

His fingers had just touched it when Karen whispered, "Wait."

Everyone in the room turned to her.

"I can't do this. I can't just watch this." There was no longer any pretense of control: her face was flushed bright red, eyes swollen almost shut with tears.

"Do you mean you don't want to—"

"Help me," she said to me. "Help me turn her over."

I moved to help her clear away the tubes and wires so she could reach under them to roll Sherry onto her right side. "She always sleeps on her side," she explained tearfully.

"I know," I answered, shaking as I held the wires and tubes away from my daughter's body like a veil.

Karen slipped her hands under Sherry's neck and hips and turned her on her side. Out of the corner of my eye I could see the doctor lay a restraining hand on the nurse's arm as she started forward.

Karen carefully arranged Sherry's legs, drawing them upward slightly, curling her like a comma, smoothing back her hair again and whispering, "I love you, baby," into her ear.

I hoped she could hear.

I hoped she couldn't.

I was about to lower the weight of tubes and wires, the weight of my daughter's life, when Karen touched my arm. She had kicked off her shoes. Instead I raised them a little higher as she lowered the rail and slipped into the narrow bed with our daughter.

I draped my burden over both of them. Karen nestled herself around Sherry's tiny, still body, cradling her, and buried her face in the soft, bed-pressed hair below the edge of the bandages. Her body was racked with silent sobs.

I rested my hand on Karen's shoulder more for my own good than hers and looked across the bed at the doctor.

Our eyes met, and I nodded just once.

He stepped to the machine and, with the touch of one finger, turned it off.

KAREN

She was so small, so light, it was like she wasn't even there. Like I was holding, trying to hold, a handful of rain.

I could feel her breath, the steady rise and fall of it under my hand, the steady warmth of her . . .

Thou shalt not grow cold

The smell of her, her shampoo . . .

May God bless and keep you always

Her breath . . .

I whispered in her ear, where only she could hear me . . .

Now I lay me down to sleep

A breath.

And then nothing.

I pray the Lord my soul to keep

I heard her saying it along with me, felt her arms around my neck as I kissed her good night, pulling the covers up to her chin.

Felt her chest stop rising in mid-breath.

And if I die before I wake

Felt the soft rain of her heartbeat under my hand stop, like a passing summer storm.

I pray the Lord my soul to take

Nothing.

It was as if I could actually feel the life pass out of her, a motion of breath, of wings, an actual physical presence I wanted to catch.

If only . . .

Was she cold? Already?

It seemed so soon . . .

Too soon . . .

I tightened my arms around her, pulling her to me, trying to pull her back inside me, where I could protect her, where I could keep her warm and safe.

I would not let her go.

I would not let her go.

I would like to start again.

I wanted that moment back, the moment that the truck pulled her away from me, the moment that I let her go . . .

In my arms, her chest fell, and I could hear the breath, her last breath, escaping from her.

Could I catch it?

No.

Just let it go.

May angels guide you

And then her chest rose. There was a wheeze as she breathed against the pressure of the machine, against the tubes in her mouth and nose.

I could feel her heart.

Beating.

Beating again?

Another breath.

And then choking . . .

Choking . . .

SIMON

The silence of the room was broken as Karen arched upright on the bed, screaming, "She's choking! She's choking!"

I leaned in, whispering, "It's all right. Just let her go—"

"She's choking!"

And from the corner of my eye I could see motion on the heart rate monitor. "Holy . . ."

The doctor had seen it too. "She's got a pulse. Janet, we have a pulse. Let's get those tubes out."

I pulled Karen off the bed as the nurse and the doctor stepped in, turning Sherry onto her back, swiftly removing the tubes from her mouth and nose.

As her airway cleared, she coughed and sputtered. "Let's turn her back onto her side," the doctor said. "In case she vomits."

As they turned her, she coughed again, a small pool forming on the pillow under her mouth and nose. The nurse cleared it away.

The heart rate monitor was still beeping out its rhythm. The doctor hastily pulled on his stethoscope and pressed it between her shoulder blades where her back was exposed. He listened for several seconds, as if he couldn't believe what he was hearing. He changed position and listened again.

As he straightened up, the nurse asked, "Doctor, what?" She couldn't even form the question.

He waved her silent, glancing at us across the bed, huddled together, shocked and confused, unable to take our eyes from our daughter.

Using the digital thermometer, he took Sherry's temperature from her inner ear. He shook his head as he stared at the readout. "Son of a bitch," he muttered, but everyone in the room could hear him.

"What is it?" I asked. "What's going on?"

"I don't know." He was too shaken to be anything but completely honest. "Spontaneous respiration has resumed. And when I listen to her breathing, I don't hear any fluid in her lungs. It's like the pneumonia is . . . gone. I'll schedule some tests."

For a moment, we looked at one another. Then all our eyes turned to rest on the small form on the bed, curled into the fetal position, looking for all the world as if she were only sleeping.

Halfway down the corridor, the stranger watched as nurses ran into the little girl's room. Seconds later, the elevator doors slid open, disgorging more doctors and nurses, all rushing into the room. Then in twos and threes they came out into the hall. Most of them were half-smiling, half-confused, not sure about what they had just witnessed.

The stranger knew.

One nurse, young, pious, the chain of her crucifix visible at the neck of her uniform, was in tears.

As he drew on his coat, he heard her say, "It's a miracle."

A miracle. Yes.

The stranger turned away.

It had begun.

November 1996

KAREN

Some mornings everything seemed normal.

I would lie in bed, letting myself wake slowly from dreams I could not remember, the house silent around me, the bed warm. I would pull on comfortable clothes—jogging pants or Simon's flannel pajama bottoms. I'd splash cool water on my face. In the hallway, I would pause outside the closed door to Sherry's room, straining to hear any sign of waking within.

It was only as I walked past the doorway to the living room that reality would reassert itself. Where once Simon and I had sat with friends, laughing and drinking wine, now the furniture was pushed against the walls, the couch and coffee table crammed into the corner, Simon's chair tucked almost into the closet. The room where we used to sit around the Christmas tree was dominated by a hospital bed and the mixed smells of antiseptic cleanliness and the thick, cloying cut flowers that failed to conceal it.

Sherry lay motionless on the bed, the covers tight around her.

Seeing her lying there, on those mornings when I had been fortunate enough to forget, would almost kill me. I had to force myself to breathe.

I wanted to mess up the bed, to make it seem as if she had stirred during the night, to hold on to the hope that she was only sleeping, that at any moment she might open her eyes, sit up and wonder why I was crying.

But she hadn't moved the night before, or the night before that. She hadn't moved since Simon and I brought her home from the hospital.

And she didn't stir as I touched her forehead with the cool back of my hand, checking her temperature.

"Hello, Princess," I said. "It looks like it's going to be a beautiful day outside. A little cold though. Mr. Squirrel will be putting on his winter coat . . ."

On the windowsill I had placed the three stones she had asked me to carry on our walk to the shopping center that morning.

"No more than three," I said.

"Four?" she asked, smiling at me, testing her limits.

"How about none?"

She stuck her tongue out, then spent several minutes carefully choosing three stones from a gravel driveway.

For a moment, as I pulled back the curtains, spilling sunlight into the room, I almost expected to turn around and see her looking up at me, shifting groggily and burrowing more deeply into her blankets.

I knew she wouldn't, but that moment, as the light fell across her, that second of possibility, was the last vestige of a normal life that remained.

HENRY

At first I tried to take care of myself. I looked for somewhere to sleep and to eat, somewhere warm where I could rest. I tried the Mustard Seed, the Salvation Army, the Upper Room, anywhere with a crowd of men gathered on the sidewalk outside— the sort of men who are used to looking up at people as they walk past without making eye contact.

Everywhere I went it was the same: I would line up for a bed and no one would see me. The man behind me would get a bunk as the volunteer passed me by. When I lined up for food, the servers in their hairnets didn't offer me anything.

I tried to speak, but nobody heard me. Even screaming got no reaction.

Those first few days, I screamed a lot.

So I stopped going to the shelters, and soon I made another discovery. Even when I found a place to lie down, in an alley or a park, I didn't sleep. I would close my eyes, feeling the tiredness in my muscles and the coldness in my bones, but I couldn't drift off. I ached with hunger, but I couldn't eat. Any food I scavenged from the Dumpsters behind restaurants or corner grocery stores sat like cardboard on my tongue. Eventually the hunger disappeared, and I stopped noticing that I was tired.

And I discovered soon enough that I wasn't being ignored: I really wasn't seen. I could stand directly in someone's path, and they would only veer around me, no recognition in their eyes.

It was like I had disappeared.

Not eating, not sleeping, not seen, I had nothing to do but walk. Along the shoreline, on the cliffs high above the surf, the cold wind in my hair, blowing through my thin clothes. I barely felt it. Along crowded downtown sidewalks, through shopping malls, bars, churches. I could feel people as they brushed against me, hear their voices, smell their perfume, their breath, their hair, their skin. They shuddered sometimes when I passed, like a chill had come over them, but they never saw me.

For the first few weeks, I kept coming back to the hospital. I would wait for Mrs. Barrett to step out, for the doctor to disappear, and I would sneak in to stand beside Sherilyn's bed. I knew I had watched another child sleeping, but I couldn't remember who. A brother, maybe? Did I have a brother? I didn't know anymore. Everything from my life before the accident had disappeared. Nothing seemed to exist for me before I watched Sherilyn float away, before that night on the cliff.

I kept walking. It was like I was looking for something, but I wasn't sure what it was, or how I would know when I found it.

SIMON

The shower turned off on the other side of the bedroom wall. Even with my eyes closed, I knew that the curtains were open, the room bright with morning. I nestled deeper under the covers.

Half-asleep, I was only vaguely aware of the bathroom door opening. Then there was a new weight on the bed, the shifting of covers, a radiating warmth alongside me.

I groaned a little and rolled onto my back.

"Are you awake?"

She slid her leg over mine, damp and hot.

I moaned this time, as she ran her fingers over my bare chest, across my stomach, gently wrapping them around my penis, which thickened at her touch.

"*You're* awake," she whispered.

"You're awake too."

"Here," she said breathily, sliding atop me. "Here." Using her hand she guided me inside herself, hot and wet. Raised herself up, settled herself atop me.

Any last remnants of sleep were burned away. "Oh God, Mary. You're gonna kill me." And I opened my eyes to this vision in the sunlight, her head thrown back as her body moved on top of me, the Inner Harbour behind her through the tall glass.

RUTH PAGE

Mrs. Barrett always had a pot of tea waiting for me when I arrived at the house in the morning.

I would let myself in with my key, hang up my coat in the hall closet and then check on Sherry. I noted her temperature, pulse and blood pressure—anything significant—on her chart before joining Mrs. Barrett in the kitchen.

The first few days she had offered me coffee, and seemed quite puzzled when I said no, thank you. Then I explained about my ulcer. The next day she had a cup of tea ready for me, the bag dropped directly into a coffee mug. The tea was almost as black as the coffee she was drinking herself.

I thanked her, keeping a smile on my face.

The next day when I got there, she had set a proper teacup and teapot on the kitchen table, with the tea bag on the edge of the saucer and the kettle on the boil.

She wasn't sleeping very much after they brought Sherry home from the hospital, and it was worse after her husband left. When she had coffee with me each morning, I couldn't help but notice the dark circles bruiselike around her eyes. Already slim, she'd lost weight, and her hair had turned brittle and dry. Her hands shook as she cradled the mug.

"Are you all right?" I asked her one morning. "Are you sleeping enough?"

She shrugged ungracefully and took a sip from her coffee. "It's hard. I know she's fine through the night, but I still wake up every two hours. I have to check on her."

"Would it be better if we arranged for a night nurse? It's not helping Sherry for you not to sleep."

She set her mug on the table, then sat for quite a long time just staring at it.

The friend in me wanted to reach out to take her hand, while the nurse in me knew I should sit back and let her work through what she needed to work through.

"No. No, it's not that. It's . . . I keep seeing the accident," she said quietly. "I lie awake and it just . . . plays. Like a song you can't get out of your head."

I nodded.

"Simon was like that with cases. Even when he'd win a big one, he'd spend weeks afterward focusing on what he *should* have said, the things he missed"—she took a sip—"It doesn't help that all of a sudden I'm alone with all this."

Leaning forward, I curled my fingers around her hand, meeting her eyes and holding them with my own.

HENRY

I got to know the city in a way that most people never get a chance to. Some mornings I would hang out at the Inner Harbour, watching tourists as they stepped off the ferries or floatplanes. I'd see some of them again over the next day or two, shopping downtown or walking through Beacon Hill Park or along the waterfront, taking the whale-watching tours out to the San Juan Islands.

I got to know people without ever meeting them. The businessmen and the people who worked in the stores all had their own routines. They went to the bank at this time, had lunch at that time, at this table. The students up at the university, the bankers on Douglas, the homeless people under the Johnson Street Bridge—I saw all of them, and none of them saw me.

I started going to the library every morning to check the paper, to see if there was any news about Sherry. I would sit at the same table every day, reading that morning's *Sentinel*.

A few days after the accident, there had been an update. Sherry's condition was "stable," but they said she was in a coma. There was a picture of Sherry and her parents in front of a Christmas tree, dressed up, smiling and happy. For a while, there were updates on the search for the driver of the truck that had hit Sherry, who seemed to have just disappeared.

The first time I read that, I sank a little lower in my chair, peering carefully around to see if anyone was watching me. Nobody even knew I was there.

The newspaper had talked with a woman named Arlene, and showed a picture of her in her apartment, not quite looking at the camera. I recognized her, but it was like I had once dreamt about her. The newspaper said that she lived with me, that we had two children. Sons. The same article mentioned that the police had contacted my parents, and asked for people to please keep their eyes open for me.

Parents, children, a girlfriend. Why couldn't I remember them?

There wasn't very much news for a while, just little things that I really had to look for. My insurance had agreed to pay out for the accident. Sherry went home with her parents. A picture of them at home, a nurse standing next to the family. Occasional updates on Sherry's condition. A brief mention of marriage difficulties, then the news that Mr. Barrett had moved out in a "trial separation." A short article about Sherry's fourth birthday, with no change in her condition.

After that, news about Sherry just faded away, replaced by the latest drug bust, the most recent pit-bull attack, a crackdown on panhandlers downtown.

But I still went to the library every day and read the paper.

SIMON

I took the bus across the bridge to the house every morning.

Mary drove me the first few times, letting me off down the block, kissing me good-bye and taking my briefcase with her to the office. But when she saw that my visits were going to be routine, she shook her head. "I can't keep driving you there," she said. "I know you need to see your daughter, but I can't."

I made a point of arriving on the 7:56 bus, which dropped me across the street from the mall, near the crosswalk where the accident had happened. I used the few minutes' walk to steel myself before going up our steps and ringing the doorbell. I had learned not to just let myself in; this was no longer my home.

"Good morning, Ruth," I said as the nurse opened the door.

"Hello, Mr. Barrett." She always smiled. I knew that I was likely not her favorite person in the world, but she never let it show. Always professional.

"Your payments coming through on time? No problems there?" I asked about the insurance every so often, letting her know that I wasn't the complete bastard that Karen and her friends believed I was.

"Oh, yes. No problem. No problem at all." She always made a point of leading me to the living room, as if I didn't know my way or couldn't be trusted on my own in the house.

"How's Sherry this morning?"

"She's doing well. We're listening to some Mozart."

The curtains were open, the blinds up. *Eine Kleine Nachtmusik* played at a dominating volume.

I leaned over the bed and kissed Sherry on the forehead, surprised to feel how warm she was under my lips.

"Good morning, sweetheart," I whispered. "Listening to Mozart this morning? Good for the brain." I glanced up at Ruth as I settled myself into the chair next to the bed.

"I'll leave you be for a little while," she said with something approaching a smile.

Some mornings I would talk to Sherry about the weather or something from TV, or I'd tell her a story she used to like. If there wasn't any music playing I would sing to her from my limited selection of lullabies and kids' songs or the folk songs I used to play in university. Eventually, I would find myself just sitting, not saying a word, listening to the gentle in and out of her breath, unconsciously counting, only later noticing that I was doing so. I would listen to the familiar noises of the house around me, the sound of water in the pipes, the furnace, footsteps and distant voices.

I would stroke her soft hair.

KAREN

After he had had a little private time with Sherry, I brought Simon coffee.

I would probably have been better off to ignore him, to stay in the kitchen or my bedroom until he went off to work. But I wanted to be the bigger person.

So I put on a happy face, stood ramrod straight in the kitchen and prepared myself for the meaningless pleasantries that should never come between a husband and wife.

When I came in he was sitting in the chair alongside the bed, his hand resting on Sherry's arm, just staring into the distance.

"Coffee?" I asked, walking around the end of the bed so I wasn't reaching across Sherry as I extended the mug toward him.

He smiled a little. "Thanks." He took the mug and held it on his lap. In the light from the window I would see that his hair was thinning. I wondered if that had started recently, or if I had just never noticed before.

"How's work?" I asked, sitting down on the couch, maintaining my distance.

"It's fine. Busy."

I nodded, wondering if he was still working as late as often as he used to, or if having Mary at home had solved that particular problem.

"How's Mary?" In my mind, the question was dripping with venom, but he only shook his head, as if he couldn't believe I was asking.

"She's fine."

"Good. That's good."

He touched the side of the mug with the back of his hand to check its temperature and blew across the surface to keep from burning his mouth. He took a sip. "Do you need anything?" he asked, somehow managing to be flat and earnest in the same breath.

My daughter.

My husband.

My family back.

My life the way it was.

I shook my head. "Nothing I can think of."

"You'll—"

"I'll let you know."

He smiled. "Good. And Sherry's . . ."

In a coma.

Gone.

"No change."

"She seems a little warm to me."

"She always seems a little warm to you. The chart's here if you want to check it." I handed him the folder.

He looked at the top sheet. "She seemed warmer," he muttered.

Setting the file down on the table, he glanced at his watch, took another swallow of coffee and stood up. "I should go," he said, sweeping the front of his suit for imaginary crumbs.

"Okay. Do you want me to call you a cab?"

Wouldn't you rather stay?

He shook his head as he crossed the floor. "That's all right. I'll walk. I didn't get a chance for a run this morning."

I tried unsuccessfully to stifle the picture that rose in my mind. "Say hello to Mary for me." Bitchy, bitchy, bitchy.

He looked at me for a long moment, then shook his head. "You've got a very strange sense of humor. I'll be by after work." He closed the door behind him.

At the clicking of the lock, my strength left me in a great rush. If he knew how difficult his visits were I could accuse him of being incredibly cruel. As it stood, all I could accuse him of being was incredibly dense.

SIMON

Leaving the house—closing the door behind me, walking down the path and through the gate to the street—was the hardest thing I had ever done, and I did it twice every day, once before work and once after. I never looked back, worried I would see Karen watching me through one of the front windows, or maybe worried I wouldn't.

On the days I walked to work, I cut through Fernwood,

taking the crow's path downtown. The twenty-minute walk gave me time to consider things without interruption. And invariably, I found myself thinking about the same things.

I had become a cliché—the older man who left his wife for a younger woman—but I certainly wasn't going to use a midlife crisis as an excuse. I didn't feel old, and Mary was certainly no ditzy trophy.

I was keenly aware of how other people viewed the situation. My secretary, Sheila, no longer spoke to me—to either of us—with anything other than deliberately exaggerated professionalism. The associates never mentioned it, but I'm sure they spoke of it.

Mary and I.

Strange how a single phrase could signal so many changes. A few months before I had been part of "Simon and Karen," almost a single proper name. Husband, wife, father, mother, family.

Mary brought me more joy than I had felt in a very long time. I felt young again, open to possibility, in a way I'd lost. No. In a way I hadn't even noticed I had lost.

It's not like I just walked away from my family. I wanted to be there for Sherry. I needed to be there with her, and twice a day wasn't really enough.

I had called Karen the first Sunday night after I left, asking if I could visit Sherry on my way to work the next morning. I was careful to keep my voice as detached as I could manage. For a long time Karen didn't say anything, then she answered, "I suppose I can't stop you."

I hadn't missed a day since.

And Mary understood.

HENRY

I spent whole days in the library. After I finished reading the morning paper, I would check out other parts of the building. The library was two full floors. Large windows on one side looked out over a glass-covered courtyard. Inside, the carpet was a dark orange-brown, worn thin in places by foot traffic. The ceiling was low, with all the ventilation and heat pipes exposed and painted brown. I was amazed by how many books and magazines and files there were, the dusty, dry smell, the billions and billions of words. I couldn't remember ever reading a book. I had no idea there were so many.

What really amazed me, though, was all the people who came in, finding books and leaving, or finding a place to sit at one of the tables and lingering, reading for hours if they wanted. Kids did their homework, people looked things up, or planned trips, notebooks open, stacks of reference books on the tables in front of them.

And then there were the others.

At first I only noticed them because they seemed so out of place. Their clothes were ratty, their beards grown in, with dirty, untrimmed hair and skin the color of concrete on a sunny day. They would take a newspaper or magazine and sit at one of the tables, slowly reading their way through from front to back. They couldn't have missed a single word. Their eyes were haunted.

It got so I recognized some of them from day to day. They always sat in the same places, and slipped away when they were finished. They never disturbed anyone and no one ever disturbed them. No one even seemed to notice them.

Just like me.

One day I was standing beside someone at one of the paperback racks, watching him choose things to read. One of the covers caught my eye. The book was dark red, and seemed familiar somehow. I pulled it from the rack to look at it. The front and back cover both said *The Catcher in the Rye* in bright yellow letters.

I held on to the book and wandered back to the chairs near the magazine section, settling myself in and starting to read. From the first line, it was like the writer was speaking directly to me. I followed the words with my finger as I read, laughing out loud in some places.

The next time I looked up, the lights were dim. I set the book on the chair and walked toward the main desk. There was no one there.

The library was closed. I had read the day away, and I was locked inside.

RUTH

It is always a delicate balance to work with families in crisis. I knew I had to be ever so careful not to become personally involved with the Barretts.

Oh, who was I kidding?

I had been personally involved from the moment I saw Sherry in that hospital bed. She looked just like she was sleeping, dressed in her pink nightshirt, head turned slightly to one side. I kept expecting her to give a little sigh and turn onto her side, suck her thumb or kick off the covers. But in the six months I had been coming, she had only moved when I moved her, for her exercises and her baths.

Her world had changed around her, and she didn't even realize it. Her father had left, moved in with his young girlfriend. Her mother cried in the kitchen when she was washing the dishes.

Karen was a good woman. I really admired her. The way she cared for her daughter, read to her, changed her. Even something as small as my cup of tea every morning was a remarkable achievement under the circumstances. If Sherry had been my daughter, I don't know what I would have done. Probably curled into a tiny ball and died.

But Karen carried on. She didn't have many friends, but she talked to her mother on the telephone regularly, and Jamie Keller from the newspaper came to the house to visit. Karen dealt with the newspaper and the television reporters well—

she was never terse, but never too open when answering their questions either. Her life revolved around her daughter.

There were times, though, when I would speak to her and she wouldn't hear. I knew exactly where she had gone. She was reliving the accident, or the night in the hospital when Sherry should have died, but didn't.

I had heard that story from several people. A number of nurses I knew claimed to have been in the room when it happened. And Dr. McKinley himself told me he still didn't honestly know why Sherry had survived.

"I could show you the file," he said. "I could show you the records from the machines. She was gone. There was no heartbeat, no respiration . . ." He shook his head.

When he spoke about Sherry's mother, his tone changed. "I couldn't believe her, crawling into the bed like that. It broke my heart, her holding her daughter as she died. I've never seen anything like that in my life."

We have to be so careful to keep our distance.

I have never hated anyone, but I imagine it would be easy to hate Mr. Barrett if you didn't know him.

But who among us can really understand why anyone else does the things they do? If we can't understand, then how on earth can we judge them? "Walk a mile in their shoes," as my mother used to say.

I was working at the house the day Karen found out about Mary. There was no screaming, no hysterics. Instead, she seemed to shut down, to shut Simon out.

He was apologizing, stuttering, trying to explain. She didn't seem to hear a word he was saying. Finally, she asked him to leave. She was calm and cold. He packed some clothes into a suitcase and a garment bag, and he carried his computer under his arm out the door to wait for his girlfriend to pick him up in her little white Volkswagen convertible.

He said good-bye to Sherry before he left. And he said good-bye to me.

I didn't expect to see him any too soon, but the following Monday, he made the first of his morning visits to the house.

I worked with Sherry Monday through Friday, but there wasn't really that much for me to do. When she first came home from the hospital, she had full-time care. I worked twelve hours each day, and other nurses came in at night and on the weekends. There was a physiotherapist every afternoon, and Dr. McKinley visited every couple of days.

I think the idea was that the insurance on the driver of the truck would pay us, and then Karen would be able to go back to work at the paper when she was ready. But Karen wasn't ready, and with Mr. Barrett and the insurance money taking care of the expenses she didn't have to work.

And then we realized that Sherry didn't require that level of care. No one could explain why, but her condition didn't deteriorate. The physiotherapist cut back his hours, to three times a week, then one, then not at all. None of the things we would normally be on the lookout for—from bedsores to muscle atrophy to infections—ever manifested. When Karen expressed an interest in taking a greater role in her daughter's care, the night and weekend nurses were let go.

I still performed my job scrupulously. I made sure that Sherry was turned regularly to prevent bedsores. I took her through her physiotherapy every day, bending her arms and legs, flexing her knees and elbows, rotating her wrists and shoulders to prevent her large muscle groups from atrophying. Every second day I gave her a full bath, carrying her into the tub and using the specially designed rack to immerse her. It was probably more often than was necessary, but the water all around her likely acted as a stimulant to her. It couldn't hurt.

On the other days, I gave her a sponge bath, carefully washing between all ten toes and all ten fingers. Every day she got a clean nightie, and every second day I changed her bedding.

I checked her thoroughly, monitoring the color of her urine and smell of her breath. I checked the feeding tube that snaked under the blankets and into her abdomen throughout the day. Karen usually took care of Sherry's feeding, but I still checked.

She was such a sweet little thing. You could tell, just by looking at her, that Sherry had been a happy one, the sort of child that lit up a room just by toddling into it. Even her motionless face spoke volumes about her—the way her lips naturally fell into a half-smile, as if she had a secret she was refusing to share.

If I claimed to be uninvolved, I wouldn't be fooling anyone.

I had retired from hospital work because it was too easy for me to get swept up into people's stories, caught up by the raw force of life and death struggling all around me. I had worked in pediatrics and it was always so difficult for me when it came time for the children to go home. Some of the parents wrote or called, usually only once, to say thank you and to give me a bit of an update. I needed more than that.

Foolish old woman. I needed to be a part of their lives, needed to know that I had made a difference to a child, to the life of a family. And that couldn't happen.

I had forced myself to take early retirement. I did have legitimate medical grounds, and all my benefits came through without any problem. The arthritis that had messed up my hips had settled into my fingers so badly that it was becoming difficult for me to keep up with the demands of the ward.

My fingers . . .

"Barrett."

"Simon. John Richards."

"How are you, sergeant?"

"Same as I ever was. Just older. You?"

"Weathering the storm."

"Like an old sailor or an old building?"

"Depends on who you ask. Do you have anything?"

"I'm sorry, Simon—"

"Come on, John. People don't just disappear."

"You know better than that. People disappear all the time. The last we've got on Henry Denton is that phone call right after the accident. Nobody's seen him since. He hasn't made contact with his girlfriend or his family. He's gone."

"So?"

"So we're keeping it open. The case'll stay open until we find him. But Simon, we can't . . . They're pulling us back."

"Uh-huh."

"I mean, the most we can do with this guy, if we ever find him, is talk to him. Maybe get a charge of leaving the scene . . ."

"You don't understand . . ."

"No, I do understand. But seeing this guy, even talking to him—it's not going to explain anything to you. It's not like it's all gonna make sense all of a sudden."

"Thanks, John."

"I wish there was more that I could tell you. I still owe you one."

"We'll see."

HENRY

It was kind of exciting being locked in the library when I wasn't supposed to be there.

It wasn't too dark. There were orange security lights, and the computer screens glowed orange or green. The shelves loomed in the shadows like entrances to a maze in a video game. I went down a few aisles, my heart beating faster, but they were the same aisles they were in the daytime.

I don't know why I had expected them to be different.

As I wandered I whistled, not a tune or anything, just whistling. I wasn't even really aware that I was doing it.

Until someone whistled back.

RUTH

I waited until I got home to make the telephone call. I let myself into the apartment, scratching both cats under their chins as I took off my shoes. I set my purse on the kitchen table before dialing. I didn't sit down; I couldn't sit.

Sarah answered after the third ring. "Hello?" Her voice was rough and weak.

"Sarah, it's Ruth." I had to stay my impulse to speak too loudly to her, as if she was deaf as well as dying.

"Ruth." I could hear the surprise in her voice. We didn't have the sort of relationship where one of us would just call out of the blue. My sister lived less than two miles from me, but for the past few years we'd only really seen each other on birthdays and Christmas. "How *are* you?"

"I'm well. How are *you?*"

"I'm not dead yet." She chuckled at her own joke, which started her into a fit of coughing I could feel in my own lungs. My hand clutched at my thick winter coat over my chest.

"Not yet," she sputtered out of the cough. "It's been a while. Are you working?"

"I am. I'm still with that family. The little girl in the coma?"

"Is she the one who was in the accident? That hit-and-run up by the mall?"

"Yes. Sherilyn Barrett."

"I heard her parents were having troubles." My sister had once had a memory like a leghold trap. It had served her well when we were working together on the ward. I had retired first. She filed for disability a few months after I did, but by the time the tumors were removed they had already metastasized, cancer clinging to her lungs "like Christmas lights," she said. The doctors had predicted six months for her, at the outside. That was three years ago. I got the impression that she stayed alive only to prove them wrong.

"They separated a few months ago."

"Only three, right? Poor little thing."

"She turned four in the summer. She's a little sweetheart. Listen, would you like to meet her?" I tried to make it sound as if the idea had just then occurred to me.

"Well, I don't . . ."

"No, it would be good for you to get out. Karen—Mrs. Barrett—goes out sometimes in the afternoon, and you could come over then."

"That would hardly be appropriate, would it?" Her voice was a hoarse wheeze. She was two years younger than I was, and dying.

"Mrs. Barrett won't mind. She's told me that if I ever wanted to have anyone over for a visit . . . You could meet her if you'd like. I just thought it might be nicer just the two of us. And Sherry."

"What have you got up your sleeve?"

Sarah was still able to see right though me.

"Nothing. I just thought it might be nice for us to have a visit. We're the only family we've got left." Our parents had died during Sarah's last year of high school. I was away at nursing school, and our older brother, John, had taken care of her until she graduated. Then she came to Victoria and stayed with me while she took her own nurse's training. John had died four years ago of lung cancer, just before Sarah was diagnosed.

The cancer was a family legacy that I had been lucky enough to dodge. Maybe because I didn't smoke two packs of cigarettes a day.

"Have you been reading those self-help books again?"

I knew she was joking with me now, and that she would

come over to the Barretts'. "Well, there is this one you might be interested in . . ." I played along.

"Okay, okay, stop. I surrender. For Christ's sake, no more self-help books!" I could hear her restraining her laughter and the choking cough it would bring. "So how do I get to this place?"

I gave her directions, and hung up after telling her she was welcome to come anytime in the afternoon. The next day was Tuesday, and Karen went to a movie most Tuesday afternoons with Jamie.

After hanging up, I raised one hand level with my eyes and held it flat, fingers extended.

There were no tremors, no shaking. Not even the slightest vibration. My hand was as steady as a rock.

Then I slowly curled it into a fist, which I clenched tightly, not releasing it for several seconds.

When I did release it, there was no pain, none of the tearing in my knuckles that I had lived with for so long, none of the dull, continuous ache that had been my companion, even at rest. There was no pain as I reached into my pocket, gripping the Barretts' house key between my thumb and forefinger, turning it from side to side, fully rotating my wrist.

There was no pain, no hesitation, no restriction of movement.

My arthritis was completely gone.

HENRY

I stopped short at the bottom of the stairwell, suddenly chilled. Somewhere above me, the whistle echoed through the empty building.

It might be the janitor. I had seen him in the distance and done my best to avoid him.

My mouth was dry as I pursed my lips and tried to whistle again. I tried a little "Dueling Banjos" this time.

In the distance I heard the next part of the song.

It wasn't different enough, though. It could have just been an echo, distorted by the books and shelves.

That's what I told myself.

I whistled a bit more and listened as the whistle came back, followed a moment later by the next line.

The silence waited for my response.

Then it hit me: someone knew I was in the library. Someone could hear me.

I took the stairs two at a time, my footfalls echoing off the bare walls. The landing on the second floor was a narrow space, clogged with paperback racks and bins of records.

I slowed just as I was about to round the corner. I peered into the reference area, the rows of tables that during the day were filled with students writing essays.

I couldn't believe my eyes.

The chairs were full and the tables piled high with books. People wandered between the shelves, taking armloads of books back to their seats. Dozens of them, all like me, shabbily dressed, dirty, unshaven. I recognized some of them from the newspaper tables.

"Had we but world enough, and time," a voice boomed out. My heart jumped in my chest. "Your coyness, boy, would be no crime . . ." There was a skittering sound, like dry leaves, as the people all started whispering at once.

"You," came the voice again, "you out on the landing . . ." My stomach dropped into a deep hole between my feet. "What are you waiting for? What are you afraid of?"

I stepped around the corner and into the reference area.

All of the men stopped their work and turned toward me, silent again, not surprised by my presence.

"Well, it's about time," the large man at the back table said, in the same resounding voice. "Of course, time is the one thing we have no shortage of."

KAREN

It was hard to say just what the hardest part was. I found myself wanting to preface every conversation with Jamie or Ruth or my mother on the telephone by saying "But the hardest part is . . ." But I couldn't make such a distinction—*everything* I prefaced with that statement would be true.

Getting out of bed, knowing what lay ahead of me in the day. Showering, washing—for who? No one cared. Eating . . .

I invited Ruth for dinner most nights, hoping to have someone to eat with, but she always declined. I could see her point.

So I ate alone. In the first few weeks after Simon left, I ate whatever was at hand: tins of soup, boxes of macaroni and cheese, ravioli, all of that crap stuff we'd give Sherry once in a while as a treat. I'd heat it up on the stove, dump it onto a plate, toss the pot into the sink.

I couldn't bear to sit at the table. The table was for family dinners, and Sherry was all the family I had left. I'd eat alongside her bed, mindlessly shoveling forkfuls into my mouth, staring out the front window, at the overgrown yard, the sidewalk, the cars going by on the street.

I made sure I did the dishes each night, but that was only because I knew Ruth would be in the kitchen the next morning.

I don't know how long I would have continued eating that garbage if it hadn't been for Ruth. One morning in early September she arrived carrying a large brown paper bag.

"I hope you don't think I'm trying to mother you," she said. Setting the grocery bag on the table, she began pulling items from it. A head of lettuce. A small cauliflower. "I know that with everything that's going on you haven't had much chance to get out to the supermarket." Several stalks of broccoli. Pale green celery. A bundle of carrots with the tops on. "So I thought I'd pick up some veggies for you while I was out doing my shopping last night." Four apples, each a different variety.

Several oranges. A grapefruit that almost rolled onto the floor. "If you want me to, I can pick up whatever you need when I go." Setting a bunch of bananas with the rest, she artfully folded the bag.

I don't think I had ever seen anything so beautiful. The table looked like a child's treasure chest. I felt a craving so deep it was primal, a desperate need for the sweetness, the fibers, the textures.

When I turned to Ruth, I realized she knew exactly what I was feeling. "Of course, if you wanted to," Ruth said, "I could stay here with Sherry and you could go for a walk, buy yourself what you needed. I know that in a lot of places, people shop every day, just for what they need. Everything so fresh." She inhaled heartily, as if swept away by the thought herself. "There's a little market not far from here, isn't there?"

I smiled at her. "What do I owe you for all this?"

She shook her head. "We'll call it insurance money."

Picking up a McIntosh, I bit, the skin exploding under my teeth, the sweetness flooding my mouth.

Ruth smiled at me and went to check on Sherry. I finished my apple in private.

So most days, early in the afternoon, I walked to the market. I loaded up the basket with what called to me as I passed: a glossy red pepper, a purple onion, snow peas, a cauliflower, grapes, a chicken breast, fresh flowers for Sherry's room. And I took my time walking home, canvas shopping bag slung over one shoulder, the warm sunlight on my face, the breeze cool against my skin.

The meals always seemed to come together as naturally as the shopping did. I lived on stir-fries over rice or noodles, maybe a piece of fruit afterward, and I ate at the table.

Every so often, though, I looked at the empty place across from me, the empty chair. These chairs were the first pieces of furniture we ever bought new, for the kitchen of our first house. This house. The house where I live alone with my silent daughter, where the man who used to be my husband visits twice each day, knocking on the door like a salesman.

We had lived here together for five years; I had been alone here for five months. Lifetimes.

When he went to the daily Masses at the cathedral, the stranger kept the collar and his Bible in the pocket of his coat. He sat near the back, in a pew of his own. He paid little attention to the sermons and homilies—what interest had he in the purported wisdoms of some provincial priest?

He was there to watch the congregation.

He knew the sort of people he was seeking. They would be there most days. They would be devout, building their lives around their faith rather than paying lip service with once-weekly observances. They would sit close to the front, close to the altar, close to the aisle. They would carry their own Bibles with them. They would be the first to their knees when told to drop.

Soldiers. He was looking for soldiers of the Lord. There were many candidates, as he knew there would be. As there always were. They would come to him when he called. They would serve.

But there had to be a first, and he knew who it would be.

He was a huge man, nearly six and a half feet tall, and solid through the body. He carried his Bible like a shield. His face, though, was soft, open. Malleable.

The man brought his mother to Sunday Mass. They walked slowly, her arm looped in his, his Bible in his other hand. He bowed his head as he walked with her, listening to the old woman, nodding. For several weeks, the stranger walked behind them. His mother called her son Leopold, but the priests at the cathedral called him Leo.

Weekdays, Leo came to the early-morning services alone. He always smiled, and as he walked up the aisle he raised his eyes to the stained glass. A little simple, perhaps, but the stranger knew there was an inner steel in the big, soft man that the stranger could shape to his purpose.

Leo was always the first to his knees, dropping with a purity of faith and a fervor no one else matched. His belief burned in him like a torch, and the stranger could feel himself warmed by the flames.

MARY

Most days, we had dinner after our run. It helped us work up an appetite, and by the time we got to the restaurant there wasn't much of a lineup.

We had started running together not long after Simon moved in. I used to do aerobics in the afternoons, and Simon would run every morning with his male colleagues and play racquetball or squash a couple of times a week. After we moved in together, though, his friendships started to fall apart. At first people came up with excuses—The kids were sick. Sorry, slept in—but then they didn't even bother. And Simon gave up, both on them and on exercise.

After a couple of weeks of Simon being surly from the lack of exercise, I suggested that we should start running together.

"You don't run," he said, lying in bed and staring at the ceiling.

"No, but I've always wanted to try it."

"Really?" He turned to look at my face.

"Really."

"That'd be great, Mary. It's always better if you've got some-one to run with. When do you want to start?"

"How about tomorrow?"

He was reaching for the alarm clock as I interrupted him. "No way. I'm not getting up at some insane hour to run. Let's go after work. You know, when I usually go to aerobics."

He withdrew his hand from the alarm clock, sliding it instead over my hip. "Thank you," he said, after a moment, his voice a mere whisper.

The tone of relief, and of appreciation, warmed me.

It took a little while before I was able to keep pace with him over his usual distance, but I think I surprised him with what good shape I was in.

"That's what aerobics four times a week will do for you," I panted after our first run, hunched over, barely able to feel my legs but refusing to let on.

Most nights, after showering, we'd retrace our route, hand in hand, the golden lights of the legislature reflecting off windows and waves.

At first we'd both felt awkward being together in public, but as summer turned to fall and beyond, we'd become comfortable. It was such a pleasure to be able to walk outside and not be afraid of who might see us.

We went to Pagliacci's on Remembrance Day. We usually went at least once a week, avoiding the weekends when you had to line up for an hour for a table. It was a Monday night, but it was a holiday for most people, and the place was packed. The walk over had been frosty.

Simon poured more wine into our glasses, sliding mine carefully toward me.

I took a sip of my wine then broached a subject I had been nervous to mention. "I was thinking that maybe we should go away for a bit."

The idea obviously took him by surprise. "What?"

"Well, it's been so busy. I mean, today was a holiday and we were in the office for what—ten hours? And last weekend?"

"I'm not arguing the need, I'm just wondering what you had in mind."

"I thought maybe pack up the car, go up to Tofino, get a room right on the beach. Maybe the Wickaninnish."

He sat back, cradling his wineglass in his right hand. "Right on the beach," he repeated. "Maybe a fireplace, whirlpool tub? When were you thinking of going? The next couple of weeks are pretty tight. What about over Christmas?"

there for a minute that maybe you were a bit tetched."

"What are . . . what are all of you doing here?" I stammered. My mouth was not quite under my control.

"Well, reading, of course." He laughed heartily, and I felt less afraid. He was a great bear of a man, with graying hair and beard still touched with red, his face full and rosy. His clothes were rumpled and plain; even looking directly at him I couldn't tell what he was wearing.

Static suddenly whirred over the PA system, then horns kicked in with a blast.

"And listening to music, apparently. Would you turn that down," he bellowed. "There's people trying to hear."

The volume fell as quickly as if he had turned the knob himself.

"Better," he muttered. "Hot Fives. Louis Armstrong. Nineteen . . . twenty-seven, I believe." He shook his head. "Great set, great set. Great man, that Satchmo."

"Who *are* you?" I asked, completely baffled. I felt like I had just stepped into a movie or a fairy tale.

"Good question," he answered, not answering. "I'm pleased that it wasn't the first thing you asked. Just don't ask me how I make a living and we'll get along fine."

"But . . ."

"The real question is, who are you?"

"I . . ." For a moment, I considered lying. "I'm Henry. Henry Denton."

"*Ah.*" He settled himself into his chair, gesturing for me to sit down across from him. A look of understanding filled his face. "Of course you are."

I sat down. "What? Who *are* you? No. Why . . . How can you see me? I thought—"

"You could also ask why you can see us, Henry, when no one else can."

My chest tightened. "You mean you're . . . People can't see you? But—"

"Can't. I told my folks I'd be up at their place from the twentieth or so. You could come too, if you like."

"What about the weekend of December seventh? We could even head up that Wednesday afternoon, make a four-day weekend of it. I figure the firm owes us a little time." He slipped past the invitation to spend Christmas with my family.

I didn't want to bring it up, but I had to ask. "Will you be okay leaving Sherry for a few days?"

"She's . . ."

He paused and I could almost hear him sifting through everything before he spoke.

"It's only for a few days. I'll let her know what's going on. Tell her when I'll be back."

"And Karen?"

"Well." He took another sip of his wine. "I don't think Karen's going to be too pleased about it. She always wanted to go to the Wickaninnish."

That thought made me strangely happy.

"So. December 4?" he asked.

I nodded. "I'll make the reservations tomorrow."

HENRY

"Well, come on," the big man called. "Time and tide wait for no man."

I hesitated in the doorway. The people were all staring at me.

"Okay, the rest of you, back to what you were doing," the big man said.

As if he had flicked a switch, everyone went back to work: back to the shelves, to their tables, their heads down in their books.

"Well," he waved me toward him. "Come on."

I made my way through the crowded room to where he sat.

"Good, good," he said, as he looked me over. "I was worried

"But why?" The big man sighed. "Not an easy question to answer. Not easy at all." He pushed back from the table, stood up and began to pace. Behind him, there was a wall of windows and through them I could see streetlights and the lights in the buildings across the street, along with a reflection of the room. I wondered what people would see if they happened to look up. Probably nothing. An empty room in a deserted building.

"There are no easy answers," he said. "Especially not as far as who I am." He gestured around the room. "Who we are"— turning his gaze back to me—"Who you are."

I pulled back. "I know who *I* am. I told you already."

"No," he interrupted gently. "You told me your name. That's got absolutely nothing to do with who you are."

I guess I looked confused. I was confused.

"Let me ask you this: why are you here?" He ran one hand over and through his beard. "Why are you here, in a closed library, in the middle of the night?"

I couldn't answer. It would have meant telling him about Sherry, about what I had done.

He watched me for a moment. "Well, what about everyone else? Why do you think everyone else is here?" He set both hands on the tabletop and leaned toward me. "Why do you think *I'm* here?"

I responded without thinking. "You already told me— you're reading."

"Clever boy." He nodded his head, grinned a little and started pacing again. "Yes, we're here because we're reading. But why are we *here?*" This time, when he looked at me, his eyes asked a deeper question. "*That's* what we're trying to figure out."

"You mean you don't know?"

He smiled. "You sound so disappointed. Do you know how few people know why they're anywhere? How few people ever find out? When they do, we turn them into saints. Or gurus." He paused. "Or gods."

"I don't understand."

He shrugged. "Of course you don't. Most people go through their entire lives without understanding, without ever stepping out of the day-to-day to really look around. But you see, we're luckier than them. We know what we are."

"What are you?" I asked, because he wanted me to.

"We, Henry? We're the damned," he answered, his eyes locking on mine. "We're doing penance for our crimes. And we don't know when that penance will end."

I looked around at the men and the stacks of books and papers. "The answer's in here?"

"The answer's in here," he said, pointing at the books on the table in front of him. "Maybe." His eyes twinkled, but I didn't think he was joking. "Who's your favorite author?"

The question took me by surprise. I struggled for a moment to remember the name of the person who wrote the book I had spent the day reading. "Saminger," I said, feeling pleased with myself.

His smile was patient, and suddenly very warm. I realized that I had gotten something wrong. "Salinger. That's a good place to start. See where he takes you."

He sat back down in his chair and opened the top book of the stack in front of him. I realized he was finished talking, that I had been given a task to do and now I was expected to do it.

"But what's . . . what do I call you?" I asked, before his attention disappeared into his book completely.

He looked up as if surprised to see me still standing there. He straightened, and when he spoke his voice was commanding, thick with a different accent. "You may call me . . . Tim." Nearby, one of the others snickered, and Tim waited expectantly.

I was missing something.

When I didn't respond, he sagged a little. "Oh great and powerful Tim," he said, waiting for recognition, his eyes bright. When it still didn't come, he sagged and slumped against his chair. "Oh, for Christ's sake," he muttered. "Monty Python? *Holy Grail?* John Cleese?"

"I don't think I've . . ."

He shook his head. "That's the trouble with youth today. No knowledge of the classics." He picked up his book, opened it again to his page. "Just call me Tim," he said as he started to read.

As I turned away, he was muttering to himself. "Great man, John Cleese. Great bit. Great bit . . ."

I made my way back downstairs to where Salinger was waiting for me.

RUTH

Sarah arrived just before Karen left to go to the movies the next afternoon. Jamie was sitting at the kitchen table with her. When the doorbell rang, I called out from Sherry's room, "I'll get it!"

I hadn't seen Sarah in weeks, and I was shocked at her deterioration. Her flesh sagged away from her cheekbones and her skin was crepey. She was dressed in a loose blue and purple floral-print blouse and navy slacks. She had obviously bought the clothes after she started to lose weight, but she still seemed to swim in them.

With her right hand she held the handle of a small, rolling oxygen tank, its plastic tubing snaking up, then splitting into each nostril. Her shaking left hand held a cigarette, which she pressed unsteadily to her lips.

I must have given her a look.

"Oh, give up, Ruth," she rasped, exhaling a blue plume of smoke. "Keep your judgments to yourself."

"I didn't say a word." I leaned forward to give her an awkward hug. She smelled terrible, a mix of stale cigarette smoke and acrid sweat, as if she hadn't bathed in weeks. "It's good to see you, Sarah," I said as I pulled away. My words hung in white clouds in the chill air.

"You too, Ruthie," she answered. "You're looking well." She took a heavy drag off her cigarette. "And don't even try. I know I look like hell." She blew out the smoke.

"You don't look . . ." She did look terrible, and she knew it. "Come on, let's go inside. I'm freezing." I added, "You'll have to leave that out here."

She gave me a withering look as she dropped her cigarette to the concrete stoop and ground it out with her foot. "Do I look like an idiot to you? Of course I'm not going to smoke in someone else's house. And around a patient . . ." She shook her head and hefted the oxygen tank up over the doorsill in a practiced, yet still uncomfortable-looking, motion.

I led her toward the kitchen.

Karen and Jamie stood up as we entered the room. "Mrs. Barrett," I started. "This is my sister, Sarah Page. Sarah, this is Mrs. Barrett."

"I'm pleased to meet you," Karen said, a little stiffly, taking Sarah's hand and shaking it. I could tell she was surprised by the way Sarah looked. I should have prepared her.

"And this is my friend Jamie Keller," Karen said. Sarah reached for Jamie's hand, forcing Jamie to reach past Karen in order to shake.

Sarah gave a watery smile. "Nice to meet you both." Her voice cracked as she spoke.

Karen's eyes flicked to mine, then away. "Ruth, I put some water on to boil when the doorbell rang."

"Thank you, Mrs. Barrett."

"We shouldn't be much later than four." They never were.

"I'll be here," I said, smiling.

Karen's eyes gleamed a little. Her spirits were always lifted by her Tuesday afternoons out of the house. "Sarah, it was very nice to meet you."

"Very nice," my sister repeated.

"I hope we'll be seeing you again."

"God willing," Sarah muttered, with the same watery smile. It made her look as if she had lost her mind.

The kettle on the stove started to whistle, and I lifted it away from the element. "Shall I make us a pot of tea?" I asked.

I heard the front door close.

"God no," Sarah said, to my surprise. "I'll be up all night. The bladder's not what it used to be." I didn't like to imagine. My younger sister.

"Let's go into the living room then. I'll introduce you to Sherry."

She followed me, the wheels of her oxygen tank squeaking along the hardwood floors. Vivaldi was playing, and I turned it down a little as we came into the living room.

"Music therapy?" she asked, teasing me the way she always did.

I shrugged. "Well, she might be able to hear."

She pulled her cart to the edge of the bed. "Oh, she is a pretty little thing, isn't she?" she cooed softly. She actually cooed.

"Yes, she is." I stepped over to the bedside, gently stroking Sherry's cheek with the back of my hand.

Sarah clung to her oxygen rig like she needed the support. "They never found the fellow who did this? The driver?"

I shook my head.

"He must have been drunk."

I shook my head again. "The police don't think so. He had just worked a night shift, and they figure he was in a hurry to get home. He had two boys of his own."

"So sad."

"Apparently he tried to go around her."

She pursed her lips. "Is there any . . . ?"

I shook my head. "No. The doctors don't think she'll ever . . ."

She nodded, saving me from having to say it. "You can touch her if you want to. Go ahead."

Sarah double-checked my face to be sure I was serious, then gingerly reached out her left hand. Her yellow fingertips trembled as she stroked Sherry's cheek. "I don't know how you do it," she said, barely above a whisper. "It must just break your heart."

"Sarah," I said seriously. "Listen, there's something I want to tell you."

She drew back from the bedside, all her attention on me. "What is it? What's wrong?"

"No, no." I shook my head. "Nothing's wrong with me. It's . . . I wanted you to come over here . . ." I took a deep breath, trying to figure out the best way to broach the subject with her. "Watch this."

Holding my hand in the air in front of her face, I clenched my fist, flexed my fingers, rotated my wrist.

It took her a moment to realize what she was seeing.

"Oh my God, Ruth," she gasped. "What happened to your arthritis?"

I hesitated before I answered. "Gone."

Her face shifted in confusion, her fingers tightening around the handle of her oxygen tank. "But how? A new medication? A new . . . Some experimental drug? Oh God, Ruth, I'm so happy for you!" Her watery eyes sparkled. "When did this happen?"

"I'm not really sure."

I had spent most of the past few days trying to answer that question, but I still hadn't been able to figure it out. The trouble with chronic pain is that it is so easy to become accustomed to it, both mentally and physically. At first it's absolutely agonizing; it's the only thing you think about, like a rock in your shoe that rubs your foot raw with every step. Then the constant rubbing, the pain and the limp all become part of the status quo, the occasional stabbing pain just a reminder.

You are set to endure, hunched against it—and when it starts to ease, you don't really notice, until the absence washes over you like a balm.

"Sometime in the past few months," was the best I could do.

"And you're only telling me now?"

"I . . . I didn't really notice right away. The pain is always better in the summer. But when the cold weather hit, it didn't come back."

"You must have known," my sister snapped. "It's not like someone was slipping the pills into your food like you were a pet cat."

"There weren't any pills."

"What?"

"There weren't any pills." I turned my eyes away, suddenly embarrassed.

"So what was it? Some sort of spontaneous remission?" She spat out the words with all the venom of a fallen true believer.

"I think . . ." I turned my gaze back to Sherry, motionless on the bed. "I think it was her."

Sarah just gaped at me.

"I know how ridiculous that sounds. I know it sounds like I'm turning into one of those old women, the ones who send in all their money to the television evangelists, but it's the only thing that makes any sense to me. My arthritis was terrible last winter. Then I started working with Sherry every day. And now," I clenched the fist again to demonstrate. "I'm not taking any pills, I haven't changed my diet. It's the only thing I can think of."

"You think this little girl healed your arthritis?" she rasped, leaning a little farther over the bed, eyeing Sherry curiously.

I nodded, bracing myself for her derisive laughter.

Instead, she asked softly, "And me? Is that why you wanted me to come over here?" For just a moment her voice was that of a sixteen-year-old girl, and I had a sudden vision of a funeral in a country churchyard in the rain, two coffins, two daughters holding one another.

I hesitated, then nodded.

"I don't believe in God," she said, looking me straight in the eye.

The remark took me by surprise. "I hadn't—This isn't about God," I stammered.

"Well, what then?"

"I don't know." I shook my head. "I just know that I'm healed." Again I clenched my fist, demonstrating, still transfixed by that simple motion, by the emotions that the movement raised in me.

"Well," she said. "I'm at the point where I'll try just about anything. How do we do this?"

"I don't know," I confessed.

She grinned at me, with her yellowing teeth. "Well that doesn't do me much good, does it?"

"Well, I'm in contact with her all day. I bathe her and turn her and—"

"I know the routine."

"So I don't know when exactly it happened."

"*If* it happened."

"Or how," I countered, glaring at her.

"Well," she said, changing her tone, studying Sherry. "What if we try this the old-fashioned way?" She gently took the covers down from Sherry's still form, freeing her arms.

"Here, let me," I said, coming around the bed to stand alongside her. "I'll take care of Sherry," I said, taking hold of her tiny arm. "You . . . maybe you should unbutton your blouse . . ."

Sarah leaned forward slowly, opening her blouse to expose her brassiere. It looked new, and loose on her diminishing frame. I gently raised Sherry's arm, supporting it under the elbow, turning her wrist to shift her hand.

For a moment, I felt guilty. I glanced at the doorway, feeling suddenly as if we were being watched. There was no one there. Guilty conscience.

As I turned back, I glanced at Sarah's face. Her eyes were closed, her lips parted, her features . . . hopeful.

I knew I would be able to handle the guilt.

Gingerly, I touched Sherry's hand to the pale, loose skin of my sister's chest, just above the barely noticeable rise of her breasts. Carefully, I applied just enough pressure to smooth the tiny palm flat against the white skin, and then I just held it there.

"Can you feel anything?" I asked.

She shook her head. "I don't know what to expect . . ."

I had no idea either. I held Sherry's hand there for just a moment longer, then removed it, tucking her gently back under the covers as Sarah buttoned her blouse. "There you go, sweetie," I told her. "All bundled up again."

Straightening up from the bed, my eyes met Sarah's and we just looked at each other for a long moment.

She smiled a little, bit her lip and shrugged.

"Well," she said.

THREE

November 27–December 5

KAREN

Simon was singing when I brought him his cup of coffee.

"Hush little baby don't say a word . . ."

The weather had turned cold almost overnight, the late gales of November blowing icy off the strait, the last of the leaves clinging to the wet pavement, the trees skeletal against the gray sky.

"Daddy's gonna buy you a mockingbird . . ."

Simon had a nice voice. Back when we were in school he even used to play a bit of guitar. We'd have people over to our place, a tiny apartment in one of the big, converted heritage houses near downtown. Friday nights of songs, soup and jugs of homemade wine.

"And if that mockingbird don't sing . . ."

But that was a long time ago. I didn't even know where his guitar was. Probably up in the attic somewhere.

He broke off mid-line as I came into the living room, setting the two mugs down on the table.

"You didn't have to stop."

He smiled. "Well . . . Listen, Karen, there's something I wanted to talk to you about." His tone was careful. Too careful.

"What? Is it Sherry?"

"No, it's nothing like that. It's just that . . . Mary and I are going away next weekend. Four days. Head up to Tofino."

"Why are you telling me this?"

"I thought you should know . . ."

I could feel a hot rush in me.

"You thought I should know that you and your girlfriend are getting away for the weekend? That's nice. Have a great time." I stood up. I couldn't bear to be in the same room with him.

"Karen . . ."

"Oh, for Christ's sake, Simon," I snapped. "What made you think that this would be a good thing to share with me?" I was trying to keep my voice under control, but it was starting to rise.

"I just wanted to let you know that I wouldn't be coming by for a few days."

"Good for you. Thanks for the heads-up."

"I thought you'd want to know."

"You thought I'd want to know?" I said, dripping sarcasm. "That's sweet. Now when I wake up alone in the middle of the night next weekend, I can think about you and your girlfriend fucking in Tofino. That's great. Thanks."

I should have left then, but I couldn't stop myself. "I hope you get a room with a fireplace. Maybe a hot tub. I imagine doing it in a bed must be getting pretty boring for you."

"Karen . . ."

"Oh, right. I forgot. She's all of what? Twenty-four? Twenty-five? Shit, you probably won't get bored with her for another ten years."

"Jesus Christ, Karen, Sherry's right here! Keep your voice down."

"The next time you're looking at her ass, be sure to check the expiration date!"

He headed for the door and I followed him. I couldn't stop.

"Simon, what you fail to see is how little I care about what you do. You may not have noticed, but I have a little more on my mind than that. Come or don't come, I don't care. Sherry doesn't care. It's all the same to us."

He stopped at the front door.

"Listen, this isn't . . . I'm just going to go."

"Fine. Whatever. That seems to be what you're best at."

"Hello?"

"Ruth? It's me."

"Sarah?"

"Yeah. Listen . . . I just had a doctor's appointment . . ."

"Are you okay?"

"Well, I started to notice some strange things a week or so ago—"

"Are you okay?"

"So I made a doctor's appointment—"

"Sarah! Are you okay?"

"It's gone, Ruth. They did X-rays, tests . . . Spontaneous remission. That's what the doctor said."

"Spontaneous remission."

"Yeah."

"Oh my God."

"Yeah. That's what I was thinking. Exactly."

"You've reached Jamie Keller, extension 328. I'm not at my desk right now, or I'm on another line. Please leave a message after the tone. If it's urgent, please dial zero to have me paged."

"Shit, Jamie, you're out. I was hoping you'd be there. I just . . . I just had this colossal fight with Simon. No, not even a fight. I just screamed at him for like twenty minutes . . . Oh, it's so stupid . . . he's going up-island with Mary for a few days . . . I just freaked out. Call me, okay?"

"Hello?"

"Hello. Is this Pam?"

"Yes. Who's this?"

"It's Sarah. Sarah Page."

"Sarah Page?"

"From the group. Sarah from the Tuesday-night group."

"Oh yes, yes. Sarah. Hello."

"How are you feeling, Pam?"

"Oh, not so good, Sarah. It's not a good day. But how are you?"

"Well, that's why I'm calling . . ."

RUTH

For the whole morning after the phone call with Sarah, I alternated between staring at Sherry and not being able to look at her. I tried to find some physical sign of what she could do, but I didn't know what I was looking for. An aura maybe. A halo. But there was nothing—just a little girl who will never wake up.

"Who are you?" I asked her at one point. She didn't answer.

Anything that I had read about healers and saints, all my Sunday-school lessons so long ago, led me to believe that I should have been able to see *something,* some trace of the divine. Her ordinariness—it scared me.

How would I tell Karen? For that matter, what would I tell Karen? That her daughter had cured my sister of cancer? My arthritis? That she could do miracles, but she would still never wake up? How she could heal others but not herself?

I bathed her carefully. Not that I was at all rough with her usually, but now I took an exaggerated care, cradling her as though she was an object of great value. I looked for some sign that I had missed, but no. It was still just the same pudgy, pale body I had washed so many times before.

This mortal vessel . . .

Karen was distracted. She had been upset yesterday morning. I had heard the raised voices from the front room as I sat in the kitchen with my second cup of tea, heard Mr. Barrett slam the door as he left. He hadn't come for his regular visit last night or this morning, and I had caught Karen checking the clock as it got later and later, until it finally became clear he wasn't coming.

She was gone three hours on her walk, and when she returned it was obvious she had been crying. I wanted to do something to comfort her, but she retreated upstairs to the privacy of her bedroom.

She was a little better this morning, but it seemed like she was trying not to let anything show. I mostly stayed with Sherry. I didn't know what else to do.

If I told her about my sister, maybe it would help to put all of this stuff with Mr. Barrett into perspective. Or maybe not. Maybe it would all be just too overwhelming. Or maybe it would be just what she needed.

How could the miraculous and the banal exist so close together?

"I'm going out," Karen said from the doorway, startling me. I hadn't heard her footsteps.

I glanced up at the clock. 11:30. That was pretty early, even for a Tuesday.

"I'm meeting Jamie for lunch downtown before the movie," she explained, as if she'd read my thoughts. "I'll be back well before five, though."

As if she needed my approval. I nodded, although it really had nothing to do with me. "All right."

She looked past me at Sherry. I had dressed her in her green nightie after her bath. "How is she today?" she asked. It wasn't like her to have to ask.

"Oh, she's doing just fine. We were just about to listen to some Bach."

She nodded. "I'm sorry, Ruth. I haven't been very . . . I've been a little stressed."

"That's fine," I said. "I know there's been some stuff going on."

She smiled. "I guess it's pretty hard to keep anything a secret around here, isn't it?"

I returned her smile, but her words struck very close to home. Secrets.

She glanced down at her watch. "Shoot. I have to go. I'm walking. Listen, thanks. I'll try to be more together tomorrow."

"Don't rush anything," I said as she was turning away.

She looked back and I forced a smile. "These things work themselves out."

"Not this time." The front door clicked shut.

I sat down next to Sherry and brushed her hair away from her face. The light coming through the windows didn't seem to penetrate as deeply into the room as it had even a few weeks before.

"That's okay, Sherry. Your mom and dad are having a little argument, but it's going to be okay. It'll all turn out okay."

I spent the next while listening to the music, leaning back in the chair, my hand touching Sherry's hair where it spread out across the pillow. I knew she could hear what was going on around her, the music, the voices. I knew she was aware of what was going on between her parents when they argued across her bed. I knew she could hear her father sing to her, and people saying her name. I wanted to ask her what I should do, how I should tell her parents what she was capable of . . .

I was awakened from a light sleep and a vague dream by the sound of the doorbell. The music had finished, and for a moment I didn't recognize where I was.

Then the doorbell rang again.

Sarah was standing on the front step. Gone was the oxygen tank, the pallor, the lifelessness. Her cheeks were flushed, her eyes bright and full of life. She held her overcoat around herself against the cold, but she seemed stronger. Taller, even.

"Hello, Ruth," she said, a little too cheerfully. "I'm sorry for not calling first. This is my friend Pam."

As bad as Sarah had looked when she arrived at the house two weeks ago, Pam looked even worse. A much younger woman, no older than thirty, she seemed withered, almost weightless. Her hair had fallen out in chunks, leaving bright spots on her scalp. She clung to my sister as if Sarah was all that was holding her to life.

"Sarah . . ." The thought of what Sarah was asking me to do chilled me.

"Can we come in, please?" She spoke with forced joviality. "It's really too cold out here for Pam."

I knew that by letting them into the house, I was condoning what would happen. I looked again at Pam and stepped aside. I couldn't leave this frail person standing on the doorstep in the cold. But I couldn't let this happen.

Pam's steps were slow and tiny. Sarah carefully guided her along, over the doorsill, into the house, supporting her weight and rubbing the back of the hand that clutched her arm. I closed the door behind them.

"You have a seat, Pam," Sarah said, walking her into the living room and settling her on the couch.

"Can we talk?" I gestured for Sarah to come back into the hallway, out of Pam's sight.

"I'm sorry, Ruth," were the first words out of her mouth. "I would have called, but I knew you would have said—"

"No?" I finished her sentence. "Sarah, what do you think you're doing? Do you know what Kar . . . Mrs. Barrett would say?"

"Have you told her? About . . ." She gestured with her head toward the front room. "About Sherry?"

"Not yet. I don't see how I can."

"She's dying, Ruth."

"What?"

"Pam. She's dying. She's in this support group that I was going to. For terminal patients."

"Sarah." I realized I didn't want to hear Pam's story. But Sarah was not going to stop.

"It started off in her breasts. She had a double mastectomy, but it's metastasized all through her now. They've taken out most of her stomach, pieces of her lungs. The doctors figure she's got no more than a couple of weeks."

"Sarah, I can't."

"Ruth, she's got two little kids. Both under five. I could show you pictures."

"Sarah . . ."

"Please?"

I was stunned: it was the first time Sarah had asked me for something in years.

I took a deep breath before speaking, knowing that I was going to regret my decision, whichever way I went.

"All right," I whispered. "We'll give it a try."

"Thank you."

"But listen," I interrupted. "This is *it*. You can't tell anybody else. This can't get around, okay?"

"Okay."

"No," I said. "This is important."

"I said okay." She looked at me unflinchingly. "I *do* understand."

"Okay," I breathed. "Let's try to get you both out of here before Mrs. Barrett comes home."

I started back toward the living room, but Sarah reached out for my arm. "Thank you," she whispered.

I knew that she wasn't talking about Pam.

SIMON

The last thing I wanted to do was to upset Mary by telling her about the fight with Karen, so I kept it to myself.

Mary worried so much. One night, when I was almost asleep, she started a conversation by saying, "Are you ever sorry you're here?"

I rolled over to face her. My eyes were dazzled by her skin, glowing in the darkness. "What?" As if I either hadn't heard or hadn't really understood.

"Are you ever sorry you're here?" she repeated, her voice small.

"Why would I be sorry to be here?" I curled my arm around her, shocked to find her cool despite the temperature of the apartment.

"Well, I feel . . . sometimes I feel like I stole you from your wife . . ." Her voice dropped even lower.

"There were problems between Karen and I before I met you."

"Yes, but if it weren't for me—"

"If it weren't for you, I'd be very unhappy right now."

"And with me?"

"With you I'm very happy."

Her eyes lit up, and after that she fell asleep quickly, but I knew that wasn't the end of it. Occasionally she would look at me and almost speak, but then she'd change her mind.

The reactions at the office hadn't helped. If anything, the tension had built, not eased. Everyone was still civil to my face, but it was different for Mary. People treated her like she wasn't even there. Sheila wouldn't acknowledge her presence. If she brought files or records to us while we were working, she would hand me everything I needed, but leave Mary's materials on the table or desk out of reach. She would bring me coffee without bringing anything for Mary. She would ask if I wanted her to order lunch for me, ignoring Mary entirely.

I spoke to Sheila about it a couple of times, and she assured me that I was mistaken, that it had been an oversight, that it wouldn't happen again. That was, of course, a lie, and we both knew it.

"How's Karen holding up?" Sheila would ask.

Karen.

I had picked up the phone half a dozen times in the forty-eight hours since the fight, punching in what used to be my home number, disconnecting each time before the phone had a chance to ring. What would I say?

I would apologize.

But I hadn't done anything wrong.

What was I thinking? Hadn't done anything wrong?

I might as well have rubbed salt in her eyes, kicked her while she was down.

Mary had been quite concerned when I told her that I wasn't going over to visit Sherry the morning after the fight.

"The doctor's going to be there."

"Well, shouldn't you be there too?"

"Karen'll let me know what he has to say." I cleared my throat. "Sometimes the doctor and I don't see quite eye to eye. It's best if I just give him the space to do his job."

She seemed to accept that as a valid reason, and didn't pursue it any further. That afternoon I deliberately let a meeting run well past five, the time I normally left to see Sherry.

"Are you still going to stop by the house?" Mary asked after the client had left.

I pretended to think about it, then shook my head. "No, I don't think so. I don't want to disturb Karen at dinnertime. Besides, I really feel like a long run tonight."

She eyed me strangely. "Don't you want to hear what the doctor said?"

Caught in my own lie. "I'll call her later."

Mary didn't say anything more, and we drove home together in silence.

The next day's excuses were even weaker.

And then it was 1:42 a.m., according to the red digits of the clock radio. Mary's breath was as regular as a metronome, and I had lain awake for almost three hours, watching the soundless changing of the numbers, listening to the distanced, muffled noises from the other tenants.

Mary shifted a little in her sleep and moaned softly.

Without disturbing her, I slid out from under the covers. By the light from the windows, I navigated out of the bedroom, shutting the door behind me before I turned on one of the table lamps in the living room.

I looked around in the low amber glow. I had been living with Mary for months, but I didn't seem to have made much of an impression. There were a few of my books stacked on the floor next to her bookshelves, but all of the art in the room was hers—reproductions of a Lichtenstein comic panel, a blue Matisse *Jazz* figure, a Navajo-style blanket. There was a small stack of my CDs on top of the stereo cabinet, but the stereo itself, the television, the furniture, the apartment, were hers. Sometimes, it was as if I was not even here. As if I were no more than a guest in her home.

I crossed the room to the CD rack. There were almost no artists that I recognized among Mary's CDs. The rack was filled with groups with names like The Orb, Prodigy, Blur, Moist and Sloan.

Each time I looked, it brought home the fact that an entire generation separated us. Although I preferred the classics, I had once taken a great deal of pride in my knowledge of music, and kept up to the minute on all the latest artists and trends, even if I didn't listen to much of it. Not to recognize any of these performers? Old.

Sighing, I turned to the stack of CDs I had bought over the last couple of months, comforted by their spines. Van Morrison. Bob Dylan. Neil Young. The Grateful Dead.

"What's that?" Mary had asked in the record store when she saw what I was carrying.

I showed her the CDs—*American Beauty. Blood on the Tracks. Astral Weeks.*

"That's all fogey music," she complained good-naturedly.

"Get outta here."

"No kidding. I mean, how old do you think you are? Fifty? This music was old when you were my age. This is the stuff my grandparents used to listen to."

Exaggeration aside, she did have a point. I had never really gotten into the music my friends liked when I was younger.

My collection resembled that of a forty-year-old—a hip forty-year-old—not the twenty-year-old student I was.

I slipped a Sinead O'Connor CD into the player, plugging in the headphones before pressing Play. This was one of the first CDs I had ever bought, when I began to make the transition to digital after Karen bought me a player for my thirtieth birthday.

The sound was immediate and true, insinuating itself directly into the middle of my cranium, "God grant me the serenity to accept the things I cannot change . . ."

Good choice.

I found myself thinking, for the first time in a very long time, about my guitar. It was a cheap little acoustic, but I had spent hours playing it as an undergrad, building calluses on my fingers, irritating Karen to no end with countless renditions of "Tangled Up in Blue." I found my fingers unconsciously curling into chords, sliding along imagined strings with a beautiful, steely rasp as I listened to the CD. Why had I stopped playing? When was the last time I had even seen the guitar, which had once stood so proudly in the corner of our tiny, book-lined living room in its battered black case?

I wished I had it now and could cradle the comforting, familiar weight of its body in my arms. Strange how things slip away.

The album was almost an hour of betrayal, of loss, and aching strength, but also understanding, great sadness and acceptance. As I listened, I became inescapably, deeply aware of two truths, beyond words, beyond the capacity of rational thought, beyond any possibility of reconciliation.

I was in love with Mary. This wasn't the silly, midlife infatuation that everyone seemed to think it was. She pulled me out of my accustomed form in ways that I hadn't thought possible. With her, I felt a sense of possibility, of potential, that I hadn't felt in years.

But that recognition was made almost unbearable by my second, simultaneous realization.

I loved Karen. Still. After everything I had done, the problems we had and everything I had subjected her to, I loved her.

I loved her, and I couldn't stand myself for hurting her. I knew I was too far gone to ever go back, but I couldn't bear to lose her.

I couldn't bear to lose her . . .

The trouble was, these words were equally true of both Karen and Mary.

I sat, in the silence of the headphones after the music ended, until the barest light of dawn began to touch the world outside the window.

HENRY

A cold hand fell on my shoulder. "Jesus Christ!" I yelped and jumped out of my chair, dropping my book, spinning to face . . .

Tim, who grinned at my distress.

"You scared the hell out of me," I mumbled, trying to recover a little dignity.

"I would have cleared my throat or something, but that seems like such a cliché."

I was pleased with myself. A month before I would have had no idea what a "cliché" was.

He pulled out the chair next to mine and sat down, gesturing for me to do the same. Leaning over, he picked up the book I had dropped and studied the cover. "*Tao Te Ching,*" he muttered. "However did you end up at that?"

I had to think for a moment. "Well, I started off with Salinger, which sent me to . . ."

He waved my words away, as if he hadn't really meant for me to answer. "What do you think of it?"

"I don't know if I really get it. I mean, I understand the

words and everything, but they just don't seem to pull together."

"That's the thing with the Oriental philosophies," he explained. "Zen, all the schools of Buddhism, Taoism . . . it all makes sense when someone else processes it for you, like Salinger. But when you go back to the sources," he gestured at the book in my hand, "you realize how very foreign, how very different the cultural framework is. And that makes the ideas really difficult for the Western mind to wrap itself around. We don't have a common vocabulary."

I nodded, mostly understanding him.

"It's good you're prepared to tackle it, but you might want to try something a little closer to home. Some Western philosophy. The Bible, perhaps."

I felt a small surge of pride at the way he was talking to me.

"Is it just the books that are keeping you down here?" he asked, his voice dropping a bit. "Or is it something else?"

"What?" I asked, pretending not to understand.

"We haven't seen too much of you," he said. "You seem to spend most of your time down here."

"Well, I've been . . ." I stammered, gesturing at the books piled on the table in front of me.

How could I explain?

I killed a little girl. Well, I didn't kill her exactly: I put her into a coma that she'll never wake up from. I tried to kill myself, but I can't seem to die. There's no way I deserve to be with other people.

I couldn't bring myself to say the words.

"I guess I'm just a slow learner," I said.

He nodded. "You'll find that a lot of us are. That's why we're here."

"Maybe in a little while."

"Whenever you're ready. No pressure. No rush." He rose to his feet, started to turn away, then changed his mind.

"It's not so bad, you know," he said.

"What?"

"What you've done. Whatever you've done. Whatever you think is so bad that you shouldn't be allowed to associate with people. It's not as bad as you think." His smile seemed more sad than happy. "It's probably not nearly as bad as some."

Without waiting for me to answer, he disappeared into the shadows of the library, leaving me to puzzle over his words.

MARY

Something was going on.

Simon had been preoccupied and secretive for days, as if there was something on his mind that he didn't want to tell me about. And he was behaving strangely, changing plans at the last minute. Not visiting with Sherry. Not sleeping. One night, I woke up at about four and he wasn't in bed. The bedroom door was closed, but I could see a splinter of light under it from the living room.

I got up and opened the door, just a crack, to look out into the living room. He was sitting naked on the floor next to the stereo, leaning against the wall with his knees up to his chest. The headphones were over his ears, his eyes closed.

I wanted to go to him, but thought somehow that I shouldn't. I stood in the doorway for several minutes. Then I went back to bed, hugging his cold pillow against me.

Just after five I woke up again. He had come into the bedroom, grabbed a pair of shorts and a shirt off the dresser, and ducked back out. A few minutes later, the front door clicked shut.

What was going on?

I stared at the white, textured ceiling. How had I ended up living with a man who had a wife and a daughter across town? I got up too and showered, mindlessly soaping, shampooing, rinsing, then got dressed and made myself a cup of coffee.

If it had been something with Karen, or anything wrong with Sherry, he would have told me. Wouldn't he? He hadn't said anything. So what had I done?

Goddamn this self-pitying crap.

I just about called Brian. If anyone could cut through the BS and help me figure out what was going on, it was Brian. But I hadn't spoken to him—to any of my friends—since Simon had moved in. How pathetic. Was I really turning into one of *those* women, the sort whose lives revolve around their men, their fucked-up relationships?

A couple of mornings later, Sunday, I was sitting in the living room, coffee cup on the table in front of me, glancing through the *New Sentinel,* when the doorknob rattled and he came in. He was wet from another solitary run, his shirt plastered to his body, his face red, his breath harsh. I wondered how far he'd gone, how hard he'd pushed himself without me.

I wondered how much I held him back.

"Good run?" I asked.

"What are you doing up?" He glanced at his watch. "I was just coming to wake you."

I shrugged, as casually as I could fake. "I woke up when you left. Couldn't go back to sleep."

"I'm sorry. I tried to be quiet. I wanted to blow out the cobwebs. I'm having problems sleeping."

"I noticed. Are you going to tell me what's going on?"

He looked at a loss for words. It was a state I don't think I had ever seen him in before. I didn't like it very much.

"Everything's fine," he finally said.

"Simon, you can talk to me."

"There's nothing—"

Then he looked at me and sighed.

"Yeah, I should have talked to you. I had a big fight with Karen the last time I visited Sherry. It got pretty loud . . ."

"And that's why you haven't been going over there?" I didn't dare allow myself to feel relief. It was Karen; it wasn't me.

He nodded, but didn't meet my eyes.

"Well, why didn't you say something?"

He was silent. "It was about me, wasn't it? That's why you didn't say anything."

"I told her about our trip next weekend."

I waited silently, expecting some revelation. When it didn't come, I asked, "And?"

"And she just lost it. Screaming. Cursing me out. It got pretty ugly." He paused, as if to shape the words before speaking them. "Right over Sherry's bed." He shook his head, as if he was having difficulty understanding the situation.

I was stunned. "That's it?"

"What?" He seemed surprised by my response.

"You kept me in the dark, you made me worry, because you had a fight with your wife?"

"Well . . ."

"Because she's pissed off that we're going away for the weekend?"

He shrugged.

"Damn it, Simon. I thought you were mad at me for something. Of course Karen's pissed off we're going away for the weekend." I shook my head. "Try to put yourself in her shoes."

"Oh, Mary," he finally said. "I'm sorry. I didn't mean to . . ."

"I thought I had done something wrong."

His chin dropped. "That's exactly what I didn't want you to think. That's why I didn't say anything. It's just . . . This is all so hard."

"Of course it is. Did you think it would be easy? What you have to remember, though, is to communicate, okay?"

I made eye contact with him, and waited until he nodded.

"Good. Now go shower." I messed his hair. "We're going for brunch."

He leaned in and kissed me gently, then he lingered for a moment, his face almost touching my own. I could feel a crackling of energy in the air between us. "You're going to be a very wise woman when you grow up," he said, his eyes dancing.

I smiled. "Maybe. But by the time that happens I'll be too busy caring for you in your old age to enjoy it."

On the nights that he hunted, the stranger did not wear the collar. There were things best done in the shadows, and times when the objects of the light were best left behind.

Victoria, he discovered, was a small town masquerading as a city. Within weeks, he was familiar with everyone he would need. He recognized them going to work and coming home, he followed their routines and sought out the secret habits they were convinced no one knew save themselves.

Secrets. He always knew where to find the people he needed, the people whose vulnerabilities he could turn into his strengths, his power. The power of secrets and lies.

Everyone had secrets, which, if confronted, they tried to explain away as mistakes, momentary lapses of judgment.

If confronted.

But secrets, the stranger knew, had their own power. Those things people hide could be used to reveal the truth, in time. Untold stories could bring other stories to the light.

The weakness of others would become his strength.

KAREN

"You probably just needed to vent." Jamie said when we met for lunch.

"Maybe."

"I mean, look at the facts: your daughter's in this horrible accident, she comes home from the hospital requiring *extraordinary* amounts of care, and within a couple of weeks Simon's up and gone, moving in with his secretary or whatever she is, who it turns out he's been sleeping with for months. I think you're entitled to vent."

"But it was so stupid."

I had wanted to call him ever since. I don't know how many times I had dialed his cell phone, hanging up before it could connect.

"I should apologize."

"Why? For calling him on his bullshit?"

"He was just trying to be polite."

"Oh, for Christ's sake, Karen. How much more of this are you going to take?"

She handed me a business card. I vaguely recognized the name. "She's one of the best," Jamie volunteered, taking a bite of her linguine. "I talked to her for a feature I was doing on the state of marriage in the 1990s. Very pro-woman. Very smart. I think you'll like her."

I stared at the name and realized that I had been introduced to her at a party with Simon at some point. For the opera, maybe? A fundraiser? One of the firm functions, whatever it was. She hadn't seemed very cutthroat, drinking a champagne cocktail.

"You're starting to sound like my mother. I'm not looking for a lawyer."

"Well, you probably should be. I mean, if Simon's behavior should prove anything to you, it's that he's moved on. You're not his priority anymore. Don't think he hasn't been talking to someone already."

I shook my head. "It's not like that. He comes to visit Sherry every day—"

"Which is exactly the sort of thing a lawyer would tell him to do. It looks good in court if he seems to be a devoted father."

"God, you're hard, Jamie."

"Someone has to be realistic."

I tucked the card into my purse, trying to forget that it was there, trying to ignore the sound of Jamie's voice in my head.

This wasn't supposed to happen to us. Not after all the lean years—the studying, the macaroni and cheese, the thin soup, the shitty basement suites and scrounging change for the bus. Everything was supposed to be smooth sailing now. We had our house, our daughter . . .

What had happened to my life?

What could I do? Simon wasn't coming back—I knew that. So what did that leave me? Fighting? Bitching? I couldn't just accept things the way they were: Stop thinking of Simon as my husband and reimagine him just as Sherry's father? Accept that he was gone, that his life was with someone else now? I couldn't. But what other choice did I have? How much could I give, could I fight, for something that wasn't going to change?

"Hello?"

"Is this Sarah?"

"Yes . . ."

"What did that little girl do to me?"

"Pam?"

"I was just at the doctor. He wants me to come in for more tests. He says he's never seen such a remission."

"Pam, slow down."

"He says it's a miracle. He actually used the word. He says that after my appointment on Friday he wasn't expecting to see me again. He thought that I would probably die over the weekend."

"Pam, what—"

"He thought I was going to die. And now the cancer's gone. All gone."

"Pam, what did you tell the doctor?"

"About what?"

"About Sherry. The little girl. What did you tell him about Sherry Barrett?"

"Nothing."

"Thank God. Pam—"

"But we have to tell someone."

"No. I promised Ruth—"

"Sarah, listen to what you're saying. This little girl cures cancer. Do you know what that means?"

"We can't—"

"People are suffering. How can we keep this a secret?"

"We have to."

"Why?"

"I promised Ruth."

"People are dying, Sarah."

"Let me talk to Ruth."

"We have to tell people."

"Let me talk to Ruth first. She took a big risk letting us . . . helping us. I can't go back on my word. Just let me talk to her. Please?"

"Okay."

"Promise me you won't say anything before I call you back?"

"All right. I promise. But get back to me soon."

"I will."

"No, I mean it. People are dying every minute."

"City desk. Todd Herbert."

"Is this the *Sentinel*?"

"Yes ma'am. City desk."

"I need to speak to someone."

"Is this a delivery question? I can transfer you to circulation. Hold on."

"No. I have a story you might be interested in."

"What sort of story, ma'am?"

"It's about that little girl. The one who was in the accident."

From: therbert@ns.ca
To: jkeller@ns.ca
Jamie—

Bit of a situation here. Woman calls me up, says she's got a story for me about a little girl who was in an accident. I figure it has to be Karen's daughter, so I let her talk. Long story short, she claims Sherry has miraculous powers, that she cured her of terminal cancer. Normally, I'd just blow this off, but the lady seems to have some pretty solid information, so I figured I'd run it past you, get your read on it before we take it any further. Have you heard anything like that? Could be guesswork, but she gave what sounded to me like a pretty solid description of Casa Barrett—right down to white carnations on the table in the room the daughter's in.

Any thoughts,

th

From: jkeller@ns.ca
To: therbert@ns.ca

Sorry, Todd—talked to Karen. I don't think there's any news here. Good human interest, maybe a short feature: followup the accident, etc. As far as miracles go, Simon and Karen wish. Apparently the woman you spoke to is the nurse's sister. They're pretty close and she's been over to visit at the house a few times. Yes, there were carnations in the room with Sherry. Don't get excited, though: according to the nurse, her sister's never been sick a day in her life. Approaching senility, apparently. I've met her myself and she's no sicker than I am. Thanks for the reminder though. I think maybe I'll

do a followup for the Life pages next Thursday.
What do you think?

Jamie

Oh—Karen says hello.

"Uh, hello. This is a message for Simon. Simon, it's
Karen. Listen, I just wanted to let you know that
Jamie's working on an article for the paper, for
next Thursday. Sort of a, you know, a human interest, 'where are they now' kinda thing . . . I know
you'll be out of town, but I thought you might want
to get a copy."

SIMON

I woke to the sound of thunder, a throaty rumbling that rattled
the bed. No, not thunder. The roar of waves, mere feet from
my head. For a moment, I was completely disconcerted.
Nothing about the room was familiar—the pale walls, the
honey-colored trim, the chair, the beige carpet stretching to
meet the sliding door onto the balcony. Then it came to me:
Tofino. The Wickaninnish.

We had driven up the night before, stopping in Nanaimo
for dinner before addressing three hours of winding wilderness
roads, the headlights illuminating only trees and undergrowth
until we emerged on the west coast of the island. We had
checked into the hotel long after dark, the clerk at the front
desk the only person in the firelit lobby.

Arriving at the room, we had fallen into bed, absolutely
exhausted. The promised view was nothing more than a reflection of the inside of the room on the clean, slick glass.

I rose from the bed, careful not to disturb Mary, who was
still asleep, facing away from me, away from the view, huddled under the white quilt. The room wasn't at all cold, but

with a single flick I ignited the gas fireplace, which purred to life.

"Oh my God."

"What?" Mary asked groggily, rustling as she turned to face me. "Oh, wow."

The hotel was built on a rocky outcropping along the water's edge, the waves crashing against the slate-black, barnacle-encrusted rocks right before our eyes. The balcony seemed to dangle precariously over the waves. The sky was cloud white, and there was nothing in the distance save a thin line of silver where the waves met the sky. Out there somewhere: Japan.

Every crashing wave spewed foam skyward, toward where we stood, always falling just short of the balcony.

Writers and painters have been attracted to this coast for almost a hundred years, and now I understood why. The sensation as I looked out at the ocean reminded me of church, the tiny Anglican chapel my mother dragged us to when I was a boy, and the breathtaking cathedrals in Europe that Karen and I had visited during our backpacking trip in university. I felt awe, wonder and fear in the face of the sublime, and a limitlessness akin to weightlessness, as if some sort of internal gravity had been lifted away. Even behind the glass, I felt tiny, nearly overwhelmed by the roar and the spray.

I could hear Mary's footsteps on the carpet as she came up behind me, sliding her arms around my waist, the softness of her bare breasts and warm belly against my back. "This is amazing," she said, looking out around me at the view.

"Yeah." I entwined my hands with hers.

She kissed me just inside my shoulder blade, resting her face there for a moment. "I'm happy we're here," she said, her voice muffled.

"I am too."

After a moment, she asked, "Do you want to go for a walk on the beach?"

"Actually, I'd like to get some breakfast." As if prompted, my stomach growled.

"Always thinking with your stomach," she said slyly. "I'll call room service."

"No, let's go out, find a little café."

"You do like going out for breakfast, don't you?"

"Best meal of the day."

"Do I have time for a quick shower?"

"No rush at all."

"Good. I'll see you in a sec."

She was just closing the bathroom door when I decided I needed a shower myself.

"Jamie? Are you there? If you're there, pick up. Shit. It's Karen. Have you seen the paper? What the hell is this? Jesus Christ, the phone's ringing off the hook, I don't know what to say. What the hell happened? Where are you? Listen, give me a call. No, never mind, you won't be able to get through— just get over here."

SIMON

It was cool outside; not cold, but the moisture in the air and the wind chilled us right through as we hurried to the car. The air was heavy with the smell of the ocean. We drove the few minutes into Tofino along the winding coast road, and parked the car in front of a little restaurant called the Cranberry Café, weathered wood with white curtains in the front windows.

Next to the door there was a busker—the typical West Coast, Generation X type with his rough goatee, knit toque, shapeless jacket and pants—driving out an old Bob Dylan song on a battered guitar. He couldn't sing, and could barely manage the chords, but he swayed, eyes half-closed, as if in a trance. I dropped a few coins into the open guitar case at his feet as we went through the restaurant door. Mary looked a bit surprised.

"Good morning," called out the heavyset girl behind the counter as we came in. "Can I get you coffee?"

"That'd be great. Where should we . . . ?" I looked around at the tables. The restaurant wasn't busy, filled mostly with what seemed to be locals, but there were a few couples like us, tourists making a long weekend of it.

She waved her hand. "Wherever you like. I'll be able to find you." Her smile was infectious.

We sat in the window, overlooking the rough street, the cracked pavement, the row of small stores. She was there with the menus and the coffeepot, filling our mugs, almost before we sat down. "So, how long are you folks in town for?"

"For the weekend."

"Are you staying in town?"

"Actually, we're up the road."

"Nice place," the waitress nodded. "Anyway, the specials are on the board," she gestured to a dusty chalkboard on the wall behind the counter. "I'll be back in a few minutes to take your order. If you get bored waiting for me, just wave."

She turned to walk away.

"Uh, before you go, do you have a copy of today's *Sentinel* that I could take a look at?"

Her smile turned teasing. "I thought you were supposed to be on vacation?" She shook her head and winked at Mary, who shrugged. "I've got one at the counter. I'll bring it when I come to get your order."

Mary looked around the restaurant. It was a cute place— tablecloths on all the tables, lots of plants, plain walls with lots of natural wood trim, decorated with watercolors. "I like this place," she whispered.

"I like you," I said without even thinking about it.

I wasn't usually prone to emotional blurtings like that.

She reached across the table and laid her hand across my own. The gesture seemed utterly natural. "I like you too." She grinned, and blushed a little. "I like *this*."

"Me too."

We sat looking out the window, until the waitress returned, setting a folded copy of the *New Sentinel* on the table in front of me. "Are you guys all ready to order?"

"I think I'll just have some pancakes—butter on the side, please."

The waitress turned to me, jotting down Mary's order. "And for you?"

"Bacon and eggs, sunny-side up, hash browns, multigrain toast and a glass of tomato juice."

She scooped the menus up and headed back to the kitchen.

The folded copy of the *New Sentinel* lay on the table between us. Mary smiled and shook her head, watching me deliberately not looking at the paper.

I took a sip of my coffee. Neither of us said anything for a long moment.

Finally, Mary broke the silence. "You might as well read it."

I shrugged. "I'm not in any hurry."

She grinned at me. "Well, I'm in a hurry. I'd like you to read it so that we can get it out of the way and get on with our weekend, okay?"

"Well, if you insist . . ." I unfolded the paper. "It's not like there's going to be anything new."

I skipped the front section entirely, guessing that the story Karen had called about would be in the Life section. "I expect it'll be the typical six months later—"

My voice caught. Under the fold, C3. A small picture of Sherry, and a headline that I couldn't believe even as I reread it.

"Holy shit," I muttered.

"What is it?"

I couldn't stop reading to explain. "Oh my God."

Victoria New Sentinel
Thursday, December 5, 1996
Miracles?
Can injured girl cure the dying?
~Todd Herbert~

According to one grateful woman, four-year-old Sherilyn Barrett is much more than the victim of a tragic accident last spring. "She's an angel," says Pamela Harding, 28. "She's a miracle."

The miracle is that Harding is alive to say anything at all. According to Harding, two months ago she was informed by her doctor that she had mere weeks to live. "It was cancer," says Harding. "I lost both breasts, but it was all through me. The doctor said that there was nothing he could do. He said that I was going to die." Today her doctor confirms that no cancer remains in her system. "It's the most amazing thing I've ever seen," says Dr. Eugene Katz, oncologist at Royal Jubilee Hospital. "There seems to have been a complete remission. I can't explain it."

But Pamela Harding thinks she can explain it. "It's a miracle, and it's all because of that little girl." According to Mrs. Harding, who is married with two young children, she was taken to the Barretts' Fernwood home by a friend who had also been healed by Sherilyn Barrett. "She told me that her lung cancer had completely disappeared. I didn't believe her, but I thought, Well, it can't hurt."

According to Harding, her contact with Barrett took place almost two weeks ago. By the following morning, her cancer had disappeared. "It's a miracle," Harding says, radiating her newfound good health. "I've got my life back, and it's all because of that little girl."

Calls to the Barrett residence went unanswered yesterday. According to Harding, "They're
trying to keep it all a secret. They don't want anyone else to know. But I had to tell you: it's a miracle, and everyone should know."

SIMON

"Simon? What is it?"

Unable to speak, I handed her the newspaper. "Here," I said, tapping the article. "This."

As Mary scanned the article, I punched in my home number as quickly as I could. Busy. Of course.

I dialed again.

"Holy shit, Simon. What is this?"

Still busy.

"I have no idea." I dialed again.

Still busy. "Goddamn it!" I slammed the phone to the table. The other patrons turned to look.

Mary stared at me as the waitress came rushing over.

"Is something wrong?" she asked, her face creased with concern.

"No." I shook my head, clearing my throat and trying to pull myself together. "Just a . . ."

Mary's eyes lowered to the table, and she shook her head. She touched the waitress's arm. "Actually, could we have our breakfast to go, please? It turns out we need to head back into town."

"Sure, sure. Of course. No problem. Right away."

"What are you doing?" I asked.

"We'll stop at the hotel, grab the stuff and head out. If we drive straight through we should be back in Victoria by"—she stopped, checking her watch—"3:30 or so."

Without even thinking about it I looked at my own watch. "Yes, but—"

"You need to be home for this. Your daughter needs you. Karen needs you."

"Mary—"

"If nothing else, they probably need a lawyer."

I could see how hard she was trying to hold on to her calm facade. "You need to be there, Simon. It's as simple as that. We'll get away some other time."

It was clear that neither of us completely believed what she was saying. We both knew that our lives had changed again in a single moment. The waitress returned with two takeout containers and neither of us said anything more.

RUTH

It was even worse than I had feared. By the time I got to the house at 8:30 that morning, the front yard was surrounded by reporters, bunched together on the sidewalk, at the edge of the lawn, in the driveway. They all turned to watch me as I drove up, and rushed toward me when I got out of the car.

"Are you the nurse?"

"Can you comment on . . . ?"

"Have you seen any . . . ?"

"Mrs. Page!"

"Ma'am, what about . . . ?"

"Has Karen Barrett ever . . . ?"

I tried to be polite, but they pressed around me, a wall of voices, shoving and pushing. I walked as quickly as I could across the front yard, opening the door with the key Mrs. Barrett had given me, slamming it behind me.

I wondered how long it would be before she asked for the key back.

All of the lights were off, except one in the kitchen.

I hung my coat on the hook. "Hello?" I called quietly. "Hello?"

Karen was sitting in the dark in Sherry's room. She didn't flinch when I turned on the light. I was the one who jumped.

"Mrs. Barrett."

She stared at me without saying a word, a folded newspaper on the table next to her.

"I've been on the phone all morning."

"Mrs. Barrett—"

"It just kept ringing and ringing. Finally I just left it off the hook."

"I can explain—"

"Can you?" she asked, turning to me. "Can you really?" Her face was pulled so tight it looked like she might tear.

I sighed. "I can try."

She stared at me, waiting.

"I didn't mean for any of this to happen." When the words started coming, I could do nothing to slow them. I told her everything, from my retirement to when I had first noticed that there was no longer any pain in my hands.

"I couldn't believe it," I said. "I had lived with that pain for so long. I'd tried all the treatments. Nothing worked. I couldn't figure out what had happened, until one day . . ." I stopped. I hadn't told anyone. I didn't want to sound ridiculous. "I was giving Sherry her bath, and I was holding her head to wash her hair, and I saw my hand on her forehead. I'm not a Bible-thumper or anything, but I couldn't . . . I couldn't think of anything else that explained it."

Then I told her about Sarah, and inviting her to the house, about Sarah's remission and about opening the door to find my sister on the doorstep with her dying friend Pam.

She didn't say anything when I was done. Unable to bear the silence, I busied myself with Sherry's routine as if it were any other morning. The curtains were drawn, but with all the reporters outside I didn't want to open them. My hands were shaking as I wrote the notes in her file.

"Did you have any problems with the reporters?" she finally asked.

"No. No. I just got into the house as fast as I could."

She stood up and peered through the crack in the curtains. "They're staying out on the sidewalk," she muttered. "I could call the police and complain about trespassing if they came into the yard."

"I didn't know that."

"When did you know about the article?" she asked, her back still turned.

I hesitated a moment. "I thought that Jamie's article was going to be in the paper today, so I bought a copy."

"You didn't know?"

"I didn't know that Pam had told."

I couldn't say anything more. I had betrayed Karen, betrayed Sherry. I stared down at the carpet.

"I'm sorry, Karen. If I hadn't invited Sarah in, none of this would have happened. But . . . she's my sister."

She sighed, and turned to face me. "Ruth, did you leave her—either of them—alone with Sherry?"

"I would never do that. They were never alone with her."

"I can't . . . I can't be lied to anymore," she said.

"I'm sorry."

"There has to be honesty here. Here," she stressed the word. "I have to know that there's someone, one person, I can count on."

She didn't seem angry; she seemed close to tears. "I'm so sick and tired of being surprised by things. Of always being the last to know. Do you know what I mean? I can't, I just can't . . ."

I nodded. "I won't. I won't lie to you again."

She nodded, and looked at me without saying anything for several seconds.

"I made tea," she said. "I'll bring it in here."

She turned to leave the room.

"Do you . . ." I stopped her. "Do you want me to come to the kitchen with you?"

She turned back to face me. "You're asking if I still trust you alone with my daughter?"

I didn't say anything.

"I'll bring the tea in here," she said.

I sat down heavily, my eyes wet.

When she came back, she set the tray on the table and reached out to me.

"Take my hand," she said.

"What?"

She wiggled her fingers a little. "Take my hand," she repeated.

Gingerly, I took hold of her extended fingers.

"Squeeze it."

"What?"

"Squeeze my hand. As hard as you can." Our eyes met, but I didn't quite understand what I saw there.

Without breaking our gaze, I squeezed her fingers as hard as I could. I saw her jaw clench, saw her flinch with the pressure, until finally she jerked her hand away. "Jesus," she muttered.

"I'm sorry," I started.

"And last winter . . ."

"You should see my cupboards at home. I had to go out and buy all those gadgets, like the can openers with the big rubber handles, so I could get a grip. But now . . ." I gestured toward the tea. "Even my ulcer isn't troubling me."

She stared at me for a moment, then turned her attention to her daughter. "And you think Sherry . . ." She drifted toward the bed, resting her hands on the rail.

Standing next to her, I just nodded.

She stared down at her daughter. "How?" she whispered.

"I don't know. For me, it just happened. I guess I was in such close contact with her all the time, washing her . . . But with Sarah, and with Pam, I thought that laying on hands might work."

"You mean they just touched her?"

I shook my head. "No, I lifted Sherry's hand . . ."

Karen pulled the sheet back from Sherry's still body. Gingerly, she picked up her right hand, carefully cradling the wrist as she turned it slightly, gazing down at the pale palm, the tiny curled fingers, the skin almost entirely free of line or mark. Karen didn't speak, just ran her thumb gently over the smoothness.

She was crying, thin rivulets of tears trailing unchecked down her cheeks, collecting at the corners of her jaw, falling soundlessly away.

"This is John Sellers for News At Noon. I'm outside the Barrett residence in Fernwood, where, sources tell us, miracles have started to happen in Victoria. I'll be joined by Pam Harding, who was apparently miraculously cured of cancer by Sherilyn Barrett last week, and Todd Herbert of the *New Sentinel* in a few moments, but first a little background . . ."

KAREN

"You need to explain," I said, holding fast to the doorknob, my body between Jamie and the house. "You need to tell me what the hell is going on."

"Karen, I had no idea."

Jamie glanced over her shoulder at the other reporters watching us from the far side of the fence and the small crowd that had gathered behind them. "Can we do this inside?"

I didn't move for a long moment, then stepped back, allowing her enough space to slide past me. I closed the door behind her and shot the deadbolt. I could hear the shouts of indignation from the sidewalk.

She started to take off her jacket. "No," I said, turning to her. "You're not staying. Not until I find out what's going on."

"Karen, how can you even think . . ."

"There's a story in *your* paper about how my daughter is some sort of healer. What am I supposed to think?"

"Damn it, Karen, I tried to protect you." Her voice came out in a squeak.

"What?"

"Can we please . . ." She started toward the kitchen, and I followed.

Ruth was at the table, and neither of them said anything when Jamie sat down across from her. I sat down between them.

"So."

Jamie shook her head. "Karen, I tried to stop this."

"So what happened?"

She glanced at Ruth. "Have you asked her?"

"I'm asking you."

She sighed. "Todd—you remember Todd—sent me an email. Said he had received a phone call from a woman who claimed that Sherry had healed her."

"Pam," Ruth said quietly.

Jamie nodded. "That's what he said. Anyway, he was asking a lot of questions, talking about how she could describe the inside of the house, right down to what flowers were on the table. White carnations."

She sniffed.

"So I told him I'd check it out. I told him that I didn't think that there was anything to it, but that I'd check it out."

I just sat and waited.

"So that day I came over, and I made a point of looking around Sherry's room."

"Oh, Jamie."

She shook her head. "No, I wanted to prove to him that this woman was making the whole thing up. I tell you, I've never been happier than when I saw that there weren't any carnations anywhere in the room."

"So what—"

"Until I looked in the garbage can," she continued, as if I hadn't said anything. "And there they were. Broken stems, all crunched up, gone brown. A bunch of carnations."

I felt like I was going to be sick. "So you told him."

She shook her head firmly. "No. No, I didn't. I tried to misdirect him. I made up something about your sister, Ruth. I didn't know anything about any Pam . . ." She dropped her head.

"But if you didn't . . . ?"

She shrugged. "I guess he didn't believe me."

"So what happened to the story you were working on."

"They killed it. They weren't interested in anything from me. At least that's what Ron Kozak said."

"The managing editor?"

She nodded. "It's a hell of a way to start a day. Being told that you've lost your objectivity. That you've betrayed your employer. It was a nice little chat. And then I packed up my desk."

"You were fired?"

"Suspended, with no fixed date of return. I got the feeling they wouldn't be calling anytime soon."

"Oh Jamie," I stood up and moved to her, intending to embrace her, but she pushed me away.

"No," she said, looking across the table at Ruth. "I need to know what's going on around here."

"This is Troy Shepherd with the CFAX News Cruiser. I'm here at the home of Karen and Sherilyn Barrett. I'm talking to Todd Herbert of the *New Sentinel*, who wrote a story in this morning's paper . . ."

KAREN

The house was dark, silent. None of us spoke, so focused were we on trying to ignore the murmur from outside the windows. We were playing a waiting game, but none among us knew what we were waiting for.

After Jamie had heard Ruth's side of the story, I borrowed

her cell phone. I dialed Simon's cell, then pressed Cancel. Instead, I called Dr. McKinley.

"I saw the paper. What's going on over there?" I could hear genuine concern in Stephen's voice.

"Well, I've got reporters camped out on the sidewalk." I pulled back the living-room curtain to check on the group and jerked back in shock, almost dropping the phone. "Jesus Christ!"

"Karen? Karen, what is it?"

About a dozen people were milling around on the front lawn, right under the window. They turned to look as I parted the curtain. Several of them rushed up to the window and pressed their hands and faces against the glass, trying to see in. Trying to see Sherry.

I dropped the curtain, but images of their faces lingered in my mind: blind eyes, scars, patches of hair, yellow skin . . .

"Karen? Are you still there?"

"I'm here."

"What's going on over there?" he asked again.

"It's, it's a little crazy. Could you . . ." I stammered, not even really sure what I was asking.

"I'm done here at two. I'll come right over."

When he arrived, I let Jamie and Ruth explain it to him, all of us sitting in the family room, away from Sherry, away from the crowds of reporters and onlookers who were separated from my daughter, it seemed, only by a curtain. When they finished, he looked between the two of them, first at Jamie, then at Ruth.

"Total remission?" he asked.

Ruth nodded. "That's what Sarah said."

Stephen looked thoughtful. "We should get her checked out by an independent physician."

"Why?" Jamie asked.

"In case this is all a big scam. So we can go to the paper with the test results, maybe get them to back off a little."

"But it's *not* a scam," Ruth said, quietly but forcefully. "It's not."

"The records can be checked. There must be tests we can do."

"On who?" Jamie asked.

"On you," he said to Ruth, who looked at the floor. "On your sister." He turned toward me. "On Sherry."

"I don't want this," I whispered, afraid that if I met anyone's gaze I would start crying again. "I just want all of this to go away."

Jamie came over and, perching herself on the arm of the chair, rubbed my back. Her hand was cold through my thin sweater, but I was grateful for her touch. "Kar, I don't think that this is going to just go away." She gestured toward the front of the house. "I don't think those people out there are just going to go away."

"I know," I whispered. "I just, I just want my old life back."

At that moment, there was a knock at the front door.

Instinctively I rose to my feet, stepped toward it, stopping as Jamie took my arm.

"Leave it," she said.

Instinct and habit were at war with rationality. I couldn't let a telephone ring unanswered either.

Stephen rose to his feet. "Let me get it."

I shook my head and pulled free of Jamie's hand. "No, I'll get it. I can't just sit here anymore."

Bracing myself, I opened the door a crack, holding tightly to the knob in case I needed to slam it shut again.

"We got here as soon as we could," Simon said. Mary was standing just behind him.

Fanned out at the foot of the steps were more of the damaged people, their ranks swollen in the dimming light.

"Can we come in?" Simon asked.

SIMON

For several seconds it seemed as if Karen might not let us into the house. She looked at me as if she didn't even recognize me, then at Mary. Finally, biting her lip, she stepped to one side and allowed us in, closing the door behind us.

Out of habit I bent down to take my shoes off. Mary followed my lead.

"Just leave them on," Karen said, walking past us toward the family room.

I led Mary into the living room to see Sherry.

"Hello, baby." I leaned over her bed, touched her face. "Daddy's here. Daddy's here."

Mary stood stiffly next to me.

"This is Mary, honey," I reached out and found Mary's hand, took it into my own. "Do you remember her from Daddy's office?" I glanced up at her, smiled a little, feeling at a loss. I turned my attention back to Sherry. "So I hear you've been getting into trouble," I teased my silent daughter. "What did Daddy tell you about that, eh?"

Straightening up, I turned to Mary. "You can talk to her, if you want. I don't know if she can hear it or not, but I like talking to her."

"It's so sad," she said, her voice rough. "She's so small . . ."

"I know. That's what everyone says."

"I should go," she said. "I should go home."

She hadn't wanted to come in at all. I'd spent most of the last hour of the drive down-island trying to persuade her. I asked, "Why?"

She shook her head. "It's not right. I shouldn't be here."

"No, it's fine," came Karen's voice from the doorway. We both jumped, turning to face her like children caught misbehaving. "You came all the way back down. You should both stay."

It was hardly the response that either of us was expecting, and I suppose our surprise was apparent in our faces. Karen took a deep breath. "I don't care . . . Just stay."

She was pale and worn, as if she might disappear into the painted wall behind her. Her eyes were darkly outlined, her face stretched taut.

"Everyone else is in the family room," she said.

I knew that Mary still wanted to leave, despite what Karen had said. Or perhaps more so because of it, I couldn't be sure. I also knew that I wanted her to stay. We walked into the family room in silence.

Karen was standing with her back to the window. "Find a seat. I'll get you some coffee."

The room felt like a minefield. "Yes," I said. "Coffee would be nice. We've been driving for hours."

Her jaw tightened. "Mary, why don't you sit here." Karen gestured back to the chair, as she crossed the room.

"Uh, no, that's okay. I'll just find a piece of floor."

I caught the sidelong glance between Jamie and Ruth as I sat down on the couch next to Dr. McKinley. Mary folded herself into a sitting position, leaning against the couch by my legs. I reached out and smoothed her hair.

There was an awkward pause. To cover as I pulled my hand away, I asked the doctor, "So where are we at right now?"

He shifted a little in his seat, and shook his head. "I don't really understand it myself. Ruth?"

After Ruth finished speaking there was a lengthy silence. It took me a long time to realize that everyone was waiting for me to say something. To have an idea. A plan.

I drained my coffee cup and rose to my feet, beginning to pace the room. I always think, and speak, more clearly if I'm in motion. "Well, leaving aside everything else," I started, then stopped short. I had no idea how to continue. "I . . ."

I looked at Mary, who smiled at me, clearly believing that I would know what to do. Looking at Karen, though, was like seeing a reflection of myself—trapped and frantic, with absolutely no idea of what to do.

"I . . ."

From the front yard, I could hear the sound of singing, voices raised in a hymn, people calling out my daughter's name.

HENRY

The library was closed for the night. Tim was in the children's section, his massive frame squeezed into one of the tiny little chairs, pulled up to one of the tiny little tables. He was chuckling over a picture book.

"Tim."

He glanced up. "Ah, Henry." He didn't seem surprised to see me, folding his book closed on the table and looking at me expectantly.

I sat down next to him. "Can I ask you a question?"

A smile touched his lips. "You just did."

"Ah. I guess I did—"

"Anyway," he interrupted.

"Anyway, I wanted to ask you." I struggled to get my focus back. "I wanted to ask you about miracles."

He raised an eyebrow, his face spreading into a smile. "What about miracles?"

I couldn't really pin it down. I wanted to know everything about miracles, everything Tim knew about them. Ever since reading the newspaper articles that morning, I needed to learn as much about miracles as I could.

"Well, just . . . what are they, to start? I mean, I know what they are, but . . ."

He paused for a moment, looking at me. "Well, there's really no single answer." His voice trailed off. "If you're King Lear, well, then, your life, sir, is a miracle. If you're having a wedding at Cana, and you have no food, then you hope there's a messiah nearby with some loaves and fishes." He waited, I think expecting me to comment, but I had nothing to say.

"But if it's a little girl you're talking about, a little girl more dead than alive, who seems to be able to heal people without being able to heal herself, well then, that's something completely different, isn't it?"

I felt the blood leaving my face, a sudden lightness as if I might pass out. "But, how . . ."

"How did I know?" He laughed. "You make such a point of reading the local paper every morning. As soon as it's out on the rod, you've got it. But you don't really read it. You just scan through, looking for something. When I saw you reading this morning, I thought you might want to talk about that little girl that you almost killed in the spring."

I still couldn't speak.

He sighed deeply. "Let's talk about miracles, then."

I nodded.

"How did it feel when you couldn't kill yourself?"

I felt like he had punched me in the face. "What?" My body tensed, ready to bolt.

"You still don't understand it, do you?" he asked.

"Understand what? I don't understand anything."

"You think you're so different from everybody else, that you're not fit to associate with anyone, that you don't even deserve to be a member of the human race." I nodded slowly. "But you see, that's why we're all here. We all have our own stories, our own secret shames."

I couldn't meet his eyes.

"So how did it feel when you couldn't kill yourself?" Tim asked again.

"I . . . it scared me. I felt angry. Sad. Frustrated."

"Trapped?"

I nodded. "Trapped."

"And yet you're immortal. Free to go anywhere, to do anything. You're virtually a god. That's a miracle, isn't it? Immortality?"

"It doesn't feel like it."

He shook his head. "No, it doesn't. But that's the flip side. That woman gets cured of cancer, gets to live a few more years with her children, and you and I and everyone in this building just want to die, but can't. When does a miracle become a curse?"

He chuckled. "I'm sorry. I'm not being very helpful, am I? I guess I don't really know the answer, any more than you really know the question." He smiled at me, but it seemed sad. "Go back to your reading. You'll find what you're looking for. Or at least something to point the way."

I nodded, not knowing what to do.

"But Henry, I do know this. Miracles don't come easy. They're not a gift. There's always a price in return. And it applies to everyone, not just us. The price of miracles is dear. You have to remember that."

I repeated it silently to myself as I walked away.

MARY

Simon was a different person when he was with his family. I had always known him to be caring and gentle, but these qualities seemed to be heightened, more sharply focused, being with Sherry. Being with Karen.

I hadn't been able to escape that realization since we arrived that afternoon.

I'd never been inside their house before. Aside from a few visits to the office when she was just a baby, I had never met his daughter.

There was a whole side of Simon I didn't know. He was so very careful, when we were together, not to call this place "home," even reflexively. He always called it "the house": "I'm going to the house." "When I was at the house this morning . . ." I guess he thought that hearing this place referred to as home would upset me. Instead, I always noticed the slight hesitation as he consciously shifted from "home" to "house" before he spoke. In his mind, this was home.

And Karen. You could see how this new disturbance in her life was wearing on her, but somehow she held herself together. I wouldn't have been able to cope with it. And to have someone like me in her house . . . What had I done to this family?

After sunset, the people on the front lawn began lighting their candles. The doctor and the nurse had left together, and the four of us sat mostly silent in the family room.

Karen rose to her feet. "I guess we need something to eat," she said, starting toward the kitchen.

"Why don't we order something in?" Jamie suggested.

Karen paused to consider the idea. "I don't know how keen I am on answering the door at this point," she concluded. "Besides, it's no big deal. I can whip something up."

As she slipped from the family room, Simon called after her. "I'll give you a hand." Jamie and I sat for a few moments, looking at one another awkwardly.

"Well, all the best parties usually end up in the kitchen," Jamie said, standing up to follow, leaving me alone.

Simon was chopping vegetables on a maple block on the kitchen table when I got there, carrots falling under a large chef's knife, a tea towel draped over one shoulder. The kitchen was bright and clean, large and well organized. Karen was at the stove with a wok. "I could open wine or something," she said.

"Yes, I think so," Simon said, glancing at me. "Let's have some wine."

It was amazing to watch them work. As Simon finished chopping the carrots and swung toward the stove, Karen stepped away, leaving a space between her body and the wok, allowing him to slide the cutting board through and to empty the carrots in, never breaking Karen's stirring. It was a dance between two people who had been partners for years.

I couldn't watch. The easy intimacy, the comfort and custom, it was all too much.

I left the kitchen, then lingered in the family room for a moment, running my eyes along the bookshelves, over the CDs and records beside the stereo. The light was still on in the living room, but it was even gloomier than it had been in the afternoon. I don't know what I was expecting, but I was surprised that Sherry was still in exactly the same position she had been earlier, that she hadn't turned in her sleep, or kicked off her blankets.

I sighed, looking down at her. She looked completely normal, as if she might, at any moment, open her eyes, sit up and start speaking.

The sound of someone clearing her throat in the corridor made me turn around. Jamie entered the room tentatively, carrying a glass of red wine in each hand. "It's really sad, isn't it," she said, looking at Sherry, handing me a glass.

"Thanks," I replied, shy at being caught at the bedside. "I was—"

"You don't smoke, do you?"

"No."

"No, of course not. You probably do aerobics or something too, right?"

"I run," I said.

"Nobody smokes anymore," she said. "I'm a social pariah." Going to the corner she picked up her purse, fumbling for a moment before coming up with a package of cigarettes and a lighter. "Normally I'd go out onto the front step." She pondered for a moment. "Maybe the backyard."

I took a sip from the wine as she left, then set the glass on the coffee table.

Nobody inside the house noticed me leave, but the eyes of the people in the yard were upon me, following me as I walked up the sidewalk to my car.

FOUR

December 6

Victoria New Sentinel
Friday, December 6, 1996
Miracle Vigil for Sherry
"Please go home" says distraught father
~Todd Herbert~

A group of several dozen seekers and pilgrims, many suffering from life-threatening diseases, kept a cold, candle-lit vigil outside the Fernwood area home of Sherilyn Barrett last night. They had been attracted by news reports that the four-year-old girl, comatose following a hit-and-run accident last April, had healed two women of cancer in the last month. "We just want to see her," said Eliza Cox, 54, of Cobble Hill. "It seems to me that if she's been chosen by God, then she's been put on Earth for a reason."

"My son is dying," said Donna Kelly, 24, of Seattle, accompanied by her six year-old son, Jeffrey, who suffers from leukemia. "There's nothing more the doctors can do. If there's any possibility that this little girl can do what the radio says she can do, then I don't mind waiting."

Cox, Kelly and the other pilgrims may not get a chance to find the answers they are looking for. In a written statement delivered late last night, Simon Barrett, Sherilyn's father, pleaded, "I'm asking you as a father, please leave my daughter alone." His words went largely unheeded by the crowd, who clustered together in the Barretts' front yard, lighting candles and waiting.

SIMON

For the second morning in a row I awoke with no idea where I was. As I opened my eyes I saw bookshelves, distorted by the angle at which I was lying. The shelves sat against a dark-green papered wall, coving into a cream ceiling—the paper Karen and I had put up when we moved into the house, before we had Sherry. The family room, flooded with morning light from the east-facing windows.

I was home, on the couch in the family room.

The moment I thought of the word *home,* I thought of Mary.

She had left without saying goodbye.

When I asked Jamie if she had seen Mary leave, she shrugged. "Maybe she just wanted to give you and Karen a little space."

Karen.

I jerked to a sitting position, the comforter falling off my shoulders. She was leaning against the doorframe. "Finally," she said. "There's coffee on. I brought the paper in." She slipped away before I could respond.

I pulled on my pants and yesterday's shirt, and put on my watch. 7:40. Running my fingers through my hair, I found Karen at the kitchen table, two coffee mugs and the morning paper in front of her. "Morning," I said.

Her eyes flicked up to me from the newspaper, then returned.

"Did you have any problem getting the paper? With the . . ." I didn't know what to call the people outside.

She shook her head. "I think I took them by surprise. I checked to see if anyone was on the step, but they all seemed to be over by Sherry's window. I cracked open the door and just grabbed it. By the time they realized I was there, I was already gone."

I gestured toward the paper. "So? What does it say?"

She wrinkled her nose. "You're not going to like this," she warned. She closed the paper and turned it toward me.

It took me a couple of seconds to register what I was seeing. Just below the banner headline were four photographs. The smallest was the picture of Sherry that we had taken at Sears on her third birthday—we had given a copy to the *New Sentinel* at the time of the accident. Somewhat larger was a picture taken at the scene of the accident, paramedics huddled around the tiny, blanketed form of our daughter.

Dominating the page was a large night shot of the people in front of the house, their faces lit from below by their candles, the orange glow of the living room visible behind them. Inset into this larger photo was a black-and-white shot of a young boy, smiling into the camera.

"Oh my God."

"That's what they're saying too," Karen muttered. "Lots of human interest. Lots of sick people." I scanned the story as she continued speaking. "They'll be posting copies of it at Lourdes."

I took a swallow of my coffee. "I don't like to think of how many people that article will attract."

"It's already started. There were ten or fifteen people out there when I got the paper, and cars have been pulling up steadily."

I shook my head.

"So what should we do?" Karen asked.

I shrugged. "I have no idea. We could get an injunction . . ."

She raised her eyebrows. "Do you want to be the one who has terminally ill kids dragged off by the police?"

"Well, it would keep them away," I joked.

She gave the beginning of a smile and took a long sip of her coffee. "So," she looked at me. "What happened to Mary last night anyway? She just sort of disappeared."

I shifted in my chair. "She must have gone home. I tried calling, but she wasn't there."

"I'm sorry," she said.

"For what?"

She waved her hand as if I should know. "For that, that whole thing with your trip up-island. That whole freak-out . . ." She seemed really uncomfortable. "I'm sorry, that's all."

"Yeah. Me too."

The silence between us was thick. Neither of us knew what to say next.

I drained my coffee and set the mug on the table. "Listen, would it be okay with you if I had a shower?"

Her eyes flashed up at me. "Oh, sure."

"I just don't really feel awake unless I—"

"No, I know," she cut me off. "I remember." She gave a wry smile. "Your clothes are where you . . . where they usually are."

"Okay." I pushed away from the table. "I'll be back in a few."

KAREN

I don't think I breathed again until I heard the shower starting in the upstairs bathroom. I hadn't known it would be so easy. Or so hard.

The last time I saw Simon I had all but thrown him out of the house. Then to have him show up when I needed him so badly—to show up with Mary.

My first impulse had been to slam the door; my next to fall into his arms. In the end, all I could do was let them in.

Them.

I couldn't even think about it.

I pulled the paper toward me and took another look at the front page. It was unsettling, seeing your life there—your own home, your daughter, your husband. All your problems, your tragedies—now public knowledge.

Setting aside the paper, I went to the living room to check on Sherry. I wanted to open the curtains to let in the cold sunlight. Instead, for the second morning in a row, I flicked on the lamp.

"I'm back, baby," I said, judging her temperature with my hand. "Your dad's in the shower. Are those people bothering you?" The crowd on the front lawn was singing again, but I couldn't make out the words. "Are you hungry? It's almost snack time. Another hour or so."

It was Friday, but with Simon spending the night, I had called Ruth and given her the day off. She had offered to come in just in case, but I had reassured her. "I think we'll be all right."

With her not coming in, I would be bathing Sherry, checking the feeding tube and changing her diapers, tracking all her vitals—just like any night or weekend. "Another busy day for us, isn't that right, sweetie? Isn't that right?"

I went to the window and peered out, pressing my eye to the crack between the frame and the blind, hoping not to be seen. Probably twenty-five people were now milling around on the front lawn. As I watched, another car pulled up in front of the house. Two elderly women gradually extricated themselves from the backseat and helped one another over the curb. They teetered past the knot of journalists on the sidewalk and into the yard, joining the crowd. A police car crawled past.

No one even seemed to be looking at the house. No one except a little boy, at the front of the crowd, eyes locked on the living-room windows, staring directly at me. He was tightly bundled in a winter coat, head covered by a red toque, and sitting on a sleeping bag. Our eyes met, and he smiled, then looked down at the ground in front of him.

I let the curtains fall back. I recognized the little boy from the front page of the paper—Jeffrey, six years old and suffering from leukemia.

At the kitchen table, I examined the group picture of the vigil outside the house, the faces in a luminous half-circle. And there he was, barely visible in one corner, partially hidden by sets of legs. He was seated exactly as he was now, his back to the camera, his attention completely focused on Sherry's window.

It was as if he hadn't moved in what—twelve hours? Fourteen? Fourteen hours on the cold ground? And for what?

For what?

SIMON

It was strange to be naked in the bedroom, after such a long time away. It felt familiar, yet at the same time alien. Some of my clothes were still in the drawers and hanging in the closet. I pulled out a pair of jeans and a shirt, socks and underwear, folding the dirty clothes I had just taken off and leaving them outside the bathroom door.

I showered using the same soap, the same shampoo, as if the last few months had been only a dream. I found one of my razors in the cupboard.

When I got back downstairs Karen was still staring at the front page of the newspaper.

"Much better," I said with a gusto I didn't entirely feel, picking up our mugs from the table. "Can I get you another cup?"

She didn't answer me for so long I began to wonder if I had actually said the words out loud. Then she looked up at me. "What are we going to do, Simon? What are we going to do?" Her eyes were desperate.

"I don't know. I feel like it's out of our hands."

She pushed the paper toward me. "Look at this," she said, tapping the photograph with an extended finger. "Look. His name's Jeffrey. He's got leukemia—"

I nodded. "I know. I read the—"

"He's only six years old, Simon. He's six years old and he's dying and he's been sitting out in front of our house all night."

"What are you saying?"

"He's got no chance. Can you imagine being six years old and being told that you're not going to get any older? That you'll never grow up?"

I wanted to reach out to her, to make it all go away, but I couldn't.

"Can you imagine having no hope?"

"Karen—"

"No hope, except for a little girl—"

"Karen—"

"What if someone told us . . . What if someone said there was someone who could help Sherry?"

"Karen, what are you trying to say?"

"How can we just let that little boy die? How can we let all of those people suffer, when—"

"We don't know that Sherry can—"

"We *do* know, Simon."

"We *don't* know," I repeated. "I would have thought that you of all people . . ."

"I know, but—"

"Fairy tales. That's what you called them, all of those stories about saints and miracles, all that dogma your mother tried to ram down your throat. Fairy tales."

"I know. But Simon," she said, "look at the evidence. Look at what happened to Ruth. And to her sister. And to that woman who reported it to the paper—Those things *happened,* and it had nothing to do with faith."

I walked over to the counter and poured myself another cup of coffee. "So what do you want to do?"

"You're angry."

I shook my head. "I'm not angry. I'm—scared. What happens if we bring him in here? What happens if . . . if Sherry *can't* do it? Can't heal him? And what if she *can?* What then? Do we let everyone in? And what does it do to Sherry, every time she . . ." I choked on the word. "Every time she heals someone?"

"But what—" Karen was cut off by a loud knock at the front door. She rose automatically from her chair, but I waved her down.

"I'll get it. It's probably a reporter."

"Be careful."

I was surprised by the concern in her voice.

"I will."

I opened the door just a crack at first.

"Mr. Barrett?" the stranger asked, meeting my furtive eye. "I'm Father Peter." He was dressed in crisply pressed black trousers, coat and vest over a black shirt, buttoned all the way to his neck, and topped with a stiff white collar. He was almost bald, save for a light trace of hair along the ridges of his scalp. He wore a pair of wire-rimmed glasses over cold gray eyes. Tall and painfully thin, his skin stretched tight over his chin and cheekbones. He wasn't an old man, but with the shaved head and the dour expression, he seemed skeletal.

"Yes?" I answered, not loosening my hold on the door.

"Mr. Barrett, I'd like to speak with you and your wife." He glanced back. The crowd was beginning to gather behind him.

"Why?"

"It would be better if we discussed that inside the house."

I opened the door, seeing little to fear in a priest. As he slipped inside I could hear voices raised outside, just beyond the stoop. "Hey . . . what about . . . Why's he . . ."

Karen was standing just beyond the foyer. The priest stepped forward, his hand extended. "Mrs. Barrett, I'm Father Peter. I'm very pleased that you're giving me this opportunity to speak with you."

She took his hand and shook it gingerly. "Do I know you?"

"I was at the hospital the night of Sherry's accident. Visiting a friend."

She thought for a moment. "I remember. Do you remember what I told you?" She didn't give him a chance to answer. "What is it that you want?"

There was a chill in the air, and the cold seemed to radiate from him.

"I'd like to meet Sherry, if I could," he said.

"Why?" Karen asked.

He sighed, impatiently. "I was sent to see you by the arch-bishop—"

"We're not Catholic," Karen said.

The priest smiled, revealing yellow teeth. "That's why he

sent me. I'm not directly affiliated with the diocese. I don't preach, I don't have a home church . . ."

"Yes, but why are you here?" I interrupted.

"The archbishop called me this morning, quite concerned about the story in the newspaper, the coverage on the television news. He asked me to stop by—informally—and try to find out what was going on." As he spoke he toyed with a coin in his left hand.

The coin caught the light, flashed through his fingers, tumbled.

Surprisingly, Karen stepped to one side. "Sherry's right through here." I followed them into the living room.

The priest went directly to Sherry's bed and turned back the covers. Karen stood to one side; I could see how tense she was. I felt the same way. He lifted Sherry's right arm, turning it to expose her palm.

"What are you doing?" I asked.

"He's looking for stigmata." Karen answered, as if she couldn't believe what she was saying.

"And there are none," he said as he checked Sherry's other hand. "That makes it considerably easier."

"That makes *what* considerably easier?" I asked.

He ignored me, tucked Sherry back in, then straightened up.

"I've come to make you an offer," he said. "The archbishop has authorized me to tell you that the Church is willing to undertake an investigation into . . . these matters." He leaned forward, his tone confiding. "You do understand that an investigation must be done."

Karen shook her head. "Why?"

"To make her into a saint," I muttered.

"No." The priest turned to me. "The investigation will find that absolutely nothing miraculous has transpired here. The newspaper will print a correction. You and your family will be left in peace. The three people who claim to have been healed by your daughter will be revealed to be"—he waved his hand as if pulling the story from the air—"fraud artists trying to take advantage of you people, or religious fanatics, or perhaps to be suffering from dementia." He was completely casual, his voice utterly flat. "Upon examining their medical records, it will be revealed that they never suffered from the conditions your daughter supposedly healed them of. Cancer, whatever." He smiled again, and I was reminded of a dog, showing its teeth.

"What are you talking about? You can't . . ." I was thinking of Ruth, of her obvious love for Sherry.

"It will be quite a scandal for a while," he continued. "But the investigation will find that neither of you had any knowledge of what was going on, that you and Sherry have been victimized." He shrugged, as if this plan made such perfect sense there was no need to explain further.

"Why?" I asked. Karen's eyes moved between the priest and me.

His tone had the exaggerated care and condescension I imagined he used to speak to a child. "For reasons you don't need to understand," he said. "The Church finds that it is in its best interests if any claim of miracles is refuted as quickly as possible. I ask you, can you imagine what it will be like as the stories of Sherry start to spread? It must be very difficult for you now, with even those few people out there, holding you prisoner in your own home. Do you know how many people visit Lourdes each year? Don't you want this problem to disappear?" He paused, an effect I recognized from the courtroom.

"That doesn't explain what the Church—"

"It's about faith," Karen said, her thoughtful gaze on the priest. "Right? What's faith worth, what's heaven worth, if there are everyday miracles? What role does the Church have if people have direct access to God?"

The priest smiled his cold smile, neither confirming nor denying what she was saying. "Mr. and Mrs. Barrett, I came here to offer you a way out of the dilemma you currently face. I urge you to consider this carefully, and consider the repercussions of any decision you make. How your life will be affected—"

"How our lives will be affected?" Karen repeated. "And what about them?" She gestured toward the window. "What about all of those people who Sherry could help? Is the Church comfortable with letting them die?"

"Mrs. Barrett," he said in measured tones. "There is no reason to believe that anything miraculous has occurred here. And frankly, the Church is not concerned with what happens to people who put their faith in snake handlers or faith healers." He started for the front door. "Those are choices people make. Your concern should be with the choices you make."

"Are you threatening us?" I asked.

The priest turned and we both stepped back despite ourselves. "Mr. Barrett, I have considerable experience with matters like these. Things can become very difficult if these situations are not resolved quickly and quietly." The darkness of his eyes left no doubt—this *was* a threat, not a warning. "I'll be checking back with you."

He opened the front door and set off down the walk as if we had just had the most casual of visits. I hurried to close the door behind him, trying to ignore the press of faces staring in. Out of the corner of my eye, I caught sight of the boy with leukemia still sitting on the front lawn, staring at Sherry's curtained window.

As I came back into the room, Karen was pacing, muttering to herself. "It's all the same old bullshit you think went out with the Dark Ages . . ."

"A lot of people think that miracles went out with the Dark Ages."

"That's not what the sisters taught us. It's not what my mother would say. Christ, when she was here last month she told me that she had asked her priest if they could do some fundraising so we could take Sherry to Lourdes. And the priest agreed." She stopped her pacing, shook her head. "I thought I'd left all of that behind. How the hell did we get into this?"

"I don't know," I said.

"The worst part is, what he was saying made sense. In a way. Wouldn't it be easier if all this just went away?"

"I was thinking the same thing."

Of their own accord, my arms opened and I found Karen in them, her arms around my waist, her head against my chest. It felt like the most natural thing in the world to stroke her back, breathe in the scent of her hair.

"What are we going to do?" she asked.

LEO TANNER

I parked the van behind the truck from the TV station. I turned off the engine and looped the springy key ring around my wrist, just like Mr. Perkins always told me. I sat there for a minute, looking at the newspaper on the other seat.

The little girl was so beautiful. Sherilyn Barrett. She looked just like an angel. Or like the Holy Mother in those paintings where she looks so peaceful, her eyes looking up to heaven.

The Holy Mother. I kissed my rosary and said a Hail Mary before I picked up the newspaper.

I read the story again, even though I knew it almost by heart already.

They didn't give the whole address, but this had to be the place. Why else would there be TV trucks on such a quiet street? Why else would all those people be in the front yard? I watched them for a minute. I wanted to be sure.

"Be careful, and you won't make any silly mistakes." That's what Mother always says. I didn't want to make a silly mistake.

I'd been waiting all morning for my lunch break so I could come, ever since Mr. Perkins showed me the newspaper in the break room when I got to work.

"I guess you'll be interested in this," he said, pointing to the picture of the little girl who looked like an angel.

I read the story while I had my coffee and a chocolate doughnut. A couple of the other guys asked me what I was reading, and I showed them, but they weren't interested. Then we had to go out to fix a broken sewer main and a flooded basement. I did all the digging and the heavy lifting, but then I had to wait for the other guys to do their jobs. So I couldn't come to the house until lunchtime. I could hardly stand it. I had to see her, to see if what the papers said was true.

Taking a deep breath, I opened the door and climbed out of the van. I made sure it was locked before I closed the door. Better safe than sorry. Mr. Perkins was really nice to let me use the van, and I didn't want anything to happen to it.

"Better safe than sorry." That's something Mother always says too.

There was a crowd of people with cameras and Bibles and cups of coffee on the sidewalk in front of the house, and I had to walk on the street to go around them.

I went through the gate and walked up to the crowd in the front yard. I tried to smile.

"Walk like a man." That's what Mother always tells me.

But I was really scared. I wasn't scared of the little girl, but I had a funny feeling like butterflies in my belly.

I stood near the back. I think I was the only one there who was alone. I smiled at the people around me, and some of them smiled back, but they all looked a bit scared. It's because I'm so big—nobody ever wants to talk to me. I had the newspaper in one hand, and my rosary in the other, so I just stood there, rolling the beads between my fingers.

"Hail Mary, full of grace . . ."

Everybody jumped when the front door opened. A priest came out of the house, and the door closed behind him. I could tell he was a priest, even though he was only wearing a collar and no robe. He looked like one. His long black coat was sort of like robes anyway.

Everyone on the lawn backed away from him. He started down the walk, but he stopped when he saw me standing in his way.

He looked me up and down from my head right to my toes. He looked at the rosary in my hand. He was playing with a nickel or a quarter. The coin was shiny in the sun.

Then he smiled at me. People don't usually do that, and I smiled back.

"Hello, Leo," he said, holding out his hand.

"How . . ." I put the newspaper under my arm and took his hand and shook it, not too hard and not too soft, just like Mother taught me. I'm always careful not to hurt people. She said, There's no reason to be a bully just because you're bigger than them.

"How do you know my name?"

He smiled again. "It's on your coveralls."

I looked down at the patch on my uniform. Leo Tanner. "Oh. I forgot about that."

He held on to my hand with both of his. "Why are you here, Leo Tanner?" he asked.

"I came to see the little girl. The one who can do miracles."

"You saw the story in the newspaper?" He put his hand on my shoulder and walked with me to the van.

I nodded. "I've got a big book about miracles at home," I told him. "I never thought I'd actually get to see someone who could do miracles for real."

"I could tell you about miracles," he said. "Would you like that?" He had a funny look on his face. I couldn't tell if he was smiling or angry.

I nodded, and then stopped.

"I'd like to learn about miracles," I said. "Could you teach me?"

This time I was sure that he was smiling.

"Thanks, Diane. I'm Bill Stewart, live at the Barrett home here in Fernwood where we've had, in the last few minutes, what may be a significant development in this story. Moments ago, Simon Barrett, father of Sherry Barrett, who you'll remember is the little girl who was in that tragic hit-and-run accident back in April, and may in fact be capable of healing, Mr. Barrett moments ago came out of the house, onto the front step for his first public appearance. Let's go to the tape."

[Simon Barrett:] "Is Donna Kelly here? Donna Kelly? Donna, I'd like to have a word with you and Jeffrey if I could. Just for a moment . . . Come right through . . ."

[Bill Stewart:] "As I said, that was a few moments ago. No one here knows what is going on. There are some in the crowd who believe that they've called Jeffrey Kelly, who is a six-year-old with terminal leukemia, there are some who believe that he has been called in to be healed by Sherry Barrett, although we have no confirmation of this. Jeffrey and his mother have apparently been here since early yesterday afternoon, maintaining a vigil, hoping that he might be healed of his terrible disease."

[Diane Oliver in studio:] "Bill, what's the mood like in the crowd?"

[Bill Stewart:] "Diane, that's an interesting question. There are a couple of dozen people here, a lot of them have been here all night. A number of them protested after Mr. Barrett closed the door, but overall the crowd is very calm. I think all of the people here are hoping for something like this to happen to them as well. There are a number of very sick people here, wanting a chance to see Sherry

Barrett. I think they're thinking that if Jeffrey Kelly has been called in to be healed, then maybe it bodes well for everyone else here."

[Diane Oliver:] "You'll keep us posted?"

[Bill Stewart:] "As things develop."

[Diane Oliver:] "Thank you, Bill. That was Bill Stewart live . . ."

KAREN

As Donna Kelly and her son, Jeffrey, stepped into the foyer, they both bent to take off their shoes. "Don't worry about that," I said.

"We really should," Donna said, helping her son with his shoes. "It's pretty muddy on your lawn."

She looked so sheepish that I smiled to reassure her. "It's a strange situation we're all in. Let's go into the family room."

She was a small woman, young and fit, and she looked like she might once have been happy. With her blond hair pulled into a ponytail, she had the air of someone who worked with kids, in a daycare or a preschool. Jeffrey was everything a six-year-old boy should be—cute and shy, blushing and turning away as Simon and I introduced ourselves to him. But there was a brittle brightness about him that I realized came from weight loss, from the taut translucency of his skin. Under the toque he was bald from his chemotherapy.

No one seemed to know what to say once we were all sitting down. I decided to lead with honesty. "We, Simon and I, we don't really know . . ." I smiled at Donna, and at Jeffrey sitting next to her, craning his head toward the living room. "We don't really know what we're doing with all of this. It sort of took us by surprise."

Donna nodded. "It must be terrible for you. I mean, I can't imagine being in the position you're in, but I know . . . I know what it's like to face losing a child. And then all this. This circus."

"That's a good word for it." I didn't point out that she was part of that circus.

"I'm sorry we were out there . . ." Donna stammered. "We were at the hotel when we saw the thing on the news and we caught a bus up to the mall right away. It was pretty easy to find your house, with the reporters and all." She looked down at her hands, folded in her lap.

"Hotel?" I asked.

"We're not from here. We live in Seattle. We're just up for a few days."

"Holiday?" Simon asked.

Donna glanced at Jeffrey. "It's . . . You know those Make-A-Wish people? Jeffy's been seeing the ads for Victoria on the TV and he wanted—they're paying for us to have a few days up here in a nice hotel. See the museums and stuff. I never would have been able to afford it on my own."

Simon looked at me out of the corner of his eye. "It can't be easy for you."

She pursed her lips. "It's hard, yeah. The medical expenses have pretty much wiped us out. I had to quit my job to take care of Jeffrey, and we moved back in with my mom."

"And his father?"

She shook her head. "High school. I haven't seen him since graduation." Donna laid a hand on Jeffrey's leg and squeezed it. "But we do okay, don't we, bud?" His thigh was so thin.

"When can we go see Sherry?" Jeffrey asked, as if discussing a visit to McDonald's. He looked around the room for someone to answer his question.

Donna patted his leg. "We'll see, baby, okay? You remember that this was a maybe, right?"

"Maybe right!" he repeated.

I looked across at Simon. He cleared his throat. "We don't really know how this works. We don't know why. Or how—"

"Mr. Barrett," she interrupted.

"Simon."

She blushed and looked down at her lap again. "Simon, I'm sorry, and please don't misunderstand me, but the why and the how of it aren't really that important to me. Is it true? Did the news get it right? Did your little girl cure that woman's cancer?"

I glanced across at Simon, then nodded. "We think so. Yes. It's true."

"Oh my God," she said.

I watched her fingers tighten on Jeffrey's thigh. After a moment he pushed her hand away. "Ow, Mommy!"

"Sorry, honey," she said, but her attention was focused entirely on Simon and me. "Would you . . . Do you think it would work on Jeffrey?"

Before I could speak, Simon answered, "We really don't know, but let's give it a try."

"Oh God," she whispered, tears streaking her face. "Thank you . . ."

Jeffrey turned toward her, his face twisted with worry. "What's wrong, Mommy? What's wrong?"

"It's nothing, hon, Mommy's just . . ."

"Hey, Jeffrey," Simon called out playfully. "Would you like to go and meet Sherry now?"

He stood up. "Yeah."

"I'm sorry," Donna sobbed after they'd left the room. "This is so stupid . . ."

"No, it's not," I said, crouching in front of her, gently touching her knees. "It's not stupid. I just hope it works . . ."

She shook her head again. "No. No. Even if, even if it doesn't, just the thought that maybe . . ."

I could hear my own thoughts in her voice. "I know. If someone were to tell me that Sherry . . . that there might be a way—" I shook my head. "We should go in there."

She smiled through her tears and nodded. As I started to stand up, she grabbed my hand, pulled it to her and kissed the back of it, then pressed it to her tear-damp cheek. "Thank you, Karen. Oh God, thank you so much."

I didn't know what to say, so I helped her up and led the way to Sherry's bedside.

Simon was explaining the feeding tube to Jeffrey. "So the food—"

"The juice," Jeffrey interrupted.

"The juice," Simon played along. "Goes down through this tube and into Sherry's tummy. So even though she can't eat, she still gets to have all the good stuff that she needs . . ."

Jeffrey nodded. "I have something like this when I'm in the hospital, but it goes in my arm."

Simon noticed us over Jeffrey's head. "Here's your mom," he said.

Jeffrey looked up. "Mom, look, this is Sherry. She was . . ." He glanced at Simon, who nodded. "She got hit by a truck and now she's never gonna wake up." He touched the side of Sherry's face, his tiny hand in perfect scale with her features. "Isn't that sad? She'll never wake up."

Glancing at me apologetically, Donna gently touched the back of her son's head. "Yes. Yes, that's very sad."

"Is that what's going to happen when I die?" he asked his mother, as if it were of no greater consequence than taking an afternoon nap, or being forced to eat his vegetables.

Donna looked like she was close to breaking. "It's something like that, honey."

Simon cleared his throat and beckoned me with a surreptitious twitch of his head.

"How do we . . . ?" he asked in a whisper. Donna was looking over at us. I smiled at her.

"Ruth said that she used Sherry's hands . . ."

He nodded and stepped forward. "Hey, Jeffrey," he called, and the little boy turned toward him. "Can I show you something else?"

Jeffrey looked at his mother, who smiled and nodded.

"Do you want to feel how soft her hand is?" Simon lifted her arm, turning her palm to face the boy. "Here, go ahead. Touch it."

Jeffrey reached out, and with a single finger touched the center of Sherry's palm, pulling back with a giggle.

"Oh, you didn't feel it!" Simon mock-scolded him. Jeffrey responded with another giggle. "Try it again."

Jeffrey shook his head, giggling still, making strange.

"Here, I know what . . ." Simon started, shifting his hold on Sherry's arm. "Close your eyes."

Jeffrey closed his eyes, then opened them again.

"No peeking," Simon warned.

When Jeffrey closed his eyes the next time, Simon covered the boy's eyes with one hand. "Hey," he protested.

"I have to make sure that you're not peeking," Simon explained. With his other hand he gently laid the palm of Sherry's hand against Jeffrey's forehead, pushing back his toque.

"What's that?" Jeffrey asked, smiling.

Donna held her breath.

"Guess," Simon said, pressing on the back of Sherry's hand.

"I don't know."

Donna's hand was at her mouth, choking back a sob.

"Come on, guess."

"I don't know!"

"Does it feel soft?"

"Uh-huh."

"Does it feel warm?"

"Uh-huh."

"Does it feel like it's got fingers?"

"Uh-huh." Jeffrey brought his hand up, touching the back of Sherry's hand. "Is that Sherry?" He traced her fingers, and I heard Donna gasp.

Blood roared in my ears.

"It is," Simon said, lifting his hand away from Jeffrey's eyes and Sherry's hand away from his forehead in the same motion.

"Aren't you a smart guy!" he joked, gently tucking Sherry back in. "Aren't you smart." He playfully pulled the toque low over Jeffrey's eyes.

Jeffrey pulled his hat up. "Is that how she's going to make me all better?"

His mother, who had bent to hug him, scooped him into her arms, crushing him to her. "I don't know, baby. We'll see. We'll see what happens."

"Thank you," she whispered.

"You're welcome, Mommy," he said.

Simon and I looked at one another across the room, both of us aware of the bridge we had just burnt.

There was no turning back.

"This is Bill Stewart, live at the Barrett residence in Victoria, where just moments ago Simon Barrett announced that he'll be holding a news conference in a half-hour. We'll bring coverage of that to you on the news at five. Meanwhile, it's been a very strange day here. A few hours ago, the front door you see behind me opened and Simon Barrett asked for Donna Kelly. Miss Kelly and her son, Jeffrey, who suffers from leukemia, entered the house. Miss Kelly left almost an hour later, carrying her son, and refusing to answer any questions. It's unclear what happened inside the house. Perhaps that's the reason for the news conference we'll have for you at five."

SIMON

It was cold on the front step. The reporters were all in position below me, a phalanx of microphones, of necks craned to get the best view, cameras raised to get the best shot. Behind them, the pilgrims stood vigil.

"Thank you for coming out this afternoon," I began, as if they were doing us a favor. "I have a brief statement, then I'll take a couple of questions." The door opened behind me, and Karen came to stand next to me.

"Ladies and gentlemen, we are the parents of a little girl who was involved in a horrible accident. Our instincts are to protect Sherry at all costs. At all costs. No parent would argue that instinct." I paused, making eye contact where I could with the journalists, as if they were a jury. "When the news broke about the miracles for which our daughter was supposedly responsible, we were taken completely by surprise. Our first instinct was to pull back, to lock the doors and do everything we could to protect Sherry from all of this." I gestured at them, at the cameras and the crowds.

"This afternoon, as you know, we spoke to Donna Kelly, and her son, Jeffrey. Jeffrey has terminal leukemia. Six years old, and no hope of growing up. We spoke to his mother, another parent whose instincts are the same as our own—to do anything she could to save her little boy."

"We still don't have enough information to confirm the rumors you have heard. I don't know if we ever will. But earlier this afternoon—" I shifted from foot to foot. "Earlier this afternoon, we attempted to replicate the conditions of those healings with Jeffrey Kelly."

I pulled myself up to my full height and directed my gaze over the fish eyes of the cameras, toward the pale faces bent toward me, eyes rapt.

"We're parents," I continued, speaking directly to the pilgrims. "And one of the things that being a parent requires us to do is to be good role models for our daughter, to teach by example. One of the things . . ." I found myself choking up, paused for a second. "One of the things we wanted to teach Sherry is that she has a responsibility, as a human being, as a member of a community, to reach out to people if they need help. Not to walk past the beaten man at the side of the road."

I took a deep breath. "We don't know if what people claim about Sherry is true or not, but we just can't just walk past." As I watched, the hope that had been building in people's faces peaked. Stress gave way to gratitude. The reporters looked stunned, as if this were the last thing they were expecting.

"So on Monday morning, at ten a.m., we're going to open the doors of this house to allow people access to Sherry. We don't know how this is going to work out." I had to raise my voice to be heard above the murmurs and whispers, the snapping of camera shutters. "We don't know how this is going to work out, so I'd like to ask for your patience and consideration as we try to come up with some sort of system. I don't know how hard this is going to be on Sherry, so we'll have to see, but I think that just a few hours a day . . . maybe starting at ten? We'll have to see. Are there any questions?"

"Mr. Barrett, Suzanne George, *New Sentinel.* Are you confirming reports that your daughter is able to heal people?"

I fought the urge to snap at her. "As I stated, we're not confirming anything. If there's any possibility, though, I think we need to be open to trying to help as many people as possible."

"Mr. or Mrs. Barrett, Brad Roberts, CBC—have you spoken to anyone from any of the churches or religious institutions about your daughter, about what's going on here?"

I glanced up to see Father Peter at the back of the crowd, studying me intently. Our eyes met. "My wife and I are agnostics. Religion doesn't enter into this."

The reporter from the *New Sentinel* started to ask another question, but the reporter from the CBC cut her off. "How can you claim that religion has nothing to do with this? If there are miracles—"

"Perhaps you should be talking to someone from one of the churches. I don't have the background to discuss the theory or the theology behind all of this. Next?"

Father Peter turned and walked down the driveway, quickly

merging with the shadows. I guessed he wouldn't need to check back with us.

"Mr. Barrett, don't you see this as exploiting your daughter?"

I started to answer, but Karen stepped forward, laying her hand on my arm. "I love my daughter so much I can't even begin to describe it. If someone told me that there was some way—some new therapy, some faith healer, whatever—if someone told me that there was a way that my daughter might be able to wake up, might be able to smile at me again, I would do anything in my power to make that happen." She took a deep breath, calming herself. "If I was in that position, and someone might be able to help, I would hope that they'd be willing to do so. That's all we're doing. If you want to view that as exploitation, that's fine." With that, she went back into the house, closing the door behind her.

"That's all for now." Ignoring the cries for "just one more question, just one more," I continued, "I'd like to ask, please, everyone go home. We'll be here at ten o'clock Monday morning, so there's no need for you to put your health further at risk by sitting out here in the cold. Go home, please. Take care of yourselves."

I ducked back inside, ignoring the voices behind me, closing them off with the front door.

From behind the curtains in the living room Karen and I watched as most of the crowd dispersed. The press left first, hopping into cars and speeding away, eager to meet deadlines and get footage edited.

I wondered which sound bite the five o'clock news would choose to run, and how the paper the next day would deal with the whole thing.

The pilgrims who had been at the house all night were slower to slip away. Some stayed to clean up, picking up their garbage, rolling up their sleeping bags before leaving the yard. Someone even cleaned up the mess of coffee cups and takeout wrappers the press had left scattered in the driveway. Someone else rolled up Jeffrey's sleeping bag and left it on the front step as they were going.

By five o'clock the yard was empty. The last pilgrim to leave shut the gate. It was as if none of it had happened.

MARY

All day I managed not to answer the phone when it rang. Instead I'd pause in the middle of whatever I was doing—a long overdue cleaning, another chapter in my book—to listen to the answering machine as he left his messages.

Five messages in the past twenty-four hours. The first an hour after I had left his house, while I was out walking along the water. "Mary? It's Simon. Are you there?"

I'd gotten into his habit of checking a clock every time something happened, making a mental note of the time, measuring my life out in increments. Just like him.

9:40 a.m. "Mary, it's Simon. What happened to you last night? You just disappeared. I was worried. Listen, give me a call on my cell . . ."

His voice was low. Not a whisper, but pitched low enough that Karen wouldn't hear him. I could picture him, sitting in their family room—

family room

—speaking softly into his tiny black phone, keeping one eye on the door, ready to cut it off should his wife appear.

I'd been through all of this before.

12:10 p.m. "Mary, it's Simon again. Are you there? Are you okay? Please call . . ."

His voice was touched by tenderness and care, by worry. I should have explained why I had to go.

But what would I have said? "I'm leaving you so that you can choose between me and your wife. I'm leaving because you want me to leave—you just don't know it yet."

I almost picked it up. Too late. He'd hung up.

3:40 p.m. "Mary, it's Simon. Listen, I know you're mad at me. I know we need to talk. Please, just call me, okay? I love you . . ."

Mad at him? Not a chance. I was too furious at myself to even think about him. What was I thinking, destroying a family like that? Taking a father away from his daughter, a husband away from his wife. Mad at you? God, no, Simon. And that last, that "I love you," as if just saying it could make everything all right.

But love was easy. I had loved Simon long before he ever moved in, long before it was even a possibility that we could have a life together. Loving him was easy.

Was easy.

5:55 p.m. "It's me . . . I've . . . It's been a really long afternoon . . . I don't know if you saw the news or not, but . . . I really need to talk to you. If you get this, please call."

I hadn't watched the news; I hadn't been doing anything except sitting around, putting CDs into the player, changing them after a few songs, unable to find anything that seemed to speak to me.

I couldn't stand to hear him in pain. I was reaching for the phone to call him when it rang. I jumped a little, then answered it. "Hello?"

"Party Girl!" came the loud, familiar voice, almost a shout over the music in the background.

"Brian?"

"Who else, Party Girl? Where have you been hiding?" He was clearly camping it up for an audience at his end of the phone. "We thought you'd died!"

"No, not dead. Just in love."

"That doesn't sound as happy as it should."

"Is it ever?"

"It's always a man, isn't it?" he said, more sympathetically.

I didn't need to answer. Brian and I had known each other since we were undergraduates, both headed for law school. The hippie girl from the small town up-island, straight As, who never did anything bad, falling in with a flaming hometown queen who lived off-campus in a house full of lesbians who kept stealing each others' girlfriends and tampons.

"How can you live like that?" I had asked him at one point.

"Honey, if I ever need a reason not to be interested in women, all I have to do is spend a few minutes in the living room."

Victoria was Brian's town, and he didn't hesitate to show me its secrets: the bars, the restaurants, the nightlife. We would study through the week, pouring all of our energy into our books, papers and exams. Then we'd go crazy on the weekends, dancing at the clubs or raves, crashing house parties, whatever. With Brian it was impossible not to have a good time. Law school went the same way—the work was harder, and we partied harder. After, I decided to go the private route, while Brian took a job at Legal Aid. Always helping out the little guys.

"Married, gay or stupid?"

I found myself smiling. Brian can always do that. "Married. And stupid, I guess."

"Is this a bad one?"

"The worst," I answered. "And you?"

"This is the lawyer, right?"

I was a little surprised, but I shouldn't have been. Just because I hadn't spoken to Brian in the past few months didn't mean that he was out of the loop. "Yeah, it's the lawyer."

"I just saw him on TV. On the news."

"Him and his wife, right?"

He ignored the question.

"Listen, Party Girl, I've got just the thing for you. Big rave, up the Peninsula somewhere. Love bus leaves at ten—"

"Brian, I'm not—"

"Listen," he said, suddenly serious, oddly maternal, his voice dropping an octave. "You need to get out, right?"

"I don't think—"

"Let me guess: you've been puttering around the apartment all day, not answering the telephone, in a cleaning tizzy, not eating, trying to think of anything else but him, right? Changing the CDs every half-hour?"

Ah, Brian. "Right."

"So you need to get out."

"Brian, I'm not up for this."

"Look, we'll dance. We'll drink some smart drinks, we'll talk, we'll just hang, okay?"

He was impossible to resist. "Well . . ."

"I'll be there at ten," he jumped in. "Wear your Day-Glo lipstick." He hung up.

As I cradled the receiver I looked at the answering machine, the red light flashing four times, pausing, then flashing again. I thought for a moment about calling, just to let him know I was okay.

Instead, I pressed the button and erased the messages.

The light went out.

KAREN

I was afraid to admit to myself how good it felt to have Simon at home. It was like what Donna had said, about getting accustomed to the worst and accepting it, and how anything else, any slight hope, was almost too much to bear.

Sitting at the table, a glass of merlot in front of me, watching him cook, I was reminded of the early days of our relationship. That first basement apartment, so tiny, so dark. We had rented it furnished with an awful cream vinyl chair and couch, a bed that felt like it had no mattress on it at all and a rickety table with two chairs. God forbid if we ever wanted to have company. We had no money, but it never felt like suffering. He could whip up a gourmet meal from a few vegetables, some noodles and the tiniest pieces of meat—all that we could afford. It was so easy to romanticize the poverty of those days, both of us in school, no TV, always working or reading or going for walks or making love. There was no sense of a real world outside that dictated our actions to us. Not the way it seemed to once we grew up.

When the telephone rang, Simon looked at it with suspicion. I couldn't blame him. I'd just hung up after a painful near-hour with my mother.

"Is it true?" she had started, without any warning or preamble.

"Mom—"

"Father Jean just called me and said he had heard from someone in Victoria—"

"Mom—"

"It *is* true, isn't it?"

I could picture her clutching her rosary beads to her heart.

"I was going to call . . ."

"Oh, Karen, you must be so happy."

"Happy?"

"To be so blessed."

I sighed, and Simon shook his head, obviously piecing together the conversation.

"I wouldn't say happy, Mom. I'm . . . the house is under siege. There are reporters and people everywhere—"

"They just want to see the miracle," she answered. "They just want their questions put to rest. Just like you."

"Mom," I said warningly, gritting my teeth.

"It's true, Karen. It's what I've always said: God doesn't depend on your belief or disbelief, He just is. And now you see proof."

"Mom, I really don't want to—"

"I've called Air Canada," she interrupted. "They can get me on a flight Monday—"

"No," I said, so firmly Simon looked startled.

"I beg your pardon?"

"I said no, Mom," I said, trying to stay calm.

"But Karen—"

"Now is not a good time, Mom. Let us . . . give us a couple of weeks to get used to this. Maybe right after New Year's."

"That's a month!"

"Mom, you were just here three weeks ago."

"But that was before—"

"Before what, Mom? Sherry's the same as she ever was."

I could hear her sigh over the phone. "I know how tough it must be for you," she said. "To have everything you believe— or don't believe, I guess—fall apart with this proof."

The conversation degenerated from there.

So when the telephone rang again, mere minutes after I had hung up, I hesitated.

"It's up to you," Simon said. "The machine will pick it up if you don't."

I decided to chance it.

"Karen, it's Jamie." I waved Simon's concern away. He turned back to his cooking. "I just saw you on the news. How are you holding up?"

"Fine, I suppose."

"Are you guys really sure about this, this whole thing with letting people in to see Sherry? It's going to turn into a zoo."

She was repeating my own fears back to me. "We don't really have a choice in the matter."

"Well, yes, you do."

"We can't just—" I couldn't finish the sentence.

"I suppose."

There was an uncomfortable silence.

"Do you need any help? I know you'll have Ruth there. But Simon?" She trailed off.

"Simon's still here." He glanced toward me at the sound of his name. "He's cooking dinner."

"Ah. Well, he's going to have to go to work, and, well, I seem to have the time . . ." I hadn't often heard Jamie at a loss for words.

"I'd really appreciate that," I said. "We've got no idea what to expect."

"I'd be happy to come over."

"Thanks, Jamie."

"Don't worry about it. I'll be there, what, eight o'clock? Just to be sure everything's all ready? Or should I come earlier?"

I couldn't help but smile. "Whenever works for you. I'm just happy you're coming."

"Me too. I'll see you Monday morning, then."

"Yeah."

"Jamie wants to help on Monday morning," I explained when I hung up.

He nodded. "Good. We'll need as much help as we can get."

"Are you going to be here?" I asked, not even realizing the enormity of my question until he glanced at me. "I mean, don't you have to go to work?"

"Actually, I thought I'd call in, take some personal time."

"Really?"

He nodded. "Really."

I was speechless for a moment. "Okay, then. Jamie will be here, and Ruth, and you and I. We should be okay."

He returned his attention to his cooking. I took a sip of my wine. "Have you spoken to Mary?" I asked before I lost my nerve.

He shook his head. "No, not yet. I've left a couple of messages."

"I'm sorry," I said.

"What? Why?"

"This must be very hard for her. And you."

He looked at me for a long moment, then nodded. "Grab a plate," he said. "Dinner's ready."

After we had been eating in silence for several minutes, I said, "Can I ask you something, Simon?"

"Of course." He was watching me warily.

I set my fork on the edge of my plate and picked up my wineglass. "You and Mary. How long had that been going on, you know, before . . ." I took a sip of my wine.

He sighed and leaned back in his chair. "I . . . it was . . . I don't know, I guess a year or so before I moved out." He spoke without looking at me, without meeting my eye.

I shook my head. "I never even suspected."

He nodded, still looking away.

"I was . . . stunned," I continued, filling up the empty spaces between us.

At this, he turned to me. "Do we have to talk about this now?" he asked quietly. "Haven't we got enough other stuff to worry about?"

"I'm sorry. I was just—"

"Don't be sorry. But let's not talk about it, okay? Not right now," he said.

I bit my lip. "Okay."

But I needed to ask him why. I needed to know why, after being together for more than fifteen years . . .

"No. Not okay," I said. "I'd like to know why."

"That's fair, I guess," he said as he stood and picked up the bottle. Filling both of our glasses, he added, "Why don't we go sit in the family room?"

HENRY

Tim was on the roof of the library, leaning against one of the ventilation shafts, looking up at the sky. The smoke from his cigar seemed to shine as it curled away, the tip an orange glow.

I had to wait for him to look up at me.

"I've been doing some reading," I said.

"Ah, yes. Well, come and sit down. Tell me what you know." He gestured at the roof, his motions a shadow against a shadow, barely visible.

I was carrying several books, and holding my place in one with my index finger, but I managed to settle myself next to him.

"Isn't it a gorgeous night? A little cold, but look at those stars."

"I've been doing some reading," I started again.

"Would you like a cigar?" he asked. "I've got a couple of extra. I steal them from the shop around the corner."

I shook my head. "No, no. I don't smoke."

He shrugged. "You're missing out. There's really nothing quite like it." He held the cigar before him at arm's length, rolling it between his fingers. "More of a meditation than a vice, really."

"I've been reading . . ." I tried again.

He sighed, took a gentle pull on his cigar. "Let me guess: you've discovered old Ahasuerus?"

"What?" I had no idea what he was talking about. I carried on, trying to keep my thoughts organized, grateful to have his attention. "There's a story," I fumbled with my books for a moment before realizing that, even with the light of the city around us, it wasn't bright enough for me to read. I had to rely on my memory. "There's a story, in the Bible—"

"*Not* in the Bible," he interrupted. "Apocryphal. Scholars seem to think it was added in the Middle Ages, but accounts go all the way back to the time of the Gospels."

I shook my head, amazed. "So you know."

"You'll find, young Henry," he said, "that there's not a lot that surprises me anymore. Not for a very long time. But tell me, what did you find?"

"There's a story, about a man who was cursed—"

"Punished."

I glanced over at him, but I couldn't read his expression in the dark. "Doomed to wander the world until the end of time because he hit Jesus when he was on his way to be crucified."

"The avenue of sorrows . . ."

"So he was cursed—"

"He didn't hit him."

"What?"

The tip of his cigar glowed as he took a long pull. "The Jew. The Wandering Jew. He didn't hit Christ. Oh, I know what the books say. This man pushed or shoved or hit or spit on

Christ as he walked the avenue of sorrows toward Calvary, dragging his cross.

"Truth is, Ahasuerus was a shopkeeper. A simple man. A wife, six kids. And that day was just like any other day. Another execution. A couple of thieves, another one of those cult figures. Jerusalem was full of them in those days.

"Crucifixions were like big festivals. There was always a parade. People would follow the Romans and the victims along the route by the hundreds. A good day for business if you were lucky enough to have a shop right on the route like Ahasuerus did."

I could almost picture it in my mind as he spoke.

"Christ was weak. He'd been beaten, he hadn't eaten in days. The cross was heavy, and he couldn't continue. So he stopped in the doorway of a shop. Right in the doorway. And the shopkeeper came out, took a look at the crowd of people following along behind the Romans, took a look at this, this criminal who was blocking the way into his store, and he told Christ to move along. Told him that he couldn't stay there." His voice dropped. "So Christ turned to him and said, 'I won't wait here. But you will. You'll wait until I return.' And he picked up his cross and carried on to Calvary."

Tim blew a big cloud of cigar smoke into the night. "The shopkeeper didn't think anything of it. Just another day. Another execution. He forgot all about it until his wife died, years later. And then his children died. Not young. They had lived their whole lives. It's a terrible thing when a child dies before his parents. It's unnatural. But the shopkeeper out-lived his children. And his grandchildren. And on his hun-dredth birthday, this shopkeeper, who had meant no offense, was still thirty-eight years old, the same age he had been on the day of Christ's crucifixion. He hadn't changed. He hadn't aged, not even as everyone he loved grew old and died around him."

"And then?"

He continued speaking into the middle distance. "He ran. There was nothing else he could do. There were obviously powerful forces at work. He had stepped between—"

"Between?"

Tim shifted. "Imagine a curtain on a stage. Out front, there are people, there's laughter, there's life. People making their entrances and exits. All of us merely players and all that. And backstage, backstage are the forces that make it all happen, the things that you don't see, the mechanics of the world. The Wandering Jew had stepped between, between life and the mystery behind the curtain. He was no longer of the world onstage. He couldn't stay.

"No one knew him. No one knew that he was the same man. No one could know. He obviously couldn't stay there. So he took another name, and he ran. And he's been running ever since."

"So this," I gestured with the book. "The story's true?"

Finally he turned to me. "You'll find that many of the stories you'll read are true. Stories like the Flying Dutchman. Thomas the Rhymer. Dorian Gray. Prester John. The Emperor Barbarossa. The lore is full of stories of people who have stepped between. And there are hundreds—thousands—about whom nothing is written."

He took a long breath through his cigar.

"You."

He was telling me what I already knew, what I had put together without being able to put into words. What I knew, without believing. "Me?"

He nodded.

"You've stepped between, Henry. Just like we all have. Whether it was when you hit that little girl with your truck or when you tried to kill yourself, you stepped between."

"I don't understand."

He shrugged. "I've had centuries to think about this, young Henry, and I don't understand it either. I just know. You've stepped between, outside of the world you knew, but still connected to it."

"Is that why no one can see me?"

He nodded. "You're not a part of that world anymore. You have your own story now. The only people who can see you, who can hear you, are people inside your story. People who have a role to play."

"People like you."

His smile disappeared. "And others. You must be careful, Henry, not to assume that you're invisible to everyone. There are people who have reason to see you. They won't always be jolly fat men with a love of books and good cigars."

I waited for him to continue. He didn't.

"Why can't I remember anything from before?"

"When you tried to die, you left your life behind, even your memories of it, but you couldn't pull away. Your story wasn't done. That's why we're here, waiting."

"Waiting? Is that it? Am I being punished for hitting that little girl? Am I waiting for the Second Coming?"

He chuckled. "It's strange to talk like that, isn't it? As if the Second Coming of Christ were a new movie or something, a finite time. I don't know what you're waiting for, Henry. I don't know what forces are at play for you. I know that the Wandering Jew is waiting to make his amends. He's waiting to apologize, to beg for forgiveness, and he has to wait for Christ to return for that to happen." The cigar had burned down to a stub, and he dropped it to the roof between his feet, where it smoked for a long moment, then slowly went dark.

"How do you know so much about this?" I asked quietly.

He rose to his feet, stretching himself against the chill that the roof had brought to his muscles. "Time," he said. "I've had a lot of time to think about it."

Then he walked in silence back to the stairwell and disappeared inside, leaving me alone with the stars and the city.

SIMON

"I don't really get it," I muttered, shaking my head, once we were sitting. Karen was on the couch and I was on the loveseat, with the wine bottle on the table between us. "I don't understand this need to talk about everything. Not just you, but everyone. Why do people think that if they know everything about a given situation, it'll be better somehow?"

She shook her head. "Maybe because knowing the truth, even if it's unpleasant, is better than not knowing. Or imagining. I just need to know why you threw everything we had away."

"I don't really understand it myself," I said. I braced myself. "This will sound stupid. Clichéd. But I suppose there's nothing really original about any of this, is there?" I sipped before continuing. "We went out for a drink after work. There was a whole crew of us. Stevens had just"—I thought for a moment—"Stevens had just won Dempster, and we all went out to celebrate." I could remember that night with perfect clarity. "Mary had been working for the firm for maybe a couple of months? No more than that. We sat next to each other. Had a few drinks."

"Did you sleep with her?"

I shook my head. "No. Not then. We just talked. She asked me, point blank, if I was jealous of Stevens. I mean, Jesus, Kyle Stevens? But for some reason, I told her the truth. I told her I was."

Taking a swallow of wine, I could picture the sweater she had been wearing, how her hair, still long at that point, was held back with a comb that came from India, the smooth skin at the base of her throat. I remembered wanting to feel the pulse beating there. More than that, though, I could remember the tremendous openness of her expression as she asked me about my jealousy; her forthrightness, her attention.

"I mean, Stevens, Christ, what a yutz. But she read it right. He was coming off the biggest case of his career, and I was jealous. And I admitted it."

"You never told me."

"No, I never did."

"But you told her."

I nodded. "Yes." I tried to figure out a way to put my thoughts into words. "She had no expectations of me. I could say, I could do anything. I felt—"

"Free," she finished.

It was the word that I had been going to use, but hearing it spoken aloud, especially in Karen's voice, I could see it wasn't right. "No. No, that's not it. I felt genuine. I felt like I could be myself."

She seemed shocked. "But we've always been honest with one another."

I didn't respond.

"I guess I should know better than to believe that, shouldn't I?" She shook her head. "So what else didn't you tell me the truth about?" she asked. "Beyond the obvious, of course."

"It's not about honesty, so much," I tried.

"Then what is it about?"

"It was about me. At least, me more than it was about us. I just . . . I felt like I hadn't been able to be myself for a long time." I waited.

The reaction I had been expecting didn't come. She blinked, trying to understand. "But I never—"

"It wasn't you," I interrupted. "This isn't, this was never about you."

"Then what *is* it about?" she asked.

"It's about us, I guess. In part. About the relationship. The roles we played—"

"What *roles?*" she asked, sliding sarcastically over my word.

I thought for a moment. "Do you remember how hard it was, back when we were trying to get pregnant?"

She nodded.

"How hard it was on you?"

"And you were there for me."

I nodded this time. "Yes. Yes, I was." I tried to smile. "But who was there for me?" She gaped at me. "That sounds stupid. Stupid and selfish and weak, but it was like I didn't have anyone. *Anyone.*"

"You had me," she said quietly, already knowing herself that this wasn't true.

I shook my head. "How could I talk to you? You were so scared, so upset. Could I have told you how scared I was? How would you have reacted?" I didn't allow her a chance to answer. She didn't need to. "It would have made everything worse." I tried to make the words, the terrible words, make sense.

She bit the inside of her lip as I spoke, staring into her glass.

"So I didn't. I couldn't. I just kept it all in. I was trying to be strong for you."

"I'm sorry," she said, without looking up.

"No, it's just . . . That was the right thing to do. I know that. It was the only thing I could do. But I ended up being stuck in that role. Always strong. You leaned on me—"

"I leaned on you," she whispered.

We sat for a long time without speaking, without looking at one another.

"Why didn't you ever say anything?" she said finally, setting her empty wineglass on the coffee table, next to the bottle. "To me, I mean."

"I didn't even know anything was wrong," I answered. "Until Mary asked me about Kyle Stevens, and then I knew that there were some things that I just couldn't talk to you about anymore. Things that, by the way we had defined our relationship, couldn't exist in it."

"And Mary was someone you could be honest with."

"She was someone I didn't have to play a role with," I corrected.

She smiled wryly at me. "It's the same thing."

I didn't know whether to agree or disagree.

It was dark when the stranger arrived at the newspaper building. He had left this stop for last; the editor of a newspaper would always be near his newsroom until the next day's issue was safely put to bed.

He had taken off the collar after leaving Bradford & Howe. The senior partner had practically genuflected when the priest had asked for a moment of his time. In the end, he had come away with everything that he wanted in exchange for no more than a few moments of private confession and counsel.

For this meeting, however, the collar would be a liability.

He knew, before he opened the door to the newspaper, how the conversation would proceed, how the lies would break into heated denials, then dissolve into pleading and panic in the face of the proof. He had seen it too many times.

And they always seemed so relieved when they learned his silence could be bought, so surprised that the cost of his silence was so low.

"Truthfully, I have no use for your money. What I need amounts to no more than a few column inches."

Within minutes, it would be accomplished. Months of planning, of waiting and watching, would have served their purpose. The stranger would walk into an office with nothing more than words—secrets—and walk out with promises.

The promises were more precious than silver.

The most powerful weapon he could wield.

KAREN

Night sounds, both familiar and strange.

The dripping of the bathtub faucet a little slower than a heartbeat; the otherworldly click, then roar as the furnace burst into life; the slow, occasional pops and wheezes as the heat pipes cooled when the furnace went off; the motor and the fan of the fridge; the occasional voices of people walking past on the sidewalk.

After dinner, after the wine, Simon and I had worked together to get Sherry ready for bed. He had carried her into the bathroom, lowering her carefully into the tub, cradling her head as her hair floated in a nimbus around her face. He had held her as I dried her with a fluffy towel, as I powdered her and slipped a nightie over her head. While I warmed her nutritional supplement, Simon reconnected the feeding tube to the pump and diapered her. He told her a story while the machine fed her and I did the dishes. Without saying much, he made up his bed on the couch in the family room.

And then it was just Sherry and me, as it had been for so many nights. Her breath was slow and hypnotic, warm against my cheek as I bent to tuck her in, to kiss her face. Headlights falling across the curtains, laying shadows across the wall.

Door locked, porch light out, hall light on by force of habit—if Sherry woke and had to go to the bathroom she would need to see her way.

I peered into the family room before I went upstairs. Simon's breath was rough and irregular. He slept with the sleeping bag pulled up to his throat, twisted onto his side on the narrow couch, face buried in one of the spare pillows.

Scrupulously shaven, even on a Friday night, eyes lightly closed.

What do you dream, Simon?

I dream of that first apartment, the funky smell from the unit down the hall that we used to joke meant that they must be "cooking dog for dinner again." I dream of the weight of your body in our first bed, the taste of you on my lips, the breadth of you inside me.

I dream of my father's funeral, the way you held me. I dream of Sherry's birth, the way you held her, your hands shaking, a look of awe, wonder and terror in your eyes, and an openness I so rarely saw there.

I dream of Mary, of her long legs spread wide and you between them, the pale half-moons of your buttocks thrusting into her, your fingers in her hair, her calling out your name in my voice.

I dream of killing you in your sleep, pressing my thumbs into your Adam's apple, the look in your eyes as you awake.

I dream of kissing you in your sleep, pressing my lips gently against your Adam's apple, the look in your eyes as you awake.

"Goodnight, Simon," I whispered.

As I walked away, my shadow followed, leaving the light from the hallway to fall on his closed eyes. He groaned a little, turned deeper into the pillow.

At the foot of the stairs I turned the light off and started up in darkness. I had gone three steps when I changed my mind and turned around.

Lifting the covers gently, I slid into Sherry's bed, nestling against her, losing myself in the smell of her, her hair, her skin, her warmth. I carefully curled one arm around her, sheltering her, protecting her. I drew her to me, and lay waiting for her to press herself against me, the way she had when she was smaller. I waited. And waited.

LEO

I did everything just like Father Peter said.

I waited until Mother had fallen asleep and then I picked him up downtown. I was real quiet when I got ready to go so I wouldn't wake her.

He was outside the cathedral like he said he would be. I didn't see him at first in the dark, so I stopped the van and waited. He opened the door without knocking. It scared me a little.

"Hello, Leo."

"Hello, Father."

He closed the door, but I didn't turn the key. He looked at me.

"I can't go anywhere until you put on your safety belt," I told him. "That's what they taught us in Young Drivers. The car doesn't move until everybody puts on their safety belts. That's the rule."

He smiled and put on the safety belt. "There," he said. "It's important to follow the rules, isn't it?"

I nodded. "Very important." I started the van. "Where should we go?"

"Do you know how to get to the water?" he asked.

"Where?"

"The waterfront at Dallas Road. Near the park, I think."

I thought for a minute. "Is that the place where people bring their dogs for walks?"

"Are there cliffs there? With benches?" he asked.

"I think so. Mother and I go there sometimes after church to watch the people with their dogs."

"Do you have a dog, Leo?"

I shook my head. "No. Not yet. Someday though. Mother says I just need to be a little older, a little more responsible. It's a big responsibility to have a pet."

"Do you know how to get there?"

I nodded, and he smiled. "Good."

We parked under one of the trees that looks like it's always being pushed by the wind. I had started to pull into a spot under the streetlight, but Father Peter said, "No, over there," pointing to the shadows. When we were walking away, I looked back and I could hardly see the van at all in the dark.

A few people were still playing with their dogs even though it was so late, but we went the other way. It was kind of scary. The bushes by the sidewalk reached over my head like a tunnel. It was so dark I could barely see anything. It sounded like the ocean was right there, just past the bushes.

When we came out of the bush tunnel we were right on top of the cliffs. I was scared to look down. Stay back and be careful. Better careful than sorry. It was cold and it was windy and I felt kind of like I had to pee.

Father Peter walked all the way to the bench at the very end of the sidewalk, playing with his coin. There was a big fat man sitting there smoking a stinky cigar. He stood up when he saw Father Peter and smiled just a little bit.

"I see you've brought your bodyguard," he said. His voice sounded funny, like he came from somewhere else.

"Leo's a friend, Tim," Father Peter said. "That is what you're calling yourself these days, yes?" The fat man nodded. "I see you've come alone. Couldn't convince one of those thieves and liars from the library to join you?" He sat down on the bench, facing the cliffs and the ocean, and the fat man sat down next to him. He took a big puff on his cigar and blew out a big cloud of smoke.

"Don't I usually come alone? It's lonely work. I'd have thought you'd know that by now."

Father Peter smiled. "Aren't you afraid of me, even a little, after all these years?"

"Should I be? Should I be afraid of you wrestling me over these cliffs? We both know we'd just end up damp, and it's too cold a night for that."

I didn't really know what the fat man was talking about, but hearing him talk about the water and the cold made me have to pee even more.

"I can't say that it's good to see you," Father Peter said.

Tim shrugged. "It should hardly be a surprise."

"It's been quite some time, though."

"Since Lima. Those little girls. The twins."

Father Peter smiled. "I remember. Terrible what happened to them. And who was it before that? That whore in Oregon?" Father Peter shook his head, still smiling. "It won't do you any good this time either."

"So you always say."

I really had to pee. I started to bounce up and down a little, but I stopped when I remembered what Mother would say about that.

"I don't know why you go on trying, Tim. I always win. That should be clear to you by now." Father Peter smiled, but I didn't think he looked very friendly. I thought that maybe he was mad at the man he called Tim. "Do you remember the French girl? The one who would be king?"

"Joan."

"Joan. Yes. You tried so hard to save her."

"Yes."

"And all you could do in the end was to watch as she burned."

"I remember you there. You were a cardinal then, I think."

"The most powerful woman in the world. A beloved leader. And they burned her. They came out in the thousands to watch her die. She saved their country, and they spat on her ashes. Because I told them to. There is no one I cannot touch."

"That was a long time ago."

Father Peter shrugged. "It's only become easier. With the little faith people have these days, all it takes is a few well-chosen words. A rumor here. A whisper there. And the problem takes care of itself."

"That doesn't mean I stop trying."

"No," Father Peter said. "No, it doesn't. How long have you been here?"

Tim looked like he was thinking. "Four years or so, I guess. It's a nice little city."

"From the very beginning."

The fat man nodded. "And you?"

"A few months. Just before the accident."

The accident? I couldn't understand what they were talking about. I had to pee really bad.

"That poor little girl."

Father Peter snorted. "I'm not here because she's a poor little girl."

The fat man looked sad. "No, you're here because you're the

worst sort of zealot. You're the sort who destroys people's lives, who kills in the name of all you believe."

"All that I was taught, you mean. I'm just doing God's will in this world. Wasn't it He who rained down fire on Sodom? Who flooded the world?"

I had to pee so bad.

"I think you've forgotten all you were taught," Tim said. "I think you've spent so much time beweeping your outcast state you've forgotten the very foundations of all you believe. The Flood? Sodom and Gomorrah? What about 'Thou shalt not kill'?"

"If it comes to that I'll not stay my hand. I'll make my own reckoning when my time comes. I will be judged—"

"And found wanting. Again."

Father Peter shrugged. I thought I might wet myself, but I didn't want to turn away.

"You would kill that child?"

What did he mean, kill?

Father Peter shrugged. "She wouldn't be the first I've put to the flames. Thou shalt not suffer a witch to live."

"She's not a witch. She's a little girl who has never done anyone wrong."

"She is an insult, an aberration. Whether she is evil, or a vessel for evil, makes no difference to me. There is only one savior, only one path to salvation. I will defend Him and the purity of His name from these pretenders, no matter the cost. This little girl cannot be allowed to spread her poison, and I will do whatever it takes to stop her, to stop her family. It's the Lord's work."

"So it has begun, then."

Father Peter nodded.

"And he's the first?" Tim gestured to me.

Father Peter nodded again. "The first of the true."

The fat man shook his head.

I couldn't stand it any longer. I turned around and ran back down the path, pulling open my pants. I was peeing almost before I stopped at the edge of the bushes. That was a close one. Steam came up from where the pee hit the ground and the leaves.

I peed for a long time, then I shook myself carefully, once twice three times, and zipped up my zipper and buttoned my button.

When I got back to the bench, Father Peter was alone. I couldn't see the fat man anywhere. "We're done here," he said quietly, not looking at me.

FIVE

December 8–9

KAREN

I slept in on Sunday morning for the first time in months.

Simon and I had spent most of Saturday working around the house: planning, cleaning, moving furniture to clear paths for access. Access to our daughter.

It had been a long time since he and I had worked side by side on anything. It felt good to break a sweat with him, to laugh at our mutual ineptitude when it came to anything remotely handy. I was surprised, though. Simon actually built a credible ramp up one side of the front porch out of a couple of sheets of plywood over some two-by-fours. When it was finished, we both jumped on it, and it held.

I had been dreaming of Simon. Nothing in particular, just the sense of being with him, of spending time with him, of being in the same bed. It had been so vivid I was surprised when I woke up alone. I was even more surprised when, rolling onto my side and glancing at the alarm clock, I saw that it was after eleven.

"Shit," I muttered, sitting up. I only calmed when I realized that Simon was downstairs.

Sherry and I weren't alone.

I pulled on a robe, cinching it around my waist before stepping into my slippers and opening the bedroom door.

I heard voices from the kitchen. I was surprised to see Simon and Ruth both sitting at the table.

They looked up as I came in. "Good morning," I said, still groggy. "Did I sleep all the way through the weekend?"

Ruth smiled and shook her head. "No, but I thought . . ."

"Ruth thought that we might like a little time out today, to run some errands, or—"

"I saw the news last night," Ruth explained. "It's going to be pretty crazy around here tomorrow, so I thought I'd come over, see if you wanted me to watch Sherry today so you could get anything done that needed doing."

"Thank you, Ruth, but I don't think so," I said, shaking my head.

Simon and Ruth exchanged a glance. "I already said yes," he said.

"Oh."

"I thought we'd get away for a couple of hours. Maybe walk downtown, have something to eat. Get out of the house while we can."

"Oh."

"We don't have to, though."

"No, no, that'll be good. I'm just . . . I'm not used to sleeping in anymore, I guess. I'll be better after I shower."

A little unsteady, I turned back to the stairs.

LEO

The next time I saw Father Peter was after Sunday Mass. He was waiting outside the cathedral when Mother and I left.

He looked like a shadow, standing by the graveyard. I think he was waiting for me, and he nodded when I came out of the door.

At first I wanted to point him out to Mother, but she was concentrating on getting down the steps. And besides, I didn't have to tell her everything. When Father Peter talked to me, I felt special, knowing that he was talking right to me, not anybody else.

We were in the van for more than an hour on Friday night and he told me about all of the miracles he knew. Some of them were new to me and the time went real fast. I was really late getting home, but I didn't wake Mother. Quiet as a church mouse.

I spoke loud to her now to be sure that she could hear me. "Mother, I'm gonna go talk to someone. Okay? Are you okay with the stairs?"

"Of course I am," she said. "I was going up and coming down these steps before you were even born. Meet me back at the car."

She didn't look to see where I was going.

Father Peter smiled when he saw me coming across the lawn to him, and I smiled back.

"Hello, Leo."

"Hello, Father. Were you inside?" I was a bit out of breath after hurrying across the lawn.

"I worshipped earlier," he said. "I came to see you."

I knew it. "Here I am."

"Would you like to talk some more?"

I looked back over my shoulder. "I would. I would. But my mother"—think think think—"I have to drop my mother off at home first. Is that all right?"

"Of course it is. Of course. Why don't we meet where we were on Friday night?"

KAREN

Simon and I walked downtown. We kept to the residential streets as far as we could, savoring the quiet. We made small talk, stayed away from anything of any importance. It was nice, sort of an informal break.

We had no destination, no place we had to be. We spent a while drifting around bookstores. I noticed Simon was gravitating away from the sections in which he usually browsed, moving from business and biography toward religion, philosophy, art. In Munro's, I found him in the poetry section, reading e. e. cummings.

"What's this?" I asked.

He jumped. "It's, ah, it's . . ." He showed me the cover.

"This is kind of unusual for you, isn't it?" I joked, only realizing what I'd said after the words were already out there. "I'm sorry. That's what you meant, isn't it? The other night?"

"I always used to read poetry," he said, color starting to rise in his cheeks. "I used to write some too. I thought you'd remember that."

"I do," I answered in a whisper, ashamed of myself. I tried to meet his eye, but he didn't look at me.

The same thing happened at A&B Sound. For a long time he had bought little but opera and classical, the sort of music that someone in his position might listen to. That afternoon, though, he bought a handful of CDs: the Grateful Dead, the latest Bob Dylan, an expensive collection of folk music. This time I concealed my surprise.

It was like that for the rest of the afternoon. We meandered from shop to shop, stopping for coffee at one point, walking along the water through the Inner Harbour, through Market Square and finally into Chinatown. We avoided the furniture stores and kitchen boutiques where we used to spend so much of our time.

Despite being on the news in the past few days, we weren't recognized.

"Are you hungry?" he asked, as we were walking through Chinatown.

"Yeah. Yeah, I am."

"Do you want to get a bite to eat?"

My first thought was of Sherry. "What time is it?"

He glanced at his wrist reflexively, then, grinning, pulled back his sleeve to reveal his naked arm. "I forgot to put my watch on this morning."

I checked my own wrist. "Sure. I guess we've got time."

"I can't stop thinking about her either."

I nodded.

"Ruth's there," he ventured. "And I've got my cell."

"Lunch would be good."

"What about right here?" He gestured at the restaurant where we had stopped. It was one of a dozen in that single block. Most of them were indistinguishable from one another, but this one stood out.

"It's been a long time," I said.

"Maybe they still do the special."

The lunch special was almost twice as expensive as it had been the last time we had eaten there, but the chairs and tables seemed to be the same. The waitress, tall, willowy and young with a tattoo in the small of her back, was different, but cut from the same cloth.

"God, we must have come here every week for a year," Simon said, sipping his ice water.

"It *was* every week," I answered, smiling. "It was the only place we could afford."

In his last year as an undergrad, Simon had worked as the night clerk in a convenience store. Three ten-hour graveyard shifts each week. I hated being alone in the apartment, so I would bring a book or some homework with me and set up in one corner of the store for the night. He'd get off at eight in the morning and we'd go back to our basement apartment and fall into bed, too tired even to make love, sleeping through most of the day.

When we woke up, we'd walk downtown, stopping at this restaurant for the all-day lunch special.

He cleared his throat. "I've been thinking about that time a lot recently. That first apartment. Working those stupid hours."

"Me too," I said.

He smiled. "It's amazing, isn't it? That we even survived."

"We were young."

"Yeah. I guess." His gaze was far away. "Still. I think it was the last time I can remember feeling that there were more doors opening in front of me than there were closing behind me."

His hand was on the table, next to the bags from the bookstore and the record store.

I was startled by how close I came to taking it in my own. And then I noticed his wedding ring.

"When did you put that back on?" I asked.

He looked down at his hand. "This morning. I don't know. I just put it on."

I nodded, unable to look away.

"Is that all right?"

"That's really up to you," I said, then I stopped myself. "No," I started again. "No, it's not. I don't want to close any doors on you . . ."

"But?" he said.

"I don't think . . . I like having you at the house. I like all this, being with you like this. But I don't think you can stay. Not now. Not yet. Not with everything we've been talking about the last couple of days."

I waited for him to argue. Instead, he nodded. "Yeah."

"I know that it's not fair, but I'm still hurt. And I'm worried that we'll slip into the same old patterns."

"No, it's fair. I've still got some things I need to figure out. It wouldn't be fair to you if I was at the house when I hadn't . . ."

I looked down at his hand, the ring, on the black tabletop. I didn't want to ask. "Will you go back to Mary's?"

He shook his head. "No. That wouldn't be fair to her. To either of you."

"Your women."

He half-smiled, and glanced at the space on his wrist where his watch should have been. "Could I stay at the house one more night? I'll find a place tomorrow . . ."

He looked so open. "Of course. It'll be good to have you there first thing. I think tomorrow's going to be a difficult day."

I looked once more at his ring, the ring he had put back on this morning, then glanced at the matching gold band I had never removed.

LEO

Father Peter was already at the edge of the cliff when I got to Dallas Road. It had taken me a little longer to get Mother settled than I thought it would. She wouldn't let me leave until I had eaten some lunch.

The wind was blowing Father Peter's coat back like a cape when I came up behind him. I didn't want to get too close to the edge so I stayed by the bench. It was even scarier than it was at night because I could see how high up we were.

The park was full of people walking after church, dogs running around with no leashes, people flying kites. The wind was cold.

"I'm sorry it took me so long to get here," I said to his back. "My mother . . ."

"That's all right," he said. "It gave me time to think."

He didn't say anything for a long time, and people walked along the sidewalk behind me. Then he said, "Why don't you come over here, Leo?"

"I, I'm a little bit scared," I answered, holding on to the back of the bench.

"You're scared? Of falling?" He held out his hand to me. The silver coin flashed in his other hand, flashing, flashing.

"Come to me, Leo. I won't let you fall."

I took a deep breath and walked toward him. Baby steps. I tried not to look over the edge as it got closer and closer. I didn't feel safe until I took his hand.

"That's good," he said. "I won't let anything happen to you. You know that."

I nodded, too scared to look away from his face.

"You know that you're safe with me."

I nodded again.

"You can look down," he said. "It's all right. I won't let anything happen to you."

I knew he wouldn't. I knew that if I did what I was told Father Peter would keep me safe.

So I looked down.

There were bushes at my feet, then the cliff and all I could see was the gray water and the rocks way down below. It looked so cold. I felt like I might throw up.

"You see?" His soft voice was close to me, almost inside my head. "I won't let anything happen to you."

"I know," I nodded, looking down at the rocks and the water.

"You were right to be scared, though," he said. "Your soul is in grave, grave peril. That little girl, all this talk about miracles. Your soul is teetering on the edge of a vast abyss, hundreds of times higher than this cliff."

I could see myself falling, and I shivered.

When I looked at him, Father Peter looked worried and a little sad.

"I can save you," he said. "I can save you from those rocks, from that endless fall."

Save me.

"I can save your soul. I can keep you safe."

I nodded. "What do I do?"

"We need to talk, you and I," he said, helping me back to the bench. "There is so much that you don't know. Are you ready to learn?"

I looked into his face, then toward the cliff. I imagined myself falling into the water, into the flames, and I nodded.

"Barrett residence."

"Karen?"

"No, I'm sorry. Mrs. Barrett isn't available to come to the phone right now. This is Ruth Page speaking."

"Oh. Is . . . is Simon there?"

"No, I'm sorry. Mr. Barrett isn't available either. Is there something I could help you with?"

"No, I . . . Will they be home soon? I need . . ."

"I'm afraid I don't know exactly when they'll be home. Is there something wrong?"

"No. No, I just . . . Can you take a message?"

"For Mrs. Barrett?"

"For either of them, I guess. It doesn't really . . ."

"Of course."

"Tell them . . . This is Donna Kelly. My son, Jeffrey . . . could you please tell them, tell them we're sorry."

"Sorry? Sorry for what? Mrs. Kelly? Are you still there? Mrs. Kelly? Hello? Hello?"

SIMON

Neither of us was particularly hungry after our late lunch in Chinatown, so we had a salad for dinner. A little lettuce, a little endive, some red cabbage and grated carrot, a honey vinaigrette—light and sweet with a touch of bitterness.

After dinner, Karen looked at me. "Would it be okay with you if I had a bath? I never feel comfortable having one when it's just Sherry and me in the house."

"Of course."

Once I was done with the dishes, I went upstairs.

Access to the attic was a pulldown ladder at the end of the corridor. The only light was a bare bulb hanging from the rafters, catching motes of dust in the air. Karen and I had talked about building an apartment up here for Sherry when she got to be a teenager. It had seemed so far in the future then—now, it seemed to belong to a distant past.

The attic wasn't cluttered: some boxes of books and clothes, an old dresser still waiting to be refinished, a trunk of Christmas decorations that my mother had given us when she sold the house. It still took me a while to find the guitar, the black case leaning in a corner in plain sight, but overlooked so often it might as well have been hidden. I dusted the case off with the dish towel I had brought up with me, then pulled the chain to turn the light off, closing the attic door behind me.

My new books and CDs were on the coffee table in the family room, alongside my watch and wallet. At one end of the couch I had stacked my pillows and the folded sleeping bag. Sitting down, I set the guitar case on my lap, flipping open the catches.

I lifted the guitar from the case and the fingers of my left hand curled around the neck. I carefully rubbed it down with a chamois, bringing the color back up to a rich, honey-colored shine. The conditions in the attic must have been all right—it hadn't warped or dried out. I changed the strings, and then spent several minutes tightening the keys, plucking each string, bringing the whole into tune.

I'd heard stories of guitars that had been destroyed by being stored for a lot less time than this one. Sometimes an unloved, untouched guitar just faded away, incapable of holding a note, flat and lifeless. Casualty of neglect.

I strummed the strings lightly. The sound was far from pure, far from clean, but that was more my rusty technique than the guitar itself. I fumbled for the chords. My fingers were stiff, and my transitions were awkward, but the guitar sounded fine. Its vibrations pulsed through my belly and filled me with a remembered warmth. The strings pressed small troughs into my fingertips as I moved through the chords, first slowly, gradually faster.

Karen had bought me my first guitar for my twentieth birthday. I didn't even play. In high school, with my father out of work, then out of the picture altogether, my mother always struggled to make ends meet. She wouldn't let me work to help out, so I dedicated myself to my studies. There just wasn't any time to waste on something as frivolous as music.

But Karen knew that a guitar was something I had always wanted.

I asked Chris, this pothead who had lived on my floor in residence, to show me some chords. After that, I practiced every night for an hour, a good break from studying. The first time I played in front of people I was drunk. I played "Tangled Up in Blue" to the crowd at one of our house parties, stumbling a little on the changes at first, but quickly getting caught up in the flow. I even sang.

"Well, you're not as bad as Bob Dylan," Karen told me that night after everyone had left. I took it as a compliment and kept playing. Soon, a couple of the other guys started bringing their guitars with them and we'd play together.

I wondered where they'd ended up.

I fumbled in the pocket of the case for my capo, fastening it to the neck of the guitar, bringing it up a bit to suit my voice. I tried to find the pitch, then took the capo off, dropping it back into the case. Apparently my voice wasn't as high as it had been.

Clearing my throat, I began to sing.

KAREN

He was playing with his whole body, leaning into the notes, the chords, bending into the song, his eyes closed. His shirt-sleeves were rolled up, and his voice strained a little to keep even close to the tune. He mumbled the words he didn't remember, or just hummed over them. I drew my robe closely around myself against the cooling of the house.

He played each song all the way through, never stopping, as if he needed to finish, needed to see each one through.

> Well met, well met, my own true love
> Well met, well met, cried he
> I've just returned from the salt, salt sea
> And it's all for the love of thee.

They were all songs I had heard a hundred times, songs that seemed more fragments of dream than of memory.

I finally crept away without him seeing me, turning off the lights as I went. As I crawled into bed, I could still hear the guitar echoing through the heat pipes, the hallways, the otherwise silent rooms, his voice weaving in and out of the notes.

For some reason, the sound of it made me feel both warm and frightened.

Victoria New Sentinel
Monday, December 9, 1996
Miracle Fraud?
Investigation reveals false healings, fraud
~City Desk~

In a surprising development late Sunday, a source close to the Catholic Church announced that an inquiry may take place into the healings attributed to four-year-old Sherilyn Barrett, comatose since a hit-and-run accident last spring. According to confidential reports, those healings may be part of an elaborate fraud devised by her parents, Karen Barrett, a former journalist, and her estranged husband, Simon Barrett, an associate with Bradford & Howe.

The *New Sentinel* spoke to one pilgrim who says she no longer expects a miracle.

"It's all about money," says Donna Kelly of Seattle. Kelly's six-year-old son, Jeffrey, suffers from leukemia, and was invited into the Barrett home on Friday. "They sit you down and give you this story about medical bills, and how all of the money goes to caring for Sherry. It's pretty clear that if you don't cough it up, they won't let you see her." Although Miss Kelly wouldn't divulge the amount she contributed, she is very clear on the cost to her. "They catch you in this untenable position. You're ready to do anything if you think there's a chance that maybe it'll save your child's life."

A source close to the Catholic Church discussed the nature of miracles. "We usually find that these supposed miracles are psychosomatic. People experience temporary recovery because they believe in the possibility of having been healed. For the sufferers, it's all about faith. People who are less scrupulous can easily take advantage of these believers. That's what makes fraudulent situations so reprehensible. That people can prey on other people's desperation, taking advantage of tragedy for their own gain, is terrible."

According to a statement released by the Barretts Friday afternoon, they will be allowing people access to their daughter and her alleged powers beginning at ten o'clock today. "It looks like a textbook situation," says the source. "You hold people off, start the rumors going, then just let the demand build. The higher the demand, the higher the price."

The Barretts could not be reached for comment, nor would they allow investigators access to examine Sherilyn. Victoria Police would not confirm whether they would investigate the situation, or if criminal charges would be pending. "It would be premature to say anything at this point."

KAREN

I awoke to a familiar but unaccustomed weight at the foot of the bed. "Simon?"

"It's me," he whispered, touching my foot through the

blankets. I could see the vaguest outline of him, sitting on the bed and looking toward the bedroom door.

"What are you doing? What time is it?" I struggled up to a sitting position.

"It's a little after seven."

"Okay."

"Can I turn on the light?" He stood up, and the mattress shifted.

"Yeah, sure," I said, fumbling for the bedside lamp.

He turned on the ceiling lamp before I had a chance to flick the switch. The light was painfully bright on my sleep-darkened eyes. "Sorry," he said as I winced.

"What's going on?"

He sat down on the bed next to me, wearing only his socks, underwear and an undershirt. "You need to look at this," he said, laying today's newspaper on my lap.

"What is it? What's . . ." The black headline, over the picture of our house stopped me cold. *Miracle Fraud?* "Oh my God," I muttered, skimming through the article.

"I'm going to guess that the unnamed church source is likely—"

"Father Peter," I finished Simon's sentence for him.

I stared at the headline. "Why would Donna Kelly say we asked her for money?"

"Maybe Father Peter made her a better offer."

"But we saved her son. Sherry saved Jeffrey's life."

"We think. We don't know that. Jeffrey might be just as bad today. Worse."

I dropped the newspaper onto the bed. "Well, I guess that's what her phone call was about yesterday."

"Father Peter likely showed up at her hotel room with a bag full of money and some variation on the line he tried to sell us. She didn't really have a choice. She's not working—"

"I know, I know," I said, shaking my head, able to imagine myself in her position. "I just can't—"

I wanted to curl up and go back to sleep, to wake up a few hours later and discover that this was all a dream.

Instead, I asked, "So what do we do now? Can we sue them, or . . ."

"We can try," he said. "It's pretty expensive to pursue a libel action."

"So what are we going to do? Nobody's going to come if they think the whole thing is a fraud." A moment later I realized what I'd just said.

"Wouldn't that be better?" Simon looked at me. "Not to have to worry about it . . . Just like Father Peter was saying the other day?"

"No," I said. "No. It might be easier, but if Sherry *can* help people, then it's not better. I want the people to come."

I waited for an argument, but he just nodded.

"That's good," he said. "Because there were four people waiting on the front step when I went out to get the paper."

"Had they seen it?" I couldn't keep track of all the things that I was feeling.

"One of them mentioned it to me," he said, shaking his head in disbelief.

"There were already people waiting?"

"As of seven o'clock."

"Sheila, it's Simon."

"Simon, I was just . . . Is everything all right?"

"It's been a strange couple of days. That's why I'm calling. I think I need to take a few personal days to try to get through the worst of this. Can you please . . ."

"Simon, I was about to call you."

"Why? What is it?"

"The senior partners want to meet with you at 9:30."

"Did they say—"

"In Mr. Fitzgerald's office."

"Oh. Well. Let them know I'll be there."

MARY

I was sitting on the leather couch in Simon's office, pretending to make notes on a yellow pad, when he opened the door. I stood up slowly, my heart rushing in my chest.

"Good morning," he said, closing the door.

"Hello," I said. "I saw the paper."

He set his briefcase on the floor. "Yeah."

I had no idea what I wanted to say. The silence stretched for almost a minute, before I asked, "So what are you going to do?"

"About what?"

"About the newspaper?"

He shrugged. He seemed distracted, not really there. "There's not a whole lot we can do. If we threaten to sue, they'll just print a correction on page H17 where no one will ever see it. And I'm not about to go suing the Catholic Church over whether or not my daughter's a saint, let alone that poor kid's mother." As he was speaking his eyes were darting around the office.

Leaning over his desk, he glanced through the pink message slips. "I tried calling you this weekend," he said, without looking up. "After you left."

"I went home. Back to my apartment. I got together with some friends Friday night."

"Why?"

The question caught me off guard. "What do you mean *why?* You were at home with your wife and daughter. I didn't think there was a whole lot of room for me in that picture."

"I needed you."

"You don't know what you need."

"What?"

"Simon, I love you," I started, as coolly as I could. "But you—you just don't know. You don't know where you're going, you don't know what you want. Who you want to be with." He started to protest, but I held up my hand. "No. Don't. I don't want to be the girl who broke up your marriage. And I don't want to be some bit on the side. Not anymore. That's why I left. If there's any chance that you're going to go back to Karen, I don't want to stand in the way, but I sure don't want to participate in it."

He stared at me, speechless.

"You didn't come," I said.

"What?"

"To the apartment. *Home.* This weekend, after I left. You called. You left messages on the machine, but you didn't come."

"I didn't know if I should," he said. "I didn't know if you wanted me there."

"Of course I wanted you there. I just wanted you there for the right reasons. I wanted you there for me, and for you, and for us, not just as a reaction to your wife."

He looked as if he wanted to argue, but he didn't. "You're right," he said, looking away.

"*You* have to decide, Simon," I said. "It's got nothing to do with me now." The truth of what I was saying startled me.

"I know."

"I've got your stuff in the car. I'll—"

"I'm not sleeping with her," he blurted.

He seemed almost like a little boy, so quick and earnest with the denial. It almost made me smile.

"Maybe you should," I said. "Maybe that's what you need. Maybe that's what you both need."

He glanced at his watch and I looked automatically to the clock on the wall. 9:25.

"I'm sorry," he said. "I have to go."

I looked at him as he straightened his tie and smoothed imaginary wrinkles from the sleeves of his jacket. "Go where?"

His face was pale. "The senior partners have requested my presence in Garrett's office."

"Mr. Fitzgerald?" I'd only met the firm's founder once, but I had heard the stories.

He nodded and faked a smile. "It'll be fine," he lied.

RUTH

There was already a crowd in front of the Barretts' house when I arrived at 8:30. Both sides of the street were lined with cars and TV vans. I was forced to park several houses down and walk.

Rather than clustering on the front lawn again, the pilgrims had formed a loose line from the foot of the front steps and along the walk. I counted three wheelchairs and two rosaries held in shaking hands. No one said anything as I walked up to the front door, though several people smiled at me.

"Are there many out there?" Karen asked as I shut the door. I was surprised to see how well she looked. I had been expecting her to be more frantic.

"A dozen or so," I answered as I hung up my coat. "But there are more people coming. Looking for places to park."

"I thought maybe there wouldn't be that many."

"Because of the newspaper article this morning?"

She nodded, starting toward the kitchen. "Did they talk to you? The *New Sentinel?*"

I shook my head. "No. And no matter what they said in that article, no one called here yesterday afternoon from the paper."

"I didn't think they had. But I'm surprised to see so many people here, considering," she said.

"I think that most people, if they're going to try something like this, they've got enough faith—"

"Or desperation—"

"Or desperation. They won't be swayed by anything they read in the paper. Did Simon see it?"

"Yes, he saw the paper." I explained. "He stayed the night again but he had to go in to the office."

"I wasn't prying."

"I know. I told him yesterday that I didn't know if I could handle having him in the house," Karen said. "I mean, I like it that he's here. It's comfortable. It's safe. It feels right."

"Well, it is right. He's your husband."

She shook her head. "No, no, it's not. Like this morning. He had to go in to the office, and all I can do is worry about him seeing Mary, talking to her. I mean, I know he's in love with her, but having him here feels so natural, like maybe we can just go back to the way we were before, but we can't. We can't go back to that."

"Why not?"

She sighed and stood up, leaning on the counter with her back to me. "Because I don't want to go back. Because what we had wasn't good, and it wasn't until he left that I realized that." When she turned to face me, I was surprised to see that she wasn't even close to tears. "And now it's all about him. All about his feelings, his problems. I'm stifling him. I'm not letting him explore himself. Be himself. What about me? Aren't I allowed to have feelings?"

"Of course you are."

"Then why won't anyone listen to them?" It was just a question; there was no self-pity in her voice.

"I'm listening."

She smiled ruefully. "I don't think you're the person I need to be telling all this to." She sat back down across from me.

"It's a start."

For a moment, her gaze drifted away. "I liked being at home with Sherry. I liked watching her grow. Watching her change. But I didn't have a choice. That's it, right there. I never got to choose. I wouldn't have gone back to work at the paper, but I never got to choose. It was always just assumed that I would stay home." She drained her cup, then set it gently on the table in front of her. "This is stupid. I'm being selfish."

I deliberately didn't say anything.

She understood. "I'm sorry. I was fishing . . ."

"As you said, I'm not the one that you need to be having this conversation with."

We were interrupted by a knock at the front door.

"It's probably just Jamie."

"You're right. You're right. What time is it?" Glancing at her watch, Karen rose to her feet. "Damn it," she muttered. "How are we—"

I stood up. "Let me get it."

KAREN

Dr. McKinley was leaning over Sherry, his back to the door, as I came into the living room.

"How is she?" I asked.

Stephen didn't turn to face me. "The same," he answered, closing the file.

"I wasn't expecting to see you this morning." I approached Sherry's bed and he shifted away, toward the couch.

"I thought I'd check in." His voice was cool. "I wasn't doing anything else."

"You're off at the hospital?"

"Indefinitely," he said, turning to face me. His face was ashen and tight, his eyes ringed with circles.

"What?"

"The hospital has suspended my privileges, 'pending a hearing,'" he explained.

"Because of the article in the paper this morning?"

He started to shake his head, then stopped. "Probably. I got called in yesterday afternoon, but it was about the same stuff as the article. The board had a few questions about my conduct 'regarding the Barrett matter.'" He grinned bitterly. "They told me that they 'knew what was going on,' but that they were willing to give me the benefit of the doubt and schedule a hearing." He shook his head slowly. "I had no idea what they were talking about. It was sort of like a Kafka story. And then I saw the paper this morning."

"Oh God, Stephen, I'm so sorry."

"So, would you mind telling me what the hell is going on around here?" he said.

I led him toward the kitchen and we sat down at the table where Ruth had refilled the teapot. I recounted the events of the weekend: the visit from Father Peter, the decision to bring Jeffrey Kelly in to see Sherry and then to open up the house.

"Has a doctor looked at this Jeffrey Kelly since?"

"I wouldn't think so. His doctor is in Seattle, and it only happened Friday afternoon, late . . ."

"Then how can they claim this is a fraud? I mean, if they haven't run any tests on him, how do they know he hasn't gone into remission?"

"Maybe they had someone check him."

"No. No, I don't think so. If there had been any tests, they would have mentioned them in the newspaper article." Another thought occurred to him. "Do you have any way of contacting Donna Kelly?"

"She gave me her number in Seattle." I was already in motion, going to a small basket on the counter. "We tried calling her yesterday, but there was no answer."

"Let's try again."

My hands shook as I punched in her telephone number. Stephen's face was still curiously blank.

The line rang once, then switched over with a sharp click and a change in the tone of the line to a recording. "We're sorry. The number you have dialed is no longer in service. Please check the number and dial again." As the message began to repeat itself, I hung up. "The number's not in service."

Stephen nodded, as if he had already guessed.

"Well, there's probably a good reason why she doesn't want to talk to you," he said.

I looked up at the clock. It was almost 9:30. "There's nothing we can do about that right now. Are you thinking of staying?"

He shrugged. "I've got no other plans."

"But what about . . ."

"I can't say that I support this, Karen. But I'm Sherry's doctor; I should keep an eye on her. And if this is actually going to help people . . ." He didn't need to finish the sentence. The words had been going through my mind like a mantra for the past several days.

If this is going to help people . . .

I nodded at him, then said, "So. Any thoughts about how we are going to do this?"

SIMON

Garrett Fitzgerald didn't rise as I entered his office. He didn't even acknowledge that I had arrived. He was sitting in his famous burgundy leather wing chair, leaning toward Martin Stoller and Stephen Ross, the senior partners, who were seated on the matching leather sofa. They glanced up as I closed the door but quickly looked away.

Garrett cleared his throat and leaned back into his chair.

I stood my ground, a few steps inside the door. There wasn't a place for me to sit that didn't require my asking permission, which I wouldn't do. I didn't say a word. The dead air in the room wasn't about to force me to start this conversation.

"You know why you're here," Garrett said.

"I can guess."

"We're very concerned. The three of us have spoken several times over the weekend, and we met first thing this morning." Garrett's voice was smooth, his phrasing delicate.

I did not take the bait.

"Simon, could you please explain to us the article on the front page of this morning's *New Sentinel?*"

"The track record of the *New Sentinel* in matters such as this—"

He sighed heavily to interrupt me and Ross burst out like a bulldog. "Simon, cut the crap. What the hell is going on here? Why the hell is the name of this firm in a story about fraud?"

There it was, on the table.

"The paper got it wrong today," I said. "The previous articles were more accurate."

"You mean to tell us that your daughter is some sort of miracle worker?" Stoller stared at me as if I'd lost my mind.

"I didn't say that. There were some occurrences that aren't easily explained. The newspaper got hold of them. I didn't even know about it until I read the paper last Thursday morning."

"Yet you're opening your home to strangers." Ross this time, flat-voiced.

"It would seem that way."

"What about this Donna Kelly and her little boy?" Stoller leapt in again. "What about your attempt to extort money from her?"

"I can assure you—"

"Well, that's not good enough, is it? Is that how you win cases? By assuring the jury that your client is innocent, and that they should just ignore any evidence to the contrary? Does that usually work for you?"

I suppressed the desire to snap back. "I believe that Karen and I are being harassed." Less than impressive.

"That's as may be, Simon." Garrett's soothing voice. "But we have to look out for the firm."

"I've done nothing to impugn the firm, Garrett." I struggled to keep my voice even.

He shook his head slowly, portentously. "You were named, Simon. We were named. And what would you have us say when the clients call? Because they have been calling. All morning.

Should we say that despite an article that mentions a police investigation, we have complete confidence in both your abilities and your integrity?" Garrett paused. "Do you expect us to lie, Simon?"

He let the words hang in the air.

"Just how long are we supposed to turn a blind eye to your indiscretions?" Stoller asked, after a long moment.

"Indiscretions?"

Ross sighed. "While you might think it's acceptable for one of our associates to have an affair with a junior member of this firm, you should be aware—"

"Gentlemen," I interrupted. "Are you asking me to leave?"

Garrett's face lifted in surprise. He seemed about to speak when Stoller interrupted.

"There's no 'asking' involved, Simon," he said. "There's no option here."

"We can't have you making a laughingstock of this firm," Ross added.

Garrett watched me in silence.

I paused for a moment, then I began to pace—the slow, deliberate steps of a final summation—but this time there was no script, no notes to follow, no jury. "I assume you're offering a severance package."

Garrett cut Ross off with a gesture, his eyes never leaving my face.

"You have absolutely no grounds to dismiss me." I didn't wait for confirmation or argument. "Given my length of service, my billings, the fact that there have been no prior complaints or reprimands and no investigation on your part into a defamatory newspaper report, I expect an amount equal to my last two years' gross salary and billings, including my bonus, to be paid out within seventy-two hours."

Stoller rose to his feet. "You've got to be—"

Garrett waved him down again.

"I also expect to maintain my medical benefits, and to have

my pension plan transferred to a fund that I'll set up. And finally, Garrett, I'll need a letter of apology from you, deeply regretting the circumstances that have arisen that have forced you to take this action, as well as a letter of reference. Carla will know all the right things to say. And, in the future, if I hear that you've been expressing any reservations to potential employers, I'll have you in court."

Stoller and Ross seemed dumbstruck.

I kept my eyes locked on Garrett, knowing that, in the end, only the two of us were playing the game.

"Pay him," he said, his eyes never leaving mine.

"What?"

"Pay him," he repeated. "Have Human Resources put the package together and have it ready for him by three this afternoon." He shook his head. "If you're in the building after three, we'll have you arrested for trespassing."

I nodded. I didn't even go back to my office.

KAREN

By the time Jamie arrived, the crowd had grown to two dozen.

"How are they?" I asked as she slipped out of her coat.

She shrugged. "Patient. I don't think they're going to be any sort of problem. I'd be more concerned with the group on the sidewalk."

"What group on the sidewalk?"

We peeked out the crack between the blind and the frame of the window. "*That* group."

Father Peter was on the sidewalk in front of the house with a group of protestors waving placards that read, WORSHIP NOT FALSE IDOLS and JESUS DIED FOR YOUR SINS. They seemed to be singing as they marched in a looping line. Father Peter was at the epicenter, his black coat pulled tightly around himself. To one side of him, a wiry young man clad only in jeans and a T-shirt, feet bare against the cold December concrete, almost buckled under the weight of a rough-hewn wooden cross twice his height. On his other side was a huge man dressed in coveralls, his arms folded across his chest.

"They're singing hymns," Jamie added in a whisper, as if they might hear her and discover our hiding place.

And then, as if that was exactly what had happened, Father Peter's stare met mine. It was all I could do not to jump back.

"He's looking right at us," Jamie said in a tense whisper. "Who is that?"

I let the curtain fall back against the window frame. "Lock the door behind me," I said, not pausing to pull on a jacket or shoes.

"Karen, where are you going? What are you doing?"

"Just lock the door behind me," I repeated, striding down the concrete steps in my socks and past the pilgrims.

I don't know where the courage came from. Anger, more than anything else. If I had stopped to think about it, I would have stayed inside. Instead, I forced my way through the even line of protestors, their song and their ranks falling to pieces around me.

Father Peter smiled coldly. "Mrs. Barrett."

"What are you doing here?"

His smile widened, revealing his yellowing teeth. "Demonstrating my right to free assembly."

"And what was that in the paper this morning?"

He stood easily a foot taller than me, and the man in the coveralls loomed over him.

"You were warned," he said, too quietly for the bystanders to hear. Then, a little louder, and for their benefit, "We won't allow you to make a mockery of our faith."

A few people in the crowd grunted their support.

"And that's how you do it? By spreading lies about us?" Letting my voice rise.

"What lies?" he demanded. "You're the one who claims that your daughter can heal the sick, but where are those people you claim she's healed? Where is the woman who first went to the newspaper? Where is this Jeffrey Kelly you claim was cured? Why isn't he here, standing up in your defense?" He held my gaze just a moment too long, enjoying himself.

"Get out of here. Get away from my house."

"We're on public property here. We'll stay."

"We'll stay," one of the protestors shouted.

The crowd started to close around me.

"I'll call the police."

His eyes gleamed. "Oh, the police will come. They're eager to speak with you and your husband."

My anger condensed into a cold, hard ball of resolve. "You want miracles?" I asked as I started back to the house. "I'll give you miracles."

Jamie opened the front door as I reached it.

"Let's start allowing some of these people in," I said. "Do you mind looking after the door while I stay near Sherry?"

"Yeah, okay. What do I do?"

"I want you to get full names, addresses, phone numbers, doctor's names, everything. We need thorough records."

She nodded. "How many should I let in? How fast?"

I hadn't even considered this. "Just a few at a time, I guess. I'll let you know."

I pulled open the front door, filling the foyer with cold, bright light. Stepping out into the chill, I leaned over the woman who was first in line, helping a young man in a wheelchair. His head lolled back and his mouth twisted into a spasming rictus, his eyes moving independently of one another as his hands jerked and jumped. She looked at me with a face touched with sadness and exhaustion.

"Would you like to come in?" I asked. My throat was thick with emotion.

As I helped her with the wheelchair, I glanced up the driveway at the long line of people waiting for a miracle. And, on the sidewalk, the dark shape of Father Peter watching it all.

RUTH

The quiet line of pilgrims shifted from the front walk through the door and foyer and into Sherry's room. They were hesitant to speak, whispering the names of their conditions or injuries to Jamie in voices no one could overhear, slipping unobtrusively into Sherry's presence for their private moment, closely watched by both Dr. McKinley and Karen.

They came in pairs when they couldn't come alone, the companion helping to support, to guide or to push, offering words of comfort or encouragement. They always asked Jamie, "How does all of this work?" "What's going to happen in there?" and then, more confidentially, leaning toward her, "Is it all for real?" Skepticism and hope were in such a delicate balance. Jamie didn't answer, just made the appropriate notes on her pad and directed them to follow the line.

Once inside Sherry's room, Karen guided the pilgrims to kneel on the pillow beside the bed if they were able, gently shifting Sherry's arm so her palm rested against their forehead.

"You're welcome to pray," Karen said quietly. "If you'd like to."

Many of the pilgrims did pray, their voices almost soundless. "Glory be to God in the highest . . . Our Father who art in heaven . . ." The others remained silent, but their eyelids lowered and I thought they were probably praying to themselves.

After a moment, Karen gently removed Sherry's hand from the pilgrim's forehead and helped the ailing to their feet.

By noon, when I looked out the front window, the line of people was as long as it had been when we'd let the first come in. A television van was parked at the curb, the camera flashing in the sun.

"Why don't you open that up?" Karen asked from behind me. I let the curtain fall as I turned to face her.

"But what about—?" I started, thinking about the crowd on the other side of the glass.

She shook hear head. "We're not hiding anything," she explained. "It'd be nice to get some light in here."

I drew back the curtains and raised the blinds. In the sunlight, I could see that her face was drawn. She held her breath every time she touched Sherry's hand to a pilgrim's forehead, as if willing something to happen while at the same time terrified that it might.

When she saw me looking at her, she smiled wearily. "I'm okay," she said.

I wasn't sure who she was trying to convince.

Midway through the afternoon, Dr. McKinley gestured at his watch and Karen nodded in understanding. It was 2:45, and Karen had decided that she would shut the door for the day at 3:00. "Ruth," she asked. "Would you mind taking over here? I'm going to choose a place to stop the line."

The feel of Sherry's hand was as familiar to me as if she were my own daughter. I followed the pattern Karen had set, bidding each of the seekers to kneel, then gently touching Sherry's hand to bowed heads, brows.

As I said "You can pray if you'd like," I watched the steady rise and fall of Sherry's chest, heard the sound of the breath passing between her slightly parted lips—her only voice.

I found myself thinking of miracles.

By three, the last pilgrims of the day had passed through. The ones Karen had turned away left silently, knowing they could return tomorrow. Or the next day. Or the next.

HENRY

I don't know what I was expecting at the Barretts' house. I had read the article in the paper and I wondered if I would arrive in time to see the police arresting them, or people throwing things at the house.

Instead, it was pretty quiet. There were people with signs on the sidewalk singing hymns, but in the lineup to see Sherry everyone spoke as if they were in the library, or clutched their crosses, mouthing silent prayers.

Sherry's mother came to the door, speaking to the crowd in a voice most of them couldn't hear. The message passed quickly down the line: it was almost three o'clock. They'd start seeing people again at ten the next morning. The crowd trickled away with little fuss.

I could picture Sherilyn running in the front yard, giggling, toward her parents. I only knew her from the hospital bed, the pictures in the papers, from the blurred shape in front of the truck, but I felt like I knew what her laugh had been like, how she ran. I felt like I carried a part of her with me.

Inside, someone closed the blinds, and I found myself staring at a reflection of the yard in the suddenly mirrored surface.

"Show's over," came the voice from the driveway, directed at me.

The man was tall, wrapped in a long black coat. A chill ran through me.

"I've startled you," he said. "Henry Denton, I presume?" He stopped just close enough to make me uncomfortable and, grinning, extended his hand.

"I . . ."

After a long moment in the cold air, he drew his hand back, tucking it into his pocket. "You're wondering why I can see you."

I could barely nod. His eyes were a flat gray, his pupils barely noticeable. He radiated cold the way a road radiates heat in the summer.

"My name is Peter," he said, extending his hand again. "I've been waiting for you."

I took his hand reluctantly.

His grip was machinelike in its steady force. Torque. His smile widened. "I knew you would come," he said, just before I pulled my hand away.

I backed up. "Who are you?" I asked, finally finding my voice. "What, what are you—?"

He stepped forward, maintaining his uncomfortable close-ness. "I told you. My name is Peter. I know your fat friend in the library. I know what you're doing here, watching this house." The wave of cold wrapped itself around me and I could feel bile rising in my throat. "Don't you think you've done enough to this family already?"

I couldn't help myself: instinct took over and I ran. I ran as far, and as fast, as I could, glancing over my shoulder to see if he was following.

He wasn't.

I slowed to a gasping walk as I neared downtown, where the sidewalks were filled with people. For once I took comfort in their blindness, in my invisibility.

Why could he see me?

I only began to calm down when the doors of the library closed behind me and night began to fall.

KAREN

It was just after five when the doorbell rang. Jamie, Ruth and Stephen had gone home.

Mary was standing on the stoop.

"Hi, Karen." She shifted. "I just, uh, thought I'd drop by and see if Simon wanted me to drop off his stuff. I tried his cell, but he's not answering."

"His stuff?"

She nodded. "From my place. Didn't he . . . ?"

I shook my head. "He's not here. I haven't talked to him since this morning."

"This morning?"

I nodded.

"When this morning?"

"He called me after his meeting."

She looked confused and glanced around herself. "After his meeting?"

I nodded and stepped to one side. "Why don't you come in?"

She hesitated for a moment, then brushed past me, in a wash of clean scent. I closed the door behind her, taking care to turn the deadbolt.

In the family room, she sat on the couch across from me. Simon's sleeping bag and pillow were at the other end.

I felt like I was really seeing her for the first time. I could understand how Simon would have fallen in love with her, that smooth face twisted with worry.

"Are you all right?" I asked.

Her voice dropped almost to a whisper.

"I don't know if I should be the one to tell you this. Simon's meeting—"

"I know they fired him, Mary," I said. "Is that what this is about?"

She nodded without meeting my eye.

Of everything that had happened since the morning of the accident, Simon being terminated by the firm was probably the least surprising, especially after the newspaper story, and what had happened to Jamie and Stephen.

His voice on the phone as he described his meeting with the senior partners had been fractured, devastated. His world was coming apart around him.

"I'm coming home," he said. "I'm on—"

"Simon." I stopped him. "Don't. Don't come home, not like this. Try to work it through, or walk it off."

"But I should be there. With Sherry and everything that's happening."

"It's fine, Simon. It's going fine."

"Are you sure?"

"You were going to be gone all day, Simon. It's fine."

I couldn't tell if he was relieved or upset.

"I haven't seen him since this morning." Mary said. "They changed the locks to his office and reassigned me. I thought he would be here." Her words seemed to bubble out of her in a single breath.

"He's not. He said he'd be staying at a hotel downtown. I'm not sure which one. There are some things he needs to work out."

"That's good."

I was stunned. "Do you really mean that?" I asked.

"When we were up in Tofino, and he saw the newspaper story"—she shook her head—"It was pretty clear that this is still his home. This is where he needed to be."

Her eyes were bright. "I know what you must think of me, but I never wanted to be the kind of person who—if Simon was going to be with me, I wanted him to want to be with me, not—"

"Not just running from something else."

Our eyes met, and she nodded.

She leaned back into the couch, spent.

I wished I could hate her.

The doorbell rang.

SIMON

The bank machine spat out several hundred dollars in twenties, which I scooped out of the basin and tucked into my wallet, keenly aware of the small group of youths hanging around the vestibule. I studied the balance. There was enough. And soon my severance would kick in.

"Spare some change?" one of the girls asked as I came out.

I shook my head. "No, not tonight." I tensed, aware of the other kids around me, half-expecting to be jumped from behind.

"Have a good night anyway," the girl said, smiling. An angel of the concrete.

"Thanks," I stammered. "You too."

It was dark and colder than it had been through the afternoon—it was hard to stop shivering. My jacket was too thin and the wind cut through it. The prostitutes were huddled in doorways, out of the wind, any exposed skin raising in chicken flesh. None of them spoke to me in the three blocks between the bank and the hotel.

The lobby of the Balmoral was almost too warm, thick with voices and cigarette smoke from the adjoining pub, one of the roughest in Victoria.

The desk was staffed by someone who appeared to be in his late teens, face pocked with acne scars, hair dyed blond and cut close to his skull. As I approached he barely looked up.

"I'd like to rent a room," I said, attempting to be casual.

"For the night?" he asked, pulling a pink registration slip from under the counter.

"Do you have weekly rates?"

He nodded, bored. "Hourly. Daily. Weekly. Monthly."

"What's the weekly rate?"

"Private or shared?"

I must have looked confused.

"Bathroom," he snapped. "Private or shared?"

"Private."

He named the price and I nodded.

"In advance."

"Sure." I filled out the registration form with the chewed ballpoint.

"You have to fill in your vehicle registration," he interjected, pointing at the appropriate line, which I had left blank. His fingernail was chewed down to the quick.

"I don't have a car."

"Hmm," he said, as if lacking a car had lowered me in his estimation.

He separated the copies of my registration form, handing me the illegible yellow copy, trading the pink copy for the key in the slot marked 316.

"Elevator's over there." He gestured vaguely toward an area behind the entrance to the pub.

My room was on the third floor around the corner from the ice machine and overlooked the street. I was surprised to find it mostly clean—it smelled of stale cigarette smoke and fresh cleanser—and mostly quiet, street noise blocked by the triple-paned glass. There were burn marks on the windowsill, and a small cigarette hole in the bedspread. When I pulled back the sheets they were worn but clean. On the wall above the head of the bed was an atrocious painting of a ship on a dark sea; facing the bed was a small television, a remote control resting atop the cable box. In the bathroom there was a single glass on the shelf, wrapped in white paper. When I unwrapped it to get a drink of water, it was so badly scratched it was textured.

I went back to the door, shot the bolt and hooked the chain.

Then I sat at the end of the bed, facing the television, my hands on my knees. My reflection was stretched and distorted, a rumpled caricature of someone I could barely recognize.

KAREN

There was a stranger at the door, squinting under the porch light.

I stepped back, bumping into Mary.

"Good evening," he said. He fumbled in his pocket for his identification. "I'm Sergeant Richards, with the Victoria Police." He was a large man, solid but starting to go soft. The sort of man who would always seem rumpled, whose suits would never fit quite right.

"You're Karen Barrett?" he asked, folding his wallet back into his pocket.

"Yes."

"I'd like to have a word, if you've got a minute."

"Come in. It's easier to talk inside."

"I waited until the reporters left," he said as I led him toward the family room. "I didn't think there was any need for anyone to read about this in the morning paper."

"Read about what?" Mary asked.

"And you are?"

Mary glanced at me, then back at the policeman. "Mary Edwards," she said, extending her hand.

He shook it firmly. "You're an attorney, right? You work with Mr. Barrett."

She nodded, then corrected both herself and him. "Until this morning."

He seemed surprised. "This morning?"

"Simon was terminated by the firm this morning," I explained.

"I'm sorry to hear that, Mrs. Barrett. I know your husband."

"Really?"

He nodded. "He did some work for me a couple of years ago. Really helped me out. Did his dismissal have anything to do with the story in the paper?"

"What do you think?"

We all sat down. "Yeah. Well, unfortunately, that's why I'm here." He took a small notebook and pen from inside his jacket and opened to a fresh page.

"Mrs. Barrett," he started, "we've received some reports that are somewhat alarming, so we wanted to talk—"

"Sergeant, is there a police investigation concerning Mr. and Mrs. Barrett?" Mary interrupted, her voice calm.

He shook his head. "No, there isn't an active investigation. We've received some reports and we wanted to look into them."

Mary nodded. "That's fine, then. But if it turns out there is a criminal investigation, I think you'll find this interview of little evidentiary value."

"And why is that?"

"Because Mrs. Barrett doesn't have an attorney present."

"You mean you don't represent Mrs. Barrett?" It was hard to tell, but it seemed like the Sergeant might be making a joke.

"Sergeant Richards, I don't represent Mrs. Barrett in any way whatsoever."

"Well, I can assure you, Miss Edwards, that there is no active criminal investigation. I've just got a few questions, starting with Donna and Jeffrey Kelly."

"That's fine," I said, leaning back into the cushions.

"Do you believe that your daughter can heal the sick?"

"I don't know. There have been a few people—Sherry's nurse, her sister—but we've never claimed that Sherry can . . . can do any of those things."

"Did you ever ask Donna Kelly for money, in exchange for using your daughter's powers to heal her son?"

"No."

"Yet Ms. Kelly claims you told her that unless she paid, you wouldn't let Jeffrey see Sherry."

"Did she tell you that herself?"

He looked up from his notebook.

"Because we've tried calling her—"

"That's probably not the best idea."

"—and we haven't been able to get in touch."

"Yeah. We're responding to published reports."

"So you haven't spoken to her either."

Richards shook his head. "So no money changed hands."

"No."

"Have you asked for money from any of the other people who have come to see your daughter?"

"No. I wouldn't have taken any if they had offered."

"And how many people would you say came through here today?"

"I'd have to check. Between thirty and forty, I think. I've got a list of their names, addresses and everything if you need it."

He wrote the figure down in his notebook. "That would be handy."

I was about to stand up, to look for Jamie's clipboard, when Mary cleared her throat.

"Have you got a fax number where we can send the list, Sergeant? We'd like to keep our files complete."

"Sure." Reaching into his pocket, he passed me a business card. "All my numbers are on there."

He closed his notebook and tucked it back into his pocket. "I think that's everything," he said. "I can't . . ." He shook his head. "You might be hearing from someone else in the department in the next few days. Depending on if there are complaints or reports." He seemed uncomfortable, shifting slightly from foot to foot.

"Mrs. Barrett. Will you be talking to Simon?"

I nodded.

"Could you get him to give me a call the next time you're talking to him?"

"Sure. I'll tell him."

"Thanks. And thanks for taking the time." He extended his hand.

After I saw him out I came back to the family room where Mary was still sitting on the couch.

"That was strange," I said.

She nodded. "Yes, it was."

For some reason, I found Mary's uncertainty disturbing.

HENRY

I was walking along the narrow corridor behind the children's section, almost ready to give up my search for Tim, when I smelled a trace of cigar smoke. I pushed open the door to the women's washroom.

Tim was sitting on the counter, leaning against the tiled wall, watching the smoke from his cigar curl up toward the exhaust fan in the ceiling.

"Someone told me to say hello to you," I said.

He looked almost unconcerned. "And?"

"A priest. He said his name was Peter."

His eyebrows rose a little. "Really? Interesting." He took another pull from his cigar and rolled it between his thumb and forefinger. "Where did you meet this man?"

I felt almost embarrassed to tell him. "I was at the Barretts' house this afternoon. I wanted to see what was going on."

"He was there?"

I nodded. "When I got there everyone was leaving, except him. He was just standing there."

"Alone?"

"I think so," I answered guardedly. "I didn't see anyone else."

He rolled the cigar thoughtfully. "That's unusual," he said quietly, more to himself than to me. "He's rarely alone."

"So you know him?"

He nodded. "What did the two of you talk about?"

Isolated images, of his cold eyes, his uneven teeth behind his thin lips. "Well, he, he knew who I was. Then he asked—Tim, how did he know who I was?"

"Your picture has been in the paper—"

"No, how did he see me?"

Sighing, Tim shifted his weight around so he was looking at me full on. "His name's not actually Peter."

"I didn't think so. And your name's not really Tim."

He shrugged. "He's a very old man who made a bad choice a long time ago and has been trying to make amends ever since."

"And you?"

"The same could be said about me. Just another old man who made a bad choice."

"There's more to it than that," I said, my voice loud in the tiled room. "There has to be."

"You'll find, Henry, that there's always more to it—"

"Oh, cut the old sage stuff, man. Who is he and what does he want?"

Tim shook his head at my anger. "I don't know what he wants, or what he has planned. I will say this, though." He leaned forward, dangling the hand holding his cigar between his knees. "He's done terrible things in the past. Or convinced others to do them."

"And what have you done?"

"Many things, Henry," he said. "Time is long. And old men forget . . ."

"That's not an answer."

"No, it's Shakespeare."

Raising the cigar to his lips, he took a gentle tug. Then another, longer. Finally, he took the cigar from his mouth and studied the cold, gray-black tip.

He was trying to relight it as I left the ladies' room.

MARY

I looked down at my plate: potatoes, grilled chicken, carrots and garlic almond beans, with a bowl of lettuce and endive salad on one side. "This all looks so good," I said.

Karen smiled a little at the compliment, but I could feel a bit of the chill returning. "Thank you for your help with it," she said politely. "Do you cook much yourself?"

"No, not too much. I've usually got so much going on, with work, and . . ." I realized suddenly how all of this might be taken by Karen, forced to stay at home with Sherry. I trailed off.

"Do you enjoy it?"

"Enjoy what?" I took a sip of my wine.

"Being a lawyer. I know that Simon loves it, but I've never really understood why." She seemed to be trying to minimize any offense I might take.

I nodded. "I love it," I said. "It's all I ever wanted to do."

"Really? It wasn't something your parents pushed you into?"

"God, no," I said. "I was born in a VW microbus in North Africa somewhere. My parents have never even been sure what country they were in when it happened. They were in one of those mobile communes, going wherever the wind took them." I shrugged. "We lived in Ireland for a few years when I was little, then came back to Canada. They opened up an organic foods store up-island. They flipped when I told them I wanted to be a lawyer. God, I might as well have told them that I wanted to be an air force pilot dropping napalm on some village somewhere."

Karen laughed. "So I guess you could say they discouraged you?"

"You could say that. They thought that I should be an artist—maybe write poetry, edit a little magazine, do raku. But I liked the stability of the law, the order." I chuckled, taking another sip of my wine, risked a joke. "I was rebellious. Started shaving my legs and everything."

Karen smiled and shook her head. "Did they ever forgive you?"

I nodded. "Oh yeah. Christmas is hard though. It's like 'This is Bob, my cross-dressing son, and this is Sparkle, she paints rocks and this is Mary—'" I dropped my voice to a dramatic whisper. "'*She's a lawyer.*'"

We both laughed for a long time.

"I'm just kidding," I finally gasped. "I don't really have any brothers or sisters."

This just started us off laughing again, and it was a long time before either of us was able to speak. The sense that there might be anything strange in the two of us sitting there over dinner had completely disappeared.

"I always wanted to write," Karen said, the smile vanishing from her face.

"I thought you wrote for the *Sentinel,* before Sherry was born?" I took a small bite of my salad.

"I did." She shook her head. "I got the job at the paper to make ends meet while Simon was in law school." She toyed with her fork. "No, I always wanted to be a *Writer.* You know, capital W. Short stories, fiction, maybe a novel." She shrugged, as if that part of her no longer existed.

"Why don't you? Write, I mean."

"I did, for a while. Well, all through school I did. I did an English degree, took courses in creative writing. I spent as much time writing stories as I did writing papers."

"Did you get anything published?"

"A few things here and there. I never really sent stuff out."

"Why not?"

"I'm not sure. I guess it seems pretty stupid now that I didn't."

"That's okay," I said.

She shook her head, staring at me. "No. No, it's not. I see you, I look at you and I realize how, how . . . jealous I am. Beginning your career. Doing what you want. So many options."

I braced myself.

"I look at you and I realize that somewhere I got off track, I guess."

"So get back on."

She gave a single, sharp laugh. "Right. In my spare time."

My turn to shrug and take another bite.

"You're really something, you know that?"

I looked up and she was smiling. I didn't speak, uncertain what she meant, what to say.

"I can see why Simon loves you," she said.

"Karen, I—"

She shook her head. "No, don't. Please don't. I know. I know it goes deeper than my husband having an affair with someone at his office. I know that there's more to it than sex, than staying late after work, lying to me on the telephone." She smiled a little at my expression. "I think I knew, even before the accident, that something was going on."

"I'm sorry," I said.

"What's he like when he's with you?" She shifted in her chair.

Stalling, I set my knife and fork on the edge of the plate, dabbed the corners of my mouth with the napkin and picked up my wineglass. I really didn't want to talk about Simon with his wife, but I couldn't see any way to avoid it. "He's, I mean, he's, well, he's just Simon, I guess . . ."

Karen leaned across the table and took my hand, squeezing it.

I took a deep breath. "It's hard to describe. I mean, I don't know what he's like with you. How that compares. With me, he's gentle, I guess. I mean, he never raises his voice. Never seems to get upset. I've seen him in court: I know how he can get. You know, how cold. How precise. How vicious. I've never seen that, except in court."

She looked at me like I was describing a stranger. I tried again. "He listens. And he talks to me. I feel like we've got . . . like we had . . . a real connection." I shook my head. "I'm sorry."

"You got him playing his guitar again."

"Guitar?"

"Yeah. The other day he went up to the attic and got his old guitar down. I hadn't heard him play since university."

"I didn't even know he played," I said.

"He's a man with a lot of secrets," she said, almost without bitterness.

"I never used to think so. I always thought that we were really open. With one another, I mean. The problem, I think, is that Simon doesn't really know himself."

She shook her head.

"That's what I told him this morning. I told him—" I braced myself. "I told him that I loved him, but that I didn't really think that he knew what he wanted, and that I didn't want to . . ."

I couldn't finish the sentence. Instead, I reached for the bottle of wine in the center of the table and filled my glass, carefully looking away from Karen.

When I looked back, her eyes were focused on my face. I couldn't even guess what she might have been thinking.

LEO

I sat in the van in the parking lot of the 7-Eleven where Father Peter had told me to wait, trying to remember everything he had said. I tried to think it through. It all made so much sense when he was talking. All that stuff about people attacking our faith, about the forces of darkness being loosed upon the earth. You just needed to watch the news at dinnertime to know that he was telling the truth.

But that little girl . . .

I kept the picture of Sherilyn Barrett from the newspaper under the work orders on my clipboard so I could look at it, look at her beautiful sweet face. How could she could be evil?

That sweet little girl . . .

But no. Father Peter said she wasn't a little girl anymore, not since the accident. That was when the Beast took her, deceiving people with these false healings, luring them away from the truth and finding a home in the darkness within them.

Evil can wear so many different faces.

Somebody knocked on the window and I jumped. I thought for a second it might be the Dark One, called by my thoughts of him.

It was Father Peter. He waved for me to follow him.

I locked the door and had to hustle to catch up. Hustle hustle hustle, don't be late.

He led me up the street and into an alley. Piles of garbage leaned against the walls of an old church. The windows were all boarded up. When I caught up to him, he was unlocking a door with a ring of keys.

"A donation," he said, as he pulled the door open. "From a true believer."

The basement was as full of garbage and mess as the alley. It looked like a bookstore or something. There were boxes of books everywhere, stacks of records and magazines falling on the floor. The air stunk like cat pee and rotting meat. I coughed a little to keep from throwing up, and Father Peter looked at me.

Something slithered through the garbage. A rat, maybe? A serpent?

"Look at this place." He shook his head. He touched a stack of books and scrunched up his face. "How could anyone who claimed to truly love God allow this to happen to one of His holy places?"

I didn't know the answer.

"One of the oldest buildings in the city, a house of God, now no better than a dung heap. There's no history here. No legacy." He shook his head. "Even the Romans left the temples alone, and we do this to ourselves."

I didn't understand what he meant, and I think he could tell.

"Someone told me that there used to be a fitness club in this building. They did aerobics where people used to come to worship. Looking for salvation in the flesh, in the sin. Vanity. And now this. Somebody selling this smut, this sleaze, in the basement of a church."

He struck a match on the wall and lit a candle. He held it high as we went farther into the basement. It smelled even worse. The candle made long shadows on the piles of garbage.

"But that's all right," he said, as if he was talking to himself. "We'll clean it out. I've known places like this before. Basements and sewers. Caves and catacombs. Sometimes what we have to do is best done in darkness, where no one can see us, don't you think, Leo?"

"I guess so." I had no idea what he was talking about.

He turned toward me, holding the candle between us. In the candlelight, his face looked even more like a skull.

"You do know what I'm talking about, don't you, Leo?" he asked, his teeth sharp and shiny. "You're a part of this now."

I nodded. I knew it. I was part of it. He trusted me.

"That's good, that's good." He seemed to look into me, without blinking. "Because there is going to come a time when I call on you, Leo. When I will have need of you. And I need to know that when that time comes, I'll be able to rely on you to do what needs to be done. I can rely on you, can't I, Leo?"

I thought of the photo of the little girl from the newspaper, of the evil that was hidden inside her, just waiting to get hold of anyone who touched her, anyone fooled by her innocence. The mask of the Beast.

I bowed my head. "You can count on me, Father."

KAREN

Closing the door and locking it, I watched as Mary edged her way through the small crowd of protestors on the sidewalk. I waited until she reached her car safely before I turned off the front light.

After feeding Sherry and changing her, checking her stats, I kissed her on the forehead, saying "Goodnight, sweetheart," then I climbed up the stairs to my bedroom.

The house was completely, absurdly still. I was aware of the silence in a way I hadn't been since just after Simon left. I went downstairs to check Sherry again. Back in bed, I couldn't find a comfortable position, twisting from side to side, flipping my pillow, throwing off the comforter to cool off, pulling it back up when I got too cold.

Finally, I gave up. Sleep wasn't coming, and I didn't want to read in bed. I pulled on my robe and went down to the kitchen.

The ceiling light turned the darkened patio door into a mirror. I kept catching glimpses of my reflection as I looked in the drawer under the phone for some paper and a pen.

Back in Sherry's room, I took the largest of her books from the basket beside the bed and set it on my lap. Centering the paper on the book, I took the cap off the pen and began to write.

"Once upon a time, there was a princess in a kingdom by the sea. Beset by . . ."

SIX

December 10–23

Victoria New Sentinel

Tuesday, December 10, 1996

Can she heal the sick?

Controversy surrounds "miracle child"

~City Desk~

The parents of four-year-old Sherilyn Barrett, comatose since a car accident last April, opened their Fernwood home to a steady line of injured and ill pilgrims yesterday. Following reports that Barrett had seemingly cured several people . . .

SIMON

I stopped short as I turned the corner onto Shakespeare at about 7:30 a.m. There was a crowd in front of the house, and judging from the garbage and the lawn chairs, they had been there all night.

They had leaned their signs against the fence, and most of them were hunched over steaming takeout cups. They were dressed for the weather, but they still seemed cold, stomping their feet and rubbing their arms.

I was in front of Cecil's place next door when they noticed me.

"It's the father!"

The crowd surged toward me, the protestors coming into focus.

A woman in a floral dress with a heavy brown coat shouted, "How can you do this to your child?"

"Why?" screamed a man with a close-cropped beard and glasses, wearing thick socks in his sandals.

"Liar!" said a pretty blond girl in her mid-teens.

I kept walking. I never thought they'd touch me. So when hands shoved my chest, grabbed my arms, I stumbled and lost my balance, almost fell.

"Sinner!"

I righted myself, then lowered my shoulder and pushed through them to the gate.

The protestors shouted behind me, waving their fists and signs, but no one followed me into the yard.

"Are you all right?" The question came from a young woman in a wheelchair, first in the line of six pilgrims at the base of the ramp. The words were thick and hesitant and it was clearly difficult for her to speak.

It took me a moment to answer. "Yes. I am," I said. "Did they do that to you too? Block your way into the yard?"

She nodded.

I let myself into the house with a key I hadn't used in months.

"Karen?" I called as I slipped off my shoes.

"I'm with Sherry."

She was smoothing a new nightgown over Sherry's legs.

"How long have those people been out there?"

"The protestors?" She drew the covers up. "Most of the night," she said. "A few of them, at least. More have been arriving since it got light."

I shook my head. "They blocked the gate. I had a hard time getting through. Apparently they've been doing it to the pilgrims as well."

"Are you all right? Is anyone hurt?"

I rested my hand on Sherry's leg, reassuring myself. "They pushed me around a bit. I'm going to call the police."

"They were already here."

"What?"

"It was a busy day."

She started by telling me about the previous day with the

pilgrims, about Dr. McKinley losing his job. I stopped her when she told me about her confrontation with Father Peter.

"Why didn't you call me?" I asked. "My cell was on."

"It wasn't exactly the best day for you either."

"I would have come."

"I know."

I didn't say anything when she told me about Mary staying for dinner, and she didn't volunteer any details. I was surprised to hear that John Richards had come to the house.

"So he just wanted to ask some questions?"

She nodded. "He said there wasn't an investigation, but that someone else might be in touch. He said you should call him."

I had already planned to, the moment she mentioned his name. "I will," I said, trying to ignore the sick feeling in my stomach. "In the meantime . . ." I squeezed Sherry's leg.

"Yeah." She picked up a bundled diaper from the bed. "Let's get ready for the day."

By 9:30, when Ruth, Stephen and Jamie had all arrived, the lineup of pilgrims reached the gate.

Shortly before ten, the television trucks and Father Peter arrived in such close succession it was as if they had planned it. No sooner had the crews readied their cameras than the protestors began singing. Up came the signs: WORSHIP NOT FALSE IDOLS. PROPHET, NOT PROFIT. There must have been two dozen of them, marching along the sidewalk, across the width of the front lawn, shouting and chanting and singing.

Father Peter stood away from the group, watching them from the rear of a plumber's van. Out of range of the cameras.

"We're ready," Karen said. I let the blind fall back against the front window and turned to face her.

"What should I do?"

"Do you want to start off by keeping records at the door? Jamie set up a clipboard yesterday."

The shouting and chanting was gaining in force and volume as the protestors tried to drive the pilgrims away from the house. The pilgrims ignored them as best they could, and the protestors increased the pressure, leering into the yard, singing hymns. The television cameras devoured it all.

Then Karen opened the front door, and the day's parade of the sick and the dying began.

I spent the morning taking down information as the pilgrims passed through the foyer. I assumed, initially, that it would be better to keep my distance, to maintain my objectivity. Dispassionate distance is one of the first skills you learn as a lawyer: don't fall for a client.

I kept my head down, my eyes focused on my clipboard, only glancing up when someone new came though the door.

"Your name is?"

I was pleased with how smoothly everything was going: by noon, I had more than twenty names on my list.

And then Lorraine Coombs touched my arm.

I was writing her name when I felt her fingers just above my wrist. Her touch was hot, sticky.

I glanced up and met her eyes, liquid blue and bright. She smiled. Her skin was bright red, damp with sweat. With one hand, she clutched the handle of her walker as if she might collapse without it. With the other, she had reached out.

I couldn't look away.

"Are you all right?" I asked.

"As good as I've been in a while," she said, still smiling.

"Can I get you anything? Water, or—"

"No, that's fine."

I set the clipboard down and tucked the pen into my pocket. "Let me help you," I said.

She took my arm, and we walked, halting step by halting step, to see Sherry.

"Thank you," she said in the doorway to Sherry's room, her face lighting up when she saw my daughter.

"You're welcome."

After that, I began to notice how each pilgrim's face lit with hope and desperation when they first saw her. None of them were reluctant, none of them reserved. They hoped—no, they believed. They believed that my daughter could save them, that her touch could help them reclaim their lives.

I envied them their faith, the clarity of their belief.

After the last pilgrim left at three, I followed Karen to the kitchen.

She had been the very embodiment of strength and balance through the day. She seemed to be everywhere at once, and nothing seemed to throw her off. She was in the front yard, talking with the pilgrims as they waited in line, learning their names, their stories. She was at the gate, helping them push past the protestors into the yard. She was in Sherry's room, checking on our girl. She was taking over from Ruth, from Dr. McKinley, from Jamie and even me, when we needed a break. I never saw her flag.

We left Ruth and Dr. McKinley working with Sherry, and Jamie sorting through the information that we had collected about the people who had come through the house. I was pouring her a cup of coffee when she asked, "It's amazing, isn't it?"

She was sitting at the table, and I set the mug in front of her.

"It is. I wasn't expecting it to be like this."

"Like what?"

I sat down across from her.

"So personal, I guess," I said, sipping my coffee. "I've seen a lot of people who were sick or hurt. I've done the best I can for them; that's been my job. But with the case work, it's so clinical, so detached. I've never felt . . . connected like this."

She smiled a little and nodded. "It's important, this. What we're doing."

"Yeah. Maybe that's what I was trying to say. It feels like I've spent my whole life focused on what was important to me, and there was a whole world out there that I wasn't even really aware of."

I was trying, but that wasn't quite what I meant.

Seeing my daughter through the eyes of the pilgrims was a revelation. I had fed Sherry and washed her and dressed her, had sung her to sleep and sung to her when I knew that she would not awaken. She was a beautiful little girl who smelled of shampoo and soap and milky skin, whose laughter had sounded like singing. I had been there at her birth. I had been there at the moment of her death, and when she had come back.

In the eyes of the pilgrims, though, she was something else, something more. At some point in the last few days, she had stopped being my little girl alone and had become a vessel for their hopes and their faith, a glowing symbol where once there had been a child who liked to fill her pockets with stones.

I struggled to reconcile the two visions of Sherry in my mind—I wanted to deny the pilgrims their beliefs, to preserve the image of my daughter as just a little girl, but I couldn't.

I tried again. "It's . . ."

"Real," she said.

Our eyes met across the table.

"Real," I said.

KAREN

"Simon's gone?" Jamie asked as I came back into the kitchen.

I nodded. "Guitar case in hand. A wandering ministrel he."

Jamie smiled.

"It was hard."

"Having him here?"

"Letting him go," I said. "I wanted him to stay."

"That wouldn't—"

I shook my head. "No. That wouldn't have been good."

"You don't want to rush into anything."

I couldn't help but smile. "Yes," I said. "Yes I do. That's the whole problem."

SIMON

I stopped at McDonald's on the walk back downtown and wolfed down a burger and fries without even tasting them. But even with the stop, the six o'clock news was just starting as I turned on the TV in my hotel room.

We were about three stories in—not breaking news, but ahead of the first commercial. The piece was short: the pilgrims from the morning, some file footage of the accident scene, Father Peter's protestors singing their hymns on the sidewalk. He was nowhere to be seen—he had a knack for disappearing when cameras turned to him.

After the story, I shut off the television.

I had arranged to meet John Richards in the hotel bar at eight, and I had no idea what to do with myself before then.

I stretched out on the bed. I was exhausted, but when I closed my eyes my mind sprang to life—no chance of sleep.

I unpacked the bag I had brought from Karen's, refolding the clothes and tucking them into the battered dresser under the TV. I stacked the books on the bedside table, reading each back cover before I put it down in hopes that something would appeal. Nothing did.

Turning the television on again, I flipped through to the top of the dial and back again. Nothing.

I took my time showering, just standing for a while in the hot water as it washed the day away. I toweled off thoroughly, put on a clean shirt, checked my watch.

6:47.

I was at a complete loss.

Hair still damp, I paced around the room, replaying the day in my mind, thinking about the pilgrims: their faces, their eyes, their hope, their faith.

Everything that had consumed me up to now seemed a thin veneer hiding the true texture of the world. A gaudy surface designed to distract, to keep me from pulling aside the curtain, to keep me from looking for the deeper truths I was sensing now.

I sat down on the bed and opened the guitar case. My fingers started picking out a blues, but I stopped myself. The idea of sitting alone in a hotel room playing "Sometimes I Feel Like a Motherless Child" was too trite to bear.

Then I remembered that among the books I had brought from the house was a collection of Child ballads. I riffled through the pages. There.

I cracked the spine and started to play.

> The wind doth blow today, my love
> And a few small drops of rain;
> I never had but one true-love
> In cold grave she was lain.

There were secrets in ancient songs like the ones Francis Child collected; secrets that I couldn't explain, that I didn't understand. They were all story songs, and you always knew where you were going, verse to verse. But there was an entire world just under the surface. A world of ghosts and angels and demons pulling the strings, all with their own stories, their own motivations, impossible for the characters—or the listeners—to fully understand.

The chords vibrated through me and it felt like every one of my cells opened to welcome the music like rain. I sang, and for a moment, I felt a part of something larger, something just beyond my understanding. Every word seemed to bring me closer.

LEO

The only light in the church basement was from the candles, stuck with their own wax to the bookshelves. When I lit them I said a Hail Mary as I waited for each wick to catch. Candles always make me think of Jesus, His brightness in a world of dark. They made me feel so proud I could be helping.

Pride. That's a deadly sin.

But it felt so right to be doing God's work. To be standing tall against the forces of evil.

Even with the candles, the room was more dark than light, and filled with people. Everyone was waiting. Everyone jumped when Father Peter stepped out of the shadows.

"I apologize for our surroundings here tonight," he said as he walked to the front. "It's not pleasant, but the need for privacy outweighs comfort." He didn't talk loud, but I could hear him all the way in the back. Nobody else was making a sound. Quiet as a church mouse. Church mice.

"I don't want to keep you in this place any longer than you have to be. I'd like to begin with a prayer."

Everyone bowed their heads. We all knew the words.

We said amen after Father Peter, then the room was quiet again.

"You all know why we're here," he began. "I'd like to take a moment to thank those of you who were with me today at that house, and to think of those who aren't with us tonight, because they are still there, doing the Lord's work in the dark of night."

A few people said, "Amen."

"If you were at the Barretts' house today, you saw those misguided souls, those who believe that Sherilyn Barrett can perform miracles. Can perform miracles! As if she were gifted at the piano, or could paint." People whispered in the dark.

"Miracles are the province of God!" He lifted his hands over his head. He punched the air and almost shouted. "And yet these people continue to insist that this little girl is somehow holy. Unbaptized, but holy. Taking money for these miracles, but she is holy!

"I have been inside that house. I have seen that little girl. I have uncovered and revealed their lies for what they really are: a cruel attempt to make money—to make money!—from the pain and suffering of other people. To take advantage of people who are too weak, too desperate, to take solace in the Lord, to put their faith in God alone. It is our job to protect these people.

"I've been in that house. I've looked at that little girl. There are no miracles there, only lies and deception.

"But they will not stop. The Barretts will not stop their lying. The truth has been revealed in the newspapers—you've all seen it. Everybody knows that they are lying, but still they prey on the weakness of the sick, the crippled, the suffering, the weak in God. They must be stopped. We must stop them!"

Father Peter bowed his head. "Let us pray for strength."

SIMON

Sergeant John Richards was waiting for me at the bar, a bowl of peanuts and a plastic cup in front of him.

He stood up and extended his hand as I approached.

"How are you, John?" I asked, sitting next to him.

"I been better," he said, settling himself back onto his stool. He looked like a boxer gone to seed, big and shambling. "Nice place you got here."

The bar at the Balmoral had a reputation as the roughest in Victoria. It stank of spilled beer and cigarette smoke, piss and vomit. There was no pretense of civility—no music, no plants, just the raised voices of its patrons, battered furniture and hazy blue light. "All the comforts of home," I said.

He waved the bartender over for me. "I'll have a—" I tried to think of a they were likely to have. "—A Canadian. A bottle."

The bartender shook his axe-shaped head. "No bottles."

"You don't have Canadian in bottles?"

"No bottles at all. No glasses." He gestured down the bar, and John lifted his plastic cup to me in a mock toast. "Safer. None of this." The bartender pointed at his own face, where it looked like someone had tried to dig his eye out with a broken bottle, leaving a twisted, livid scar and a white orb in the socket.

"All right. Just a pint of Canadian."

He pulled the beer and slid it to me. When I opened my wallet he glanced at John and shook his head at me, waving away my five-dollar bill.

"So are you a regular?" I asked after the bartender turned away.

John shrugged.

I took a swallow of the weak beer. "So what's up, John? Karen told me you came by the house."

"Yeah. I wanted to . . ." His gravelly voice was low, and I leaned toward him to hear. "I'm sorry I had to do that."

I shrugged. "I figured we'd hear from the police, after the story in the paper."

His voice dropped further. "I owe you a lot, Simon." He stared down at the bar.

"Don't sweat it, John. I just did what anybody would have done."

He glanced up at me sharply, locking eyes. I wondered how long he'd been sitting at the bar. "Don't say that. It's not true. Because of you I've still got a job, I've got a pension, I've got my family."

I nodded, uncomfortable with his vehemence. "Sure. Okay."

"That's why I wanted to be the one to go to your house. I thought maybe I could . . . I dunno. I thought I might be able to help. Take a bit of the heat." He shook his head.

"What's going on, John?" I asked, steeling myself for his answer.

"Charlie . . . you know Charlie, right?"

I nodded. Charlie Hopkins was John's partner.

"Charlie's got this girlfriend, works over at Monty's sometimes. Dances on the circuit. He sees her when she's in town. Sends her flowers. Nice girl. Clean. No drugs. She makes Charlie happy. Not the sort of girl you want your wife finding out about, though."

"Ah."

"Yeah. You know."

I did.

"Anyway, so Charlie's got this girl. And yesterday he comes in all twitchy. I ask him what's up but he doesn't say anything. Not at first. But Charlie, he knows a little something about what you did for me, so he pulls me aside and he tells me about this telephone call."

I could see where this was going. "Shit."

"Yeah. He got this phone call at home Sunday afternoon. His wife is sitting right there and this guy starts talking about Clarice, and how if Charlie didn't want his wife to find out . . . Your name came up. Your little girl."

"Right."

John nodded, drained his glass and waved for another. "Thing is, I'm walkin' around the station today after Charlie tells me this and nobody's making eye contact. Everybody's twitchy. And I start to think that maybe there were a lot of phone calls on Sunday afternoon. And then the story in the paper came up at the morning briefing. You've never seen a squadroom so quiet."

"What are you telling me, John?"

"I'm telling you to be careful. I don't know who you pissed off, but somebody's got it in for you."

I had a fairly good idea. "Are we in danger?"

"I dunno. I can't get a read on it. All Charlie said was that the person who called him told him to be on the lookout for you and your family. And not in the serve and protect kind of way."

I couldn't bring myself to take another drink. It was all I could do to hold down my dinner.

Victoria New Sentinel
Friday, December 13, 1996
Waiting for a Miracle
Religious seekers disturb neighborhood
~City Desk~

More than a week after the *New Sentinel* first broke the story of miracles attributed to four-year-old Sherilyn Barrett—and despite conflicting reports concerning her ability to heal the sick—pilgrims continue to arrive daily at the comatose girl's Fernwood home. The increased traffic is creating problems for the normally quiet neighborhood.

"It's like a circus over there," says Cecil White, who lives next door to the Barretts. "The people waiting to see Sherry are fine," says White, who calls himself a friend of the family. "It's the ones on the sidewalk who are the problem."

The house has been besieged by demonstrators since early this week, protesting what they feel is a deception on the part of the Barretts.

"I've called the police on them a couple of times," says White. "They're out there all night, singing and shouting. They call themselves good Christians, but good Christians would let an old man get a good night's sleep."

SIMON

I was guardedly optimistic as I walked toward the house and saw that the crowd of protestors was no longer blocking the gate. They were partway down the sidewalk—I didn't have to fight my way through them. I didn't even notice the graffiti until I was in the front yard.

WHORE CHILD

Scrawled on the front wall in black spray paint, bordered by a pair of crosses, the words screamed at me.

SATAN

A crowd of the pilgrims were gathered at the painted wall, talking in whispers, pointing up to where the vandal had sprayed the words across Sherry's window and wall.

I burst through the door and into the silence of the house.

"Simon, what—" Karen came out of the kitchen as I slammed the door behind me and headed for Sherry's bed.

"Are you all right? Simon, what is it?"

Nothing was changed from the day before. The light glowed beside the bed where Sherry lay, covers folded on her chest.

I released a breath I hadn't even realized I was holding. "Sherry's all right."

"Of course she is. I just checked on her," Karen said. "Simon, what's wrong?"

I stepped around the bed and opened the blinds. Karen gasped as the morning light struggled vainly past the words WHORE CHILD and SATAN, the writing backward through the glass. Trails of paint trickled from the letters like black blood.

"Oh my God." One hand rose to her throat as she stepped toward the window. She knocked one of Sherry's stones to the floor and bent to pick it up.

"It must be Father Peter." She set the stone back on the sill.

"Or his crowd." I looked out, expecting to see the skeletal priest looking back at me from the sidewalk. Instead, I met the eyes of several pilgrims. I tugged on the cord, lowering the blind.

"I'm going to call the police," Karen said, turning away from the window. "They can't ignore vandalism, can they?"

"Let me," I offered. "I'll talk to John."

I made the call from the kitchen, sitting at one end of the table.

"Sergeant Richards," I told the switchboard. He picked up after three rings.

"Richards."

"It's Simon Barrett."

The phone was silent in my hand.

"Hello, Mr. Barrett."

"You're there early."

There was another long silence. "I'm just coming in. Is there something I can help you with?" His voice was flat.

"Is something wrong, John?" I knew, even before I asked.

"Just busy, Mr. Barrett. Is there something I can help you with?" Mr. Barrett. As if he didn't know me.

"I'm sorry for disturbing you, sergeant. There's been some vandalism at the house."

"I'll transfer you to the reports desk."

"John—"

"It's Sergeant Richards, Mr. Barrett."

"Oh."

"I'm transferring you now, Mr. Barrett." He paused.

"Somebody called you, didn't they?"

He answered in a whisper. "They know, Simon. They know everything."

"Who are 'they'?"

He ignored the question. "You and your family aren't . . . I can't help you. I can't talk to you. Do you understand what I'm saying?"

Karen was staring at me, trying to make sense of my side of the conversation. "I think so."

"If a police cruiser stops in front of your house, Simon, they're not there because you called them. Do you understand that?"

"Yes," I whispered.

"Do you want me to transfer you, Mr. Barrett?"

"No, thank you."

The phone died in my hand.

"That didn't go well," Karen said.

"No, it didn't." I recounted John's side of the conversation. "It's the same thing that happened with Jamie at the newspaper, with my job and Stephen at the hospital. It's Father Peter."

Karen was pale.

"This is what he was talking about when we let him into the house that day. The 'repercussions' of our decision." I shook my head; I still couldn't believe I had let him in. "What else could it be?"

"Right."

I started to rummage through the cupboard under the sink.

"What are you doing?" she asked.

"Looking for a bucket and some gloves." I set a bottle of cleaner on the counter. "I thought I'd try to get some of the paint off."

She looked at me as if she couldn't believe what she was seeing.

"What?"

She shook her head. "Nothing."

The stranger was silent and still in the center of the crowd. The black letters on the white wall, covering the window, almost made him smile.

It was crass and crude, but he couldn't always control the details—and it served its purpose. Most times, all he had to do was put the spark to the tinder, fan the flames to life and let the wind take the fire where it would.

Would it be enough? He thought it might be.

Over time, the stranger had learned what worked: a steady escalation of pressure until spirits broke.

In these days of little faith, a vague threat and a promise of money was usually enough, and the pretenders were never heard from again. Sometimes, where traces of belief still lingered, he had to go further. Without livelihood, and with their positions in the community under attack, most people found it easier to walk away, to abandon their delusions and fade into obscurity.

It had been a very long time since he had been forced to call his soldiers to direct action. This pressure would be enough. This family had no faith, nothing to guide them. They were barely a family: why should they persevere?

He allowed himself to smile as the front door opened and the husband emerged, his face a grim mask. The husband stared at the stranger as he closed the door behind him, rattling the handle to ensure it was locked.

The stranger's face broke into a smile as the husband began to scrub at the wall. Such fools, to think they could so easily clean the stain on their house, on their souls.

RUTH

Simon was hunched over the sink with the water running when I came into the kitchen. "Am I in your way?" he asked.

"I can wait."

"It could be a while. I can't get this paint off." He squirted dish detergent into his palm, then scrubbed with a small brush.

"It was still wet?"

He shook his head, attacking his nails. "No, it's these little flecks. They stick—" He threw the brush into the sink and rinsed his hands under the water. "Forget it. I'll take care of it later."

"Did you get most of it off? Of the house, I mean."

He nodded. "I can't believe people," he said.

"They're just confused."

"They're sheep. And that priest. Just standing there, staring."

I spoke softly, trying to calm him. "They're doing what they're told because they think it's the right thing to do."

"I think I've heard that excuse a time or two. It always starts with a little paint."

"Sometimes it's the truth."

He looked at me strangely. "What made you so forgiving?"

"It's not for me to judge."

"No," he said, shaking his head and leaning forward. "I mean," his voice dropped. "When did it happen?"

I tried to pretend that I didn't know exactly what he was talking about. "What do you mean?"

"You never used to cross yourself. And you're wearing—" He gestured toward me. "I never noticed you wearing a crucifix before."

My hand rose to my throat.

"You try to keep it covered, but I've seen it. When did this—"

I cut him off. "When do you suppose?"

"Right. But I didn't know you were Catholic."

"I'm not. I mean, I wasn't. I was baptized in the United Church. But there's a bit more room for the miraculous—"

"Not if you listen to our friend out there." He gestured toward the front of the house.

"That's why I didn't say anything. I know how Karen feels about the Church, and she's told me about her mother, and with Father Peter . . . I don't think that he and I pray to the same God."

Simon nodded as if he understood.

"When I was a girl, growing up in Henderson, the church was the center of everything. It wasn't a matter of belief, it was just there. Bake sales and swap meets. Weddings, wakes and funerals. Christenings. It *was* the community."

"When I came to Victoria, I didn't feel connected to the church anymore. I had never really believed, so it wasn't a matter of losing my faith. I just didn't need that sort of enforced community. I was too busy building my own. But then . . ." I hadn't spoken to anyone about the way things had changed for me since Sherry had healed me. "What happened with Sherry opened my eyes. When she healed my sister, it made me see that there's more to the world than just all this. Things we don't always understand."

"Like what?"

"Like a little girl in the other room who can heal the sick, who stays *well* herself, but can't wake herself up. Why is that, do you think?"

He shook his head.

I smiled. "I don't know either. I'm looking for the answers."

"I understand." His voice was almost a whisper.

"In the meantime, though, we should probably help some of those people find what they've come looking for."

KAREN

By six o'clock I was alone. I ate, straightened the kitchen and washed the dishes. My bones ached. I was exhausted, but I knew that if I tried to go to bed early, I would just lie awake for hours.

I mixed up a supplement and fed Sherry. Her lips were dry and I moistened them with water from the bottle by the bed, then gently dabbed them with balm. On my way back through the house I turned on any lights that weren't already burning. No matter how bright the rooms were, it felt dark. I hit power on the stereo in the family room. I needed the sound, but I couldn't decide who I wanted to listen to, so I left the radio playing. My clothes pinched and pulled, as if they—or my skin—suddenly weren't my own.

There was only one thing to do: I sat beside Sherry's bed, took out my notebook and began to write.

In the last week, I had almost filled a notebook.

I would never show anyone most of what I wrote: rhythmic, rhyming poems almost like nursery rhymes, but threaded with a darker story; fairy tales, but set in the modern world; fables in which the morals were predominantly fatalistic, not uplifting.

I was writing letters to myself, trying to make sense of everything that had happened since the accident. I had fought so long against the idea of miracles, of the divine, but now I wondered. I held my confusion up to the light, trying to allow myself to see in a different way.

My writing seemed marked by the metronomic regularity of my daughter's breathing. In the distance, I could hear the faint conversation of the protestors on the sidewalk, but they were a world away. Between thoughts or paragraphs, or verses, I looked up at my girl, her lips parted in sleep.

"How are you, baby?" I asked in a whisper, as if she might wake. "Do you want to hear what Mommy's been working on?"

I began to read. "When the spring came and the air filled with the scent of flowers, Mr. Squirrel took off his winter coat and ventured from his house, little knowing that today his life would change forever . . ."

Hours later I awoke, slumped in the chair, pages clutched to my chest. Turning her carefully on her side, I slid under the covers with her, and slept until the morning light against the blinds woke me.

Victoria New Sentinel
Thursday, December 19, 1996
Miracle Casualty
Tempers flare at Fernwood home
~City Desk~

Police and an ambulance were called to the home of four-year-old Sherry Barrett yesterday afternoon when a forty-five-year-old man, suffering from multiple sclerosis, was injured by protestors while attempting to see the little girl.

Witnesses reported a struggle occurred when protestors tried to restrict the man's entry to the Barrett property and the man was pushed to the sidewalk, suffering injuries to his head and back. His name was not released to the media, and the Barrett family could not be reached for comment.

HENRY

Even into the night there were people in front of the Barretts' house, marching, holding their signs proudly, even though there was no one to see them.

I stayed in the shadows, not knowing anymore who might be able to see me, not wanting to risk meeting Peter again. From the dark of the hedge I could watch both the house and people on the sidewalk.

I caught sight of Mrs. Barrett every now and then, the outline of her against the blinds in the front room as she cared for Sherry. It felt a little strange, almost like I was a peeping Tom or something, but it wasn't like that. Not at all.

After midnight all the lights went out inside the house. The protestors set down their signs and sat in a circle on the concrete with candles in front of them, holding hands. Some of them slept in sleeping bags or under blankets, while others kept watch.

I could hear the faint sound of whistling from down the block, then a dark figure walked up the middle of the street and stopped in front of the driveway gate, just outside the pool of light thrown by the streetlamp.

Was he one of the protestors? I couldn't tell. He seemed—

I realized suddenly that he was watching me.

His voice cut through the still air so loudly that I was amazed that lights didn't start turning on in all of the houses on the block, that the protestors didn't hear. "Aren't you cold, my boy?"

"Tim?" I whispered, hurrying toward him. "What are you doing here?"

It wasn't until I saw that he was bundled up in a winter coat with scarf and gloves that I noticed the cold.

"Freezing my ass off," he answered, rubbing his gloves together. "And you, out here in your shirtsleeves." He shook his head, then burst out laughing. "I was just about to tell you that you should be careful or you'll catch your death."

I didn't find the joke so funny. "What are you doing here?"

"I thought I would see where you were going every night. I thought it might be here."

"I just—"

"Henry," he said, cutting me off. "I've got something important to tell you." The humor had left his eyes. "Here, step into the light." Pulling off a glove, he reached into his jacket pocket and pulled out a crumpled piece of paper. There was an address on it, written in spidery black ink. Downtown. Not too far away from the library.

"What's this?" I asked.

"It's a church. An old church where your friend Father Peter holds meetings every night."

I flinched, and glanced over at the protestors. "You want me to go to a meeting with Father Peter? Why would I do that?"

"For the same reason that you spend every night here, watching over this family." He took a deep breath, his face tight with concern. "You know you have a role in this."

"But I don't want to have anything to do with—"

"I know."

"What's he got to do with the Barretts anyway? What aren't you telling me?"

"You can't imagine the terrible things he's done, Henry." He shook his head and laid one hand on my shoulder, squeezing. "His actions can't be traced back to him directly, but when things do happen, he's usually around. He's been spotted in the backgrounds of photographs, or people mention seeing him days or hours before . . . I've seen what he's done. I think you need to go to one of his meetings," he said.

"Why?"

He sighed. "Because it is always better to know one's enemy than to simply hope he'll go away."

"Then why don't you go?"

"This isn't about me, Henry," he answered.

No, it was about me. And the Barretts. Sherry.

"What's he going to do to them?"

He gestured toward the note in my hand. "I don't know."

"So I'm . . ." My voice trailed off as the full realization hit me. "I have to stop it, don't I? That's why I'm here. Whatever it is he's planning to do, I have to stop it."

"You don't *have* to do anything, Henry," Tim said. "If you want to, you can just walk away from all this. But if you were going to do that, you wouldn't be out here in the cold every night, would you? Here," he added, undoing and pulling off his coat. "You hang on to this." He held the coat out to me.

I realized how cold I had been as I slipped into it, his warmth surrounding me. "Aren't you going to be cold?"

"I'm keeping the gloves." He smiled. "Don't worry about it. I'll just steal another from the lost and found. You need it more than I do."

My cold fingers fumbled with the buttons, but once it was done up, the coat felt like armor.

MARY

When I opened my apartment door, it took me a moment to accept that Simon was really there, standing in the hallway. It had only been ten days, but it felt like a lifetime.

"Hey," I said, holding the doorknob tightly.

He shifted from foot to foot. "I guess this is a bit of a surprise."

"A bit."

Part of me wanted to slam the door. Another part wanted to invite him in—to erase the time and the distance between us.

I was afraid he was going to say that he wanted to come back, that leaving had been a mistake. I was afraid he was going to say that it was over, that he was happy with Karen. I was afraid of how I would respond to whatever he said.

I *so* wanted to close the door.

"I tried you at the office, and they said you were no longer with them."

I nodded.

"Did they fire you? Was it because of us, or Sherry, or—"

"I left." Stepping back, I allowed the door to swing open. "Why don't you . . . ?"

He nodded and stepped inside.

It was strange to have him in the apartment again. "What's done is done. I don't want to talk about it."

"You worked so hard," he continued, as if he hadn't heard me.

"I didn't want to be there after what they did to you," I blurted. "I know how stupid that sounds. I tried to give two weeks' notice the day after they fired you and they told me to leave, immediately. Paid out my two weeks."

I pre-empted the lecture I knew was coming. "I know it was stupid. I know that I've thrown away, well, maybe my whole career. But I'm happier now. I'm going to be doing work that matters."

"You've got a new job already?"

"After the holidays I'll be starting with Legal Aid. My friend Brian from school hooked me up."

"That's a good direction for you."

"No lecture about being naïve and idealistic?"

"I don't think you're naïve. And I'm starting to think that maybe idealism isn't such a bad thing."

"I think it's the right thing for me right now."

"I'm glad," he said. "I'm glad it's working out for you."

He looked down at the carpet.

"I wanted to say I'm sorry," he said, without meeting my eye. "It wasn't fair, what I did to you. Drawing you into all of this, then leaving you up in the air."

I touched the back of his hand, and he looked up. "I'm a big girl, Simon. I went into this with my eyes open. You don't get involved with a married man assuming that it's all going to work out perfectly. I never thought we'd be permanent. I never thought that you'd leave Karen. Or Sherry." I smiled a little, and then simply asked, "Are you back with Karen?"

He shrugged. "I don't know. I've been at the house help-ing, but I'm staying at the Balmoral. It's all still up in the air."

"But you want to be."

"I'm trying."

I thought I'd feel devastated to hear him say that. Instead, I felt relieved.

For a long time he stared out the window over my left shoulder as I chased words round my head, trying to figure out how to say everything that I needed to say.

"I should go," he finally said.

I nodded, unable to muster anything else. I was happy for him, and I was happy for myself, happy that this, at last, had turned out right. But I still felt on the verge of crying as his hand closed around the doorknob.

"Simon."

He turned to face me, his hand still on the knob.

I wanted to go to him, to feel myself against him this one last time, smell him, taste the salt of him.

Instead, I whispered, "I hope you work it out. I hope you'll be happy."

He smiled at me. Then he turned away, closing my apart-ment door softly as he left. The click as the bolt slid into place seemed to echo through the sudden stillness.

I stared at the door, realizing, for what seemed like the first time, that part of life was never getting a chance to say all that you should say to someone before they are gone.

HENRY

I came in just as Father Peter was stepping onto the small plat-form at the far end of the room. His bodyguard stood several steps behind him. I moved to one side, partly hidden by a set of shelves and thankful that the candlelight was too dim for him to see me.

"Great God in Heaven," he said loudly. "Please look down on this your enterprise and favor us with your blessing."

The room was packed, everyone with their heads bowed.

"Our Lord Jesus, please forgive us our sins and betrayals, and bless us in this your work. Oh Holy Spirit, please bathe us in your glory, and anoint us for this your task. Amen."

The crowd echoed "Amen" and lifted their heads.

"They have not learned," he started, picking up from a speech that clearly everyone knew but me. "The people keep coming, lining up to sell their souls to that family. Nothing we do or say seems to stop them."

To look at his followers, I could have been in a library on a Saturday afternoon. Everyone looked so normal. An over-weight woman in her fifties clutched her purse tight against her chest, while the young man next to her looked like a student, with short hair and wire-framed glasses. A woman with dark hair held a sleeping baby on her shoulder, and three children—two boys and a girl, all fair-haired and under the age of ten—knelt at the very front, their eyes lifted to him as he spoke.

"I'm not angry at those people they are calling 'pilgrims.' The Lord said, 'Forgive them, Father, they know not what they do.' We must forgive those whose illness brings them low, makes them vulnerable to evil.

"I feel sorry for those people. They think they are putting themselves in the hands of the Lord. They clutch their Bibles"—he lifted his up—"they whisper prayers, they kneel . . . They *kneel* before that little girl. Thou shalt worship no false idols before me! That's the word of God, and yet these people, these people kneel before a little girl, like the Israelites before the golden calf! It is our job to protect these people, from the Barretts and from themselves!"

The older woman clasped her hands and shut her eyes tight, while the young mother swayed in place.

"We must be strong. We must be devout in our beliefs, and

courageous in our actions. I have gathered you here because our church, our God, is under attack, and we, as the soldiers of the Lord, must go to battle in its defense."

The student and several other people shouted in agreement, their faces lighting up.

"We have been gentle. We have been kind. We have tried to persuade and to remind, to turn people back to the path of true faith, of righteousness. But so long as that family opens their doors, so long as that child is whored out by her own family, our words mean nothing. How can the soft words of the righteous compete with the promises of evil?"

The crowd leaned toward him, flexing itself like a single muscle. The children in the front folded their hands and closed their eyes in prayer.

"It is time to act. It is time to take steps against the source of the evil. The time for words is over. Now is the time for action! Who is with me? Who will stand with me?"

I couldn't take it anymore. I ran for the door as people started calling out to him.

The wind had picked up—it drove cold and merciless right through the bulky winter coat—but it felt good. It drove out the smell of that rotting basement. It rid my ears of his voice.

I walked as fast as I could up the dark side-alley toward the main street.

Under a streetlight, I started to feel a little better. The lamp posts were decorated for Christmas with lights and ribbons, and I slowed down a bit, drawing the coat up around my neck. I couldn't work up the nerve to look behind me, afraid Father Peter had spotted me. I passed a few people on the sidewalk— they didn't look like fanatics, but I had discovered that most fanatics don't. The people in that church basement were as normal-looking as anyone I had ever seen, but they all had the same violence in their eyes that Father Peter did, caught up in his passion.

And what about Father Peter's bodyguard? When I looked up during Father Peter's speech, it seemed like the huge man had been staring back at me.

He could see me, too. I was sure of it.

Even at a distance he had Father Peter's eyes, narrow and dark, but glowing in the half-light, in the flicker of the candles.

He watched me like a dog, tensing itself to pounce.

The attack would come, I was sure.

I just didn't know when.

"Karen, it's Jamie. It's a little past seven, Friday morning. December whatever. Twentieth, I guess. Uhm, listen, I'm not going to be able to make it to the house today. I've got something on the go. I don't want to get your hopes up, but . . . Listen, I'll tell you later, okay? Talk to you soon."

SIMON

I didn't think anything of it when Father Peter and his bodyguard joined the protestors the next morning before we opened the house. I heard a motor on the street and looked between the blinds of Sherry's window as the plumbing company van that Father Peter's thug drove pulled to a stop. The doors opened and a small group climbed out, carrying signs.

I had just turned away from the window when the glass exploded behind me.

Without thinking, I threw myself at Sherry, covering her with my body as glass sprayed into the room, a series of dull thuds echoing from the walls.

Rocks. They were throwing rocks at the house.

I could hear Karen running down the hall from the kitchen. Something flew through the window and shattered against the coffee table. Shattered.

Bottles. Not rocks. They were throwing bottles.

"Get down, Karen," I called to her. "No—get out. Get out of the way."

Fumbling with the covers, I lifted Sherry, cradling her head to my chest, and carried her across the room, sheltering her with my body. She was surprisingly heavy. Shards of broken glass tore into my socked feet and I stumbled. Another bottle flew into the room, crashing against the wall at the head of the bed, spraying Sherry's sheets with jagged diamonds.

In the hallway, Karen's eyes were wide with shock and worry. She reached for Sherry. "Simon, is she—?"

I rushed past her into the seeming security of the family room.

KAREN

I fell to my knees at the side of the couch where he set Sherry down. "Is she all right?"

"I think so. I don't know." He stepped away from her, and I saw the blood spotting her face.

"She's bleeding," he said in the same moment. "I wasn't quick enough." Tracing his fingers over her forehead, streaking blood along her pale skin.

"It's okay," I said. The fragments of glass had barely broken the skin. "This doesn't look too bad, and Stephen will be here any minute now."

Nausea rose in my throat—I could still hear the sound of bottles smashing against the house. But that sound was a world away. All that mattered was that my baby was safe.

"Are you okay, Simon?"

I waited for him to reply, then realized I was alone in the room. "Simon?" His bloody footprints led out of the family room, toward the front door.

I heard the click as the door opened, then Simon's voice. "Hey, what do you think—?"

The door closed. And then nothing.

RUTH

The pilgrims were huddled against the hedge when I pulled up to the house, and the protestors were in the middle of the lawn. I wondered if Karen was calling the police to report them for trespassing.

I parked across the street, and was halfway to the sidewalk when I realized that the protestors were throwing bottles. Sherry's window was broken.

I didn't know where to go. I couldn't get to the house, but I didn't want to just leave the pilgrims. They seemed so scared, cowering and huddling together.

The police. They'd have to come if I called.

I was about to run next door when the front door opened and Simon came out in his socks.

He raised his hand to shield his eyes from the winter morning light. "Hey," he called. "What do you think—?"

As he spoke, the biggest of the protestors, the one who usually stood with Father Peter, threw a bottle, which caught the light as it spun through the air. Simon couldn't see it. I could.

The bottle shattered against his head. He stood for a moment, rocking on his feet as if he couldn't understand what was happening to him, then crumpled slowly to the stoop.

"Simon!" The protestors scattered as I ran through the yard.

By the time I got to him, his face was masked in blood. His breath bubbled red between his lips.

Please let the door be open.

I pushed it with my hip as I bent to grasp Simon's shoulders. I pulled him inside without looking up.

Karen was there. "Oh my God! Simon!"

"Towels," I snapped at her. "Bring me some towels." I looked up. "And close the door."

She slammed it and disappeared down the hallway.

I cleared his mouth. I hoped that all the blood was from the scalp wound and he hadn't suffered any internal injuries from the fall.

Karen returned with the towels as I ran my fingers over the back of his skull. There was a bump from the fall on the crown of his head—not too serious. I pressed a towel against the wound on his forehead.

Karen clutched at his hand, stared helplessly at the blood on his face.

"Karen," I said. "Karen! I can't do this on my own."

She bit her lip, then picked up a towel and began to wipe the blood from the side of her husband's face.

"It's not as bad as it looks," I said.

"That's good. That's good."

"There's always lots of blood from head wounds."

His forehead was still positively gushing blood, but it didn't look like it went too deep. He'd need stitches, but two inches in either direction and he could have been blinded or . . . I pressed the towel to the wound.

"I'm going to check his feet." She moved down his body.

"His feet?"

Craning my head, I saw that his socks were bloodsoaked too. She pulled them off and glass tinkled on the tile floor.

"What happened?"

She dabbed at his feet with the towel. "He walked through the glass to get Sherry out."

"Where is she?"

"She's in the family room."

"Is she hurt?"

"Little cuts. She's okay." She took another look at his feet. "They're really badly cut. And there's glass embedded in them."

"Let's—"

The front door burst open. "Karen? Ruth?" Dr. McKinley almost tripped over us as he came through the door. He dropped to his knees. "What happened?"

SIMON

I awoke on the floor of the foyer with shocking suddenness. One moment I was standing on the front porch, catching the glint of something coming at me, then I was flat on my back, looking up at Karen and Ruth.

"What—" I struggled to rise, but the weight of hands on my shoulders pressed me back down.

"Just rest a moment," Ruth said, from what seemed like a long distance away. "Almost done."

I felt the softness of a hand on my cheek. Karen's. I let my eyes close.

Sharp pain in my right foot. I flinched and pulled away.

"That's got it," Stephen said, swimming into view. "I've bandaged . . . Oh, I see our patient is awake."

"He's been in and out," Ruth said.

"How are you doing?" Stephen asked, leaning over me.

It was hard to talk. My lips felt thick, and my face seemed stretched taut. "Sherry. Where's—?"

"She's okay. The doctor checked her." That was Karen.

"What happened—?"

"You got hit." He lifted my left eyelid with his thumb. "With a bottle." A bright light flashed into my eye, and I tried to look away. My left eyelid closed and there was a gentle pressure on my forehead before my right eye was forced open and the light flashed again. "Ruth, can you give me a hand?"

"I can do it," Karen said.

"We're going to move you into the kitchen," Stephen explained. "I want you to try to sit up, and Karen and I—"

"I can walk," I protested.

"That's one of the things we're going to check," he said as he shifted me to a sitting position. "But right now your feet are probably a little tender."

I had no idea what he was talking about until I tried to stand up and my knees buckled with the pain. I would have fallen if he and Karen hadn't been there to support me.

After we had hobbled to a chair at the kitchen table, Stephen ran a series of tests—vision and reflexes and memory and cognition—as Karen explained again what had happened. It took me a moment to realize that she was holding my hand. Ruth brought me a glass of water, cautioning me to take small sips. When Stephen took his stitching kit from his medical bag, Karen blanched and offered to get me a new pair of socks.

The tug of the thread through the tight skin of my forehead made me feel like I was going to vomit.

"You're doing fine," Stephen muttered in what had to be automatic reassurance. I didn't feel fine.

"Just a couple more."

"So do you travel everywhere with a needle and thread, doctor?" I asked him. I hoped that it sounded like a joke—I meant it as a joke.

"What did you think I was around here for, my good looks?"

I smiled, with some difficulty. "No, I think that's my job description."

He finished up, snipping the thread, and took a long look at me. "You may need to find some other employment, at least for a while." As he repacked his bag, he said, "It's quick and dirty. You'll need to get it looked at. Maybe a cosmetic surgeon."

"Thanks, Stephen," I said.

"Are you okay with these?" Karen asked. She held up a pair of white cotton socks.

I nodded and bent over to slide them on.

"Do you want me to?" Karen offered.

I shook my head, then reconsidered. "Please."

She was careful, but I had to close my eyes against a sudden dizziness.

"Are you okay?" Stephen asked.

"Woozy."

"Take it nice and slow."

I nodded. "I'll be fine." I took a deep, cleansing breath and opened my eyes. The first thing I saw was the concern on Karen's face. "I'll be fine," I said, to her alone.

She tried to smile.

"Is Sherry . . . ?"

"She's okay. A few cuts, but just minor ones. Stephen checked her over."

"That's good."

I looked up at Stephen and Ruth behind Karen.

"You all should get back to work, though," I said. "No need to worry about me."

"No," Karen said. "We can't. Sherry's room is a disaster."

"But what about the pilgrims?"

"Simon, we have to think about ourselves, about Sherry. It's not safe."

"That's what he wants," I said. "That's what he's wanted from the beginning."

"He's still out there," Ruth said. "Watching the house. Most of his people ran when you got hit, but he stayed."

Bracing myself against the table, I stood up.

"What are you doing?" Karen asked.

"I'm going out there," I said, walking slowly out of the kitchen.

"What?"

My feet were throbbing, and the walls seemed to inhale and exhale around me. "I'm going out there," I repeated. "We can't just let him—"

"What if they start up again?"

I stopped in the foyer to force my feet into my shoes. I was shocked to see the smears of blood on the floor, and a small pool of congealing red near the front door. My blood, staining the cold tiles of my home.

Karen was staring at the blood. I couldn't read her expression.

"I have to," I said. "If we just let this go, then . . ." I didn't know how to finish, so I just opened the door.

"Wait," Karen said. She was putting on her shoes, and pulling a jacket down from the hook. Her face was hard, determined.

I thought of telling her to stay in the house, that it was too dangerous. But I realized I wanted her to come with me, I wanted us to be together. I needed her strength and her fierce determination.

I held the door for her.

KAREN

The air was crystalline and cold, the silence so profound it felt like the world might shatter with a single word. It was still early; there were no reporters or television vans on the street.

Father Peter looked as if he was expecting us. Alone on the sidewalk, he played with his coin and didn't move as we crossed the lawn past the pilgrims who followed us with their eyes.

"You look terrible," Father Peter said to Simon with mock concern.

"I have you to thank for that, don't I?" Simon asked.

"Me? I threw no stones. But this is what happens when you put your family directly in harm's way."

Simon ignored the comment.

"I want to tell you what's going to happen next." Simon took a deep breath. "In a few minutes, Karen and I are going to go back into the house, and while I clean up the blood and the broken glass and fix the window, Karen is going to invite these people"—he gestured at the pilgrims—"in to see our daughter."

He took a step toward Father Peter. The priest stepped back.

"And that's what we'll do every day. If you or your friends spray-paint obscenities on our walls, we'll scrub them off, and the people will come. If you break our windows, we'll fix them, and the people will come. If you hurt us, we'll wash off the blood, slap on some bandages and the people will come." He pulled his hair back with one hand to show the priest the gash with its row of stitches. "Do you see this? That's what we'll do. Every day. Any wound you inflict, we'll stitch up. We're not going to stop, no matter what you do. This work is too important. Too many lives are at stake."

I stepped forward, lending Simon whatever strength I could.

"Including your own, Mr. Barrett," the priest whispered. "Do you think it was an accident that you were struck by a bottle this morning?" His eyes were bright, unblinking. "Do you actually believe that God didn't guide the hand of him who threw it?

"One such as yourself," he hissed, "ignorant of the Lord's work, of the teachings of the faith, can perhaps be forgiven for not understanding. Perhaps someone who has chosen to ignore those teachings," his eyes flicked to me, "might tell you what happens to those who oppose the Lord's work."

He waited a long moment.

"They burn, Mr. Barrett. They drown. The Lord drowned a whole world when it displeased him. He burned cities full of sinners. Are you willing to burn for something in which you do not even believe, Mr. Barrett? Are you willing to consign your daughter to the flames?"

He folded his hands piously in front of him. "I'll let you go back to your work, as I go back to mine."

He turned and walked away down the sidewalk. He didn't look back.

Simon swayed on his feet. "I think," he said, his face white as chalk. "I think I need to sit down."

SIMON

"You should see a doctor."

"What?" I lifted my head from the pillow as Karen sat next to me on the bed.

Our bed.

"I did see a doctor." Moving made my head swim, and I lay back down.

"You've been out all day. Stephen actually checked on you a couple of times."

"All day?" I struggled to sit up. The effort set off fireworks behind my eyes. "What time is it?"

"About 4:30. Everyone's gone home," Karen answered.

"Oh, shit, Karen, I'm sorry. I only meant to lie down for a second."

She smiled and put her hand on my leg. "You've been through a lot."

"How did everything go?"

"It went fine. It took us a while to clean up the mess, so we didn't start letting people in until noon."

"How's Sherry?"

She stopped rubbing my leg. "She's fine," she said, then paused. "But something strange has happened. Can you make it down the stairs to see her?"

I followed her with tentative steps, trying to figure out if there was any way I could walk to avoid the cuts on my feet. I couldn't find any, but it wasn't as painful as I had feared.

Sherry was back in her own bed.

"You got the window fixed already?"

She shrugged. "I called, some guys came, the window got fixed. But that's not what I wanted to show you. Here. . . ."

I couldn't see what Karen wanted me to see. Sherry looked like she always did, her lips parted in sleep, her breathing regular, her cheeks smooth.

I glanced sharply at Karen. She nodded.

Not trusting what I was seeing, I traced my daughter's cheeks with the tips of my fingers. Perfectly smooth.

"She was—"

"Yes."

Before I had stepped onto the porch, my daughter's face had been cut in a dozen places. And now . . .

"When did this happen?"

She was about to answer when the doorbell rang. She glanced up sharply, and I knew exactly what she was feeling.

But it was Jamie, standing on the front porch with an older woman and a bearded man with a camera. "Karen, Simon, this is . . . Listen, this is Amy Moore. She's a medical consultant for the *Globe and Mail*. And Don Neale, a photographer who is working with us today."

"Working with us? Jamie, what's this about?"

Jamie reached forward and squeezed Karen's upper arm. "Over the last week or so I've been doing some follow-ups with some of the people who have been coming to see Sherry. I didn't want to say anything until I had it nailed."

Karen said, "You'd better come in."

Jamie kept talking, "I've spent the last two days interviewing doctors to confirm what people were telling me. I'm working on a story for the Monday paper, and I'm wondering if you'd like to comment"—she reached into her folio and extracted several file folders—"on these reports from five doctors confirming spontaneous remissions and inexplicable recoveries in patients who have been to see Sherry in the last ten days?"

The Globe and Mail
Monday, December 23, 1996
Spontaneous Healing
Sick, dying go into remission after
paying visits to comatose girl
~Jamie Keller, special to *The Globe and Mail*~
Doctors in Victoria, B.C., confirmed late last week
that five patients with chronic or terminal conditions who visited four-year-old Sherilyn Barrett,
comatose since a car accident last spring, have
demonstrated clear and remarkable recoveries.

"Of course I'm not going to use the word miracle," said oncologist James Gibson, who spoke to
The Globe and Mail with the permission of his patient
Tanya Ross. "What is clear is that there has been a
remarkable spontaneous remission that I am at
a loss to explain."
Other doctors confirmed . . .

LEO

"It was supposed to be over," Father Peter said, looking at the newspaper again.

We were in the van in the alley by the church. We weren't going yet, but I had the motor running so the heater would work.

"It's too soon," he said. "I thought I had enough time—"

I had no idea what he was talking about, but he looked angry. Angrier than I had ever seen him.

"Spontaneous remissions. How can that be? How did it get this far, Leo? From where do they draw their strength?"

"From hell," I said, without even thinking about it. I looked at him to see if I was right.

He was smiling at me. "Of course," he said. "Of course. That's it. And we know what the righteous do with devils like this, don't we, Leo?"

"We fight them," I said. I tried to remember what he had said at one of the meetings. "We bring the light of the Lord, the flaming sword—"

My watch beeped. "We should go," I said. "It's almost ten o'clock."

"And we can't be late," Father Peter said. "Not today. There will be too many questions. From this." He rattled the news-paper. "Those weak of faith and limited of vision will be doubting—"

"Like Thomas."

"Like Thomas. But not you. You're one of us, aren't you, Leo? One of the righteous. The pure of heart. No doubts, no reservations."

I nodded and stepped on the gas.

"And what do the righteous do, Leo? They fight and they keep fighting. Even when the battle seems lost. Even when the devils seem to have won. They fight until they drop."

I nodded. I didn't know exactly what he meant, but I knew that I would keep fighting. I would never give up.

"This will be the last day, Leo. The last day at the house, I promise you that. This story says that they're shutting down for the holidays, that after today they won't allow anyone in to see Sherilyn until the twenty-seventh.

"That gives us three days, Leo. Three days to ensure that they never reopen that house. Three days to bring the wrath of almighty God down on that house of sinners."

When I looked over at him, he was smiling.

SEVEN

Christmas

The telephone on the bedside table rang well before seven, but I was already awake. I don't think I had slept at all, just watched the red digital numbers on the clock change.

I already knew who it was. "Hello?"

There was some whispered shushing and laughter, and I smiled. I could picture what was happening on the other end of the line. "We wish you a merry Christmas," came the massed voices of my family, two time zones away. "We wish you a merry Christmas . . ."

I could see them all, tatty sweaters and unbrushed hair, clustered around the telephone in the kitchen, the living room a blizzard of torn paper and candy-crazed children. My family did this every Christmas: called all of the relations who couldn't be home. When we were teenagers, my brother Barry and I had started calling it the Cunningham Tubercular Choir. Nobody in my family could carry a tune; Simon's rudimentary folksinging had really stood out.

Simon.

"And a Happy New Year!" The song dissolved into a round of cheering and shouted Merry Christmases before Mom claimed the receiver for herself. "Merry Christmas, honey. And Merry Christmas to our Sherry too."

"Merry Christmas, Mom." Tears filled my eyes despite myself. "Is everybody there?"

"Oh, yes," she said. "Everybody and their dog." I could see her sitting at the table. She would have brought out the Christmas dishes for the holidays, and the table would be covered with a red cloth, a little the worse for wear after

Christmas Eve dinner. "I wish I was with you in Victoria, though."

"You'll be here next week."

"But it must be so hard for you—"

"I know how important it is for everyone to be home for Christmas, Mom. We're fine."

"I just worry about you, that's all."

"So who's there?"

She let me change the subject. "Well, Chris finally brought that Heather girl he's been seeing."

"And how's that?"

"She seems very nice. A bit quiet. He's wandering around like he just won the lottery, though."

I could imagine. "Did Stan's kids come?"

"They're with their mom. He'll pick them up at the bus in time for dinner."

"That's good." I snuggled deeper under the blankets.

She waited a moment. "And how are you?"

"Just waking up," I lied.

"You shouldn't lie to your mother."

I smiled.

"You could never sleep on Christmas Eve. I hardly think you'd start this year."

"I used to listen to you and Dad putting the presents out. Arguing. Remember that year you guys had to put together that air-hockey table for Stevie?" My room had been right above the living room, and I heard every word of the argument.

There was a burst of crying in the background. "That's Franny," my mother said. "She's a bit overwhelmed."

"Yeah."

"And how is our little Sherry?"

I shifted in the bed. "I haven't been down yet," I confessed. "She was fine at midnight."

"Was Santa Claus good to her?"

I had to close my eyes and squeeze my face tight to keep from bursting into tears.

"Yes," I managed to say.

"I lit a candle for her last night."

"Thank you," I said, and I meant it.

"I lit one for you too." She was silent for a long moment, waiting for me to say something. "I wish I could be there for you."

"Don't worry about us," I said, a little glad that she was worrying.

"I just don't like the idea of you being alone on Christmas. It doesn't seem right."

"We'll be all right. I decorated the tree yesterday, and I rented *It's a Wonderful Life* to watch this afternoon. Simon's coming for dinner." I tried to slip that in so she wouldn't notice.

She didn't say anything for several seconds. Then, "That's interesting."

"Let's leave it alone, Mom."

"He ran out on you and Sherry when you needed him most, and you're inviting him for Christmas dinner?"

"Mom."

"Karen, I know you're lonely but this, this is—"

"Mom."

"I won't say anything. You know me. I know how to keep my peace."

I did know her, and braced myself.

"I just think it's a big mistake. I don't know why you haven't been in contact with a lawyer—"

"Jesus, Mom."

"Language, Karen," she scolded. "Not another word. Not from me." A distant crash claimed her attention. "Listen to that. The kids are wanting some breakfast and have started to take the dogs hostage. I should go. Give me a call a bit later when you're up and about. Give a kiss to Sherry."

"I will."

"I love you, Karen."

"I love you too, Mom,"

We both hung up without saying good-bye, like always. My relationship with my mother was an ongoing telephone conversation.

SIMON

I stopped on the front porch with my key in my hand. I'm not sure why, but it didn't feel right to let myself in today.

I rang the doorbell, and stood up straight, shifting the weight of the bag in my hand.

Karen opened the door quickly, as if she had been waiting. "Hi," she said, smiling almost shyly. She was wearing a light gray dress that seemed to float around her, touching her curves, falling to her knees. Her cheeks were pink—was she blushing?—and she was wearing lipstick. There was perfume in the air.

"Hi," I said, like an idiot. "You look lovely."

Her cheeks got pinker. "Thank you," she said. "You made it through okay?" She gestured toward the sidewalk.

"It was fine. All they're doing today is reading the Bible to each other."

"Maybe the article in Monday's paper took some of the wind out of their sails." She stepped back from the door. "Come on in," she said. "You must be freezing."

For a long moment I felt like all of this was new, that I had never been in this house, that I was meeting this beautiful woman for the first time. The night seemed portentous, full of promise.

"You brought presents," she said.

"Ho ho ho," I slipped off my shoes and hung my coat.

"You look," she started awkwardly. "I meant to say before, you look nice too."

I smiled, not sure of how to respond.

"And how's your head?"

I swept the hair back from my forehead. I knew what she was seeing—I had stared at it long enough in the mirror. Where a few days before there had been a jagged split, roughly stitched, now there was only the faintest white line.

I hadn't even noticed the change until I woke up in my hotel room the morning after the attack and started to peel the dressing from my feet. The bandages were stiff with blood, but underneath my feet were entirely healed: not a trace of the cuts remained.

A quick glance in the scratched mirror confirmed my suspicion. The wound on my forehead had vanished as well, leaving behind only a thin line and, on the pillow, a smear of blood and a length of black thread, still knotted from Stephen's stitches.

Karen surprised me by touching my forehead, running her fingers lightly over the skin.

"Does that hurt?"

Her touch was so sudden, so unexpected, I could barely speak. "No, not at all. It's . . ."

"Healed," she finished for me. "I don't even think it's going to scar."

I shook my head. "No, I don't think so either."

She sighed and shook her head.

"Do you want something to drink?" she asked, changing the subject. "There's mulled wine."

I could smell the spices.

"I'd love some. Do you need a hand?"

She shook her head and touched my arm as if to stop me from following her. "I'll be right back. You go say Merry Christmas to your daughter."

I could still feel her touch after she turned away.

Coming from the family she did, Christmas was a big deal for Karen, so I wasn't surprised to see that she had rearranged the room, sliding the couch over and moving the chairs to clear the corner where we always put the Christmas tree. It was a beautiful tree, almost brushing the ceiling, filling the room with a fresh smell of pine. There was a poinsettia on the coffee table, and along the windowsill Karen had placed pictures of Sherry with the Santa Claus from the mall. You could see her grow from year to year, until the pictures stopped.

And there she was, still in the middle of it all.

"Hey, pretty girl." I crouched at the side of her bed, setting my bag on the floor so I could smooth the hair away from her forehead. "How are you doing?" Karen had dressed her in a white flannel nightie with reindeer and snowmen playing along the front. "Merry Christmas, baby. I've got some presents in here for you." I pulled packages out of the bag and set them on the bed next to her. "We'll open them a little later."

I stacked the other gifts I'd bought under the tree. I was still looking at it when Karen came back with the warm wine in Christmas mugs.

Strings of white lights flashed slowly from deep within the dark branches, all hung with familiar ornaments. I fingered one, a Renaissance snowflake that we had bought at gift shop at the Met in New York one year. "Nice tree," I said.

"Thanks." She sat down on the couch and I sat down next to her.

We fell silent, looking at Sherry, looking at the tree, looking down at our mugs. Neither of us knew what to say. Was she feeling as strange, as pleasantly confused, as I was?

"This is very good," I finally ventured, after another sip of the wine.

"Are you hungry? We can eat whenever you like. I just need half an hour. or forty-five minutes' notice. Are you hungry now?" The words spilled from her.

"A little," I confessed. "What's for dinner?"

"Whatever you like. Young's is delivering until eight."

She let the words hang in the air with a strange expression of vulnerability, waiting to see how I would react.

The first Christmas Karen and I had spent on our own in Victoria, rather than making the frantic flight to visit her family—our annual Guilt Trip, as we had come to call them, separate bedrooms and family singalongs—we had ordered Chinese, rounding it off with a couple of bottles of wine and a night of lovemaking under the tree. The dinner had become a Christmas tradition, the way some families go to church.

I smiled. "Do you want me to call?"

Her tension seemed to break. She shook her head and got up. "No, I'll call." As she left the room, she turned back. "You can pay." She grinned at me.

My heart was beating almost in time with the blinking of the lights.

LEO

Father Peter told me to meet him in the church basement after Mother went to bed. He told me that he would leave the side door open for me.

I bought two turkey dinners from the grocery store, and Mother heated them up in the oven after Mass. She said the blessing. I didn't say anything when she asked God to watch over that "precious little girl." I just smiled at her and said "Amen." Loose lips sink ships.

I closed the side door behind me. It took me a second to see him in the dark. "Merry Christmas, Father."

He grunted. "Christmas."

"Don't you like Christmas? It's the birthday of Jesus."

"We don't have time to talk about that. We need to talk about what comes next. Our holy mission."

Of course. Our mission.

"I need your advice."

I smiled. He wanted my advice. "All right."

His teeth were shiny in the candlelight. "I knew I could rely on you, Leo," he said. "I knew that from the first time I saw you. Do you know what tomorrow is?"

I was sure I knew the answer. "Boxing Day?"

He shook his head. "Saint Stephen's Day. Do you know the story of Saint Stephen?"

I knew that it was one of the churches in town, but I didn't want to make any more stupid mistakes, so I didn't answer.

"Saint Stephen was the first Christian martyr. The first of us to be killed for the truth, the first to die in the service of God."

I nodded as if I knew that already.

"We've tried to stop them, haven't we, Leo? We've tried every other means. But now, these big-city newspapers are spreading the lies too! We need to stop them, Leo. We need to stop the Barretts before they can spread their poison any further. We need to find someone to take the next step in this battle, Leo. We need to find someone who is willing to follow in Saint Stephen's footsteps."

I listened very carefully.

"Think back to the meetings, Leo. Was there anyone you noticed who looked like they might be brave enough to take on this fight against the darkness?"

I tried to think of all the people who had come to the church, but the only face I could see in my head was the man who tried to hide, who didn't pray.

"Is there someone who believes strongly enough to be a tool in the hand of the Lord?"

"I—"

"We're looking for a lion, Leo." He was talking like he hadn't even heard me. "A lion of God, willing to kill or die in the Lord's name."

My heart began to race.

"It has to be someone strong, someone powerful. Someone strong enough and pure of heart, to fight off the devils who will try to stop them."

A lion. Leo.

"I could, I could be the lion of God."

He shook his head. "I couldn't ask that of you. The dangers are too great, I couldn't—"

"You're not asking. I'm offering. I'm offering my life to the Lord." I stood up taller. "I want to do this. Please? Let me be your lion. Let me do this."

He nodded. "All right," he said. He was so proud of me. "Are you absolutely sure?"

"I'm sure."

"You're willing to be the lion of God?"

"I think God wants me to be. I felt him take my hand when I was throwing that bottle. I think God wants me to be his lion."

"I think so too." He put his hand on my shoulder. "In a few hours, it will be Saint Stephen's Day, and we'll go forth. We'll finish this battle with the Barretts."

KAREN

Simon picked up my plate from the coffee table and stacked it on his own. "Do you want anything else? Coffee?" he asked, standing up.

"Just a fortune cookie."

He smiled. "Okay. I'll be right back."

"And bring the wine," I called after him.

I flushed Sherry's feeding tube while he was gone and tucked her under the covers before looking out the front blinds.

"Should I take them out some leftovers?" Simon asked, coming back into the room.

"There's no one there to eat," I said, my words misting the glass.

"What?"

I turned to face him. "They're all gone."

"Maybe they didn't want to miss their turkey dinners."

He was joking, but there was something unsettling about the sudden absence of the protestors.

"It's kind of strange not having them out there."

"I could get used to it."

I didn't know whether I should hope that this might be the end, that maybe they would leave us alone now. I settled for temporary gratitude.

He set the wine on the coffee table and held his hands out toward me, a fortune cookie hidden in each. "Pick one," he said.

I touched the back of his right hand, and it opened.

I suppressed a laugh as I read. "God, they're getting predictable with these. 'Fortune favors the bold,'" I read.

"In bed," Simon added, observing our traditional fortune-cookie game.

"In bed," I echoed. "Fortune favors the bold in bed."

"So let's see what I've got." He broke the remaining cookie. "What the? 'The only time people prefer crunchy to smooth is in peanut butter.'"

"There's no sensible way to make that dirty."

"Actually, there's no way to make that sensible."

He tossed the slip of paper onto the table and crouched beside the tree. "Should we do the presents now? There's actually quite a bit under here."

"I saved the stuff from my family so we could open them together. Don't get your hopes up, though. I don't think anyone sent you anything."

"I would imagine." He sorted the presents into piles. "Did anything come here from my mom?"

I shook my head. "She called from Maui to wish us a merry Christmas, and to tell us that the gifts should be coming in the mail in the next few days."

"Good old mom."

"Yeah. I didn't hear from your dad."

"I did."

I was stunned. "What? When?"

"I called him."

I couldn't get over the thought of Simon calling his father, on Christmas no less. "And how was he?"

"The same. Unhappy. Alone." He sorted through the gifts. "It was good to talk to him, though."

His voice had dropped as he mentioned his father. I knew how hard it must have been for him to call.

"Shall we open Sherry's first?"

"Sure." I felt like I'd been opening presents for Sherry for weeks: letters from people too sick to visit the house, parcels from people who had read her story, gifts from people who had been to see her. Every day more packages came from people we had never met: stuffed animals and nighties, children's Bibles and baubles. Now I left the letters in a sack by the bed—I hadn't had time to open them—but I had donated the parcels to a gift drive sponsored by one of the radio stations. I didn't think anyone would mind making a different child happy.

Simon had brought her a CD of children's music by Fred Penner and a collection of picture books. Santa and I had brought her new pajamas and a book by Robert Munsch.

"You've got a lot of reading to do, hon," I said.

Simon rubbed my back.

"These are nice," he said, examining the slippers that my mother had sent me while I unwrapped the rest of the gifts from my family. "There's something oddly familiar about them, though."

"That's because they're exactly the same as the pair she gave me last year."

"And the year before that," he added. "Ad infinitum."

Simon and I kept our packages from each other until the end.

"A harmonica," he said, turning it over in his hands.

"I thought if you were doing the whole folksinger thing, you might as well go all the way."

"Thanks," he said. "This'll irritate the hell out of 314 and 318."

"So should I open these now?" I asked, looking at the pair of packages marked "from Simon."

He shrugged. "It's no big deal."

"Your wrapping's gotten better," I joked. When we were together, wrapping had always been one of my responsibilities.

"I had them wrapped at the store. More wine?"

I nodded and extended my glass to him. "Is there a special order these should be opened in?"

He shook his head. "Doesn't really matter. But I guess— open the big one first."

I picked up the package. "This feels suspiciously like a book."

"Just open it," he smiled. "No fair guessing."

I peeled the paper off carefully, revealing a beautiful, soft plum leather binding, tooled with a Celtic design. "It's gorgeous," I said, cradling it in my hands. It was a slipcover, with a plain sketchbook inside.

"I know how much you love notebooks, but you never use the fancy ones with the good paper. What are you doing, saving them for a rainy day?"

"They're too nice."

"Exactly. This way you can have a nice notebook that you can actually use."

"Thank you, Simon. I love it."

He shrugged, but I could see how pleased he was. "You've got one more," he pointed out.

I picked up the smaller package and opened it just as carefully, already suspecting its contents. Simon has always had a hard time resisting thematic gifts.

"It's German," Simon explained as I took the fountain pen from the gift box. "It's got a good weight, doesn't it?"

I nodded, making small circles in the air with the nib.

"Try it," Simon urged. "I had them fill it before they wrapped it up."

I looked around for a piece of paper, then sat back as Simon opened the notebook on the table in front of me. "Here," he said. "That's what it's for."

The pen laid down a beautiful wet green line. "That's gorgeous, Simon. The ink . . ."

"I've got the bottle in my jacket pocket."

"I don't know what to say."

"Just use it," he said. "The pen and the notebook. I want you to use them. Really use them."

"Thank you," I said, leaning in and kissing him quickly on the mouth before I realized what I was doing.

"You've given up so much, lost so much. I was so happy when you told me that you had started writing again. I don't want you to lose that." His eyes held mine until I nodded.

"Good," he said. "Merry Christmas, Karen."

He stood up.

"What are you doing?"

"I thought I'd clean up this mess," he said, plucking handfuls of paper from the floor. I turned the notebook over in my hands, feeling the leather warm to my touch.

"This *is* beautiful," I repeated as he crumpled the paper into the garbage next to Sherry's bed.

"I'm glad you like it," he said, arranging the teddy bear my brother Steve's family had sent into the crook of Sherry's arm, touching her cheek with the back of his hand.

"I'd like you to stay," I whispered. I wasn't sure if I had spoken loud enough for him to hear.

He straightened slightly.

I had wanted to say it for a while; the wine made the words a little easier.

He turned away from Sherry to face me.

"Tonight. I'd like you to stay tonight. With me. We can talk about tomorrow in the morning. But—"

He took two steps toward me.

"—I was alone last night. I don't want to be alone tonight."

For a moment he looked like he was about to launch into a speech. Then our eyes met, and he nodded.

"Fortune favors the bold," he said, picking up his glass.

LEO

I waited inside Mr. Perkins's van around the corner from the Barretts' house. It smelled like gas, but I liked it. It reminded me of what I was here to do.

I had Sherry's picture from the newspaper in my lap, and I held on to my rosary. I said the Hail Mary over and over again as I stared at the picture.

Hail Mary, full of grace.

I felt sorry for the people they had fooled. Thank God for Father Peter, who saw the truth that the sheep couldn't see. Someone brave enough to do something important. Something to save those too stupid to save themselves.

Blessed art thou among women.

I was so lucky I met him when I did, before I could have my head muddled and confused by meeting the Barretts. Before I had actually knelt by that child of the devil. I would have knelt.

And blessed is the fruit of thy womb, Jesus.

All my life I tried to do what is right. I go to Mass whenever I can. I go to confession. I say a blessing before every meal, and a prayer before I go to sleep. I take care of Mother now that she can't take care of herself.

But this. Tonight. Tonight I will be a lion of God, a warrior, bringing the battle home to those evil enough to try to destroy His children. Tricksters and crooks. Evil. Tonight I will be a lion for God.

Pray for us sinners now and at the hour of our death.

SIMON

In the past few weeks with my family, I had learned to savor the little things; to hold on to the moments of grace as they came. Like walking through the still house with Karen, turning off all the lights except for the Christmas tree in the living room, making sure all the doors and windows were locked.

Like the weight of my daughter in my arms as I carried her up the stairs, as I laid her down in her old bed, close to our room.

Like the warmth of my daughter's skin as I kissed her forehead and whispered, "Good night."

Like following my wife down the hallway, my body tingling.

Like the momentary pause as we both looked around the bedroom as if seeing it for the first time.

"Do you want to . . . ?" she gestured toward the bathroom.

I shook my head. "You go ahead."

"I won't take long." A moment later I heard the water in the sink, the rattling of the hook on the back of the door as she took down her robe. The sounds of our life together.

I let myself sink into the bedside chair and rubbed the heels of my hands into my eyes. It was late, but I didn't feel tired. In fact, I felt electric.

The toilet flushed and the door opened and Karen stepped out, her housecoat loosely belted. "I opened a new toothbrush for you. It's on the counter. It's blue."

I brushed my teeth and washed my face. When I opened the hamper to drop in my dirty shirt, I saw her panties at the top of the pile. They were warm, and soft to the touch.

LEO

No moon. No stars.

No sound.

The lights were off inside the house except for the blinking

Christmas tree. The other faithful had been told to leave. All was still.

Oh holy night.

The witching hour. That's what Mother called it: the witching hour. No good Christian had any business being out at this time of night.

What did she know? This was the holiest time of the night on the holiest night of the year, a time for all good Christians to stand up and be counted, if they were good enough, and true.

I leaned against the van for just a minute, feeling the lion of God inside me trying to get out. I had to remember to slow down, to do everything right, just the way Father Peter told me.

I opened the back door of the van as quietly as I could. I could barely breathe with the stink, but I knew what I had to do.

I zipped my coat up high around my mouth. That's better.

I picked up the gas can.

I didn't shut the van door. I didn't hide or skulk. I walked like a man through the gate, right up to the front door. The gas can was heavy, but not for me. Not for the lion.

The porch light wasn't on. There was no security light, nothing. It was just like Father Peter had said it would be. I felt a little scared as I walked up the ramp, but mostly I felt strong. I felt like I could do anything.

I splashed the door with gas from the can. I tried my best to stay dry, but some of it splashed on my coveralls and the stink filled my nose and made me feel like I might throw up. But I didn't stop. I splashed the walls with gas, up and down, all the way along the flowerbeds and around the corner down the side to the back of the house.

When the can was empty I threw it into the hedge. It didn't matter. It would all be over before anybody found it.

When I got back to the van I was shaking—I felt so good to be doing God's work! Just one more step.

He had tried to warn them. They knew that they were sinning, and that they would be punished. Father Peter had told them.

One more step.

First a prayer, then the fire.

SIMON

She was already in bed when I came out, the comforter pulled up around her neck, her housecoat draped over the chair. It took me several seconds to realize that she was lying on the wrong side. I had always slept on the side of the bed closest to the bathroom. I walked around to the far side of the bed and lifted the covers, sliding in alongside her.

The sheets were smooth, cool and familiar.

"This is kind of weird," she said, her voice low.

"Yeah." It was as if there was a bubble around us, a delicate, shimmering globe that the wrong word, the wrong action, the wrong thought, could destroy.

"It feels . . ."

"New," I finished, unsure of where the word had come from. She nodded. "Yeah. New."

"Like those nights in the dorm: covers up to our necks, Donna in bed just across the room—"

"Trying to be so quiet," she added.

"Not getting any sleep."

"I always wonder how we survived that year. Falling asleep in class—"

"When we went to class at all."

Her hand found my hip. Her fingertips were hot.

It was strange to cross the distance between us. As I reached out, Karen's eyes closed a little and her breathing sharpened.

We both kept our hands the same safe space, the nonpresumptive area of hip and abdomen, careful not to trespass where we were not yet certain we belonged. We hovered in a soft, trancelike state, neither of us quite prepared to take it further.

Then cautiously, I slid my hand until the base of my palm brushed gently against the cool side of her breast, bare and surprising.

Her eyes met mine.

I raised my eyebrows playfully.

And immediately regretted it.

Karen pulled away without physically moving, her jaw tensing.

"What is it?" I asked, lowering my hand again to the safer area near her hip.

"I'm not . . ." She shook her head against the pillow. "I'm too tired to make any sense. I'm sorry."

I didn't move, just waited for her to continue.

"I, I don't want . . . I don't know what I want. I just . . . Could you please just hold me? I'd like, I just want to feel you against me. Is that okay?"

I lifted my hand to her hair, smoothing it. "Of course it's okay," I said. "Of course it is."

She came into my embrace, the space between us disappearing, my arms around her, hers around me. We fit together perfectly, as we always had: she curving where I was rigid, soft where I was coarse. Our foreheads touched, the remaining space between us bridged by our breath.

"When you touch me like this," she said. I felt her words more than heard them. Smelled them in sweet mint.

"What?" I asked after she had been silent for a long time.

"It's the same way you touch Sherry. Smoothing her hair back."

"I'm sorry," I said, afraid that I had hurt her in some way.

"No, no, no. I like it. I like the way it makes me feel." She pulled herself even closer against me.

"How does it make you feel?" I asked.

"Safe," she said, and on that word, on that single syllable, her voice broke like the edge of a wave. Her back shuddered with sobs. I didn't try to stop her, to comfort her with whispered words. Instead, I stroked her back, the buttons of her spine. I cupped the round base of her skull in my hand, gently stroking her soft hair as she cried against me, her tears hot on my cheeks, salty in my mouth.

As she cried, I could feel growing there, as had once before, a presence between us: the tiny perfect form of Sherry nestled between her parents' bodies. Our bodies were shaped by her absence, by the almost unbearable weight of her loss.

LEO

Father Peter had filled the glass bottle at the church. When he pushed in the rag his lips were moving. I thought he was praying, but I couldn't hear the words.

When he handed me the bottle, he had asked, "Are you sure that you can bear this burden?"

I hefted the bottle in my hand. I remembered how it felt when God had guided my hand when I threw the bottle at Mr. Barrett. I imagined the flames, and the lion inside me roared. "Yes, I'm sure."

"I knew you would be," he said. "This is for you. Use it well."

I felt for the lighter in my pocket as I stepped onto the Barretts' front lawn.

My breath made a fog and my fingers hurt from the cold. It didn't matter. In a minute I would be warmed and cleansed by God's fire.

I struck the lighter and touched it to the rag. It burst into blue flame with a loud pop that scared me a little.

It was hot on my face as I closed my eyes, as I prayed for God to guide my hand.

I drew back my arm. "Hail Mary," I whispered, letting the bottle fly.

The flames were blue in the night sky.

Something moved in the corner of my eye.

The bottle tumbled once in the air.

The man came out of the shadows and threw himself in the direction of the bottle, reaching out, like he thought he might catch it. But the glass smacked against his shoulder, spraying burning gas all over him.

His arm and chest burst into flames, and around his feet the grass burned where the gas had spilled. He kicked the bottle away and he screamed and fell on the ground.

He rolled and rolled, trying to put out the fire, but the flames didn't go out, and he screamed again and again.

I knew why the flames weren't going out. I knew who he was, how much he loved the flames.

I threw myself at the devil, swinging my fists. The heat of his flames tried to drive me away, but I didn't give up. I kept hitting and hitting.

"Stop it," the devil screamed, rolling away from me, pulling at his burning coat. "Stop it!"

Flames were eating at part of his face, but I knew him. His long hair, his beard, his eyes. He was the one from the meeting, the devil who wouldn't bow his head to pray.

"Devil," I shouted, throwing myself at him again.

KAREN

"Simon? Do you hear that?"

He was already rolling out from under the covers and crossing to the window. There was a hint of light as he drew back the curtain. I pulled the sheet with me to cover myself as I leaned toward the glass.

At first, I didn't know what I was seeing. There was a fire— no, someone was on fire! And someone—was that Father Peter's bodyguard?—was punching him, kicking him, as he tried to roll away, as he writhed in the flames—

The scene vanished as the room filled with light. Simon was by the door, pulling on his pants.

I dropped the sheet and pulled open a drawer for something to wear. "Was that Father Peter's—?"

"I think so." He tugged a T-shirt over his head, and he started through the door. "It looks like he's trying to kill someone."

"What should we—?"

"Call the police."

I grabbed the cordless phone and followed him, looking into Sherry's room before racing down the stairs.

HENRY

So much pain, all at once. I couldn't—

I kept rolling on the ground, trying to smother the flames. I could smell burning meat, and I knew it was me. My face, my arm. If I could just get Tim's coat off.

Then there was a blow and a cracking in my chest and I couldn't breathe. Another burst of pain. Another kick.

"Stop it!" I cried out. Every word pulled at the burned skin on my face.

I opened one eye, and closed it again as I rolled away. If I could just—

My right hand didn't work anymore. When I tried to move my fingers, the pain was crippling.

Fumbling with the zipper with my left, I shrugged the coat off that shoulder. I shrugged again, but it was stuck.

I opened my eye again.

The fabric of the coat had melted and clung to my skin like glue. If I pulled it off, it would take the skin right off my arm with it.

I couldn't leave it.

Bracing myself, I started to pull.

"Go back to hell, you devil!" More blows rained down on me. I heard a crunch and saw a bright light and I was suddenly choking on blood. My nose . . .

He was still coming at me, arms flailing.

I stumbled away and pulled off the coat, peeling the burnt skin from my arm. My scream stopped the big man in his path.

I couldn't breathe, and my eye clouded over with the pain. My entire arm was an open wound, so tender that the movement of air across it felt like fresh flames.

Then he punched me again, and again, wherever he could reach. I reeled and stumbled and fell.

"Go back to hell!" he shouted, drawing back to kick me again.

The pain was too much to bear.

And then there was a sudden brilliance. He looked behind him at the house. The porch light! The porch light was on.

He ran toward his van. It took me a moment to get my bearings. Grass. Concrete. I was at the edge of the driveway. And right there—

As the van door opened and closed, I pulled myself across the driveway and into the shadow of the hedge.

Then I surrendered to the dark.

KAREN

Simon's adrenaline carried him out the front door and partway down the ramp before he stopped, clutching the flashlight like a club. I was only a few steps behind.

"There's no one here," I said. I hung up before the phone connected.

"Look." Down the street, taillights shone in the dark, and a cloud of steam rose from the exhaust as the van pulled away.

For a moment I thought Simon might run after the moving vehicle. Instead, he walked to the base of the ramp and looked around the yard.

"What the hell?" he muttered.

I was closer to the house and smelled it first. "Do you smell that?"

He lifted his head. "What?"

The reek burned my nose. "Oh, God," he muttered. Crouching, he touched the door just under the knob.

The lower half of the door was wet. Simon touched a finger to the wetness and brought it to his nose. "It's gas."

"On our door?"

"Check on Sherry," he said, turning on the flashlight and starting down the ramp again. "Lock the door."

My head was swimming as I checked our girl again. I couldn't tell if it was the fumes or the danger we were in. They had soaked our door with gasoline. What were they trying to do?

Simon looked flushed and scared when he came in. "There's gasoline all over the house. And I found these on the lawn where they were fighting." He had an empty soda bottle in one hand, and a winter coat, partially burnt, in the other.

"Is that—?"

He nodded, a sheen of sweat breaking out on his face. "Yeah. A bottle bomb." He hefted the bottle in his hand.

"Father Peter."

He nodded slowly. "It looks like they planned to burn down the house, but—"

"But somebody stopped them. Whoever he was fighting with."

Simon nodded. "It looks like he's pretty badly hurt," he said, turning the coat over in his hands. Half of it had melted into a gnarled clump of plastic.

"Is he still out there?"

Simon shook his head. "I couldn't find him."

The thought was numbing. Someone had tried to burn down our house. Someone had tried to kill us all. This wasn't a warning.

"Should I call the police?" I asked. I still had the phone in my hand.

"I don't—" He bit his lip and shook his head, trying to figure out what to do.

"No," I said, setting the phone down. "Probably not. So what are we going to do?"

"The gas—we could hose it off," he ventured.

"Will that be enough?"

He shrugged. "It's a start."

"Let's try it."

He shook his head. "I'll do it," he said. "I'd feel better if one of us stayed inside with Sherry."

"That makes sense. Just be careful."

It took him the better part of an hour to wash down the walls using the garden hose. I spent the time upstairs in Sherry's room, curled up in the chair beside her bed.

When would we ever feel safe again? How could someone do this? The answers just weren't coming. How could someone who professed their faith, their love for God, as loudly as Father Peter even consider something like this?

I thought of the God I remembered from when I was a little girl, and I couldn't force the ideas into anything that resembled sense.

"That'll do for a start," Simon said from the doorway. He had taken off his shoes and coat. He was chilled and damp and out of breath.

"Do you think anything we do will be enough?"

LEO

I don't know how Father Peter knew, but he took one look at me and said, "You failed."

Walk like a man.

I nodded, and bowed my head. I didn't want to see his face when he got mad at me.

"What happened?" he asked.

I looked up at him. He didn't look angry. He looked like he might start to cry.

"I did everything just right. Everything just like you told me. I poured the gas—"

"I'm sure you did well, Leo. But what happened?"

"There was . . . I saw him at the meeting. He was at the back, and he didn't pray. And he was there. He stopped the bottle, and I knew . . . He was a devil, Father. He was a devil and I fought him and I would have, I would have killed him, but the lights went on and—"

"The lights went on?"

I nodded. "In the yard."

"Did they see you?"

Did they . . . Didn't he care about the devil? "I don't think so."

He shook his head and turned away. "Thank you, Leo," he said. "You did very well."

"I can go back," I said. "I can go back and try again." I knew I could do it.

"It's too late," he said. "It's over."

"It's not over," I said, pulling at his coat. "I can go back. I can do it."

"It's too late," he said again. "They've seen you. They know what we tried to do. Tim knows. They'll be ready. Someone will be waiting. It's over."

I didn't understand. What did the fat man have to do with any of this? Was he a devil too? And how could Father Peter just say it was over? There was so much left to do. "What about the sinners? What about saving the people from that girl, from that demon? What about the devil?"

"It's over, Leo."

"It's not over," I shouted. "The righteous fight, and they fight until they drop. That's what you said. I can do it. I know I can do it."

He looked at me for a long time. He shook his head. "It's time to go home, Leo."

Then he turned and walked away down the alley.

"It's not over," I yelled. "I'll do it. I'll show you."

He didn't look back.

"You can't just walk away. You can't leave me. I'm sorry. I'm sorry. I'll do better next time. I will. Just don't . . ."

He turned at the end of the alley.

I could do it. I'd show him. I was the Lion. I could do anything.

SIMON

I kissed Karen on the forehead and watched as she climbed the stairs.

Double-checking that I had a key in my pocket and the flashlight, I locked the front door behind me.

It was cold outside, and I was grateful for the old ski jacket Karen had found for me. The porch light cast a pool of security across what had once been the front lawn. The feet of hundreds of pilgrims had left it a bare, dirty patch, gleaming with frost in the dim light. I could see my breath, and I pushed my hands deeply into my jacket pockets.

It was only one night, a few hours really. In the morning we would call a security company, hire someone to watch the house. We should have done it weeks ago.

I took a slow walk around the place. I paid careful attention to the basement windows, playing the light over the glass and along the frames to ensure they hadn't been opened. The smell of gas was still strong, but not overwhelming. We could all be dead now, the house in flames. I couldn't bear to think about it.

On the porch, I sat with my back to the door, keeping a keen eye on the yard and the sidewalk and street beyond. It was perfectly still, perfectly silent.

Silent night. Appropriate.

I sat there till dawn, protecting my family. I thought about Sherry, snugged tight in her own bed. I thought about my wife. I watched my breath rise into the cloudless sky. Every fifteen minutes or so I walked around the house, checking.

I'd never been so happy to see the sun rise. I lingered on the front porch in the warm glow, watching as the light crept across the yard.

And then I heard footsteps on the sidewalk, the determined click of hard heels.

The sun was bright over the horizon, and I was looking right into it, not seeing anything. I heard the rattle of the gate, and the footsteps coming closer.

All I could see was a shadow against the light, the dark of a long coat. I stepped forward, tightening my grip around the flashlight.

"Mr. Barrett?" The voice startled me. "It's Father Peter."

EIGHT

Saint Stephen's Day

I must have passed out in the bushes. The next thing I knew, it was morning, and the curtains were open inside the Barrett house.

When I sat up, every part of me screamed with pain. The ground seemed to swim around me. My arm was raw and oozing and I couldn't see out of one eye. That side of my face was numb. I didn't want to think of how bad the burns must be for me not to feel them at all.

I could feel where he had hit me, though. My nose was broken, and I'd lost a tooth. I could taste my own blood and I wanted to find somewhere warm, somewhere to rest.

I pulled myself to my feet. I needed to get back to the library. I needed Tim to look at my wounds.

I stumbled toward downtown, stopping every so often to rest. It hurt to lift my head, and I watched the sidewalk as I lurched from side to side.

I wasn't paying attention, and somehow I lost my way. I found myself surrounded by noise and crowds, people rushing along the sidewalks with shopping bags held tight to them. I couldn't bear the press and push, the noise, the smell.

I collapsed in a bus shelter on Douglas.

At first, he was just another face in the crowd, another child being dragged along by an adult. From the scowl I could tell he was being propelled against his will. He had a shock of blond hair, clothes a little too big, as if inherited from an older brother, a turned-up nose, green eyes.

Green eyes.

Something about those eyes drew me back to him. Something I should have been able to remember, but couldn't.

As he passed the bus shelter, it came to me.

He had his mother's eyes.

"Connor!" I called out, stepping into the sidewalk. The tide of the crowd pulled him away, pulled the three of them away. "Connor!"

Three of them. A mother, two children.

"Dylan!" I stumbled down the sidewalk after them.

I caught glimpses: Connor's hair, the side of Arlene's face, Dylan pulling on the door as they went into the Eaton Centre. But I couldn't catch up. By the time I got inside the mall, they had disappeared. I ran to the railing, but I couldn't see them either below me or above.

"Connor!" I called out. "Dylan!"

No one turned. No one heard.

A flood of memories tore me apart. A life so like a dream returned to me with the force of a blow.

Arlene.

Dylan.

Connor.

All here. Now.

I rode the escalators up and down. I hobbled from one end of the mall to the other, looking into stores. I checked the bathrooms upstairs and down. I ran onto Government Street, looking for Arlene's familiar ponytail in the sea of shoppers.

They were gone. But I knew where I could find them.

Home.

I remembered.

I remembered everything.

How could I have forgotten?

KAREN

"Are you sure?" I asked, still groggy from the sudden waking.

Simon nodded. There were dark half-moons under his eyes. "He introduced himself."

"He just came up to the door?"

He was pacing at the end of the bed and he nodded again. "Scared the hell out of me."

"You were outside? Still?"

"Yes."

"What did he say?"

"Nothing." He shook his head. "Just that he needed to talk to us."

"Where is he now?" I asked.

"He's still on the front porch. I told him I was coming to get you."

I threw the blankets off, a little stunned by the news, and went to the closet.

"What should we do?" Simon asked, not looking away as I dressed.

I pulled on a sweater. "I think we should hear what he has to say."

"Are we going to invite him in, or . . ."

"We've let everyone else in," I said as we went downstairs.

When I opened the front door, I relaxed immediately. This man was as far from the threatening specter who had tried to kill my daughter as you could imagine. His face was ruddy on top of his white collar, his hand firm in mine, and he smiled as he spoke. "Mrs. Barrett? I'm Father Peter. Father Peter Shaughnessy. I was contacted by the diocese." He smelled a bit of aftershave, and his voice had a hint of an accent, and the warmth of someone who spent his life talking to people.

"Are you all right?" he asked as we shook hands, meeting my eyes.

I glanced at Simon. "I guess we were expecting someone else."

He smiled reassuringly. "No, it's just me," he said. "I'm sorry I couldn't come sooner."

HENRY

When I got to the library, I found Tim sitting cross-legged on the counter of the ladies' room, his head bowed over the large book open on his lap.

"Tim," I said quietly, not recognizing my own voice. The door closed behind me with a soft thud. I recognized the book as a Bible. His finger was tracing along the inner column as he read.

"Henry," he said, looking up at me. "Good Christ, you look awful."

I didn't even try to smile.

He straightened his legs and slid off the counter. "Let me look at you," he said, leaning toward my face. "What happened?"

I stepped away from him. "That doesn't matter," I said. "I need to talk to you."

"Clearly," he said, stepping toward me again, staring at the burns on my face. "What happened to you?"

"Last night, at the Barretts'."

"Father Peter did this? But how?" He seemed uncertain for the first time since we had met.

"No, not him. His bodyguard. He tried to burn down the house."

"And you got burned?" He was acting as if he didn't believe what he was seeing.

"Yes, but that's not—I need to ask you about my family."

"You don't have a family," he said. "None of us do."

"No, I do," I protested. "I just saw them. My sons. Arlene. I just saw them."

He backed up a little and looked even more confused. "You're remembering?"

"I remember it all. Arlene, the boys, the job. My parents. Everything."

"But that's—did they see you?" he asked.

Hesitating just a moment, I shook my head. "No," I said.

He seemed comforted by the word. "No. Of course they didn't."

"But it was crowded and . . ."

He shook his head. "I'm sorry, Henry," he said. "I know it's hard. It's probably the hardest thing to get used to. I wish I could tell you how to make it better."

"Why did I remember them? Why now?"

He shook his head. "I don't know." He looked intently at my burned face. "But you should try to forget them. Again. Deliberately. Forget that whole life."

"But I don't want to forget them. I want to see them."

He shook his head. "You can't. There's no going back."

"Why not? What if this is what I was supposed to do? You're always talking about amends. Maybe I was supposed to help save Sherry and her family, and that's why I can remember my life. I saved them. Last night. Maybe I've been given my life back. As a reward . . ."

"Then why couldn't they see you?"

"I don't . . ."

"Even if they could see you, what would you say? Where do you say you've been? How do you explain what's happened to you? All of this." He gestured at my face, my arm. "And even if you can make your wife hear you, what happens then? You're not really alive anymore. You don't eat. You don't sleep. You don't die."

"I'm not feeling too immortal right now."

He went on as if he hadn't heard me. "Are you ready to watch your wife grow old before your eyes? To watch your children crippled by time? What will you say when your grandchildren die, and you haven't aged?"

"But maybe they . . . I don't know. It doesn't matter. She'll understand."

"Henry, it's not a good idea."

"I'm sorry, Tim," I said. "They're my family. They're my life."

"They *were* your life," he corrected me. "Not anymore."

His eyes fixed on me a moment, then he slowly raised his hands, palms upward and open, gently shaking his head. "I don't understand everything, Henry. I don't know what's happening to you. But this isn't your path, and I think you know that. Still, I'm not going to stand in your way."

"I'll make it work. I'll get my old life back. You'll see."

He shook his head. "I'm sorry, Henry," he said, as I turned away.

KAREN

I'm sure I flinched when the real Father Peter first touched Sherry, tracing his fingers over her forehead, down the softness of her cheeks. It was a reflex, really, nothing to do with the man himself. The air of calm that surrounded him had quickly put my fears to rest.

"Is she always so warm?"

Simon, Ruth and I were watching him closely. He had wanted us to tell him our story before he saw Sherry, and Ruth had arrived while we were having coffee in the kitchen. She said she knew we hadn't planned on opening the house on Boxing Day, but had come just to check on things.

"She feels warm to the touch, but it's not fever," Ruth said, reaching for her chart. "Her temperature is normal, consistently."

Father Peter glanced at her. "Don't you find that unusual? Wouldn't you expect her metabolic rate to be slower? Anything I've read about comatose states—"

Ruth nodded. "We thought the same. And yet her pulse rate, blood pressure, temperature, blood glucose, they're all normal. We've never had any problem with bedsores or secondary infection."

"What do you suppose that means?"

Ruth looked like she was about to answer, then stopped herself, shaking her head. "I don't know."

Father Peter regarded her for a moment. "I don't either." He turned back to Sherry. "She's a very pretty little girl."

As he shifted around to the head of the bed, he stumbled over the sack of mail. He crouched to take a look.

"We've received lots of letters for Sherry. Asking, asking her to . . . you know," I said.

"All of these are petitions?"

I nodded.

"There must be hundreds here." He tucked his handful back into the top of the sack.

"A lot of people saw her on the news. Or read about her."

"What are you doing with them?"

"Nothing. We haven't had the time to think about how to handle them."

"It is a bit much to deal with, isn't it?" He smiled at me. "When you get time, you could try reading them to her."

He glanced at Ruth. "You may as well try."

She nodded back.

He leaned in close enough to kiss Sherry's forehead, but turned his head instead to smell her skin, a long sniff.

"What sort of soap do you use?"

"Just water. We didn't want to use anything too strong."

I trailed off when I saw him nodding, his head still inclined over Sherry. "Of course not, of course not. You wouldn't want anything very strong at all. Tell me," he asked, straightening up. "Have you noticed any strange smells around her?"

"Smells?" I repeated, "I don't think so. Why do you—?"

"Lilies," Ruth said.

I turned to look at her.

"Yes, yes," the priest said. "I had thought lavender, but I think you're right. Lilies. Have you noticed it often?"

"All the time. I just thought it was the way she smelled."

"Of course," the priest said. "And after a while you'd get used to it. Not notice it. Did you know, though, that in the folklore"—he used the word as if it were the best of several bad choices—"saints are often recognized by how they smell?" He was watching me intently. "Sandalwood. Jasmine. Various flowers. And this was when people didn't consider bathing, or did it only occasionally."

It was as if a shadow had passed over the room, discouraging speech.

"Lilies are for purity," Ruth said softly behind me. "For peace."

LEO

I went right to the library as soon as Mother was up and had had her breakfast. I couldn't go in. The doors were locked, and a sign said that it was closed for the holiday. I was glad that I wore my winter coat. It was going to be cold waiting for the devil to arrive.

This was where Father Peter said the fat man Tim was staying. I didn't know if he was a devil, or if the devil was working with him, but I thought that the fat man would know where to find him. He would tell me, or I would destroy him. I would destroy all of them.

First the devils.

And then the Barretts.

I practiced flicking the lighter a few times, and I thought of the whole building full of paper. How it would burn. I would destroy him. I would send him straight back to hell.

I'd wait however long it took.

KAREN

Father Peter straightened up and turned toward us, brushing his palms along his jacket. "You're not used to hearing your daughter referred to as a saint, are you? Surely someone has suggested—"

Simon interrupted him. "We deliberately don't use that word," he said. "I think the first time that word was used in this house was by someone with the same name as you, just before he tried to ruin all of our lives."

"Somebody threatened you? Is that what you meant when you said you were expecting someone else?"

I took Simon's hand. Neither of us spoke.

"Was he a tall man?" Father Peter asked, in a voice both excited and startled. "Very thin? Almost cadaverlike? Pale and—"

"You know him?"

"I know *of* him. Our paths have crossed. We may have met once, I'm not sure."

"He implied to us that he was close to the diocese. That he represented them in some not-quite-official capacity," Simon said.

Father Peter shook his head. "No. No, that's not true at all. This man, if he's the one I believe him to be, is in no way affiliated with the Church."

"Then who is he?" I asked. "Who is he working for?"

"The short answers are all 'I don't know.'" The disappointment must have registered in my face, because he hurried to continue. "I *do* know that a man—you'll have to forgive me for this, because it sounds like those man-in-black stories one hears about UFO sightings. There have been reports, over the years, of a man matching this Father Peter's description often interfering with a . . . a possible saint."

"Interfering how?" I asked.

"Usually he tries to discredit the subject in the community and in the church. He keeps his distance, using the press and the police and more fervent locals to apply pressure."

I glanced at Simon, who shook his head grimly.

"I was involved in a case several years ago . . . This was in the U.S. A small town in Oregon. A young woman seemed to have the gift of healing, through the laying on of hands." He looked down at Sherry's still body, then shook his head as he turned back to me. "By the time I got there, she was dead."

"Father Peter killed her?" Simon asked.

He shook his head. "No, it's not that simple. She killed herself. The local newspaper had begun running stories. Well, she was nineteen, she had had a number of lovers, both male and female, several of whom spoke to the press. Her parents hadn't been aware." He shrugged his shoulders. "I was too late. I got into town just before the funeral. I didn't really have any need to contact the family at that point, but their priest introduced us after the funeral. It was the girl's sister who mentioned that I was the second Father Peter they had met."

"So his name really is Father Peter," Simon concluded.

He shook his head. "No, I don't think so. Usually, he's referred to simply as the Stranger. I think he just used 'Father Peter' because he knew that I would be coming, and he wanted to create confusion and tension. Like he did here."

"How would he know that?" I asked.

"Because I'm the one who gets sent, in North America at least. When we get reports of occurrences like this, I'm asked to look into it. My counterpart in Europe is named Joseph. I don't think it's any coincidence that when reports come back from Europe about the Stranger, he's usually calling himself Father Joseph."

"But who is he?" Simon asked.

Father Peter frowned. "We don't know," he confessed. "I wish we did. There are some who believe—" He stopped cold on the word as he rethought what he had been about to say. "It seems that there are reports of contacts with this man, or another who bears quite a striking resemblance to him, going back several hundred years."

LEO

It was cold work waiting on the devil.

I never thought Father Peter would be the one to come.

He came out of the dark looking just like a shadow, wrapped up in his long black coat. He walked across the square so fast it looked like he wasn't even going to stop at the door.

I hid behind the big plant, holding tightly to the lighter, and watched him as he pushed on the doors.

What was he doing here? Was he going to fight the devil and his friends himself?

Why wouldn't he have wanted me here with him?

The locked doors opened without a sound. No alarms went off. No watchmen came running.

I wanted to run after him, to tell him that I was there to help him in his fight against the devils.

I followed him into the library. Quiet as a church mouse.

RUTH

I tucked the covers gently around Sherry's neck. "You've had a big day, haven't you? We'll let you get some rest." I kissed her on the forehead. I was glad that Karen had asked me to stay while she and Simon talked with Father Peter. Changing Sherry and taking her vitals took me no time at all, and it gave me a chance to be with her.

I had missed this, our time alone together.

There was something comforting in just sitting with her, listening to the soft regularity of her breath.

I inhaled deeply—the lilies and the milky, sleepy smell of a baby—as I sat down in the chair at the head of her bed, marveling at how quickly I had become accustomed to living without pain. Bless you, child. I smiled at the thought—how strange it was to ask for a blessing for her when it was I who had been blessed by being near her.

A low murmur of voices came from the family room. Family. It was good to see the two of them together, to see Simon at home.

As I leaned back and closed my eyes, my fingers trailed over the sack of mail, knocking a few letters to the floor. Opening my eyes as I bent to retrieve them, I happened to glance up at Sherry. I don't think it was my imagination or a trick of the light: from that perspective it seemed like there was a nimbus, a golden glow, surrounding her, touching her with a divine light.

"Foolish old woman," I scolded myself, out loud, but I couldn't look away from her. Closing my fingers around an envelope, I gently rose. As quickly as it had appeared, the glow disappeared, leaving only a small child asleep, a lamp burning beside her.

My hands were shaking when I opened the envelope. I couldn't get that glow and the serene expression on her face out of my mind. I wanted to share the experience of it with as many people as I could.

The envelope fell to the floor as I unfolded the letter. The paper looked like it had been torn from a school notebook, and the printing was rough and uneven.

"Dear Sherry," I began to read, both my voice and my hands shaking. "My name is John. I am eleven years old. I am writing because the doctors told my mom and dad that I only have six months to live . . ."

HENRY

Limping home was like going back in time. I fell into the old patterns without even thinking about it: the shortcuts across side streets and schoolyards, walking up the narrow roads between Blanshard and Quadra to avoid the worst of the hills. I had to stop several times each block to let the dizziness pass.

Our apartment was in the second building from the corner, one of the first-floor, sub-ground specials that rented cheap. Fully furnished in vinyl and sprung mattresses, it was all we could afford and still have money to eat. Arlene couldn't work and look after the boys too, so we got by on what I made at the gas station. When you're a parent, you do what you have to do.

From the sidewalk, I could see that the white curtains were closed, backlit from within.

I couldn't help smiling, even as my open eye filled with tears.

It was fate. I had been put in that bus shelter this morning to see them, to be reminded, to be given my life back again. To have whatever spell had been cast over me broken.

It was the only explanation I could think of: I had been rewarded for helping the Barretts. I had made my amends, suffered my punishment, and the family in the brightly lit apartment—my family—was my reward.

I punched the intercom button for 108 with my left hand, keeping my injured hand buried in the front pocket of the hoodie that I had borrowed from the lost and found.

A moment later the speaker crackled to life. "Who's there?" came a young boy's voice.

I pushed the talk button. "It's me, Dylan. It's your daddy. Let me in." My voice sounded strange, thick and lispy.

"Hello? Hello? Who's there, please?"

"Dylan, it's me, hon. It's your dad. Press the button." I could feel a cold trickle of fear tracing its way down my spine.

"Who's there, baby?" Arlene's disembodied voice sounded tinny and distant.

"It rang, Mommy. It rang, but nobody said anything," he explained, his voice growing fainter as she lifted the receiver away. "Nobody said—"

There was a harsh click as the receiver was set back into the base on the wall.

I stared blankly at the panel, the cold trickle threatening to become a flood.

I started punching the black buttons on the intercom panel at random, just punching them, ignoring the inquisitive voices from the speaker, waiting, waiting—

There! As the buzzer sounded, pushed by someone too lazy or trusting to bother checking, I grabbed the door handle and let myself in.

"What will you say?" Tim had asked. "How will you explain?"

I had thought about that the entire walk. I would tell Arlene the truth. I would tell her about the accident, about running away afterward. I would tell her about the state of shock I had been in, the confusion, the amnesia.

I would tell her about the library, and the men who lived there who had taken me in, who had kept me safe. I would tell her about Tim, about the books I had been reading, about finally seeing her and the boys downtown and how they had brought me home at last.

I could hear the sound of the television, the boys playing behind our door. I knocked.

Dylan called out, "Mom, there's someone at the door!"

"She knows, stupid," Connor said, and I could picture him giving his little brother a shove.

"Don't call your brother that." Arlene's footsteps came toward the door. "And stop pushing him."

The chain rattled and the door cracked open. Arlene's green eye looked out into the corridor.

I forced a smile, feeling the tight pull of the burned skin, trying to ignore the racing of my heart. "Hi," I said. "It's me." I steeled myself for her response.

The door opened a little more. Arlene looked directly at me, but there was no shock, or surprise, or recognition. There was no trace of anything at all.

Despite the sick feeling in my belly, I tried again. "It's me. I'm home."

She stepped out into the corridor, almost brushing against me. She was beautiful, her dark hair pulled back into a high

ponytail, her skin clear, eyes puzzled. She was wearing a blue
T-shirt and gray jogging pants, what she always wore around
the house, but cleaner, less ragged than usual. She had lost
weight—she looked like a runner again, like she did in high
school. She looked like someone you wanted to spend your
whole life with.

I could smell her soap and the light perfume of her skin, and
feel the warmth emanating from her body. "Arlene," I called,
even though she was right there. Her brows knit in confusion.

"It's me," I said, my voice cracking. "Arlene!"

I waved my left arm in front of her face, lurched directly
into her field of vision. She stepped back, as if she could sense
my presence, then, shaking her head, turned back into the
apartment.

"Who was it, Mommy?" I heard Dylan ask. I could see him
inside the door, huddled against the wall. Connor was standing next to him, craning his neck to see but obeying the rule to
stay inside the apartment until Mommy or Daddy said it was
okay. Where Connor looked like his mother, Dylan looked like
me: the brown eyes, the small nose, the brown hair you had to
fight to get to lie flat. "Dylan," I cried, stumbling forward.

"No one, hon," Arlene answered him, closing her hand
around the doorknob. "Some joker playing a prank."

"A joker," he giggled as the door started to swing shut.

"Dylan," I called again. The door closed in my face.

I sagged against it, pressing my burnt face against the cool
of the paint. "Dylan," I whispered. "Arlene." Tears streamed
hot down my face, and I couldn't control my trembling. I was
cold. So cold.

So maybe that was it. Maybe the last eight months had just
been a dream, and I was actually dead, floating through limbo.
Maybe everyone in the library, everyone I had met, had been a
spirit. Maybe I had died on that cliff, or on the rocks below,
and I had been wandering ever since, seeking . . . what? What
do ghosts seek? Revenge? Redemption? Forgiveness?

I wanted to pound on the door. I wanted to be heard. I wanted to will myself to be seen. I wanted to explain to Arlene what had happened.

But when I raised my hand to knock, I couldn't. I couldn't bring myself to see her again, knowing that I would never be able to make her see me. I couldn't bear the idea of seeing her again without being able to touch her, of seeing the boys without being able to hold them.

What was I going to do? Was I just going to wander aimlessly, waiting for some mysterious salvation, for something to break my curse? Was that my destiny? To live in limbo for generations, haunted by that little girl, some modern-day Wandering Jew?

And then I knew what Tim didn't know. He had been trying to teach me, all these months, about my future. About *his* past and what he thought was *my* destiny.

For him, whose past had been spent waiting, the future would hold more of the same.

But not for me. The truth had been right in front of me the whole time, but I hadn't seen it. Until now.

I wasn't doomed to live forever, wandering the earth, waiting to make my amends. That was Tim's destiny.

I had made my amends.

I didn't have to wait an eternity to beg forgiveness. My forgiveness was right here.

KAREN

After midnight. The house was silent, save for the coughing and knocking of the heat pipes as they cooled, and the choking noises Simon and I made as we tried to stifle our laughter.

"This is a first," he whispered. "With a priest in the room next door."

"It's what every good Catholic girl dreams of," I answered, burying my laughter in the pillow.

It felt good to laugh with him. To be naked and smiling and sweating and happy. To be together.

"Shh."

"He's asleep," he whispered.

"How can you be so sure?"

"He would have pounded on the wall if he wasn't."

That set us both off again, and I had to bury my face in the pillow. Simon rubbed my back and tangled his fingers in my hair.

"I love you," he whispered.

I turned onto my side to face him. "I love you too." I brushed my fingertips along his face.

"Do you ever . . ." He stopped himself cold.

"What?"

"I don't . . . this probably isn't the time."

"You might as well say it now—it's out there."

"I was just . . . Do you ever think about having another baby?"

His words knocked the wind out of me. I struggled to catch my breath.

"I wasn't even going to bring it up. I've just been thinking about it. I know, it's insane. After everything we went through the first time, and everything that's happening with Sherry." He shook his head as if he didn't agree with what he was saying. "I just . . ."

"I used to think about it," I confessed. "I haven't recently. Not with everything that's happened. That's still happening."

"I know."

"I wouldn't want to try to replace Sherry."

"I don't think that's what it would be," he said. "I wouldn't want to do that either. But this . . . I want to have a baby. I know that it sounds crazy, and I know that we've got a lot to work out between us, but it just feels right to me. I say the words out loud and they sound right."

"Don't you remember the last time, though?" I asked. "All the tests, all the trying. I don't know if I could go through that again. Not with everything else." I thought of Sherry, sleeping downstairs for the first night since the attack on the house.

He shook his head, his eyes soft. "I know. I'm not saying that I'm even really considering it. I'd like us to . . . I just feel open to it, to the possibility."

The possibility.

LEO

Father Peter floated like a shadow into the library, but the fat man Tim blocked his path. He stopped, and the two of them just stared at each other.

I hid behind a set of shelves where I could see both of them. I wanted to be close. I wanted to be there if Father Peter needed me.

I tightened my grip on the lighter.

I wanted to be close enough to see what he would do to these devils. The thought made me smile, made me feel warm after the cold wait.

The two men were still looking at each other.

I waited for Father Peter to strike out, to bring the devil down.

Instead, the fat man smiled, and Father Peter bowed his head.

"Gloating?" Father Peter asked him.

The fat man shook his head. "Just waiting."

"I'd be gloating."

"You usually do. But I'm not you. And there have been far too many innocent people hurt for me to take any delight in how things have turned out."

"It's been a long time since you've won. I suppose you were due."

Tim shook his head. "I don't view this as a game. Besides, it had very little to do with me. Henry's a very bright boy. Thinks for himself. And the family was strong. Stronger than I expected."

"Much stronger. And it's done now. *He's* arrived, bringing the bright light and protective arms of the Church. He's at the house right now. If I had had one more night . . ."

"They would have been ready for you."

"I suppose they would. Still—"

"I've long wondered," Tim said, pointing at the coin in Father Peter's hand. "Is that one of them?"

Father Peter nodded, looking at the coin. "I spent a lifetime trying to find this," he said. "Do you have any idea how hard that was? Searching an empire for a single piece of silver?"

"How do you know you found the right one?"

"Well, there were a number of them." Father Peter smiled, showing his teeth. "But I could tell, right away. It burns. From the first moment I picked it up, it has burned me. But I can't put it down."

Tim looked in my direction, then away. Had he seen me? I crouched lower behind the bookshelves, but it was like he knew I was there, listening.

After a second, Father Peter said, "You can't keep up this fight forever."

"And you can?" Tim smiled. "How many times have we two met? How many alleys? Hillsides? Libraries? Sewers? A wise man once said that the best definition of insanity was performing the same action over and over again, expecting different results."

Father Peter stopped smiling. "The same could be said of you. What makes you so sure you're right? And so sure I'm wrong?"

"The difference is that I made a mistake once, out of ignorance," Tim said. "Everything I've done since then has been to try to make amends."

"To earn forgiveness."

"To protect the innocents." Tim smiled. "And yes, to earn forgiveness."

"Some of us have a higher calling," Father Peter said. I had heard him say those words dozens of times. "There are things more important than oneself."

"But that's your failing," Tim said. "You made a mistake a long time ago, and you think you've spent that time trying to make amends, but you just keep making the same mistake again and again."

"It's not a mistake. It's you who doesn't see. Who doesn't understand. I made a mistake, yes. I failed Him. But I have been given the chance to make amends."

"By killing children?"

"By keeping the way clear for His return. By dealing with those pretenders and false prophets who draw people away from the true savior. I stand by my judgment."

"You always have," Tim agreed. "But has it ever occurred to you that one of those false prophets you destroy could be Him? That you're killing Him all over again?"

"Don't be ridiculous. I would know Him."

"You didn't before."

He frowned. "There were other factors."

"How many times can you hang for that handful of silver?"

Handful of silver?

"Is that really what you think?" he asked. "I thought you were too smart to believe the slander, especially considering everything that's been said about you over the years. Do you honestly believe that I hanged myself out of guilt? Surely you know me better than that."

And throwing down the pieces of silver, he went and hanged himself . . .

It couldn't be . . .

"Then why did you?"

Father Peter shook his head. "I hanged myself to try to find Him. He was always talking about the life everlasting. I thought that if I died, I might find Him there. I thought I would be able to ask for His forgiveness. Instead"—he shook his head—"I had to find another way to atone."

Tim looked my way again. "And how do you think you will be judged, on the day the trumpet sounds? You who have caused so much pain, so many deaths."

"I have been true to Him. I have stood up for His name when all around me—"

"For His name," Tim said. "But what of what He taught? What of the innocents you have killed in His name?"

"I've only known one miraculous innocent," Father Peter said.

"And you've spent your lifetimes trying to atone for your betrayal, to protect His memory. A memory that doesn't need your protection."

"You're not going to change my mind."

"I know," Tim said. His voice was sad. "And my work here is done."

Father Peter nodded. "So what now, Ahasuerus?" he asked.

"Now we move on."

"I thought so. When?"

"Tonight. Right now. We're all ready. I was just waiting to tie up a couple of loose ends. Waiting for you, for one."

"As usual."

"As usual."

"Are you going to wait for Henry Denton?"

Tim shook his head. "He's gone. He's got a rough road ahead of him, but I think he'll find his way. He'll be able to find us if he still needs us."

"And where are you headed to this time?" Father Peter asked.

"I'm not sure. We've been trying to figure that out. You?"

He shrugged. "I'll drift a bit. More of the same."

They stared at each other for a long silent moment.

"I'd like this to be over," Father Peter said quietly. It didn't sound like his voice.

He started to walk away, then turned back toward Tim again. "Do you think we'll ever be able to sit down together, you and I? Have a drink? Eat? Breathe?"

Tim smiled, but his eyes looked sad. "Next year in Jerusalem?"

He shook his head and turned away with his hand still raised. "Good night, Ahasuerus," he said, but he didn't look back.

The dark of his coat looked like wings as he walked away.

"Goodnight, Judas," Tim whispered, standing there alone in the darkness, watching him go.

Judas.

The name seemed to rip something inside me.

Judas.

My knees felt like rubber, and I had to grab the shelf to keep from falling over.

Tim turned to look right at me. I took a step back, trying to hide in the dark.

"Mr. Tanner, I presume?" he said. "Please come out from the shadows. Time is growing short, and we have much to talk about."

SIMON

"I'm not sure about this," Karen whispered as we crept down the stairs.

I don't know who had thought of it first, but we had sat up in bed and turned on one of the lamps and talked for hours, talked in circles. We had talked ourselves out.

"I'm not either," I said, holding her hand.

In the end, we had got up and pulled on our robes.

At the doorway to the living room, I was stopped by the enormity of what we were considering. In the silvery light through the blinds I saw the shape of her body barely lifting the sheets. We couldn't. We just couldn't . . .

"Are you okay?" Karen asked.

"I'm not sure," I answered. "You?"

"I'm not sure either."

From the window came a light pattering, almost but not quite like rain. Without thinking, I drew the curtain aside. Karen joined me and we peered out, our breath misting against the glass.

Outside, the world was transformed. Wet snow was falling, not yet covering the ground, but spiralling and refracting under the streetlight, shimmering like a galaxy, like a benediction in our front yard. With what we were about to do, it felt almost sacred.

"That's so beautiful," Karen whispered.

I let the curtain fall back into place, brushing the three stones that Karen kept on the sill, and turned to face our daughter, my eyes still dazzled by the snow-bright midnight.

Turning on the lamp, I noticed, for the first time, that Sherry had grown since the accident, that her body was longer in the bed, that her hair was longer too. I wondered how long she would keep growing. Twenty years from now, would we be standing alongside the beautiful young woman we had always imagined her becoming, knowing that she would always be the three-year-old she was the day of the accident? I shook my head against the tears I could feel forming. I couldn't cry. If I started to cry, we would never get through this.

Blowing into my hands to warm them, I gently stroked her hair. "Hi, baby," I whispered. "How are you tonight? You had a big day today, didn't you?"

I wanted to explain to her, to reassure her that everything was all right, but how could I do that? How do you explain to a little girl that her parents' happiness depends on her? It was so unfair. If there was any other way, we wouldn't even consider this.

Instead, I started to sing, quietly, my voice tremulous and near to breaking. "Hush, little baby, don't say a word, daddy's gonna buy you a mockingbird . . ."

Karen was fighting back tears.

"I'm sorry, baby," I said to Sherry as I gently drew back her covers. "I know it's cold. It'll only be for a minute." As I spoke, I was praying that she understood. At the same time I was hoping that she was completely unaware.

"Simon, I . . ." Karen's fingers dug into my arm.

"We don't have to do this," I said.

She looked down at Sherry and shook her head. "No, I think we do."

I met her eye and nodded. "Do you want . . . ?"

She shook her head. "No, you. You first."

I knelt beside the bed, leaning my head against the cool sheets for a long moment, trying to build my courage. Finally, I straightened up.

"And if that mockingbird don't sing," I shifted her hand gently to my forehead, closing my eyes. "Daddy's gonna buy you a diamond ring," I couldn't stop my tears. Unlike the daddy in the song, I could do nothing to help her. Instead, she was helping me. Us.

I kept her hand against my forehead for a full minute, holding in my mind the image of Karen's face at the very moment of Sherry's birth, the pure joy as the sticky, curded bundle of blood and breath was pressed into her arms, that moment when our eyes made contact over the slick head of our daughter.

Our daughter.

I don't know what I was expecting: a blinding flash, perhaps; a revelation, or a healing glow. I didn't feel anything except cold. But as I took her hand away, laying it gently on her covers, I felt comforted, as if someone had whispered to me, "It's all right. Everything's going to be all right."

I chose to believe that.

As we traded places, Karen kissed me, quickly, full on the mouth.

For a moment she stood uncertainly at the bedside, then she untied the loose knot of the belt of her robe and allowed it to fall open.

"Hi, baby," she said quietly. "Are you cold? I'm cold. I'm sorry. This will only take a minute."

She lifted Sherry's hand with the tender care I remembered her using when she bathed Sherry as a baby, cradled her wrist as she turned her palm and laid it gently on the soft skin of her belly. She closed her eyes and held Sherry's hand there for the space of several breaths, tears running in rivulets down her cheeks.

After she laid Sherry's arm back down and tucked her under her blankets, she threw herself into my arms, and we cried there in the pool of golden light surrounding our daughter.

Before turning off the light, we each kissed Sherry on the forehead. So fragile. It was as if she was only sleeping, as if she might open her eyes at any moment.

"Good night, sweetie," I whispered, taking in the floral scent of her. "Sweet dreams."

I walked Karen to the foot of the stairs. "I'll be right up," I said. "I just want to check the doors and windows."

"Are you okay?"

"Not really," I said. No secrets between us. Not anymore. "But I will be."

"Do you want me to wait for you?"

I shook my head. "I'll be right up."

She laid her hand over mine. "I love you."

"I love you too."

She walked back upstairs in the darkness as I methodically checked the front and back doors, as I double-checked that the windows were locked. The snow was coming down heavier, a thin crust now covering the ground.

I was about to let the curtain fall back into place when I saw the figure under the streetlight, silhouetted in the falling snow. He was pudgy, in a too-large coat that nearly dragged on the ground. The smoke from his cigar pooled upward with the snow. Another man, taller, broad across the shoulders in a blue ski jacket, followed him. Then another, similarly ill-kempt, then another, and another all walking past the house. The last man, huge and gangly, stared into the yard as he passed. He looked almost like the false Father Peter's assistant, but I couldn't quite see him in the dim light, and he disappeared into the dark before I could be sure. In the end, more than a dozen men passed. Street people, I thought. Rousted from somewhere they had been sleeping, searching for another resting place out of the cold.

It occurred to me to call after them, to invite them in, to give them shelter for the duration of the storm, but by the time the thought had fully formed, they had gone, slipping from the pool of the streetlight back into the shadows.

I made my way silently up the stairs, past the closed door of Sherry's old room, through which I could hear the snoring priest, and into the bedroom. Gently draping my robe over the chair, I slid into bed and pressed myself against Karen.

She moaned a little as my cool body came into contact with her warmth. "Where did you go?" she asked slowly, in a drawl that was more asleep than awake.

"I was checking the windows and doors."

"Mmm. Thank you."

"You're welcome. Hey, listen . . . It's snowing harder now."

"Sherry'll like that," she replied drowsily. "Maybe we'll go for a walk in the morning, make angels."

I thought that I had cried myself out downstairs, but hot tears coursed down my cheeks, spilling into her hair. I wished for sleep. I wished that I could meet Karen wherever she was, in that world where our daughter was whole, where in the morning they would be making snow angels in the yard.

NINE

The Price of Miracles

———

December 27

I was awakened by a soft tapping at the door. "Father Peter?" asked a male voice.

At first, I didn't recognize the tiny bed, the animal-print wallpaper, the mobile slowly spinning above my head. Then it all returned to me. "Yes, Simon," I answered. "I'm awake."

"Do you prefer coffee or tea?"

I had fallen asleep with the window open a crack, and the air was cold on my face, but I was very comfortable under the weight of Sherilyn's quilt. "Coffee, please, Simon," I answered. "I'll be right down."

His footfalls faded as I swung my legs out of the bed. Something was different from the day before, something subtle. The air seemed brighter, cleaner.

Snow had fallen overnight, blanketing the yard in several inches of thick, heavy white. Snow was still falling, large wet flakes the size of silver dollars, plummeting, rather than drifting, toward the ground. The street was unplowed, bisected by a single set of tire ruts, the sidewalk marred only by a few sets of footprints.

I dressed quickly, checking my watch as I put it on. It was just before nine. I was not accustomed to sleeping in.

Simon was sitting at the kitchen table reading the local paper. He looked up as I came into the room. "Well, I don't think we're off to a very auspicious start for you," he said.

"I'm sorry?"

Karen was bustling around the kitchen, and I wasn't quite sure what to do with myself.

She waved me to the chair across from Simon, setting a cup

of coffee on the place mat in front of it. "Simon's worried that with the snow we won't have many people out today." She gestured toward the chair again. "Go ahead, sit. Did you look outside? Ruth and Stephen already called to say they wouldn't be able to make it in."

I nodded from the chair. "It's still really coming down. I don't think you have to worry, though. I think people will come through . . . well, snow or high water."

Karen smiled.

By the time I had eaten some fruit and cereal for breakfast, there was a line of about ten people waiting in the front yard, pressed against the house under the eaves.

"Should we just send them home?" Karen asked.

Simon shook his head. "No," he said. "We can't do that. We can't just send them home after they've come through the snow."

"We can't just leave them outside either."

"No," he stretched the word out as he shook his head. "There probably won't be that many people today. We can have them wait in the family room." He glanced at me. "Father Peter will be with Sherry, so you and I can trade off. Whoever's looking after the people in the family room can check the front every so often in case more arrive. How does that sound?"

So Karen and I stood in the living-room doorway as Simon showed the pilgrims into the house. They left their wet coats and shoes in the foyer. A few of them craned their necks, trying to look past us to see Sherry, but most of them just followed Simon, their eyes on the floor in front of them. They all seemed to be both optimistic and embarrassed, as if they were ashamed at being forced to seek out such help, but unable or unwilling to not take the risk. I had seen it before.

Karen had already taken care of Sherry's needs: she had been fed and her diaper and bedding were clean, her hair was combed back and she was wearing a clean gown in pink flannel. Karen very carefully pulled back the covers, folding them near Sherry's waist, as I sat down in the chair nearest the window, opening my notebook onto my lap and taking my pen from my pocket.

"So this is what you do?" Karen asked as I was organizing myself. Leaning behind the chair, she plugged in the lights and the dark Christmas tree in the corner burst into life.

"I'm sorry?"

"Your job. It's to go around, collect evidence, disprove reports of miracles." Her tone was maybe a little critical, but mostly curious.

"Or to prove them."

"Does that happen often?" she asked, turning the rod for the blinds, the bright, clear winter light spilling through the sheers into the room.

"That I get a chance to prove that a miracle has actually happened?"

She nodded.

"Very rarely."

"I didn't think so," she said.

I shook my head. "No, it's not like that. Most families, most people put into a situation like you're in with Sherry, don't handle it nearly so well. There's an impulse to pull away, to run from what a lot of people consider such a huge responsibility, such an overwhelming obligation. Very few people open their lives to the needy. We wish more did.

"And of course," I continued. "The other Father Peter does everything in his power to encourage people to turn away. Or to run. Many times I've had reports of miracles—of healings or visitations—and by the time I arrive at the scene, the family has moved, leaving no forwarding address."

"I don't think we could do that," she said. "Just turn our backs."

"But you can see the temptation?"

She hesitated for a moment, then nodded.

"I still don't like the word *miracle,* though," she said. "It just smells to much like church to me. Too much incense and candle wax."

I was smiling at her, about to respond, when I noticed the figure in the doorway behind her. "Hello," I said. I didn't recognize him from the group of pilgrims we had escorted to the family room.

"Did Simon send you in already?" Karen asked.

The man stayed silent. He was in his mid-twenties, not overly tall, wearing faded, dirty jeans, battered sneakers and a burgundy sweatshirt. His face was mostly hidden in the shadow of the hood. His right hand was tucked into the front pocket of the sweatshirt, and he stood hunched over, as if in pain.

"You can see me," he finally said.

Karen took a step toward him and I rose to my feet, setting my notebook and pen on the chair. "Did Simon get your information?" she asked.

"No," he said, his voice gruff, his tone like that of someone surprised at being spoken to. "I came to see Sherry."

"Well, you have to sign in . . ." Karen started.

"I knocked at the door," the man explained. "No one answered."

"I guess we didn't hear," Karen answered.

He turned toward Sherry.

Karen put herself between the man and her daughter.

"Can I see her?" he asked. His voice had dropped to a whisper.

With his left hand, he fumbled with his hood and pulled it off. He had the disheveled look of someone who had been living on the street for a while—tangled shoulder-length hair, uncombed for what looked like weeks, a long, tangled beard—but the right side of his face was a raw burn, fresh and oozing. His right eye was swollen shut from the wound, which extended down his neck.

He was completely focused on Sherry, and he didn't even seem to notice our attention. He looked at her with a deep anguish that radiated from him in waves.

"You . . . You're burned," Karen said, her voice dropping. She stepped toward him, raising her hand.

"Your arm too," she said, not releasing his gaze. "And here." She traced her fingers along the right side of her body, mirroring him. Her eyes were wide, and her face brightened, as if something suddenly made sense to her.

He nodded, slowly.

"You were here," she whispered. "Two nights ago. You stopped the man with the bomb. You got burned." She reached out, almost touching his face. "You saved us."

He turned back to Sherry on the bed.

"Simon," she called, not quite shouting, but loud enough to be heard.

"I just want to see her," he said quietly, stopping inches from Karen, craning his neck. "I *need* to see her."

"Simon," she called again.

I stepped forward. "Listen, if we can—"

"What's wrong?" All three of us turned to face Simon, outlined in the doorway.

Her face was tight with uncertainty, and she didn't move from her position between the man and her daughter. "This is . . . this is the man from the other night—"

Simon was looking at the man. "It's you," he said, stepping toward him. His jaw was set, his face hard. The man seemed confused.

"He wants—"

"You don't recognize him?"

"What?"

"I'm not," he sputtered as Simon took hold of his left arm and turned him toward Karen. "I just came to see—"

Karen looked at him, trying to see past the beard, the burns.

"I'm sorry," he said quietly. "I didn't see your daughter."

He glanced between the two of them, then his gaze stopped on Karen. "I didn't see Sherry," he repeated. "I came, I came to say I'm—"

"It is you, isn't it?" Karen asked.

Their eyes locked. "Yes," he whispered.

Before she could speak, he stepped forward again. "I've been . . . I wanted to come. I wanted to see Sherry. I came to say I was sorry."

Simon shook his head. "You can't just—"

"I'm glad you came, Henry," came a voice from behind us.

The tiny, high voice seemed to echo through the room, and we all turned to face the small bed where Sherilyn Barrett had spoken.

She was sitting up, staring at us. Her eyes were curiously dark against her pale skin.

"Oh, God, Sherry," Karen gasped, stumbling toward the bed.

Everything seemed to slow down in the moment that Karen pulled her daughter into her arms, squeezing her and rocking gently in place. Sherry's arms were around her neck, and after a moment her fingers began to toy with her mother's hair.

"Oh, Sherry." Karen couldn't stop her tears, but the sob, when it bubbled up, sounded like laughter. "Sherry."

"Don't cry, Mommy," Sherry whispered into her neck. "It's all right."

Karen pulled away from her a little so she could make eye contact when she told her, "No, honey, it's just . . . Mommy's so happy." She cradled one of her daughter's cheeks, letting her fingers linger.

"I know," Sherry said, touching her mother's cheek in return. Her fingers came away wet with tears.

Simon stared, his eyes wide, mouth gaping before his hand covered the lower half of his face, hiding a sob. He fell toward the bed, taking his family into his arms.

His eyes met Karen's as he buried his face in Sherry's hair, breathing her in. Both of their smiles seemed caught somewhere between ecstasy and despair.

"I love you, baby," he whispered into his daughter's ear.

She squirmed at the tickle of his breath.

"I love you too, Daddy," she said. "Can you sing me a song?"

"Anything," he said, meeting Karen's eyes again. Her hand found his on Sherry's lap, and they clutched at one another. "Anything you want."

"I like that one about the mockingbird."

As the Barretts huddled together, Henry Denton took several halting steps to the edge of the bed and crouched there, clutching the covers in his hands.

Sherry looked down at him, and her parents exchanged a glance over her head.

The tiny girl, pale and small, lifted her gaze from the broken man before her and turned back to her parents. "Call her Lily," she said. "I'd like it if you called her Lily."

Karen made a sound that was somewhere between a sharp laugh and a sob, and tightened her hand around Simon's.

"Henry," Sherry said, as though he and she were the only people in the room. She leaned toward him.

He lifted his head. "I'm sorry," he said to Sherry, not flinching from her wide, dark gaze. "I came to ask your . . ." His face was streaked and stained with tears, his open eye filled with confusion and fear that seemed to melt away as she raised her hand to him.

With the lightest of touches, she drew her fingertips across the twisted red flesh on his face. She smiled. "No more ouches."

The wound seemed to recede as she drew her hand away. At first, her fingers left faint streaks of unblemished skin behind them, but the whiteness spread quickly, the livid red skin healing at her touch. Within seconds, there was no trace of the burn on Denton's face, and I imagined the cool balm of her touch traveling down his arm and chest, leaving new, clear skin behind.

"I knew you'd come," she said softly. "I was waiting for you." He smiled gratefully before bowing his head to her, almost touching his forehead to the white sheet.

She took a long look around the room, her gaze lingering on her parents. It was impossible to read her expression: I want to call it beatific, but there was a hint of resolve there, as well as a touch of sadness.

She knew.

Sherry lowered her hand gently to the crown of Henry Denton's head, slowly enough that we could watch his tangled hair give under its weight.

I think that we all realized what was happening at the same moment. Karen gasped, "Sherry?" as Simon raised his hand as if trying to stop her, but none of us were able to interfere, none of us knowing, or even able to guess at, the consequences of what we were witnessing.

Sherry knew.

"It's all right, Henry." As her fingers touched his head, her eyelids slowly lowered.

It was like an electrical current passed through them both, as if when she touched him, when she told him it was all right, a circuit was completed.

A single spasm passed first through Henry Denton, who crumpled to the carpet.

Then the girl's back arched, and a force seemed to push her parents away from her. At that moment, I felt a pulse thrum through me, the pressure of a sound too low to hear. The light dimmed as the breath rushed out of me and the force brought me to my knees. I struggled for a moment, but the next breath I drew was as sweet as the air after a summer storm.

The light grew bright again, and Sherry sagged, motionless, onto her bed.

For a moment, the silence seemed deeper than that of an empty church. I felt connected to the world. I could feel Simon and Karen on the bed, and I knew that the pilgrims down the hall were on their knees with me. I could hear the falling of the snowflakes in the cold white light outside the window. It sounded like the dryness of wings, the gentle pressure of a final breath. The air filled with the smell of lilies.

"Sherry?" Karen choked, her voice raw and desperate, struggling toward her daughter.

Before I even touched the cool skin of Sherry's throat, I knew it was too late. Her chest wasn't rising; there was no pulse under my fingers.

"Sherry?" Karen whispered, her voice breaking into sobs as she pulled her daughter into her arms. She slumped onto the bed holding the girl close, pressing her face into her hair, cradling her head as she wept. Simon took them both into his arms, and they held one another in the white glow of the room, their daughter still between them.

Neither of them seemed to notice the expression of peace and serenity—of release and comfort—the little girl wore. Nor did they notice, then, that the body of Henry Daniel Denton had disappeared from the room, leaving no trace. It was as if he had never even crossed the threshold.

File # 5485.2
Barrett, Sherilyn Amber
—Final Report (excerpt)—
Father Peter Shaughnessy
April 24, 1997

. . . It is appropriate that I am completing and sub-
mitting this report today, a year to the day since the
accident that injured three-year-old Sherilyn Amber
Barrett and initiated the strange series of events in
Victoria, British Columbia, that culminated with her
death on the morning of December 27, 1996.

I have spent the four months since her death
both working on this investigation and assisting the
Barrett family, and their friends, in dealing with
Sherilyn's death.

You will find, attached, testimony from more
than 150 people who witnessed Sherilyn Barrett's
healing powers, including petitioners and their
medical practitioners, who testify to the complete
recovery and remission of those who came in contact with Sherilyn. I will solicit further testimony
from these witnesses at the first and fifth anniver-
saries of their contact, as is the norm in these cases.

Of the twelve people waiting in the Barrett
home that morning, we have received reports of
seven full recoveries; I am awaiting replies from
the remaining petitioners. By mid-January, the
Barretts were receiving letters and reports of
recoveries from as far away as Toronto, Halifax and
the American South. These people had all written
to Sherilyn; their letters of petition were found at
her bedside, still sealed.

Pilgrims continue to wait at the Barrett home
even now, months later, their numbers having

increased after Sherilyn's death. Some of them also report spontaneous recoveries, although such incidents are less common.

I do not know how to make sense of the things I have seen, nor what meaning to ascribe to those events in which I was a participant, however minor.

I have delayed completing this report, hoping that time would provide me with the clarity and distance to help me to understand the events I witnessed and to recount them objectively. Time has not, however, accorded me understanding or distance. I find that I cannot be objective where Sherilyn Barrett is concerned: I owe her too much.

I would like to attach to this report a more personal concern. I have discussed this with my confessor, and have decided that, although personal of nature, this note should form part of the official record.

In August of 1996, I was diagnosed with prostate cancer, which had metastasized. The doctors informed me that it would likely be terminal within a year, and I determined that I would resign my position on December 31, 1996. The inquiry into the miracles attributed to Sherilyn Barrett was to be my last.

Following the events of December 27, however, the cancer disappeared. As of last week, I have been in complete remission for four months. My doctors are "cautiously optimistic," and will monitor my situation. I, however, am certain: I was cured by Sherilyn Barrett on the morning of December 27.

CODA

April 24, 1997

I go with them to visit the grave. They can't see me. They have no idea I'm here. But I want to be with them. It's been one year since the accident, and I want to be with them, today of all days.

I follow behind them through the parking lot, through the gate and along the winding pathways.

They're holding hands, and they walk slowly, not saying anything.

They stop at the side of the grave, and he hugs her to his shoulder. They still don't speak. They just look at the grave with its small white stone, and the pile of flowers and letters and stuffed animals that people have left.

Sherilyn Amber Barrett

Beloved daughter, beloved friend

August 1, 1992–December 27, 1996

I can't look at it for too long. It makes me too sad. Too sad for them.

It's a beautiful spring day. In this place of death, the world is full of life. You can almost hear it singing, all around. The daffodils are waking up after their long winter naps, and their yellow and white heads dance between the rows of gravestones. The grass is green and bright and damp. Mr. Squirrel will be taking off his winter coat.

It rained last night, but this morning it's warm and the sky is clear and blue and beautiful.

I'm wearing my sky-blue dress, because it matches the sky.

Without letting go of Mommy's hand, Daddy crouches beside the flowers and teddy bears. "Baby," he chokes, tears running down his cheeks. His hand shakes as he reaches into his jacket pocket and carefully puts a stone atop the grave marker. "Oh, baby . . ."

After Daddy stands back up, Mommy crouches carefully. She uses Daddy for balance as she puts a stone of her own on my grave, near a picture of me, gently brushing the white marker with her fingertips the same way she used to tickle my cheeks. As she stands up, her hand goes to the small swelling of her belly, and she turns herself into Daddy's arms.

There were three stones I gave to Mommy before the accident. There were three stones in Mommy's pocket when the truck hit me, three stones on the windowsill of the winter room where the people came to see me, the room where I died. The last stone, I know, is in her pocket again, near her heart, near the heart of their unborn child, the girl they will call Lily.

My sister.

Lily.

For peace.

Praise for
Song for a Whale

"At its luminous heart, *Song for a Whale* is a tale about longing for connection and finding it in the most magical and unexpected of places. **Fascinating, brave, and tender, this is a story like no other about a song like no other. A triumph.**"
—Katherine Applegate, Newbery Award–winning author of *The One and Only Ivan*

"*Song for a Whale* is **beautifully written** and is such **an important story** for kids with big struggles in their lives. **I fell into Iris's world from the first chapter.**"
—Millicent Simmonds, actress
(*Wonderstruck* and *A Quiet Place*)

"A **quick-moving, suspenseful** plot.... **Iris's adventures will engross readers.**"
—*Kirkus Reviews*

"The strength of the book is its **strong portrayal of Iris as a Deaf girl in a hearing world.**"
—*Booklist*

"This finely crafted novel **affectingly illuminates issues of loneliness, belonging, and the power of communication.**"
—*Publishers Weekly*

"**An uplifting tale.**"
—*SLJ*

ALSO BY LYNNE KELLY

Chained

1

Until last summer I thought the only thing I had in common with that whale on the beach was a name.

I sat with Grandpa after collecting shells and driftwood scattered along the shore, and wildflowers from the dunes. The shells and driftwood were for Grandma, and the flowers were for the whale. Grandpa had asked how school was going, and I told him it was the same, which wasn't good. I'd been at that school for two years and still felt like the new kid.

Grandpa patted the sand next to him. *"Did you know she was probably deaf too?"* he signed.

I didn't have to ask who he meant. The whale had been buried there for eleven years, and my parents had told me enough times about what happened that day.

I shook my head. I hadn't known that, and I didn't know why Grandpa was changing the subject. Maybe he didn't know what to tell me anymore about school.

The whale had beached herself the same day I was born. When she was spotted in the shallow waters of the Gulf, some people stood on the shore and watched her approach. My grandma ran into the cold February water and tried to push her away from land, as if she could make a forty-ton animal change her mind about where she wanted to go. That was really dangerous. Even though the whale was weak by then, one good whack with a tail or flipper could have knocked Grandma out. I don't know what I would've done— jumped in like she did or just stood there.

"She wasn't born deaf like we were," Grandpa continued. *"The scientists who studied her said it had just happened. Maybe she'd been swimming near an explosion from an oil rig or a bomb test."*

When Grandpa told a story, I saw it as clearly as if it were happening right there in front of me. His signing hands showed me the whale in an ocean that suddenly went quiet, swimming over there, over there, over there, trying to find the sounds again. Maybe that was why she'd been there on our Gulf of Mexico beach instead of in deep ocean waters where she belonged. Sei whales didn't swim so close to shore. Only her, on that day.

"A whale can't find its way through a world without

sound," Grandpa added. *"The ocean is dark, and it covers most of the earth, and whales live in all of it. The sounds guide them through that, and they talk to one another across oceans."*

With the familiar sounds of the ocean gone, the whale was lost in her new silent world. A rescue group came to the beach and tried to save the whale, and they called her Iris. Grandma asked my parents to give the name to me, too, since I'd entered the world as the whale was leaving it.

After the marine biologists learned all they could from her, she was buried right there on the beach, along with the unanswered questions about what had brought her to that shore.

We lived on that coast until the summer after second grade, when my family moved to Houston for my dad's new job. Since then, we went back just once or twice a summer. The good thing about our new home was that it was closer to my grandparents. I liked being able to spend more time with them, especially since they were both Deaf like me. But we all missed the beach, and I missed being around kids like me. My old school had just a few Deaf kids, but that was enough. We had our classes together, and we had one another.

"But it's different for us," Grandpa signed. "Out here, there's more light, and all we need is our own small space to feel at home. Sometimes it takes time to figure things out. But you'll do it. You'll find your way."

I wish I'd asked him then how long that would take.

2

I'd come to the conclusion that sending me to the office was Ms. Conn's only joy in life. That made me responsible for her happiness, in a way, but I tried to slip into class without her noticing. I was only a minute late this time, and I had a really good reason.

She pointed toward the front office before I could drop into my chair.

When I got back to the room with my tardy pass, Ms. Conn said to my interpreter, Mr. Charles, "Tell Iris to move over next to Nina so she can catch her up." She usually talked around me like that. Mr. Charles had told her so many times that she could just talk *to* me, and he would interpret the message instead of always saying "Tell Iris . . ." Finally he gave up reminding her. She was never going to get it.

Also, I didn't need help catching up, and I for sure didn't want it from Nina.

"*I'll catch myself up*," I signed. When Mr. Charles voiced that for Ms. Conn, her face turned even meaner than usual, which I hadn't thought was possible. She didn't say anything else—just jerked a pointed finger to the space next to Nina's desk.

The plan made sense to Ms. Conn because she thought Nina was the smartest person in class, and Nina thought she knew sign language. She'd checked out a library book about it, so that made her an expert. Some people have the kind of confidence that lets them get away with being clueless.

Nina signed something to me as I slid my desk over to her territory.

I asked Mr. Charles, "*Did she just call herself a giant squirrel?*"

He clamped his lips together and looked away while answering, "*I think she meant 'great partner.'*"

That was what I'd figured, but trying to make Mr. Charles laugh was one of my favorite things.

I leaned over to the next row to look at Clarissa Gold's book. Mr. Charles interpreted my question when I asked Clarissa what we were working on. Nina tried to barge in with her flapping hands and made-up sign language. When I ignored her she got dangerously close to my face. As if I couldn't see her. My eyes stayed on Mr. Charles, since he actually did know what he was doing. Nina's hands were like a swarm of flies I wanted to swat away, so it felt good to flick the wrist of an open hand to sign *"Stop it"* to her. After Mr. Charles interpreted that, he added that it might be distracting to have two people signing at the same time. Usually he didn't jump in like that because he wanted me to take care of things for myself, so Nina must have been annoying him, too.

After a few minutes Ms. Conn came by to ask Nina, "Are you doing okay, helping Iris?"

"Yes, I think she's catching on," she answered.

Catching on. I looked back down at my work so I wouldn't turn into one of those cartoon characters with steam shooting out of their ears. After I scribbled down the last answer in the workbook, I slammed it closed and signed, *"Finished."*

I was about to take out my phone so I could read the new issue of *Antique Radio Magazine* I'd downloaded that morning. If I opened a book on my desk, I could probably read some of the magazine by looking down at the phone on my lap.

While my hand was sliding into my backpack, Ms. Conn said something to me and pointed at her mouth. She'd tried that before, as if that would magically help me understand her. One night at dinner I told my parents, *"Hey, I'm not Deaf anymore. Ms. Conn pointed to her lips while she talked, and everything was perfectly clear. Can't believe you didn't think of it."*

On the first day of school, Ms. Conn tried to hold Mr. Charles's hands still to force me to read her lips instead of watching his signing. I didn't catch what Mr. Charles said to her, but she let go of his hands like she'd touched a hot stove, and didn't try that ever again.

We ignored the lip pointing, and Mr. Charles interpreted what Ms. Conn said: I'd have to redo my poetry assignment from last week. That didn't make sense. The poem I'd turned in was really good.

When Ms. Conn returned with my paper, she looked like she'd just bitten into a sour pickle. A normal expression for her, but right then, it looked like she was smelling something really bad at the same time she was biting that pickle.

The red ink was the first thing I noticed when Ms. Conn handed back my paper. In the margin were the words *This does not rhyme!*

Which wasn't true. The poem came from a sign language storytelling game I used to do with Grandpa. One of us would start a story, and we'd take turns adding to it, one sign at a time. The trick was our hands had to keep the same shape for the whole story. Like if we started out with a closed fist, every sign for the rest of the story had to be made with a fist too. We'd go on and on like that until one of us couldn't think of something to add without breaking the handshape rule.

My favorite story started with a tree, full with leaves. A leaf blew away with a gust of wind, then landed in a river, floated down a stream, and onto the bank. It ended with a bird swooping in to grab the leaf to add to her nest in another tree. We told that story with our hands open like the number five the whole way through.

It didn't look the same on paper. Paper is flat, so I couldn't use all the space above and below and around it that I needed to tell the story right. And the words in English don't have the same shapes as they do in sign language. But here's how it looked when I wrote it down:

Leaves waving
Blowing, twirling
Floating current
Land on a riverbank
Mother bird grabs the leaf
And builds a new nest.

Sure, it didn't rhyme the way English words do, but I thought maybe it would be okay to turn in if I explained all that. At the top of the paper I'd written a note about the poem. I wondered if Ms. Conn had even read that part.

A red line crossed through the poem, ruining it. I took out my own red pen and glared at Ms. Conn. Below her *This does not rhyme!* message, I wrote *It does to me.*

Ever since Grandpa died, I'd wondered if he could still see me, if he was with me in some way. Right then, I hoped more than anything that he was nowhere near me. I didn't want him to see what Ms. Conn had done to our story. To us.

Everyone turned and looked at me as I crumpled the paper into a ball. Nina held a finger to her lips as always, like it was her job to remind me that things made noise and that I wasn't supposed to do any of them. But I did not throw the paper at her face. I flung it across the room, where it landed in the trash can, followed by the tree and the leaves and the river and the bird with her new nest, all slashed to pieces by a red line.

3

Even though electronics is a science-y thing, science was the one class where I wasn't reading about it on the sly. Usually I paid attention to what was going on in there because I liked science and my teacher, Sofia Alamilla. I even liked the way her name rolled off my hand like a wave when I spelled it out.

Ms. Alamilla wrote the letters *Hz* on the board. "Remember what this stands for?" she asked.

A few hands went up, and Ms. Alamilla called on me. I spelled out *"h-e-r-t-z,"* and Mr. Charles voiced "hertz" for her and the class.

"That's right," said Ms. Alamilla. "And what does it measure?"

"The frequency of sound."

I wondered why Ms. Alamilla was reviewing frequencies. We'd taken the test on it months ago.

"I found something that ties in nicely with what

we're studying now," she said, as if she'd heard me. "It's about a special whale, and you'll see why the frequency of his song is important."

Ms. Alamilla pressed some keys on the computer at her desk, and her eyeglasses reflected the video that played. The projector screen in front of the room showed a big blue square with "No Signal" in one corner.

I was heading to Ms. Alamilla's desk even before she signed *"Please help"* to me. After restarting the video and pausing it, I connected the computer to the projector's signal, then clicked the "CC" at the bottom of the screen to turn on the closed-captioning.

The video started out with a whale swimming in the ocean. Because of the captions, I could read the words on the screen instead of from Mr. Charles's hands. The dark gray-blue body of the whale filled up the screen, his tail waving up and down.

The narrator in the video talked about a whale called Blue 55, who swam around by himself and not in a pod like most whales. As far as anyone knew, it had always been that way; he didn't have any friends or a family to swim with or talk to. He was a type of baleen whale— the kind that ate plankton and small fish, not the kind with teeth that ate squid and seals. But he was a hybrid. His mother was a blue whale, and his father was a fin whale.

"The problem," said the narrator, "is Blue 55's unique voice. Most whales call out at frequencies of thirty-five hertz and lower, while this lonely whale's sounds are at around fifty-five hertz."

Only about twenty hertz off, but it made a big difference. He was speaking a language that only he knew.

"Furthermore, his song is in a unique pattern; even if other whales can hear him, they don't understand what he's saying. Blue 55 likely couldn't communicate with his own parents."

My stomach tightened into a ball. I wanted another whale on the screen to swim up to Blue 55, or at least look at him.

"The strange calls of Blue 55 were first detected by naval sonar in the late 1980s. Marine biologists figured out what was making the sounds and why the whale was all alone in the ocean."

I didn't notice until the words on the screen blurred that my eyes were watery. Mr. Charles handed me a tissue from his pocket. Maybe I'd sniffled or something.

"Allergies," I signed without looking away from the video.

The narrator went on to say that researchers from a marine sanctuary had tried to put a tracker on Blue 55 the year before so they could follow his migration pattern, which was also weird and unlike other whales'. They did get a sample of his skin to test. That was how they figured out his parents had been different species. Before they could attach the tracker to him, he dove down and swam away. He wouldn't need to resurface for a breath for another twenty minutes. Without a tracker on him, the only way anyone ever knew where he was swimming was from underwater microphones that picked up his song.

I didn't remember standing up, but when the video ended and Ms. Alamilla started talking, I had to look down to see Mr. Charles. Everyone's eyes were on me as I slid back down into my chair. My textbook was on the floor—I must have knocked it off my desk when I stood up. I left it at my feet.

"Can you imagine that?" Ms. Alamilla asked. "Swimming around for all those years, unable to communicate with anyone?"

Yes.

She said something else about frequencies, but I

wasn't paying attention anymore. I looked through Mr. Charles, as if I could still see that whale on the screen.

Blue 55 didn't have a pod of friends or a family who spoke his language. But he still sang. He was calling and calling, and no one heard him.

4

He hadn't always swum alone. Long ago, when the loudest sounds in the ocean were the songs of whales, he'd had a pod.

Those first whales had tried to talk to him. Every day they worked to change their songs to something like his.

He returned their calls, but his sounds meant nothing to them.

He heard the other whales. But nothing he sang back made sense. They thought he didn't understand.

They communicated to one another past him, through him, across him. Like he was a coral reef or a kelp forest they passed by. But he heard all of it.

He understood them when they despaired, giving up on ever hearing him, and when they lamented he would never be able to contribute to the pod. He couldn't warn them of a coming predator or announce the scent of waters that were good for feeding.

Yes, I can, he bellowed. *There, waves full of krill.* He turned to show them the way. He sang his message, struggling to match the sounds of the whales around him. But the sea grabbed his song and dragged it away, too high for the others to reach.

One night, when he awoke to float to the surface for a breath, he found himself alone. After so much time, with so many songs unheard, his family had left him.

He called out *Where are you?* and *What will I do now?* knowing no answer would come, knowing the sounds held meaning only for himself.

5

At lunch I sat at a table with other people, but still alone.
I could actually read lips all right—not that I'd ever tell
Ms. Conn. No matter how good I was, there'd be no way
to catch everything. Too many sounds look the same,
and in a group of people, it's impossible to pick up more
than a word or two here and there. It's even worse if
they're eating. Some kids tried to remember to look at
me when they talked. Then they'd get into a conversation with everyone else, too fast for me to keep up. A
couple of the kids knew the sign language alphabet
and would spell out sentences letter by letter. That took
forever, so I'd tell them to just go ahead and write it.
Whenever I spelled something back, they didn't catch
it anyway, unless I slowed down so much that by the
time I got to the end of the sentence, they'd forgotten
the beginning.

Some people at my table were in my science class.

I was still thinking about the whale called Blue 55, and wondered if they were too. It didn't look like anyone was talking about him. I wanted to ask if they thought he liked swimming around by himself or if he wanted friends. Maybe he'd tried singing like the other whales and couldn't do it, or he was happy singing his own song.

Nina walked by with some of her friends and waved like she wanted to tell me something super important. Even when I understood her, she never said anything important. But she had seen the Blue 55 video, and obviously she was interested in sign language. I took a deep breath and decided to give it a try.

As clearly as possible I signed to her, *"What did you think of that whale?"*

Nina pointed at my lunch and signed something that made absolutely no sense. I couldn't even figure out what she was trying to get at.

Maybe the message was jumbled because she was excited and signing too fast, as if her hands couldn't keep up with her brain.

I held up a hand to try to slow her down. Numbers and letters were easy enough to understand, so I shook a letter *B* to sign *"Blue,"* then tapped the air twice with a five handshape. *Blue 55.* I shrugged a little and raised my eyebrows with a question. It should've been perfectly clear I was asking, "So, what did you think of that whale?"

Somehow, she still didn't seem to get it, and I didn't understand whatever she was trying to say. Nothing that looked like *"whale"* or *"ocean"* or *"song."*

I gave up and turned to Sanjay, who was sitting across from me and talking about a new level he'd unlocked in a video game or something like that. Out of the corner of my eye, I saw Nina signing even more furiously. Her friends backed away to avoid getting smacked in the face by her flailing arms. Even though she was the one making a scene, I was getting the attention. Sanjay pointed to tell me I should be looking at Nina, but I waved him off, as if I were dying to know the rest of his video game story. I took a quick glance to see if Nina had given up yet. My face burned as she moved in closer. Great. This girl couldn't recognize a hint if it ran up and set her hands on fire. I reached into my backpack and ripped a piece of paper from a notebook.

"What's everyone doing this weekend?" was the first thing I thought of to start a new conversation. Nina was right next to me. I knew this not from looking at her, but from the breeze created by her hands waving at the side of my head. Finally I turned to look, because

everyone was pointing by then. What I witnessed was amazing. Not even one sign made sense. I signed to Nina, *"I don't understand you,"* then turned back to the group. Still she didn't give up. She leaned over, forcing me to see her, and signed with her hands right in my face. I couldn't take it anymore. My face burned hotter. Everyone looked at me like I was the dumb one for not understanding.

I pushed her away and signed, *"Leave me alone!"* I didn't mean to push her so hard, but she ended up crashing into the people at the next table and landing on the floor. Nina's mouth was open wide, as if she were yelling. She must have been making a lot of noise since people from all the way across the cafeteria stood up for a better view. The lunch duty teachers made their way to our table then, their faces full of concern. One of their mouths formed the words "What happened?"

A teacher helped Nina up. She rubbed her elbow where she'd landed but seemed fine otherwise. I stood up and swung my backpack over my shoulder. Even though the bell hadn't rung, I headed to the principal's office. That was where they were going to send me anyway.

6

The secretary was picking up the phone when she saw me coming, and I waved to her on my way into Principal Shelton's office. Ms. Shelton wasn't there, so I went ahead and rearranged the furniture. I slid the black chair over to one side of the desk. Mr. Charles would sit there, so I could see both him and Ms. Shelton at the same time. I sank into my favorite chair and stared at the ceiling while I waited.

Ms. Shelton came in and sat behind her desk, then held out her arms, as if she were saying, *"Well?"*

I shrugged. No point in chatting until Mr. Charles got there. I reached up to the pendant I wore around my neck, the one made from an old Zenith radio knob. They used to emboss the wooden knobs with a raised Z-shape lightning bolt. In my room at home, I had a collection of antique radios. I did some repair work for Mr. Gunnar's antique shop, and sometimes—okay, a lot of times—I ended up buying radios from him after I fixed them. I'd made the pendant so I'd have a piece of my collection with me even when I was away from home. While we waited I traced the jagged edges of the letter with my fingertip.

Mr. Charles came in a few minutes later. *"Welcome,"* I signed as he took the seat across from me.

I pointed to a picture on Ms. Shelton's desk that I hadn't seen before. *"New grandbaby?"*

"Yes, that's Henry," she said after Mr. Charles interpreted my question. "Now, tell me what happened in the cafeteria."

Ms. Shelton knew what happened; I was sure of that. She always wanted to get my side of the story. One of those things they teach in principal school—find out what happened, then question the kid to see if they lie about it. Mr. Charles interpreted between Ms. Shelton and me as I filled her in.

"Nina was only trying to ask what you were having for lunch," she said.

I actually slapped myself in the forehead. All this because Nina wanted to know what kind of sandwich I had?

"She was trying to make conversation with you, Iris. To be friendly."

"No she's not," I signed. *"She's trying to show off and pretend she knows something she doesn't. She needs to keep her hands out of my face."*

Ms. Shelton reminded me of the school's zero tolerance policy for fighting. I tried to argue that I was only removing someone's hands from my personal space, but it was no use. At school that counted as fighting.

"This isn't fair." I slumped back in the chair and looked out the window at the parking lot.

Mr. Charles waved to get my attention and interpreted the rest of what Ms. Shelton said.

"The other students at the lunch table did say that you tried to get Nina to stop when she got so close to you. We'll talk to her about respecting personal space. If it happens again, tell a teacher instead of shoving someone."

"Okay." I left it at that. Ms. Shelton probably wouldn't like it if I pointed out that shoving was a lot quicker than flagging down a teacher and scribbling a note to explain what was going on.

I'd have in-school suspension for the next two days, starting right then. That meant I'd sit in one room all day, and my teachers would send my work there. Fine with me. Regular suspension would've been even better. At home I could fly through my schoolwork and then start on some radio repairs. That was probably

24

why they didn't do it—because they'd figured out it was too much like a vacation.

Then Ms. Shelton slipped in the worst part. "And you'll have to apologize to Nina when you return to class."

Maybe she'd forget about that.

By the end of school day, I had a text from Mom. *Get straight home after school.* Of course Ms. Shelton had called to let her know of my sentencing. I biked toward home after school, but I wasn't in a big hurry to get there. My parents had told me I'd be in Serious Trouble if I got sent to the principal's office again, even though there was a whole month left of school. I wasn't sure what they meant by "Serious Trouble," but some things were better left a mystery.

That morning I'd been working on a radio repair for Mr. Gunnar, a mint-colored Zenith from the 1950s. That was why I was a little late getting to school. I was so close to fixing it, but then I realized I didn't have what I needed to finish the job. Mr. Gunnar wasn't in a hurry—he always told me to take the time I needed to do the job right. But I couldn't stand to leave anything sitting around broken. It chased me until I couldn't ignore it anymore.

The junkyard was on the way home. Sort of.

At the gate of Moe's Junk Emporium, I hopped off my bike even before it stopped rolling. My eyes scanned the dead appliances section as I ran up the sidewalk. Always so many dishwashers and washing machines. But there . . . There was a monster-size TV/radio/record player set. Not that it had a big screen; I mean, it was thick. You'd have to set it at least three feet away from the wall.

I ran over for a closer look. Made by Admiral; in the 1950s, I was pretty sure. The set featured decades of dust that had sunk into the scratches of the wood cabinet, and tatters of cloth hanging from the speaker. Hopefully the insides were in better shape. The TV and record player weren't much use, but the radio might have the exact parts I needed.

I took out my phone to text Grandpa. It was the kind of thing he'd pick up for me before someone else grabbed it. I typed a few words before I caught myself. Sometimes I'd think of something to tell him, before remembering he wasn't there to answer me. Then I felt bad for forgetting. Shouldn't I always feel it? Missing him?

After erasing the message I changed it to *Wish you were still here.* Even though he wouldn't receive it, I clicked send before slipping the phone back into my pocket. He seemed closer then, like just sending that short message would somehow let him know I was thinking of him. *I haven't forgotten you. Sometimes I just don't remember you're not here.*

My brother, Tristan, could drive me back later to get the set, but it might be gone by then. If I asked Mom or Dad to pick it up, they'd wonder why I was at Moe's instead of at home.

I'd ask Moe to hold it for me. He knew me well enough by now, so it'd take just a minute to tell him I was interested in the set. But when I ran into the trailer that served as the office, Moe wasn't behind the desk smoking a cigar like he always was. Some guy a little older than Tristan sat there, watching a TV show where people threw chairs at one another. The patch on his blue work shirt read "Jimmy Joe."

Jimmy Joe stood up and said something when he noticed me in the doorway. I never liked talking to people I didn't know. This was an emergency, so I would. But by "talk," I mean "write notes back and forth." I hated the way people looked at me when they didn't understand my Deaf accent. Since I didn't know if I talked very well, I'd rather not do it. Plus, I never liked the way my voice felt. As much as I loved feeling sound from a radio speaker, vibrations in my throat annoyed me, as if they didn't belong there. Kind of like how I loved electronics, but not on my own ears.

At the desk I scribbled on a notepad: *Can you save that Admiral set out there for me? I'll come back for it later.*

He looked back at me after reading the note, and his face was a question. I pointed to my ear and then shook my head to let him know that these ears were as busted as everything else around there.

His eyes widened like they did with most people. A second of panic like they're not sure what to do with me or like I might explode in front of them.

"Can you, uh, read lips? Or talk?" he asked, pointing back and forth from his mouth to mine.

Maybe, I thought, *but how about just reading that note in your hand?* I tapped the paper he was holding.

He recovered, then pointed out the window. "It don't work." His mouth was really wide when he formed the words. He was probably yelling. He shook his head and waved his hands to emphasize the point.

I held back an eye roll. Of course it didn't work. Even if it worked, it wouldn't really work. Those old antenna TVs haven't been able to get a signal for years.

After taking back the note I wrote, *For parts.*

When he read that, his eyebrows rose from scared to impressed.

I'll ask my dad, Jimmy Joe wrote back. *Doctor appointment. He'll be back soon.*

So Moe was his dad. From what I'd witnessed during my time as a junkyard customer, Moe started each day with a can of Budweiser and a Whole Hog breakfast sandwich from The Cattle Prod, in addition to the cigar, so a doctor visit was probably a good idea. Too bad he didn't pick a more convenient day to start caring about his health.

I added, *Tell him it's for Iris. Thanks!* While Jimmy Joe read that, I tore another page from the pad, wrote my name on it, then ripped a piece of tape from the dispenser on the desk. Without waiting for a response, I ran outside and slapped the Iris Bailey note on the Admiral. It was almost mine. Even though I was in Serious Trouble, I smiled the whole way home.

7

Tristan wasn't home yet when I got back there, but more importantly, neither was Mom. I'd have a chance to work on my radios before she came in to lecture me.

I ran upstairs to my room, where my radio collection filled shelves across three walls. I'd have to add a new shelf soon. Tools and electronics parts and wires covered the workbench I'd made out of an old door. My mom said it looked like a robot factory exploded in my room, but I knew where to find everything.

Most people were surprised when they found out I fixed old radios, but that was because most people don't notice that sound moves. If it's strong enough, it can move anything. Its waves can break glass or shake the ground or deafen a whale.

Even if they're not strong, sound waves tremble radios, too. That was why I didn't need to hear one to know if it was working. With my hand on the speaker, the vibrations let me know if a radio was playing music or crackling with static or sitting there like a box of rocks.

For me, listening to the radios was never the point. Each one of those sitting on my shelves was a reminder of something I'd done right. They weren't working until I got my hands into them. Whenever I fixed something, I felt like I'd won a contest.

I sat down next to my bed and touched the side of the Philco 38-690 cabinet radio like I did every day when I got home and every morning before I left. Of all the antique radios in my collection, this was my favorite. Since it was almost four feet tall, it sat on the floor instead of on a shelf like the others. It was from the 1930s and, in my professional opinion, the best radio ever made. Only three thousand ever existed.

For a long time I'd only seen the 38-690 in pictures. Then one day there it was, behind the counter at Mr. Gunnar's antique shop. My eyes almost fell out of my head when Mr. Gunnar said he was going to throw it away. Sure, it was in rough shape. Really rough. But I couldn't let him get rid of it. I asked if I could take it as payment for a repair I'd brought him. He said that wouldn't be fair, so he paid me *and* gave me the radio. Then I sort of felt like I was stealing from an old man.

Even though he might change his mind, I told Mr. Gunnar what the Philco could be worth if I restored it. Maybe he didn't know what he had.

A cloud of dust flew up when he patted the radio's scratched wooden cabinet. "If you do all the work this thing is going to need, you deserve to keep it."

For the next five months, I worked to bring the Philco back from the dead. When I finally finished, static hummed against my palms. With the smallest turn of the dial, the smooth rhythm of music flowed from the speaker, vibrating the whole cabinet of the radio. If anyone had asked why I was sitting there crying with my arms around a radio, I wouldn't have known how to explain it. I couldn't stop thinking about how many years it had sat quietly collecting dust and how close it had come to being thrown in the garbage because no one thought it was worth listening to.

Usually I left it on overnight, even though that would wear it out faster. While I was in bed, I could reach over and feel the vibrations against my hand and fall asleep wondering who was singing and who was listening.

The floor shook a little, announcing Mom coming up the stairs. I sat there, waiting to find out what my punishment would be. Probably I wouldn't be allowed to use my phone or visit my friend Wendell for a while.

When the door opened I turned to her and signed, *"I know, Serious Trouble. But—"*

She pointed around my room before I could explain that what had happened at school wasn't my fault. *"All of this,"* she signed, *"is out of here."*

"What?"

"Get some sheets and towels and wrap them up if you want, but as soon as Tristan gets home, you're going to help us carry everything out to the garage."

I gripped the edge of the Philco, as if I could keep it from leaving my side. *"No, that isn't fair!"*

"You said you'd stay out of trouble. We warned you about this."

"I didn't know you meant I'd lose my radios." I waved my arms at my collection. *"I didn't know you'd take everything I have."*

"You're being dramatic. It isn't everything you have. Anyway," she added before I could interrupt her, *"we have to do something to get your attention. Maybe you'll take us seriously when we say you have to learn to get along with people and follow the rules. That girl's parents are really upset with the school."*

"It's not the school's fault. Or my fault. They should be mad at themselves for raising an annoying daughter."

"It can't always be someone else's fault. If people annoy you, you have to figure out a better way to deal with it."

"Easy for you to say. There isn't a better way when everyone ignores you." Warm tears dampened my fingertips when my signing hands touched my face. I wiped my hands on my jeans. Just then, I remembered the Admiral set. I couldn't believe I'd forgotten about it. Mom's announcement about taking my radios must have short-circuited my brain.

"I have to pick up a TV from the junkyard." Hopefully she wouldn't ask when I'd been at Moe's, but I had to risk it.

"No, we're not going out to get you a new thing to add to the exact collection you're grounded from. You have enough junk anyway."

It didn't matter that I had a lot of junk. I didn't have that particular item. I tried to explain it, but Mom turned to leave. The conversation was over.

Before she walked out I waved my hand to get her attention. "When can I have my stuff back?"

"A little at a time, starting Monday."

"What will I do all weekend?"

"You can visit Wendell, and we'll go to Grandma's on

Saturday. You're not grounded from everything, just your electronics."

Which was everything.

When Tristan got home he told me I didn't have to help carry my things out. He knew how much it would hurt. *"Mom and I will take care of it."*

I shook my head as I slid one of my smaller radios into a pillowcase. *"That's okay. But thanks."* I really didn't want to do it, but I also didn't want to miss out on one more chance to hold my radios before they were put away.

After we hauled my stuff to the garage, I went back up to my room, which wasn't really my room anymore. The shelves were bare. So was the worktable, which just a few hours earlier had been piled with electronics parts. A thin layer of dust outlined all that was missing. An imprint in the carpet next to my bed marked where the Philco should have been.

I lay down in bed and turned toward the wall so I wouldn't have to face the emptiness.

Tristan came in later to check on me. I turned when he sat at the edge of the bed and touched my shoulder.

"You okay?" he signed.

I rolled onto my back. *"No. I will never be okay."*

"I'm sorry."

"It isn't fair. I need my stuff. It's work anyway, like for Mr. Gunnar. So they're grounding me from work, which is stupid."

"Yeah, I told Mom that. I think they want you to hang out with people instead of radios so much."

"I do hang out with people." Tristan didn't respond to that. Maybe he didn't believe me. He was always doing things with friends.

"It's just for a couple days."

"But there's this radio I really need. Mom won't let me pick it up, even if I promise not to work on it yet."

"Where is it?"

"Moe's." I sat up. "Will you go get it for me? Please? It looks heavy since it's in a cabinet with a TV and record player, but you're strong enough to load it into your truck."

He said what looked like "Ummm . . ." and ran a hand through his hair. Unlike me, he could do that without getting his hand stuck. He had Dad's smooth light brown hair, instead of thick dark curls like Mom and me. All I got from Dad was pale skin that turned pink and more freckled in the sun, instead of Mom's, which tanned.

"Please," I signed again. "Do you know how many vacuum tubes are in there?"

"No idea. How many?"

"I don't know. More than I need. I was going to look it up. Plus tube sockets, wires, transformers, caps . . ."

Tristan laughed and threw his hands up in surrender, which, as it happens, looks like the sign for "give up." *"Okay, okay. But then what? You don't think Mom and Dad will notice?"*

"Hide it in the garage with everything else. Then we'll bring it up to my closet when they're not here."

"Okay, hold on. Be right back." He signed *"hold"* like he was clutching something in his fist and not by pointing an index finger up like people do all the time, as if they were saying *Wait a minute* and then never getting back to you. Tristan knew I hated that.

After a few minutes Tristan came back and waved me to the doorway. *"Let's go."*

"Me? Go where?"

"I just chugged the last of the milk and then told Mom I'd go out to pick up more."

I jumped up and slid into my shoes. Milk wasn't the only thing we'd be picking up.

Moe was back at his usual place behind the desk in the junk-yard's office trailer.

"How was the doctor appointment?" I asked.

Tristan voiced my question, and Moe answered, "I'm healthy as a horse."

Not any horse I'd want to ride, but I wasn't going to mention that. *"How much for the Admiral set?"*

Even though Tristan was there, Moe communicated with me like he always did and held up two fingers on one hand and five on the other.

I pretended to consider the twenty-five-dollar offer, as if I wasn't desperate enough to pay whatever he asked. Before we left home I'd grabbed two twenties from my repair money envelope.

I held up two fingers on one hand and formed the other into an *O* handshape.

Moe nodded and gave me a thumbs-up, then followed us outside after I handed him a twenty. He helped Tristan lift up the set and load it into the truck. Before hopping into the passenger seat, I shook Moe's hand and hugged Tristan. I'd have to force myself to stop smiling when we got home so Mom wouldn't wonder why I was so happy.

We were pulling into the driveway when I tapped Tristan on the shoulder and signed, *"Milk!"* The reason for the trip, as far as Mom knew. He backed out and hurried to the gas station.

"Want anything?" he asked when we were inside.

"I'm almost out of gummy worms," I answered.

He squeezed my shoulder and signed, *"Pick out whatever you want."*

The hard part was when we got home. Tristan always parked in the driveway, since our two-car garage had room for only one car and a bunch of stuff. We slid the TV onto a flattened cardboard box and shoved it into the garage, stopping a couple times along the way to give my arms a rest. Finally we got it safely in the corner and covered it with garage junk. Tomorrow it would be in my closet where it belonged, and my room wouldn't feel so empty anymore.

8

The weekend of my grounding dragged by even worse than I'd expected. My friend Wendell was out of town with his family, so I couldn't hang out at his house. Tristan and his friend Adam had moved the TV/radio/record player to my closet. Now and then I'd open the door to take a peek, but I couldn't crack it open yet. After clearing out my room, I didn't even have a screwdriver left. Still, I felt better just knowing the Admiral set was close by, waiting for me.

While lying on my bed with my phone, I searched online for the whale. Ever since Ms. Alamilla had showed us that video in class, I'd been thinking about Blue 55 and the people who tried to tag him with the tracker.

I couldn't remember the name of the sanctuary from the video, but it came up after a quick search about Blue 55's tagging.

The "Meet Our Residents" page on the sanctuary's website showed a picture of each animal that lived there, along with a description. Either the sanctuary staff had found them injured or sick, or someone had called for help when they found them hurt in the water or on the beach. The animals lived either in large sea pens or indoor pools until they were healthy enough to return to the wild. Most of the animals were birds or seals and sea lions. One dolphin they'd have to move indoors if they couldn't release him before winter hit Alaska.

For some, the sanctuary would always be their home. The eagle who was blind in one eye couldn't hunt for food in the wild. He probably didn't understand why he couldn't fly outdoors anymore. The otter orphans had an indoor-outdoor pool to swim in. They'd have to live at the sanctuary forever too. They had lost their mothers when they were so young that they hadn't learned how to be otters. I wondered about the animals who'd been taken in when they were older and still remembered their old homes. The sanctuary staff would release them close to where they'd been found, in hopes they'd find their families. They couldn't promise it would happen, though. The released animals might have to make it on their own.

At the top of a page labeled "The Staff" was a picture of a few people in light blue shirts with their arms around one another, smiling in front of the sanctuary. The caption of the photo said that it was the expedition team that tried to tag Blue 55 the year before.

After scrolling through some of the posts, I found one about the failed attempt to tag Blue 55. The tracker they wanted to put on him would collect information not just about where he swam, but other things too, like his heart rate. It would also record his song. They'd share information about him on their website if they ever did tag him. Now I really wished they'd tagged him. If they shared what they recorded from that, I'd get to feel his song and heartbeat through a computer speaker.

A picture showed Blue 55's back arching out of the water, next to a small boat. Mounted to the front of the boat was a metal platform with railings on either side. A woman wearing a stocking cap and a green fleece jacket stood at the edge of the platform, holding a long metal pole outstretched toward the whale. It looked like she'd topple over the railing and into the ocean if she leaned over any farther to reach him. The caption read: "Near miss: Blue 55 takes a dive before sanctuary staffer Andi Rivera can attach a tracking device."

The tracker at the end of the pole looked close

enough to brush the whale's back. A grimace lined Andi's face, either from effort or disappointment. The next photo showed water cascading down Blue 55's huge tail as he started his deep dive. Andi had been so close to him before he slipped away. Maybe she was only interested in him as a scientist, but she tried so hard to reach him; maybe she really cared about him, too.

If Blue 55 followed the route he usually did, he'd be near the sanctuary soon. A new post said that the team would try again to tag him. They didn't say what they would do differently next time, so they could get close enough to attach the tracker before he swam away. Maybe there was a way to get him to stick around a little longer.

At the bottom of the page was a link to more information about Blue 55's communication. That article used piano keys to describe whale song frequencies. If you sit down at a piano and hit the lowest key, the very first one on the left, that plays the frequency of 27.5 hertz. That's the frequency of most baleen whale songs. They sing lower than that, too—like twenty hertz or ten hertz—but pianos didn't have a key that played that low. Count over to key number thirteen, and you'll play fifty-five hertz—Blue 55's frequency, and the reason he couldn't talk to any other whale.

Already I was thinking of a way to reach out to him. At my desk I grabbed a scrap of paper to jot down some notes. I didn't know yet how it would work, but maybe the people who wanted to tag Blue 55 could find a way to sing back to him and hold his attention with something that sounded a bit like himself.

As I wrote, a thought came up that crumbled the edges of my plan. Maybe he was like that sei whale on the beach, except that he'd found a way to survive.

On the sanctuary's post about Blue 55's communication, I scanned the comments section to see if anyone wondered the same thing I had. No one suggested it yet, so I scrolled back up and left a comment.

Maybe the whale is deaf.

9

On the way to Oak Manor to visit Grandma on Saturday, Tristan touched my shoulder and signed, *"Hungry?"* He smiled like something was funny.

Actually, I was starving. *"Yeah, why?"*

"Your stomach is rumbling like an airplane engine."

I covered my stomach with my hands to muffle the sound and smiled back at him. *"I doubt that. An airplane engine is over one hundred decibels."* However loud a stomach rumble was, it had to be a lot less than that.

That morning I'd been too nervous to eat breakfast. Normally I was excited to visit Grandma. Other than Wendell, she was the only Deaf person I got to talk to anymore.

Lately it was like I needed a bridge to get to her. One of us would say something; then the conversation would fizzle out, and we were back to sitting there trying to come up with something else to say. It used to be that when I got together with my grandparents, we'd sign nonstop, catching up on everything in our lives and laughing at our own jokes and stories that made sense only in sign language. Maybe Grandpa had been our bridge, and we didn't notice it until he was gone.

Grandma had moved to Oak Manor just a few weeks earlier. Before that she still lived in the house she'd shared with Grandpa for forever. One day, about a month after Grandpa died, she didn't answer the door when we went to visit her. She didn't reply to text messages either. Her car wasn't in the garage.

We let ourselves in with the spare key that Mom had, then searched the house. I checked the study. On her desk was a lamp I'd made her out of an old wine bottle. I'd filled it with shells and sea glass we'd found at the beach. Next to that was a picture of Grandpa and me building a sandcastle.

Grandma, where are you? I looked up then at a framed picture on the wall and felt like she was teasing me with an answer. Below the picture of a whale swimming in the ocean was a quote from her favorite book, *Moby-Dick:* "I know not all that may be coming, but be it what it will, I'll go to it laughing."

I found Mom in Grandma's room, sitting on the bed with her phone.

"*Maybe she's at the beach,*" I suggested.

Mom shook her head. "*She never drives that far. I'm checking with her friends to see if they know anything. I'm sure she's fine.*" Before she pulled me in for a hug, I caught the expression on her face. It matched the worry I felt.

Dad finally called the police.

An hour later the police called back. They found Grandma more than one hundred miles away at the Gulf Coast, walking the stretch of beach where we used to live.

After she got back home, she tried to explain that she'd left because she was like Ishmael in *Moby-Dick*. Sometimes she had too much of a drizzly November in her soul and had to get to the sea. She used to travel with Grandpa all the time, she said, and everyone should stop making such a big deal over it.

"*Why didn't you at least tell us where you were going?*" Mom asked her.

"*Because you would've talked me out of it.*" No one argued with that.

Mom finally convinced her to move to Oak Manor, which was an apartment complex for old people. Grandma said the house was too big for one person to take care of anyway, so she'd go. I didn't believe her.

She looked like she just didn't feel strong enough to keep fighting. Sometimes that was the easier choice.

My parents promised to take her to the beach in the summer, maybe, when they weren't so busy with work.

Sometimes I worried that Grandma wouldn't make it until summer. Her November had gone on for three months already, and it seemed like she might be stuck there wandering and shivering forever. So there was something I couldn't fix.

Before we went through the sliding glass doors at Oak Manor, Mom gave me a tight hug that lasted a few seconds longer than most. Then she stepped back and smoothed my hair and signed, *"I love you."* She did that every time we visited Grandma. Just to me, never to Tristan.

"Love you, too, Mom."

Tristan and I headed upstairs with Dad, while Mom went to the social worker's office to ask if Grandma was making friends yet.

It was almost noon when we got to Grandma's apartment, but she looked like she'd just rolled out of bed. She wore a pair of sweatpants and a gray T-shirt she'd probably slept in. After giving each of us a hug, she invited us to come in and sit down.

"Where's Mom?" she asked.

"She'll be up in a minute," I answered. "Talking to the staff downstairs."

Grandma smiled. "About your uncooperative grandmother."

"So that's where Iris gets it." Dad laughed at his own joke.

Grandma sat next to me on the couch and asked, "How's school?"

"The same," I answered.

"Sorry to hear that." She turned to my dad and signed, "Maybe Iris could transfer to Bridgewood and be around other Deaf students." She signed slowly for my dad and used her voice, too. She could hear a little, and people who knew her could mostly understand what she said. And Dad never had learned sign language very well. He could get by okay, but it wasn't like we could have a real conversation. I didn't expect him to know it as well as Mom. She had Deaf parents, so she was signing before she could talk. I just wished he put more effort into learning it. He said he'd always been more of a "numbers person" than a "words person" and that it was hard to learn a new language. Seems like having a kid you could barely talk to would be harder.

I held my breath, wondering if Dad might agree with her. Bridgewood was a district with a big deaf education program about a twenty-minute drive from our neighborhood. Deaf kids, like my friend Wendell, from three school districts went there. But Mom insisted on me going to Timber Oaks with all my "neighborhood friends." I'd pointed out to her that I didn't have any of those anyway, but it didn't help. She wanted to stick with the plan she'd come up with when we first moved to town.

Once in a while Grandma brought up my going to Bridgewood. Maybe Dad would agree with her this time, without Mom there to say I should keep going to school with the same people I'd been with all along. Dad didn't seem to care much either way. If he thought Grandma had a good idea, maybe he'd mention it to Mom later.

Dad said something while throwing in a couple of signs like *"think"* and *"ship"* and then waved his hand. From what I could piece together from the signs and what I read on his mouth, it was something like "I think that ship has sailed." He used figures of speech all the time, even though most of them didn't make sense in sign language. Usually I could figure out what he meant, like if I'd read the phrase in a book or it was one he said a lot. Once in a while an English expression was similar to one in sign language. Like if you pretend you're pulling a hair from your head, that's like the English phrase "by a hair." Usually they didn't match up so nicely.

"What do you mean?" I didn't see why he thought it was too late for me to switch school districts. Why should I stay in the same place just because I'd been there for so long?

"Nothing," Dad signed. *"It's not important."* He looked at Grandma and said, "Iris has gotten used to her school."

Heat rushed to my face. I probably looked sunburned. This was a conversation about my school, and Dad wanted to leave me out of it. Even worse than talking around me was talking *about* me like I wasn't there.

"Really?" Grandma asked. She didn't look like she was waiting for an answer. Her eyes shifted over to me.

I leaned forward and waved my arm so Dad would look at me again. *"It's important to me."*

"You know, it's like 'train gone,'" signed Tristan.

"I know that," I signed. *"I meant, why is Dad saying that about school?"*

"Train?" Dad asked.

I almost had to sit on my hands to keep from answering, *"Nothing. It's not important."*

"Remember? That's how you do that phrase in sign

language," Tristan answered. *"Instead of saying, 'That ship has sailed' or 'You missed the boat.'"*

"I've shown you that before," I told Dad. *"But that's not the point."* Why had that ship sailed? I'd be starting junior high next year anyway. Might as well hop on the next boat or train or whatever with people I could talk to.

Mom walked in then with some flyers.

"Hi, Mom," she signed, and came over to the couch to give Grandma a hug.

Grandma gave her a small smile and signed, *"I know, I'm in trouble."*

"You're not in trouble," Mom said. *"But I was hoping you'd be socializing more. It isn't good for you to be by yourself all the time."*

Tristan sat on the floor in front of the couch and took a flyer from Mom.

"I know," Grandma said. *"I never feel like doing anything. I'll get out sometime."*

"Look." Tristan pointed out some events on the calendar. *"They have a lot of stuff going on. Movie nights, games, a field trip to the zoo."*

"Nothing's the same without Grandpa."

One reason my parents suggested Oak Manor to

Grandma—besides all the staff who'd help keep an eye on her—was that there was a Deaf group who did things together. She chatted with a couple of them, but that was it. Grandma and Grandpa always seemed so outgoing, so fun. All that had drained out of her now that he wasn't around anymore.

They'd met in college, where they were in a Deaf theater group together. Sometimes the plays they performed were all in sign language, and they'd have interpreters speaking the parts for "the sign language impaired." Other times they interpreted plays for the school, after rehearsing for weeks with the cast. They were so good at bringing a play to life that it wasn't just deaf people in the audience who loved watching them—everyone did. That was what they'd told me, anyway.

Mom brushed a lock of Grandma's hair back with her hand. *"You're not taking care of yourself."* She found a hairbrush in the bathroom, then sat on the other side of Grandma and motioned for her to turn toward me so she could brush her hair. Grandma's hair had been a long silvery waterfall for as long as I could remember. All the tangles in it that day made me wonder how long it had been since she'd brushed it.

I rubbed the lightning bolt Z on my necklace. There we were again, so close but with the Gulf of Mexico between us.

Maybe there was a way Grandpa could still bridge us together.

"Handshape game?" I asked.

Grandma shook her head. *"That was Grandpa's thing."*

"And now it'll be our thing." I waited, ready for her to argue back.

"Okay. What shape?"

I held up my index fingers.

Grandma nodded and motioned for me to start.

I looked up and drew the sun in the sky, squinting to show its brightness.

Grandma looked up too, then shook her head and put a finger to her lips. *"There is no sun."*

Fine, then, it'd be nighttime. I showed a star in the sky.

Grandma added, *"It's the only star."*

Why couldn't I have picked any other shape, one that wouldn't lend itself to such lonely signs? I wanted to erase everything and then open my hands to show a sky full of stars, but that would break the pattern I'd started. I'd make it work.

I looked up as if I could see it. *"No, there's a shooting star."* I drew its path zipping across the sky.

Grandma showed the shooting star traveling farther and farther away. She pointed to the first star, alone in the sky again.

My turn. Two people walked together, side by side. One of them pointed out the star, and they both looked up and smiled.

On Grandma's turn, one of those people flew up to the sky to join that star, leaving the other person all alone.

I didn't want the game to end that way, leaving that person standing on the earth all alone watching a star. But I couldn't think of what else to add to the story.

I lost.

10

By the time I got home from Grandma's, a reply to my comment on the sanctuary's post was waiting for me.

Great point, Iris. We wondered about that too, but we think Blue 55 wouldn't sing at all if he were deaf. Sometimes he swims long distances to other whales, so it seems like he's following their sounds. Perhaps he has something like tone deafness, and he just can't tell he isn't singing like the others. Or for some reason he's not able to produce the same sounds.

Sometimes he's quiet for weeks at a time, and we worry that he's given up (or that he's no longer alive), but then he starts singing again. It seems he keeps trying to communicate, but there's nothing out there that understands his songs.

So he wasn't deaf; he just couldn't match the calls of the whales around him.

Before reading the rest of the message, I checked the expedition team's photos again to see who'd replied to me. The name at the top of the reply read "Andi Rivera." Andi was the woman in the photo who'd tried to tag Blue 55 the year before. The picture of the team posing together in their blue shirts showed a better view of her. Her long black hair was pulled back into a ponytail, and she looked like she was laughing. The sun, or the cold wind, had turned the cheeks of her brown face rosy.

We might never find out why whales sing, but as a scientist, I'm always thinking and looking for answers. Why Blue 55 sings when no other whale answers back is an even bigger mystery. Maybe he just likes to sing, and it doesn't matter that it's an unusual song. A lot of people think that Blue 55 is lonely. But I wonder, do we believe that because we're the ones who are lonely?

11

Ms. Shelton didn't forget about the apology thing. She told Ms. Conn I had to apologize to Nina before returning to class. Mr. Charles helped me come up with what to tell her. Even though it was Nina's fault, "Sorry you bothered me so much I had to shove you" wasn't going to work.

Mr. Charles walked with me to Nina's desk to interpret. *"Sorry I hurt you."*

She smiled a little and signed something that looked like *"pie."*

"All right," Mr. Charles corrected while biting his lip.

As soon as I got home that afternoon, I raced upstairs. Finally I'd have my radios back. Some of them, anyway. Enough to work on. For a while I stood in my bedroom doorway, looking around at the few items that were back on the shelves where they belonged.

First I had to put my workshop back in order. Mom had returned the tools and parts but didn't know where anything belonged. The Admiral set was too heavy for me to drag into my room, so I sat on the closet floor with my screwdriver. After I opened the back panel, I sat there for a minute and stared at the dust-covered parts. The work would go faster if I didn't have my thick leather gloves on, but I told my parents I'd always wear them. Unplugged or not, the radios I worked on weren't as safe as new models. Back when that old stuff was made, it was your own dumb fault if you died of electrocution.

At first glance I could tell that at least a couple of the vacuum tubes weren't any good. No obvious cracks, but the cloudy white coating inside the glass tubes let me know it was time to toss them. They'd look pretty on a Christmas tree, but I'd throw them into the recycling bin. Mom had told me enough already with the busted vacuum tube–ornaments.

Even so, that old set turned out to be worth all the trouble. When I finished the cleaning and testing of the tubes, I had five good ones.

No guarantee they'd fit the Zenith radio, though. Sometimes parts that looked like they'd match up per-fectly turned out not to fit at all.

But it worked. The new tubes slid into place like they belonged there.

Before screwing on the back panel of the Zenith, I checked everything one more time, then plugged it in. Then I stood there admiring the radio. Whenever I was pretty sure a radio was fixed, I liked to wait a minute before turning it on. It was like closing a really good book just before the final page to make it last.

Now to check. I turned on the radio for a few seconds, then switched it off and stepped back. No smoke, so I hadn't blown anything up. Nothing in the air but the smell of old radio. My favorite smell. It reminded me of attics and campfires and the antique books in Mr. Gunnar's store. I'd read that the smell was just radio parts and dust warmed up by electricity, but it was more than that. It was like the radio was remembering every home it had ever been in.

I reached over to turn it back on, then placed my hand on the speaker. Static hummed against my fingers. Almost there. The slightest turn of the knob, and the vibrations smoothed out. There was the music.

Usually I didn't think about what music sounded like. But right then, with my hand on the radio, I wondered if any note of the song vibrating the speaker sounded like Blue 55.

At my computer I searched for more about the whale. A website about whale migration came up, with maps showing where different species of whales swam throughout the year. A lot of whales were hanging around California or Alaska for the summer since that was where the food was. When it got colder they'd swim back to Hawaii or Mexico or some other warm place.

The most interesting part was how the scientists made those maps. A few whales had trackers on them, like the one that Andi from the sanctuary tried to put on Blue 55. But the scientists knew where most of the whales were because of underwater microphones in oceans all over the world. They listened to the songs and knew what kind of whale sang them. Then they'd add to the map, showing a humpback pod in Massachusetts or a minke whale in Norway. The whales' songs were like footprints they left in the ocean.

This worked even if the whales were far away. Sound traveled farther in water than in air, so a whale song could be heard from hundreds of miles away, maybe more.

Blue 55 had a map all his own. He traveled the same waters as some other whales, but at different times. Sometimes there were gaps in his route, when no microphone picked up his song. Either he wasn't singing then or other noise in the ocean drowned out his calls. A dotted blue line on the map showed the best guess of where he was.

Sometimes he took a completely different route, one that no other whale ever did. The lines on the other whales' maps were smooth, curving up or down coastlines. Blue 55 took a more jagged route. He'd start swimming one way, then for some reason change direction and go off to the side or back the way he'd just been.

I traced the blue line with my finger. *What are you looking for?*

Below each map was a recording of the whales' songs. When I clicked on a sound file, colored lines on a graph rose and fell, showing the volume and frequency of the songs that played.

I ran downstairs to bring up the website on Mom's computer, since it had speakers plugged into it. With the volume turned up, I rested my hand on a speaker and clicked on each sound file. The low calls of the normal whales vibrated more strongly against my hand than 55's did. It didn't feel like a huge difference, though. I wished I could understand the songs and figure out what they were saying, or at least why they couldn't talk to one another.

I couldn't imagine trying for so long to reach out to someone else when there was never a reply. Either he was still waiting for someone to answer back or hearing his own song was enough for him.

With my hand on the computer's speaker, I closed my eyes as the song fluttered against my fingers. This was different from anything I'd felt through a radio speaker before. Not like any other music, and not like talking, either.

A steady vibration tickled my palm as Blue 55 sang out a long call that seemed like it would never end. Then the speaker pulsed when he switched to short bursts of sound. While keeping one hand on the speaker, I placed the other over my heart to feel the matching rhythms of my heartbeat and the whale song.

On another website, I found a picture of Blue 55, taken by a photographer with an underwater camera. It looked like one of the images from the video Ms. Alamilla showed us. A profile of his face, with the black oval of his eye centered on the photo. It hadn't been so long ago that I first saw him in that video, but it felt like I'd always known him. I clicked print on the photo so I could tack it to my wall.

While the printer ran I swiveled the chair around to the window and watched Tristan and his friends playing basketball in the driveway. My eyes darted from one to the other, trying to grab any scrap of conversation as they dribbled and passed the ball and shot baskets. They all laughed and high-fived their friend Pablo over something he said. Tristan aimed for the hoop but then started laughing again, doubled over this time.

I turned back to the printer. The guys were probably laughing about something dumb anyway.

When I clicked on the sound file again, one hand felt the song playing through the speaker, and the other hand held a picture of who was singing.

12

Mr. Gunnar smiled and waved when I carried the Zenith into the shop. I set it on the counter and waited while he rang up a customer buying a creepy old doll.

"It really works?" he said after the customer left. Mr. Gunnar used to have such a bushy mustache that talking to him was like trying to lip-read a walrus. He kept it trimmed now so it didn't hang over his upper lip anymore.

I nodded and invited him to check it out. Sometimes the radios needed a little more adjusting after I thought I was finished. I knew when a radio was working, but couldn't always tell if the sound was clear enough. Some static was too faint for me to feel crackling against the speakers.

Mr. Gunnar's smile let me know I got it right. He shook his head and laughed, then he looked at me so

I could see his mouth. To make things clearer he threw in a few signs he'd learned from me.

"I admit, I wasn't sure you could fix this one." He tied a price tag to the cord, then handed me the radio. After putting it on a shelf, I wandered around the store to see if there was anything I needed. Mr. Gunnar gave me an employee discount, even though I wasn't an official employee.

That store was where I first got interested in electronics. Grandpa and I would pick up things like old lamps and toys and take them home to work on them together. Sometimes we'd take parts from different lamps and make a whole new one, like the bottle lamp I made for Grandma. Then I started not just fixing things, but making things. I built an alarm clock that shook my mattress in the morning, all with parts I picked up at Moe's. I made an alarm clock for Tristan, too. He could hear just fine, but he was such a deep sleeper, nothing could wake him. At first I gave him an alarm clock I'd connected to a truck horn. It did wake him up, but it also woke my parents, who said they nearly had heart attacks when it went off. I made him another one out of an old toy police car that drove around his room blaring its siren until he got up to turn it off.

One day when Grandma and Grandpa were shopping for furniture, I discovered the radios. I pushed buttons and turned knobs, trying to figure out how they worked. Mr. Gunnar took the time to explain what he could, pointing at radio parts and jotting down notes on some scrap paper. Even better, he gave me a broken old radio to take home to work on. After he handed it to me and saw how excited I was, he held up a hand like he had to warn me of something. *It'll be a challenge,* he wrote.

Well, that did it. I didn't know whether he meant that it'd be a challenge for *anyone* to repair that radio, or for me because I wouldn't hear when it started working. Either way, I was taking it home. Lately I'd been feeling like I could fix anything. I was ready for a challenge.

He added to the note, *The best way to learn how something works is to take it apart and put it back together.* I don't know what made him think I was smart enough to do that, but he did.

It took a lot of work, and I almost gave up a few times, but eventually, I did get that radio fixed. More importantly, it taught me how radios worked. I'd lost count of how many I'd repaired since then. I would've missed out on all that if I hadn't been there with my grandparents that day. Without that store and Mr. Gunnar, I wouldn't know I was good at anything.

After shelving the Zenith, I didn't find anything I needed, so I went back to the front counter empty-handed. As Mr. Gunnar wrote out the check for my repair payment, something in the display case caught my eye. I held up a hand to stop him, then tapped the glass over the item. He smiled and pulled a giant key ring from his pocket so he could unlock the case, then looked at me to see if he was removing the right thing. I held out my hand, and he placed the gold circle on my palm.

It looked like an old pocket watch. Etched into the cover was an ocean scene, with a whale leaping out of the water next to a sailing ship.

With a fingertip I traced the black outline of the whale. Mr. Gunnar reached over and unlatched the cover, revealing not a watch but a compass.

"Still works," he signed.

A compass. Even better than a watch. I closed the cover and ran my finger over the etching again, wondering about who it had belonged to. A ship captain, I guessed, because of the design. Before computers and GPS, people navigated with compasses and the stars in the sky.

Finding that whale compass felt like a good sign. Like maybe it'd bring me good luck in figuring out a way to talk to Blue 55. I held it up to let Mr. Gunnar know to subtract the price from what he owed me.

"Something different!" he said, then signed the check. "Ready to sell me that Philco?" he asked before I left. He didn't need to sign or write that down because he asked that every time. He was sort of teasing. Sure, he'd love to have the Philco back, but he also knew I'd never part with it.

13

Wendell's house was just a short bike ride from Mr. Gunnar's shop. Before leaving home I'd stuffed my notes about frequencies and piano keys into the front pocket of my jeans.

Wendell's nine-year-old sister, Eleanor, was practicing tennis in the driveway as usual, a bundle of black braids flying behind her as she served a ball to the garage door and chased after it for the return. One got past her, and I grabbed it as it rolled toward the street.

"Looking good," I signed after tossing it back to her. Eleanor's goal was to be a better tennis player than Venus and Serena Williams put together. Not just because they'd be old by the time she could play them. She wanted to be good enough to beat them any time.

She set the ball and racket down to free up her hands. *"Thanks. Getting ready for a match this weekend."* Eleanor signed like a Deaf person even though she was hearing. Wendell was the only one in their family who'd ever been deaf, as far as anyone knew. Their parents started learning sign language right after Wendell was born, and they signed all the time at home. His mom was even a teacher of the deaf at Bridgewood Junior High, where Wendell would go next year.

"You'll do great. Wendell here?"

She pointed into the house while taking a gulp from her water bottle. Summer had hit Houston already, and Eleanor's brown face was shining with sweat. *"He's changing the stars,"* she signed after setting her bottle back down.

Through the glass panel on the front door, I saw the flicker of the strobe light when I pressed the doorbell, followed by the tall figure of Wendell's mom. We had a flashing doorbell at home too so I'd know when someone was at the door. I'd wired mine so that lamps in the living room and my bedroom blinked on and off when someone rang the doorbell.

Ms. Jackson answered the door and smiled. *"Great to see you,"* she signed. *"Wendell's upstairs."*

I thanked her and ran up to Wendell's room, where he stood on a wooden ladder, pulling sticky plastic stars from the ceiling. His T-shirt read "You Are Here," with an arrow pointing to a spot in the Milky Way.

I didn't have to ask what he was doing; he was always rearranging the stars to match the current night sky.

He gave me a one-handed *"What's up?"* with the hand that wasn't holding a star chart.

"Can I play the piano?" I asked.

"Probably not very well."

I put a hand on one hip and signed, *"I'm serious,"* even though I was trying not to laugh. *"I mean, I want to check something out on the piano."*

He climbed down from the ladder and led me into his family's library, which was also their piano room.

We sat on the bench together and he asked, *"So what's the thing you have to check out?"*

I handed him the slip of paper from my pocket.

"It's about this whale."

"What kind of whale?"

"Not a kind of whale, just one specific whale. I learned about him in science." I placed a hand on top of the piano, and Wendell did the same thing.

At the top of the page I'd written *regular whales 28 Hz, 1st piano key. 35 Hz, 5th key.* With one finger I struck the key on the far left. The low sound vibrated against my palm. I played it a few times so we could get to know the sound. Then I did the same thing with each key up to the fifth one, a black one that played thirty-five hertz. Blue and fin whales didn't sing much higher than that.

On the next line of the page I'd written *55 Hz, 13th piano key.*

I counted over starting from the first key, until I landed on number thirteen, a white key this time. I played the note a few times, and the vibration tickled my palm again, a bit lighter than the others.

"So this whale," I explained to Wendell. *"That's what he sounds like."* I hit the key again. *"But here's what he's supposed to sound like."* I struck the first key again. *"So he can't talk to other whales."*

Wendell placed both hands on top of the piano, as I alternated between the two notes. *"Not much of a difference,"* he signed.

"It's a big difference for whales."

He was right—it didn't feel like much of a difference. Less than a foot apart on the keyboard, but it separated Blue 55 from all other whales. I thought back to my visit with Grandma and how we sat right next to each other on the couch and couldn't think of what to say.

The befuddled face of Wendell's father peeked into the room. He looked like a taller version of Wendell, but with a bald brown head instead of a buzz cut.

Wendell raised his arms so his dad could see his signs over the top of the piano. *"It's our new act. We're going on the road as dueling pianists."*

"It'll be great." Mr. Jackson laughed and added, *"As long as your audience is deaf too."* Wendell rolled his eyes like he was annoyed, but then laughed too. His dad was used to signing all the time, and he could jump in on any conversation with us. Wendell told me before that he'd gladly trade for a dad who didn't say anything unless he had to, but I knew he didn't mean it.

"So he can't sing lower or something?" Wendell asked after his dad left.

"No. He's been swimming around by himself for a long time, so I think if he could talk to other whales, he would."

"Or he's a loner and doesn't want to." Wendell nudged my shoulder. I didn't ask him why.

"I don't know, maybe. I think he just can't."

"And other whales can't hear him?"

"If they can, they don't know what he's saying."

I played each note again, focusing on the difference, and wished I could lower the piano into the ocean and play that note for Blue 55. *"I want to find a way to talk to him."*

"To the whale?"

"Yes, the whale."

"How?"

"That's what I have to figure out."

"Then what?"

"I don't know that, either. Not yet."

We took turns playing the keys, while each of us rested a hand on the piano.

"Why do you want to talk to him?" Wendell asked.

I didn't know how to answer him, how to explain that this whale swam in an ocean surrounded by other whales he couldn't talk to, that there was no pod or single whale who understood him—not even his own parents—and that I wanted to create a song that would let him know he wasn't alone. I couldn't fully explain it to myself, either. I tried to come up with something to compare it to, like the pull of a tide, or something Wendell would understand better, like the gravity of a black hole drawing in everything around it.

"He keeps singing this song, and everything in the ocean swims by him, as if he's not there. He thinks no one understands him. I want to let him know he's wrong about that."

14

A pod of humpbacks swam past. He hadn't met them before; he was sure of that. He would remember. A whale remembers everything, even the things he tries very hard to forget.

Maybe he could join them. He approached from the side, swimming at the edge of the migrating family. For a time he would hang back, gliding silently alongside them. Later, if they didn't object, he would drift closer.

He had tried this before, each time hoping he would be allowed to stay, even if they couldn't understand his music. The pods who'd recently lost a member were the easiest to join. He knew them by their songs made of low, mournful tones, announcing their grief to the ocean. They swam with an empty space, carrying the shadow of a whale who used to be. Whether they craved a new whale to fill the emptiness or didn't have the strength to slap a tail to tell him to leave, he didn't know.

He created music the same way they did: forcing breath into spaces in his body, circulating the air until breath and space turned into song.

Still, the sound wasn't right. The tones didn't match the ones around him.

They had heard. He knew by the way they glanced back. With time, maybe they would understand just one sound, the smallest ripple of his song. And that would be enough.

15

I dreamed that Blue 55 sang to me. When I woke up, my hand still rested on top of the Philco.

Maybe the radio station had been playing a song with notes that hit fifty-five hertz. I wanted to feel them again. But the vibrations from the radio had changed to the choppy rhythm of talking, and the whale song from my dream had slipped away.

After that I couldn't fall back to sleep. I kept thinking about Blue 55's song, and wanted to feel it again. A search on my phone took me to an article called "Making Music with Whales," which had pictures of weird sheet music. I'd had to sit through enough music classes in elementary school to know what it should look like. Instead of black dots or circles for each note, these pictures showed music scales with colored lines and shapes over them. At first glance it looked like someone had splattered paint, making a colorful chain of islands across the page. As I looked more carefully, the shapes became more defined. One shape looked like a wobbly heart, another like a bird.

Sheet music for whale songs. Maybe I'd found a way to understand the whales' music without hearing it.

The colored splotches and lines represented the parts of the songs. Plain black dots weren't enough to show what a whale song sounded like. They sang more complicated songs than humans could compose. The colorful splotches covered more of the music scale than human music, with different notes flowing together in each part of the song.

The humpback's songs were the most complex, with lots of colors and shapes dancing up and down the musical scale. The songs of most whales stayed near the same lines of the scale instead of zigzagging from very low to very high, and didn't have as many colors. It was like most whales were playing one instrument and the humpbacks played a whole symphony. Their sheet music showed a song with an orange-pink-purple-red-and-blue pattern over and over, but the whales stretched them out as they went on, before starting the song over again with short bursts of sound.

The article even had sheet music for Blue 55. Some

of the colors were the same as the other whales', but they were higher on the musical scale and in a different pattern. His song was in a blue-purple-and-red pattern, adding a part at the end of each section that looked like wavy lines on the sheet music. Sometimes those waves were blue; sometimes red or purple. But he'd always sing the wavy-line part of the song before starting the pattern over again.

Same shape, different colors. Like Grandpa's poems—the same handshapes but different signs. Blue 55's own rhyme.

The notes on the page swirled together with the plan I'd started thinking of before I went to Wendell's to play the piano.

I found a chart online that listed musical instruments and the frequencies they played. Not many instruments could get as low as fifty-five hertz. Even though it was a high sound for a whale, it was low for humans. The tuba could play it, and the bass trombone. And a harpsichord, whatever that was. I printed out the chart, along with the sheet music.

I tacked Blue 55's song next to his picture on the wall. The song wasn't like any other, and no other whale understood it. But it was his. Maybe it didn't look like much on paper, but there was another way it was like Grandpa's poems: the whale needed space above and below and all around him to sing his song.

When I was in third grade, I had to go to music class with my homeroom. We followed a rotation for PE, library, music, and art. I had to be dragged out of the library when it was time to leave. In art I could paint or draw what I couldn't say. PE was something to put up with. But in music I would daydream while the class learned about musical notes or whatever, or I'd have to sign the songs along with Mr. Charles. The day the teacher handed out recorders for us to play, I asked Mom to get me out of the class. Playing music was worthless. From then on I had extra library time when the rest of my class went to music.

Then there I was, at the end of my sixth-grade year, standing in front of a door that read MUSIC ROOM. That morning I'd stopped by to ask the music teacher, Mr. Russell, if I could talk to him about a project. He said he'd have some time after school.

Before opening the door, I reached up and touched the whale compass, which I'd been wearing as a necklace. The day I brought it home from Mr. Gunnar's,

I dug through my jewelry box for a gold chain. Everything was either too short or the wrong color, except the one around my neck holding the radio knob. I unhooked the chain and threaded it through the loop at the top of the compass. As I hooked the clasp around my neck, I wondered if that ship captain who owned it ever found his way home.

A message on Mr. Russell's whiteboard read *Back after bus duty.* While I waited I browsed the posters of instruments on the walls. I pulled my notes about musical instruments and frequencies from my pocket, then touched the holes on the picture of the bass saxophone on the "Brass" poster. Someone who knew which holes to cover or uncover while blowing into the instrument would be able to play a note that Blue 55 would hear.

Mr. Russell waved his hand near me to let me know that he was back, then said, "Hooooow caaaaan I heeeellllp yooou?"

Normally his slow, exaggerated talking would annoy me, but my excitement about my plan pushed that aside. I handed Mr. Russell my notes, along with the sheet music for Blue 55's song. At the bottom of the page I'd written *I want to record a song for this whale.* He sat at his desk to look over everything, then flipped back to the beginning and read it again. I didn't notice until he glanced at my hand that my fingers were drumming his desk.

When he started to talk, I handed him a marker and pointed to the whiteboard.

Fascinating, he wrote. *I can put something together for you with some of the band and orchestra students. It won't sound so good to humans, but it could be a big hit for whales.* He laughed.

With a red marker I wrote, *Thanks. When can I come back to record it?*

A few students were coming into the music room with their instrument cases.

Tomorrow after school? he wrote. *It won't take long since it's only a couple of notes, just oddly played.*

Perfect. Once I got a sound file of the recording, I'd have the biggest part of what I needed. The plan to reach out to Blue 55 was coming together.

I smiled and wrote *Thank you!* on the board before leaving.

Mr. Russell hadn't asked what class my project was for, or even if it was for a class at all. That was okay. This was more important than any class.

Dear Andi,

Thanks for answering my questions so fast. Can you send me a recording of the sanctuary's animals, for a project I'm working on?

If you could send me a sound file of whatever you record, that would really help.

Thanks,

Iris Bailey

16

The students who would play 55's song took their places in the music room the next day. Many of the students sat off to the side to observe. Even the lowest notes of violins, clarinets, and trumpets were too high for Blue 55. I was surprised a tuba player wasn't participating. That was one of the few instruments I'd listed, since it could play notes even lower than 55's. But Mr. Russell said that the note I needed was hard to play, and he didn't have a student who could do it. So it took more skill than I'd thought, if you couldn't just play the note by holding your hands in the right place and blowing into the mouthpiece alone.

Before you leave I'll show you a way you can create that sound on a phone or tablet, he wrote on a sticky note.

Listed on the whiteboard were the instruments participating and the notes they'd play. I waited in a chair at the front of the room while the group did a couple of practice rounds. It looked like the students were checking something on their phones or some other small device after playing a note, sometimes shaking their heads and playing again. Mr. Russell played the piano and pointed to each student in turn, directing them to play the notes that matched fifty-five hertz. They played the ones just above or below that, too, since Blue 55 sometimes sang a little higher or lower. A few students watching the performance covered their ears. Hopefully it would sound better to 55.

Behind the rows of blue plastic chairs were the students with larger instruments. A boy with shaggy blond hair played the bass saxophone. I recognized Angelica Freeman because she lived a few houses down from me. She moved the fingers of one hand along the neck of an upright bass, the instrument I'd always thought of as an overgrown violin. Her other hand worked the bow back and forth across the strings.

After a few minutes Mr. Russell said something to the group, then stood up from the piano bench and wrote *Ready for the real thing* on the board. Mr. Russell turned on the microphones and stereo equipment. Later he'd email me the recording of the song.

If the room didn't have deep wall-to-wall carpet, I could have taken off my shoes to feel the vibrations of the music, like of the bass drum that sat on the floor.

I wondered what all those instruments sounded like together, then reminded myself it was like the song of 55 I'd felt on the computer speakers at home. I just wished I could feel it then.

Instead of sitting down again after pressing the record button, Mr. Russell pointed to me, then to the piano bench.

I pointed to my chest. *"Me?"*

He nodded, then wrote, *It's your song. Only fair you get to play it.* I smiled and sat at the bench. Playing Blue 55's song was even better than hearing it. Mr. Russell made a tapping motion near the correct key, but I already knew which note to play. I placed a finger on the thirteenth key, then looked up to wait for his cue.

When he waved his hands, I tapped the piano key over and over, while the other students played their notes. I played the twelfth and the fourteenth keys also, to add the sounds just above and below fifty-five hertz.

Mr. Russell raised a hand, then made a fist. After we paused the recording, everyone applauded, even the students who'd been covering their ears. Maybe they were just clapping because it was over, but I didn't mind. We had the song that would tell 55 someone was out there.

As the students took their seats for their regular

practice, Mr. Russell showed me an app on his tablet. He held the phone near the piano and pointed to the thirteenth key. When I tapped it, the phone's microphone picked up the sound. Wavy lines appeared on the screen, along with the name of the note: A1. Best of all, a readout of the frequency, fifty-five hertz, appeared next to the sound wave with each strike of the key. Mr. Russell pointed to the students to show me that they were using similar apps. That was how they knew if they hit the right note. Already I felt closer to Blue 55, from playing that sound like the one he sang.

Mr. Russell showed me how to adjust a wheel on the screen to select any musical instrument. That was what he meant when he said I could play the tuba note myself. He spun the wheel to "Tuba," then showed me which note to tap. Purple lines of a sound wave, and "55 Hz" appeared in the middle of the screen. I should've known there'd be an app that would allow me to play the song. Instead of working with the music students, I could have created the song myself. But it wasn't so bad, working with them. Now that they knew about Blue 55 too, it was like he had more people listening to him.

Before I left, I drew a smiling whale on the whiteboard saying "Thanks everyone!" Some of the kids smiled and waved to me as I left, and Angelica gave me a thumbs-up.

Okay, maybe playing music wasn't worthless.

While I waited at home for Mr. Russell to finish band practice and email me the file, I tried out the tuner app he'd showed me. I worked in the study so I could use the computer speakers. Usually Mom worked at home doing graphic design, but that day she was at a meeting with a company she did some work for.

Whenever I found a note that was around fifty-five hertz, I recorded the sound on the computer. I scrolled through the selection of instruments, some of which I'd never heard of, like the euphonium. By playing with the plus and minus buttons marked "Octave," I got a few more instruments to hit the right sound. I threw in a few notes from fifty to sixty hertz to give Blue 55 a little variety.

How long could practice go on? Just when I was thinking Mr. Russell had forgotten about me, the email came through.

I opened the attached file and hit play. The vibrations coming from the speaker reminded me of 55's song. Maybe it would remind 55 of his song too.

The other sound files I needed were in a new email from Andi.

Dear Iris,

Great to hear from you again. I made underwater recordings today with the hydrophones, and I've attached the file here. Often it's noisier than what I recorded for you, but we don't have any cruise ships coming in today, so it's mostly natural sounds here, such as humpback and blue whales, orcas, seals, and the wind on the ocean surface.

Good luck with your project. I'm interested in hearing more about it.

Andi

Yep, you'll be hearing about it, Andi.

The recording was only about five minutes long. I'd have to do some editing so Blue 55 would have a longer song to listen to. After I dragged the clips from Mr. Russell and Andi into a new file, I copied them over and over so they'd replay for an hour.

Hopefully it would be enough. I placed my hand over the speaker and closed my eyes while the song played. I'd thought before that playing 55's real song wouldn't do any good because he'd recognize it as his own, but I wondered what would happen if it was mixed in with this new music. I added a clip of Blue 55's recording to the middle of the song I'd just arranged.

There ... Something familiar yet different; a bit of his own song woven in with the new one. It was impossible to make the song exactly like 55's, but I did my best to stretch out the notes or clip them so they'd match the pattern of his music. I'd read that whale songs were made up of units, like single moans, chirps, or cries put together to build phrases. A bunch of phrases made a theme. Like spoken words that make up sentences and then paragraphs. Or like signs that made up phrases, then conversations or poems or stories. Maybe 55 would know this story was for him.

After all that work, I had to sit there for a while to figure out my reply. This would be the most important message I'd ever written. It had to be just right.

Dear Andi,

Thanks so much for sending the recording of the sanctuary animals. It's just what I needed for my project.

I haven't stopped thinking about Blue 55 since I first learned about him from my science teacher, Sofia Alamilla.

My hands hovered over the keyboard. I wanted to tell her my plan without making it seem like I thought I was smarter than the sanctuary staff.

Since it didn't work out last time you tried to put a tracker on him, I thought you might like this idea I came up with.

I told her how I'd worked with the musicians at school to record a song at Blue 55's frequency, and then mixed it with his own song and the sounds of the sanctuary animals.

A sound file of the song is attached here. What you could do is play it while you're on the boat, and plug a set of waterproof speakers into whatever device you're using. Then you can drop the speakers into the water, and 55 will hear the song. You said he swims to other whales, right? And they're not even singing the same songs. I'm sure when he hears something that sounds like him, he'll follow, and he'll want to hang around for a while.

I thought about how whenever I was with another Deaf person, we'd take forever saying our goodbyes. It annoyed everyone else as they stood in the doorway waiting for us to finally say goodbye and mean it. We'd almost get there, then think of something else to tell each other. If you don't know when you'll get to talk to someone like you again, you don't want your time together to end.

Whenever he's near your sanctuary, this song can help him feel at home. Maybe other sanctuaries could play it too, like when he migrates to warmer areas. He won't feel so alone hearing something like himself out there.

I don't know how many times I reread that email to make sure it looked right. It had to be professional, but casual, too, as if we sort of knew each other and were working for the same thing. I kept editing the message, changing words here and there and then changing them back again. Finally I did it. I held my breath and clicked send.

Your song is on the way, Blue 55.

17

I wanted to see Wendell in person to update him about the whale song. After school the next day, I called on the videophone to ask if I could come over. He said if I hurried, I could ride with him and his mom to the junior high. Ms. Jackson had been absent from work that day because of some meetings, so she wanted to stop by her classroom to prepare for the next day.

On the long drive to Bridgewood Junior High, I told Wendell all about recording Blue 55 a song and sending it to the sanctuary.

"That's so cool! Did you hear back yet?"

"Not yet. It hasn't been that long, though." I tried not to worry about not getting a message from Andi yet. Even though it hadn't been a whole day, I kept checking my email for a reply. What if my idea really wasn't that great? Just because the song would be at 55's frequency, that didn't mean it would make sense to him.

An image popped into my head of Nina's waving hands asking a whale, *"Hey, how's the plankton?"* Creating something that annoyed Blue 55 would be worse than not making the song at all.

The junior high started later than we did, so students were still in class when we got to Bridgewood. On the way to Ms. Jackson's classroom, I stopped and backed up when some signing hands in a science classroom caught my eye. An interpreter signed to one group of students at a tall black table as the teacher talked to them. They weren't the only Deaf students in the room. At another table three students signed to one another as they worked. I wanted to jump in on the conversation about the electrical circuit they were building. Ms. Jackson went on to her class while Wendell waited for me in the hallway.

A woman approached the Deaf students and signed to them. It didn't seem like she was an interpreter. She just joined in on their discussion and asked what they'd do next.

"Who's that woman?" I asked Wendell.

"Ms. Martinez. The classes with a lot of Deaf students have a Deaf ed teacher in the room along with the regular teacher."

"She signs like a Deaf person."

"Probably because she's Deaf."

"They have Deaf teachers here?"

"Yeah, a few."

Wendell took my hand and pulled me away from the science class. Two students walked by us in the halls, signing with each other. They waved hi to Wendell as they passed.

I'd known that most Deaf kids went to Bridgewood, but I didn't expect to see so many. They'd be able to sign with one another all the time, like during class or PE games or in the hallways. At the lunch table.

Ms. Jackson was leaving her classroom with some books and a file folder when we got there.

"I'm going to the workroom to make copies for tomorrow's lessons. You two can wait here."

Everyone in the room knew Wendell since he'd been there with his mom before.

After he introduced me I wandered around and scanned the bookshelves while Wendell chatted with the other people in the room. A few kids sat at a half-circle table with another teacher who shared the room with Ms. Jackson. Other students worked at their own desks or computers. In one corner of the room, a TV topped with a videophone sat on a wheeled black cart.

I pulled a book from the shelf. It looked old, with just

a plain off-white cover, but it was the title that drew me in: *American Sign Language: A History.* I hadn't noticed Wendell standing next to me until he moved his hands.

"My mom uses that when she teaches Deaf history."

"Deaf history?"

"Yeah, it's interesting."

I'd never thought about Deaf people having a history or where our language came from. Wendell reached for the book and flipped to the beginning. I scanned the page he'd turned to, then read the caption beneath a picture of a white-haired man dressed in black, signing with a little girl.

"France?" I signed.

He nodded. *"Some French people came here and used their sign language to teach Deaf kids. There was just one school for a long time, so Deaf people from all over the country went there and shared their own signs with one another."*

"And that's the sign language we use now?"

"It took a while, and it changes all the time, but yeah, that became ASL."

A new language. From groups who couldn't understand one another at first. Why hadn't I known about that?

Maybe Blue 55 and I would understand each other, just a little. Just one sound.

Wendell was signing with the other students and the teacher, telling them about Blue 55. They looked over at me and signed things like *"Really?"* and *"That's great!"* The teacher asked, *"Will you let us know how it works out?"*

I told her I would.

The junior high wasn't even Wendell's school yet, but he interacted with the other kids as if he were already going there. Next year, as a student, he'd know even more people. It must have been like that for him all the time, being able to talk to people around him so easily.

I'd thought about asking Mom again if I could go to school at Bridgewood. She'd probably say no. I hadn't brought it up for a long time, because I didn't like the way her face changed when I did. Kind of like when we visited Grandma, and she held me a little longer and looked at me like I was going somewhere far away. Maybe I could try again to convince her that it would be better here, that this is where I belonged.

I set the ASL history book down so I could join the conversation with the other students, but I missed what Wendell had just signed. Then I missed what they answered back. Somehow they were all keeping up with whatever they were talking about. I tried to tell myself I was just a little lost because I'd been looking down at the book when they started their conversation. But if that were it, I'd be able to catch up right away. Instead, I felt like I was tumbling in the murky water of the Gulf after a wave knocked me over.

After watching their conversation for a minute, I picked up a little more. Wendell was signing faster than he usually did with me. That wasn't the only difference. A few of the signs he was using were new to me. No one else at the table looked confused.

They turned to me like they were waiting for me to answer a question.

I shrugged at Wendell. *"I didn't catch what you were talking about."*

One of the students waved me off and signed, *"Train gone, sorry."* I'd missed out, and it was too much trouble to catch me up.

Wendell laughed a little and signed, *"Oh, sorry. I forgot to sign like an old person for you."*

I flinched like he'd slapped me. The other students laughed with him. Wendell stopped when he saw my face, then gave the others a small head shake.

"Sorry," he signed.

"*It's okay*," I told him, even though it wasn't true. I put the ASL history book back on the shelf. Maybe I wouldn't fit in here after all.

Wendell tapped my shoulder. I'd been looking out the window of the van while Mrs. Jackson drove us back home. "*Are you mad? I'm really sorry. I don't really think about it. I just sign a different way with you than I do at Bridgewood. You do that too, right? Like you don't sign the same way with your dad as you do with your mom or grandma or me.*"

Well, that didn't help, bringing up how I have to sign differently for Dad to understand. I shook my head to let Wendell know he didn't need to apologize. "*It's okay,*" I signed again. It wasn't really okay, but it also wasn't his fault. We didn't see each other every day, and I wasn't around other Deaf people our age like he was. Most of my conversations had been with my grandparents or with Mr. Charles. So I wasn't mad at Wendell for signing differently for me than he did with other kids. I was mad that he had to do it at all.

18

I was about to go downstairs for dinner when the message
I'd been waiting for came in.

Dear Iris,

Sorry it took so long to get back to you. I was
intrigued by your idea right away but wanted to
run it by the rest of the team first. Great news—we
will play your song for Blue 55 when we try again
to tag him with the tracker!

We'll also place a speaker in the deep waters of
the sanctuary to see how he responds.

I couldn't believe it. That sanctuary staff all the way
in Alaska had talked about me and the song I'd made.
They liked my plan. I'd been afraid to hope they'd actually use it. Andi was a real scientist who cared about
Blue 55, and she had listened to me.

This all depends on whether he's nearby, of course, and if we can find him. No one's heard him singing lately, so we're not sure where he is. Hopefully he'll start singing again if he's around.

Ask your parents for permission to give me your mailing address, and I'll be glad to send you a sanctuary T-shirt. We'll mention you on our Facebook page, and when it's time for the expedition to go out, click on the link to the live webcast so you can see your plan in action. And if you're ever around Appleton, Alaska (no one ever is, but just in case), stop by the sanctuary, and we'll give you a tour.

I'm so impressed by the work you've done. You're thinking like a scientist—you discovered a problem and worked out a way to solve it.

Thanks again for writing to us with your idea, Iris. We're looking forward to trying it out so we can learn more about Blue 55.

Andi

I was so excited that I jumped up and ran a circle around my room, stopping in front of the picture of Blue 55 on the wall. *"I made a song for you. I hope you'll like it."* My hand brushed the picture of the whale's face, then dropped to my side. As happy as I was that

Blue 55 would hear the song, it didn't seem right to just watch online when it happened. While the sanctuary staff got to meet Blue 55, I'd be sitting at home in front of a computer screen. That wasn't enough. I should be there when he heard the song.

Dear Andi,

I'm so happy you're actually going to use the song! Even though Blue 55 has never heard it, it's a song he's looking for. I'm sure of it. Thanks so much for writing back and for inviting me to your sanctuary. I'll ask my parents if I can go soon so I can be there when Blue 55 is.

Can I join you on the expedition? I'll be glad to help out. That way you can focus on tracking him, and I'll take care of the speakers and the song. I've been working with radios for a long time, so I'm used to handling electronics stuff. It's almost the end of the school year, so nothing much is going on anymore because we're done learning things. And my parents won't mind me missing a few days of school for such an educational trip.

I didn't add that my school sure wouldn't mind if I missed a few days either.

I guess that's it for now. Let me know when you think Blue 55 will be there!

Iris

Maybe Andi was only being polite when she told me to stop by if I was ever in the area, but I was going. I would meet that whale.

As soon as we sat down to dinner, I told my family about Blue 55, how it all started with the video in Sofia Alamilla's class, and about Andi and her team that tried to tag him.

Mom interpreted some of what I said for Dad since he didn't understand everything. I tried to slow down for him, but I couldn't stop my hands from flying. Then I told them about all the work I did studying Blue 55's song and how I'd figured out how to make a new song for him with the music from school and the tuner app.

"And . . ." I signed that part slowly, and looked around the table to make sure I had their attention. "*Blue 55 should be near the sanctuary again soon. The staff will try to tag him again, and they'll play my song underwater so he'll hang around longer.*"

"*Really?*" Tristan signed. "*That's impressive!*"

"That's great you were able to help them," said Mom. "You must have worked really hard on that."

Dad still looked a little lost, but signed, "Yes, great!"

They did seem impressed, but I wasn't sure they really understood what a big deal this was. Maybe I hadn't gotten across how long he'd been swimming alone and that nothing else sang like he did.

They'd get it when I told them the best part. "And guess what? Andi—she's the woman who will tag him— thought my idea was so good, she invited me to visit the sanctuary!" I left out the part about her saying I should stop by for a tour if my family ever happened to be in Appleton, Alaska. That was good enough of an invitation for me. We had to go.

Mom and Dad gave each other a look like they were trying to figure out what to say. Sometimes they tried to talk without moving their mouths when I was nearby, so I couldn't read their lips. Now it looked like they were communicating silently, though.

"That was nice of her," signed Mom. "Maybe someday we'll take a trip to Alaska, and you can see the sanctuary."

"Someday" meant never. "But we have to go soon," I explained, "when the whale will be there."

"Don't worry," Dad signed. "He has other whales around him all the time, right?"

They'd totally missed the point. If they understood what a big deal this was, they'd take it seriously. This whale was finally going to hear a song like his own, and I'm the one who made it. I was ready to answer any questions they had about Blue 55 or the sanctuary or the song. They didn't ask about any of it. Dad probably hadn't even *caught* most of it. I should have explained it better. This was the most important thing I'd ever do, and it was turning out all wrong.

After a deep breath I forced myself to slow down when I answered Dad. This would work out if I could be less excited, more patient. *"But they can't understand him. That's the problem. Even when other whales are nearby they don't know what he's saying."* My hands showed Dad the swimming whale, all alone in the ocean. Singing, while nothing answered back. Then one day there was a song. A song like his. I turned to the side and held a hand up to my ear like I was hearing the song myself.

When I finished, Dad looked up like he was thinking about my explanation, then said, "Sounds like that whale needs speech therapy." He laughed at his own joke, then said something else with his face downward.

I waved to get his attention, then signed, *"What?"*

He took a spoonful of his chili and signed, *"Nothing."* That was one sign he knew well.

"It isn't nothing. You mean I'm not important enough to include."

He looked at Mom for an interpretation, but I signed to her, *"Don't interpret anymore."* Dad's chest heaved with a sigh, so he must have understood that part.

"What if you couldn't talk to anyone around you? What if you tried, but no one understood?"

Dad glanced at Mom again, but she just reached for her glass. The water in the glass shook when I slapped the table. Dad signed, *"I can't understand you. You need to slow down."*

I signed faster. *"It doesn't matter what I do. You don't understand anyway! What if your whole life was like this? What if you were that whale, in an ocean with no one to talk to?"*

He shook his head and went back to his dinner.

Mom signed to me, *"Sweetie, I'm sorry you're upset, but we can't just drop everything and go to Alaska. We'll watch the expedition online. You can invite Wendell over, and everyone will see how you helped the whale."* She added, *"I'll make popcorn,"* like that would make everything better.

"No, this isn't fair! I'm the one who made the song. It was my idea to play it for him. I'll help pay for the trip." I had no idea what a trip to Alaska would cost, but I had some money in the bank from my repair work.

No one said anything for a while, and then Tristan touched my arm. "Hey. It is great, what you're doing for that whale. The important thing is that he'll get to hear your song, right?"

"Yes, but I should be there when he hears it. I need to see him. . . ."

"He isn't one of your radios."

"What?"

"The whale," Tristan signed. "I know you don't like to leave anything broken. Make sure that's not the reason you want to do this. You can't go in there and fix him like he's a radio."

"I know that!" I signed it like I was smacking the air. What was he even talking about? "But I have to go there! I want him to know that someone hears him."

I went on like that, not stopping to wipe the tears from my face, signing so fast that Tristan couldn't keep up with me. Maybe even Mom couldn't, but I didn't slow down. I didn't care anymore. I was like Blue 55, shouting into the void of the ocean, at a frequency too high for anyone to reach.

19

The new pod was leaving him.

The youngest of the group stayed back, swimming around him in a circle, then floating nearby as the others called him. The calf was too young to have found his own song yet. He called to the large whale who swam alone, trying out clicks and chirps and fragments of a howl. With time they might understand each other.

That worried the pod. They didn't want the strange sounds piercing the waters around them, didn't want their calf singing the song they didn't understand. It was dangerous. How would he alert them when he needed help?

The humpback family called out, determined to

leave yet unwilling to move on without the calf. With a final chirp, the young whale turned to join them.

For a moment the larger whale followed, knowing he wouldn't be allowed but not ready to let go. It had been so long since he'd sung with a calf. There had been others in his own family, back when he himself was a calf too.

The pod swam ahead, tails thrashing if he got too close.

If he had remained quiet, would they have let him stay? For a time he did hold on to his song, then revealed it little by little as his trust grew. The more he sang, the farther they drifted from him, and the tighter they encircled the calf.

A storm brewed in the ocean, but he wouldn't flee the area like the others. It was in storms that he sang loudest. He was like all the others then, unable to hear his song over the wind and the crashing waves.

He swam into the rough waters, bellowing his unheard songs into the void of the ocean. Maybe the churning and the pounding and the rolling water that carried his sounds away would rearrange them into a new composition another would hear.

20

After I calmed down I decided I wouldn't let my family's response bother me. They just didn't get it yet. I'd firm up a plan with Andi, then try again with Mom and Dad. When they saw the proof that a real scientist was impressed by my idea and wanted me to come help out at the sanctuary, there's no way they'd say no. They'd see how important it was.

When an email from Andi came in later that night, I almost started packing a bag for Alaska. Then I read the message:

Dear Iris,

I'm so sorry if I gave you the idea that you should hop on a plane and fly here right now. That would be really hard for your family to do. It's a long way to go on short notice. (Plus, you might get here, and then there's nothing to see anyway, if Blue

55 doesn't show up. Sometimes science is kind of boring like that—you do a lot of planning and work, and then nature doesn't cooperate like you wish it would.) If your parents bring you sometime, that's great, but they'll want to take some time to plan the trip.

But please know that the view you'll have on a computer at home will be the same one the other members of the team will have, or even better! Tagging a whale is important work, but it is dangerous. We have to get really close to the whale to put the tracker on him. A slap from his tail could knock us out of the boat. Only one other person from the team will be out there with me, and that's the guy steering the boat. Everyone else who's been working on the expedition will be inside the sanctuary, watching on a video screen. Or they'll watch from outside on the dock, but they won't see much from there. You'll be able to see everything our cameras pick up from underwater and on the boat. Afterward I'll be happy to send you the information we get from 55's tracker. That way you'll know where he is and when he's singing, too.

Again, thank you so much for all the work you

did on this and for sending us the song. I'd love to talk to you more about it, and I hope we'll keep in touch. I know you're going to do great things, and I'll be interested in seeing what other work you do for animals in the future.

Andi

I yanked 55's sheet music off my wall so hard that the corners ripped and pushpins flew out of their holes. Before tearing the page to pieces, I stopped myself. It wasn't his fault. This was Blue 55's song. Whatever he was saying, whatever this language was, it was his.

Still, I wouldn't be able to look at it anymore. I folded it up, along with his picture, and buried it in the bottom drawer of my desk.

Wendell didn't have his own phone yet, so we had to chat online instead of texting. The chat window on the computer showed a red dot next to his name. I'd send a message anyway for him to read whenever he got online.

I heard back from the sanctuary. After that I didn't know what else to say. The dot next to his name stayed red as I sat there slumped in my chair. Finally I gave up and flopped into bed.

Mom came upstairs later to tell me that Wendell was on the videophone. I shook my head to let her know I'd talk to him another time. Lifting my arms to have a conversation would take too much effort.

A string of messages from Wendell was waiting for me when I got online the next morning.

What did they say?

Did they like your song? Are they going to play it?

Well??????

Are you alive????

In the chat window I typed, *Hey. Sorry, I didn't want to talk yesterday. But yeah, I heard back. They love my idea.*

I waited while he typed a response. *That's great! So then what was wrong yesterday?*

They invited me to visit sometime, and I want to be there to meet the whale. My parents say it's too far away. I'll get a T-shirt from the sanctuary. Oh, and a shout-out from the boat. While they're meeting the whale. Using the song that I gave them.

Wendell didn't type anything for a while, then wrote, *I'm sorry, Iris. That's not fair. It's your idea, right? So you should get to go.*

I'd gone to bed feeling like I'd never be happy again,

but I smiled a little then. Even though Wendell couldn't do anything to change what happened, it helped to have someone understand how unfair it was.

Thanks, Wendell. I'll be okay, I guess. But I'll be really mad about it for a while. They'll show the expedition online, but I don't think I'll watch.

Yeah, I wouldn't either. Well, come over again whenever you want. Jupiter and its moons will be visible soon.

Thanks, see you later.

Dad came in and sat on the edge of the bed while I was wrapping up my conversation with Wendell. He was holding a set of computer speakers.

When I swiveled my chair around, Dad pointed at the computer. I waved him over and stood next to the chair so he could sit.

He plugged in the speakers, then brought up a YouTube video of an old record player. Not as old as the one in my Admiral set, but still pretty old. Instead of a round record like ones I'd seen, this had a square record spinning on the turntable. In the middle of the record was a line drawing of a humpback whale.

I placed a hand on the speaker as the record played. The vibrations reminded me of some of the whale songs I'd found online.

Dad opened up the notepad on the computer. His

typing was a lot faster and made more sense than his signing.

My parents got this in a magazine when I was a kid. He clicked back to the video and pointed to the title, "Songs of the Humpback Whale, *National Geographic,* 1979." Then he pointed to himself and pretended he was putting on headphones. *"Every day,"* he signed.

We sat there for a while, him listening to the whale songs and me feeling the song through the speaker, both of us watching the spinning record in the video. Dad raised and lowered his hand to show me how the song flowed from low to high and back again, in waves. I remembered from the sheet music I'd looked at that the humpbacks were the symphony players. The description of the video said their sounds ranged from very low to very high. So didn't they sometimes hit fifty-five hertz? As they sang from twenty to one hundred to thousands of hertz, small parts of their songs had to sound like Blue 55's. I wondered if he ever recognized any of their sounds when he was close enough to hear them. A few notes of a song, at least.

Before this, no one knew they had such complex songs, Dad typed. *There used to be a lot more whale hunting. After hearing them, people protested against hunting whales. There was more to them than anyone knew.*

So their songs saved them. That was how powerful they were.

I wanted to find them too, he added.

"*The whales?*" I signed.

He nodded. "*That's how you sign it, like a letter* Y*?*"

"*Yeah, see how it looks like the shape of a whale's tail?*"

He held out his right hand, with just the thumb and pinkie sticking out. I showed him how to move the hand up and down in waves, to look like the tail of a swimming whale, while making a horizon with the other arm.

Maybe this was Dad's way of apologizing to me for what happened at dinner. I was still mad I wasn't going to get to go to Alaska to meet the whale, but this was something we'd be able to talk about. We'd never had that before—something we were both interested in. I hadn't thought that reaching out to Blue 55 would help me reach out to Dad, too. But that was before I knew he was interested in whale songs. He must have understood how important they were to me now, since he came up to my room to tell me how he used to listen to them.

I was about to ask him more about the songs on the record when he typed, *I wish you could hear them.*

I wanted to tell Dad that I could hear the whales,

just not in the same way he did. I didn't know how to explain that so he'd understand.

Every day I tried to forget about Blue 55. No more reading about whales or the sanctuary expedition. For a while I wore the wooden Zenith knob alone on my necklace, but I put the compass back on since I missed the weight of it resting on my chest. I still liked to think about the people who might have used it a long time ago to find their way.

Mr. Gunnar gave me his most hopeless case, an ancient radio that should have been left for dead ages ago. But I'd figure it out. With radios it was clear how the parts communicated. And whenever I fixed it, I'd know. That was how electronics were—either the thing worked or it didn't. There wasn't any guessing about that.

It took scientists a long time to figure out how whales make their sounds. They don't open their mouths and sing like people do. The singing happens inside the spaces in their bodies, by pushing air into their throats and sinuses.

When I reached into the radio, the old wire insulation crumbled into dust in my hands. Even if I got everything working, a bare metal wire could burn up all the work I'd done. I dug through the bundle of wires on my workbench, looking for replacements.

Was Blue 55 singing right then? Did anyone hear him?

I set the radio aside and went to my desk. My end-of-the-year research paper for Ms. Conn was due soon, and I hadn't started yet. I'd chosen radio communication as my topic, then asked her if I could change it to whales. Not that I didn't care about radios, but I could put all my whale research to use for my report.

If I asked to change my topic again, Ms. Conn's face would turn inside out with sour pickleness. But I couldn't write about whales anymore. When I turned it in, I'd tell her I'd changed my mind.

I brought up my favorite sites about radio history to take some notes. *FM radio signals can be detected thirty to forty miles away.*

That wasn't so impressive, now that I knew how far a whale song could travel. It could drift even farther than hundreds of miles. A song could reach up from the waves and halfway across the country, beating in time with someone's heart and pulling her to the ocean.

The sanctuary people finding him wouldn't be the same. Someone who heard him, who understood him, needed to be there.

I shook my head to clear away the thought. Then I shook out my hands too, trying to release the grip that Blue 55 had on me. There wasn't any point in thinking about him anymore. It would have to be enough that I'd helped him. I'd stick to what I was good at—fixing things—and forget all about that whale.

The website I brought up had examples of emergency communication using radios and telegraphs. I'd add one of the stories to my report.

One farmer connected his farm radio into his tractor battery when the radio's battery died. He heard the news about a coming storm just in time to get his family safely into the root cellar.

Then there was a shopkeeper who sent his daughter out of town to keep her away from the newspaper reporter she loved. After the reporter's "Matilda, please marry me" telegram reached her, they each took a minister to a telegraph station and were married by Morse code before Matilda returned home.

A soldier in a prisoner-of-war camp made a radio with a scrap of wood, a razor blade, a pencil, a safety pin, and a piece of wire from the fence surrounding the camp. At night he listened to reports about the war and passed the news along to his fellow prisoners.

I pulled 55's picture and sheet music from my desk

drawer where I'd hidden them, then tacked them back into place on the wall.

People who were desperate to communicate always found a way.

I'd find a way.

21

What if I could get there somehow? If I showed up at the sanctuary when it was time for the expedition, they'd see I was serious, that I wasn't just some kid doing a project. Even if I couldn't get on the boat, I'd be at the sanctuary when they tagged Blue 55. I'd see him swimming in the bay while the song played.

A twelve-year-old could fly alone. If I left in the morning on a school day, my family wouldn't notice I was missing until after I'd landed. But the closest airport was almost a three-hour drive from the sanctuary.

I studied the map on the computer screen. An airline ticket would let me cover almost all the distance between 55 and me. The hard part was the last 150 miles. If only I could grab on to 55's song and let it carry me to him. I was afraid one day soon I wouldn't feel his music anymore.

I didn't know how it would all work out yet, but I had

to try to get to him. I'd go as far as I could and then take a shuttle or a bus to get as close to the sanctuary as possible. Maybe I'd get caught by then. It wouldn't be hard for my parents to figure out where I was headed. But I couldn't give up on Blue 55.

Buying a plane ticket was a whole different issue. My radio repair money wouldn't take me very far. Even if I had enough, I'd have to buy the ticket with a credit card. I leaned back in my chair and glanced up at my shelves of radios, then sat on the floor next to my bed. An idea was creeping into my head that I didn't like but couldn't push away. I brought up 55's song on my phone, feeling the vibrations on my hand as it played. Hadn't I made him a promise?

With the edge of my shirt I polished my fingerprints off the side of the Philco.

My email to Mr. Gunnar was short, but it felt like it took me an hour to click send.

I'd always said I'd never sell my radios, except in case of an emergency.

I posted a few of the radios on eBay, as two-day auctions so the money would get into my account faster.

The next day after school, I hurried home to pick up the Philco. I wrapped it in an old bedsheet so it wouldn't get scratched. And maybe so I wouldn't have to look at it.

Tristan said he'd take me to the antiques shop. When he saw me in my room next to the sheet-wrapped radio he asked, *"Isn't that—"*

"Yeah," I signed before he could finish. *"Mr. Gunnar really wants to buy it. I don't mind letting it go."* I looked away so he wouldn't see how much the lie hurt. But at the same time, it was true. Letting go of the radios would let me reach for something I loved even more.

"Can you carry it for me? I'll wait in the truck." I slipped past him and ran downstairs.

Mr. Gunnar looked so happy when we walked through the door, he must have been worried I wouldn't show up. I couldn't really believe it myself.

When I was older I'd look for a Philco to buy again. Maybe from a kid like me who had a really good reason to sell it. An emergency.

I peeled away the sheet and held the sides of the cabinet one last time. Probably for a little too long, because Mr. Gunnar looked at me and raised his eyebrows like he was asking a question. I let go.

He knelt down and checked out the radio on all sides. His face showed me he was impressed. He plugged it in and turned it on, then smiled as he listened to the music.

Mr. Gunnar's open hand circled his face, then closed. *"Beautiful."* He thanked me and reached for his checkbook.

"Thank you," I signed to him before I left. I hurried out of the store ahead of Tristan, trying to outrun the thought that I could still change my mind.

"Wow, you really did it," Tristan signed when he got back into the truck.

"Can you take me to the bank?"

We pulled into one of the drive-through lanes, and Tristan put a deposit slip and the check into a plastic tube for me.

I ran my finger around the face of the compass and looked out the window, pretending not to notice Tristan staring at me. Then he tapped my arm, which I couldn't ignore.

"Sure you're okay?" he asked.

"Of course." I gave what I hoped was a convincing smile, and I sat back in my seat like I did this every day.

No big deal.

22

Later that week I stopped at the bank across the street from school. I'd gone with my mom or dad enough times to know what to do. My parents always showed a driver's license, which of course I didn't have, so I brought a copy of my birth certificate from Mom's desk. I'd get my money from my account, then go get some of those prepaid credit cards I'd seen on the racks at Walgreen's. I'd never paid much attention to them before, so I didn't know what amounts they went up to. I'd buy however many I needed until they added up to enough money for a plane ticket.

Instead of my usual outfit of jeans and whatever clean T-shirt I grabbed, I wore my black pants and a white shirt with buttons. I strode into the bank like it was totally normal for me to go in alone.

At the side counter I picked up a withdrawal slip and filled it out like I always did when I was with my parents. Except I was writing down a much bigger number than I ever had.

While I waited my turn in line, I told myself to quit fidgeting. I'd look nervous if I played with the corner of the withdrawal slip or fiddled with my necklace. Forcing myself to stand still with my hands at my sides made me look like a mannequin. I took a deep breath and imagined the vibration of Blue 55's song playing against my hands.

Finally the customer ahead of me finished whatever he was doing. I stepped up to the counter and handed the teller my withdrawal slip. I tried to look taller as she looked from the paper to me. She said something to me, and I guessed it was about an ID, so I unfolded my birth certificate and slid it over to her. She said something else I didn't catch, so I picked up the chained-up pen on the counter and motioned for her to write down what she wanted.

On the back of a blank deposit slip she wrote, *Are your parents here? One of them has to sign to withdraw money from this kind of account.*

I forced myself not to cry after I read the note. This was money I'd earned, from repair work and selling my radios. I should be able to take it out myself. I smiled like this wasn't a problem at all and wrote, *They're really busy with work and couldn't come. I'll have them sign it and come back later.*

After reading that the teller shook her head and added, *No, I mean they have to be here to show an ID and sign their name.*

I shoved the withdrawal slip and birth certificate into my backpack, then wrote on the note, *Oh right, I forgot. We'll come back later. Thanks!*

On my way out I smiled and waved at her, then signed something that would get me in Serious Trouble if anyone nearby knew sign language.

Now what? The whole point of parting with my radios was to have money to find Blue 55, and I couldn't touch it. Even if I asked my parents to withdraw some money for a radio or some parts, they would never believe I needed that much. When they'd noticed my missing radios, I told them I wanted to save up to buy more that needed fixing, since I liked repairing them. It was a little true, since I did plan to buy more radios when I had enough money. But right then, the whale was more important.

I got on my bike outside the bank but didn't turn toward home. I needed to talk to someone who understood me.

Grandma took her time answering the door, then gave me a hug and sat in her rocking chair by the window.

For a while I sat there looking out the window with her, staring at whatever she was always staring at. Nothing but trees and a parking lot, as far as I could tell.

Even though Grandma wasn't looking at me, I picked up my hands and poured out everything I'd been holding on to, all that I'd tried to do and failed at. I told her about Blue 55, the song I'd created, the trip I'd planned, the radios I'd sold, and the money in the bank I couldn't touch. Maybe it was so easy to let all that out because Grandma wasn't watching anyway, or because she'd understand how I felt. Maybe it was some of both.

But she should know that I needed her to see me, that there was a reason I went there to tell her all this. If she just looked my way, she'd see the pain on my face. I didn't expect her to fix it. She could just tell me she was sorry it happened. I'd feel better just knowing someone understood that disappointment and let me know that I'd be okay. Instead it was like I wasn't even there.

"And you know what else isn't fair?" I added, when she kept staring out the window. *"You're not the only one*

who misses Grandpa. But we can't all sit around being sad about him. Mom and Dad have to work, and Tristan and I have to go to school."

My hands finally dropped to my lap. I didn't know how to express the ache of getting so close to the whale and then missing him, as if he dove below the surface just as my fingers brushed the skin of his back. Maybe Grandma knew a sign for that kind of pain, but I didn't. It wasn't like the sign for *"hurt"* I use for a scraped knee or a headache, and it wasn't the twist at the heart that shows grief. Losing someone I'd never met wasn't the same as losing Grandpa. The closest thing would be the touch to the heart, like something piercing it. But that could also mean something that's touching or moving in a good way, because it's so beautiful.

Grandma turned to me and signed, *"What part of Alaska?"*

It took me a moment to realize she'd asked me a question. I didn't think she'd been paying attention at all.

"Oh, it's—" I held up a hand to represent the state of Alaska, then pointed at a spot along the southern coast—*"a little town called Appleton."* Not that it mattered anymore. Hopefully she saw enough to understand that I wasn't going. An ache crept into my stomach at the thought of explaining it again.

The night before, Mom came to my room to talk to me again about Blue 55. We'd avoided the subject since the dinner conversation that went so horribly wrong, and she was hoping to help me feel better. It didn't work.

Plus, she corrected me when I signed that I missed the whale, which annoyed me even more. I'd signed it with a touch to the chin; the *"miss"* sign for when someone you care about is gone. It didn't feel like the wrong sign. Even though I'd never met Blue 55, I did miss him. Mom showed me that the sign for *"miss"* I'd meant was the one with an open hand closing into a fist in front of the face, kind of like you're trying to catch a fly. The sign for something you tried to catch and couldn't, like when Blue 55 slipped away from Andi before she could tag him.

Yes, I was going to miss out on seeing Blue 55, but that wasn't what I meant. The *"miss"* sign I'd used was also like the sign for "disappointed," and I'd never understood why. Now it made sense. The meanings weren't so far apart. Someone you want to be with is far away, or something you wish for isn't going to come true.

"I know where that is," Grandma signed, pulling me back to our conversation.

"What, Appleton? How?"

"*Some cruise ships stop there. I remember from when Grandpa and I were planning one.*"

Grandma and Grandpa went on cruises sometimes, but I didn't remember one to Alaska. "*When did you go?*"

"*We were thinking about it for our anniversary next year.*"

I hadn't known they were planning an anniversary cruise. They almost made it fifty years.

"*Grandpa always wanted to touch a glacier.*" Grandma didn't turn back to the window, but kept looking right at me. She hadn't done that for a long time.

I didn't know what to say to her about that cruise. I'd bring it up to Mom. Not because it would change her mind about going to Alaska soon—she'd made it clear that was ridiculous. But I'd try to convince her that we had to go someday. Not "someday" as in some imaginary time that would never come, but for real. I'd get to tour the sanctuary. Blue 55 wouldn't be there, but I'd see the place where he'd heard my song. And we'd find a glacier to touch, for Grandpa.

"*Let's go,*" Grandma signed.

At first I thought she was thinking the same thing I was, that we could talk to my parents about planning a family trip. But Grandma didn't add *"someday."* Her chair wasn't rocking anymore. She leaned toward me, hands on the armrests of the chair.

"You mean ..." I couldn't finish the sentence, too afraid to hope for what she was suggesting. Even if I understood her correctly, I didn't see how it would work. Mom had already said we weren't going. It looked like Grandma had a different idea swirling in her head, though.

"So, what do you think?" she asked.

I shook my head and laughed, still not believing it. Like Andi said, Alaska is really far away, and people need time to plan a trip like that. But Grandma was one of those people who jumped into things like she did that day on the beach with the sei whale.

She didn't look away, and she didn't look like she was kidding.

Maybe I wouldn't have to miss out on meeting Blue 55. It would be for just a short time, a glimpse of him after such a long trip, but I'd have that to hold on to. And then I wouldn't miss him so much.

I squeezed Grandma's hand, then answered, *"I think it's time to get to sea."*

23

Grandma said not to worry about my money in the bank. *"Save it for something else. This is my treat."*

Instead of flying into the closest airport and trying to drive three hours, possibly through snow and ice, Grandma's plan was to get on a cruise ship that would take us right to Appleton.

We found just one ship with an available cabin and an Appleton stop, and we'd have to leave earlier than planned.

"How will we do it?" I asked. *"Like when it's time to leave, what will I tell Mom?"*

Grandma sat back to think, then picked up the activities calendar from her coffee table. *"We can't tell her what we're doing, exactly."*

"Right, there's no way she'd let us go. Not while I still have school, anyway."

"Or ever." Grandma pointed to her calendar, on the

date we needed to leave. *"Look, there's a day trip to Surf-side Beach. I'll tell your mom I'd like you to join me. It'd be good for us."*

"Think she'll say yes?" I couldn't believe we were actually planning this. It didn't seem real yet. More like a game. A really fun game.

Grandma shrugged. *"I'll talk her into it. We'll be with a group of people, and she knows how much I love the ocean. We'll be telling the truth about going to the beach anyway. We won't mention yet that we're going to one a little farther away."*

"A little?"

She looked back at the computer screen and clicked "Book my cruise." *"Just four thousand miles. No big deal."*

I smiled as I signed, *"Serious Trouble. We are both going to be in Serious Trouble."*

"Worth it," Grandma signed.

I couldn't leave without saying goodbye to Wendell. When I messaged to ask if he could come over, he wrote back, *Not unless you have a better telescope than I do. Come check out Jupiter.*

Mr. Jackson let me in at the front door and pointed upstairs. *"Great view up there."*

From the upstairs game room, I stepped out onto

the balcony and sat down next to Wendell. He didn't take his eye from the telescope until I touched his shoulder.

I reached down and clicked on Wendell's flashlight. He'd painted the lens red so the light wouldn't wash out the night sky and make the stars harder to see.

After the visit to the junior high, I'd wondered every day what Wendell was doing at his own school. Maybe he was learning the same things I was, but from a Deaf teacher, or he was signing with a bunch of friends at lunch, or joking with another student he passed in the hallway. If I were with them every day, I could be part of that. Even if we did sign a little differently, I'd sign more like the other kids after hanging around them more.

I shook the wish out of my head and tried to refocus. Changing schools would be impossible now. Mom wouldn't let me out of her sight again after she found out I took off to Alaska with Grandma.

I still couldn't believe Mom had said yes to the trip. I'd watched from upstairs when Grandma came over to talk to Mom about it. She kept a straight face the whole time and didn't give anything away. She really was a good actor. Before she left she got Mom to sign a permission slip. I held my breath as I backed into my room so Mom wouldn't hear me exhale. It felt like a loud sigh of relief I was holding in.

I looked up at the sky and asked Wendell, *"Which one is Jupiter?"*

"See that one that looks like a really bright star?"

"Yeah."

"But see how it doesn't twinkle like the stars?"

I hadn't noticed it before. What looked like a bright star was a solid light, not flickering like the others.

"If you see one like that," he continued, *"it's a planet. They're a lot closer than stars. It's all the atmosphere the stars' light has to travel through that makes them look twinkly."*

I looked through the telescope at the planet.

"That's awesome."

He pointed out the moons surrounding Jupiter. *"There's Io, Europa, Ganymede, and Callisto. It has a bunch more, but those are the ones we can see."*

While he took another turn looking through the telescope, I sat back and thought about what to tell him. I touched his shoulder again so he'd look at me.

"I have some news. About that whale, Blue 55. I'm going to go meet him after all. I'll try to anyway."

"Wow, really? That's great! Your parents changed their minds about going?"

"Well, no. They don't know about this."

"You're going by yourself?"

"With Grandma. She figured out a way we could get there. If Blue 55 shows up at the sanctuary, I'll be there to see him."

Wendell looked away and shook his head like he couldn't believe what I was telling him. I hardly believed it myself. It didn't seem real yet.

"And then what?" he asked.

"What do you mean?"

"I mean, after you find the whale. What will you do then?"

"I'm not sure. But I think the song will let him know he's not alone, and I want to be there for that."

Wendell didn't say anything for a while; he just stared at the sky. Maybe I'd made a huge mistake, and he was going to tell his parents, and they would tell my parents. Mom would put a stop to the trip before it started.

He looked through the telescope again, then asked, "Did you know there used to be another giant planet?"

"Another one?"

"Yeah, in addition to Jupiter, Saturn, Uranus, and Neptune, there was a fifth giant gas planet out there."

"What happened?"

"*Jupiter knocked it out of orbit. One day it got too close, and Jupiter sent it hurtling out of the solar system.*"

I looked up at the sky. "*Really rude, Jupiter.*" Then I asked Wendell, "*So where is it now?*"

"*No one knows. Maybe another star pulled it onto a new orbit, and it's in that solar system now. Maybe it even has its own moons circling it. Or it's still out there on its own, flying past everything, on the same path Jupiter knocked it onto.*" He shrugged and looked away. "*I know this is dumb, but sometimes I wonder about that planet. If I had a way of finding it, I'd go.*"

He hugged me then. I couldn't remember the last time we'd hugged, if ever. Maybe when we were little kids. I wanted to tell him that wasn't a dumb idea at all, but to do that I'd have to let go of him.

Wendell stepped back so I could see him again. "*Good luck. Let me know when you find your whale.*"

24

Each morning that week I tossed a few things into my back-pack for the trip. Then after school I'd stop by Grand-ma's to move them to her closet. Her set of suitcases fit one inside the other like nesting dolls. We sat on the floor near her closet and added items to the small suitcase each day. The medium-size suitcase had been packed with Grandma's things since the day after she bought the tickets.

I'd been reading "What to Pack for Your Alaskan Vacation" articles so I'd know what to bring. People forget things when they travel to Alaska. They don't pack enough for the cold weather, thinking, *How bad can it be in the summer?* But it's a lot colder there, especially at night. Traveling on a boat is even worse, with all the wind. A good coat wasn't enough. You had to have gloves and a scarf and a hat and thick socks.

Of course I didn't have all those things, living in

Houston. In the corner of a dresser drawer was a pair of gloves I'd hardly worn. Even in winter I got by with my hands in my pockets. My sock supply was made up of those thin white ones that came six pairs to a package from Target. I'd packed extra pairs so I could double up. My gray sweatshirt had a hood. That would work for a hat. Plus, my hair was thick enough to protect me from the cold even if I went sledding across the Arctic tundra.

Before I left home that Saturday morning, I threw the last few things into my backpack. I gave an extra-long hug to each of my parents before leaving to meet Grandma. Dad asked if I was okay.

"Doing great," I answered, which was true. This was the most important thing I'd ever done. I was nervous, but mostly excited.

"Have fun at the beach," Mom told me. *"Call if you need anything."*

All I could do was nod for an answer before walking out the front door.

Maybe they would worry till I got back, but my leaving would be a relief in a way. No more explaining things for Dad, no more of him having to explain things to me. They'd have a kind of vacation too.

Tristan was in the driveway with Adam, looking

under the hood of Adam's truck. That was not unusual. The truck was always breaking down. Once, I leaned against it when Tristan started it up. It'd shaken like it was running on a lawn mower engine.

"What's wrong with it?" I asked. *"I know it's a long list, but what are you working on now?"*

"It won't start," Tristan answered. *"Maybe needs a new battery."*

"Smells weird," I told him. *"Like a BBQ grill. Not in a good way."*

"Yeah, Adam dropped a cheeseburger last time he worked on the car. It's really stuck in there. So what do you think?"

"I think he shouldn't eat the rest of that cheeseburger if you get it out of there."

He grabbed a set of jumper cables from the bed of the truck. As soon as I lifted the plastic covers over the battery terminals for him, I saw the problem. I pointed at the caked-on corrosion. *"Clean those off and maybe it'll start."*

Adam chuckled and rolled his eyes when Tristan told him what I'd said. I didn't miss the look of warning that Tristan gave him. "That's not a big deal," Adam said. "There's something else wrong."

On any other day I'd have grabbed the alternator

wire and carried it around in my backpack till Adam admitted I was right. But I'd be far away from there in a few hours, and Mom and Dad didn't need his dumb truck sitting in our driveway all week.

"Those battery wires don't even know they're connected to anything. Clean it with some baking soda or pour a Coke on it." After Tristan interpreted that, I asked him, *"Want to go get a breakfast taco? I have some time before I meet Grandma."*

He shook his head. *"I'll stay here and help fix this. We'll go tomorrow, okay?"*

"I'm telling you, pour a Coke on it and it'll start right up."

"Okay, we'll try that. Talk to you later."

I almost told him right then that I wouldn't be around tomorrow, or the next day, or a few days after that. But I just got on my bike and rode away.

There were plenty of Mexican restaurants around, and I'd been to all of them. The best breakfast tacos were at Carlos's Gas 'Em Up. One side was a convenience store, and the other was set up as a café. The owner, Carlos, and his whole family worked there.

I ordered a potato-egg-and-cheese taco, plus a small coffee—something more grown-up than my usual chocolate milk. After one bitter sip I tossed it in the trash can, then used a napkin to scrape the taste off my tongue. How could anyone drink that stuff? I went back to the counter for a chocolate milk.

As I sat there and ate, I looked around at the people who were reading the news or chatting with one another before work. I was dying to tell someone what I was about to do. I'd never held on to a secret this big, and it was bursting to get out. I went ahead and signed it right there to the whole room. No one would understand anyway, so it was a way of letting the secret out while still keeping it.

After finishing the last bite of my taco, I crumpled up the foil wrapper and signed, *"I should get going. Don't want to miss my flight. On my way to meet a whale."*

As I left the parking lot I saw Tristan and Adam driving up the road in Adam's truck. Obviously they'd fixed it and decided they had time for breakfast tacos after all. I almost went back. Maybe if they saw me, Tristan would've signed something like *"You were right."*

That was the only reason I thought about turning around. Not so I could say goodbye to him or anything.

25

Even though it was still early, I pedaled as fast as I could to Grandma's. It'd be good to have a little extra time in case there were any glitches in our plan. Sometimes projects took longer than expected. Like the Philco radio. My stomach tightened with sadness. I missed resting my hand on it at night and feeling the vibrations from the radio programs. And then there was the fact I couldn't even touch the money I got from selling it.

I shook my head. Nothing I could do about the radio. Maybe I'd buy it back from Mr. Gunnar, unless someone else got to it first.

Grandma flung the door open as soon as I pressed the doorbell. She had to have been standing there waiting, or she'd leaped to the door as soon as the doorbell light flashed. She wore a flowery green dress and a long necklace with flower charms alternating in green and gold all around the chain. Her hair was brushed into the long silvery waterfall.

After opening up the suitcases on the floor of Grandma's closet, we checked our lists to make sure we weren't missing anything. The last thing we did before leaving the apartment was staple a blue tag from the cruise line around each suitcase handle. Seeing our names printed next to the cabin number on those tags made all our plans more real. We were doing this. Later that day we'd be rolling those bags onto the cruise ship.

When the elevator opened at the first floor of the building, we turned right, toward the side exit, instead of left, toward the front desk. The staff would have questions if they saw us heading to the front door with suitcases.

We loaded the luggage into the car without anyone stopping to talk to us.

"Ready to go?" Grandma asked after getting into the driver's seat.

"Let's go find that whale," I answered.

Then I grabbed the armrest as the car peeled out of the parking lot and raced toward the freeway.

"Slow down!" I signed with only one hand so I could hang on with the other. Grandma didn't slow down; just

changed lanes to fly past other cars. Maybe this was a bad idea. She hadn't driven much lately, and not on the freeway. If we got stopped by the police or wrecked the car, we wouldn't even make it to the airport.

Grandma laughed. *"I'm ready to start our adventure!"*

"Watch the road!" I didn't sign anything else after that, so I wouldn't give her a reason to take a hand off the wheel or her eyes off the freeway.

We made it to the airport alive. I released my grip on the armrest and slumped back to catch my breath when Grandma eased into a parking space.

After getting through the long security lines, we still had plenty of time to reach our gate. I wanted to take Grandma's hand and run onto the plane already, but we still had an hour before boarding.

We stopped at a coffee shop, where Grandma ordered a coffee and I got a lemonade iced tea. A little more grown-up than regular lemonade, but without the coffee taste. We shared a mammoth-size blueberry muffin. It was so delicious, I wondered if airport food was really that good or if everything tasted better because of the trip we were about to take. As we chatted I noticed Grandma's signing was faster, more excited than it had been lately. It matched the way she looked that day, as if the color was coming back to her signs too. She signed almost like she used to when Grandpa was around, and I wondered if she felt like he were with us. I had to eat without glancing down at my food so I wouldn't miss anything.

It didn't seem as if we'd been sitting at the coffee shop for long, but when I checked, I saw it was time to board.

We were almost in the last row of the flight since we'd bought the tickets so late. Grandma offered me the window seat, but I told her it was hers. I wanted her to enjoy the adventure as much as possible. Without her I wouldn't be there.

Under the settings on my phone, I found where to disable the GPS. I asked Grandma for hers so I could do the same thing. I didn't want my parents to worry about me, but I didn't want them tracking us down either.

"Hold on, I'll send your mom a message first." She handed me the phone after sending the text.

"What did you tell her?" I asked after turning off the GPS.

"I told her not to worry, that we're going farther than Surfside and will be gone a few days longer."

We smiled at each other and held hands as the

plane rolled down the runway and took off. This wasn't a game or a wish or a plan about a trip anymore. We were really going. Grandma was happier than I'd seen her for a long time.

This trip would kill two birds with one stone, as Dad would say. I'd meet the whale, and Grandma would be back to herself again.

After landing in San Francisco and picking up our luggage, we shuttled to the cruise terminal, where huge white ships sat in the water, waiting for passengers to board. I found ours and pointed it out to Grandma. The *Siren*. The ship that would sail me to Blue 55.

It was still too early to board, so we looked around for something to do. I'd been too excited until then to notice I was hungry, but my stomach was rumbling. *Like an airplane taking off.* I covered my stomach, even though Tristan wasn't there to hear it.

"*Lunch?*" I pointed to a seafood place with outdoor seating and a view of the ocean. Grandma took my hand and led the way. The restaurant hostess seated us at a small table on a dock. We opened the menus and pointed to the same thing—a big platter with samples of every appetizer.

As I watched the waves next to us, I realized there was a smell I liked even better than old radio.

The ocean.

Checking in for the cruise was a lot like going through an airport again, only worse because we were so close to the ship. I wasn't going to breathe until we were safely aboard. Each part of the check-in process and every person in front of us was one more thing blocking my path to Blue 55.

After getting through the long line for the check-in counter, a woman with big blond hair gave us our cruise cards, which looked a lot like credit cards. They would be scanned when we bought something on board, and every time we got on or off the ship.

We thanked the woman at the counter, then moved over to yet another line to board the ship. The attendant at the end of that line held what looked like an alien gun, and we showed her our cards like the people in front of us had. She waved the gun to scan the bar codes on our cards before handing them back to us.

On our way to the metal ramp that led to the ship, a crew member stopped us for a picture. A sign on the wall in front of us read "Bon Voyage" next to a big picture of glaciers and blue water. Grandma put her arm around me, and we faced the camera, with the Alaskan backdrop behind us.

Finally it was really happening. Even though I was a few days away from meeting 55, I felt like I'd already accomplished something. At the end of the metal ramp that led to the ship, I stopped.

"All right?" Grandma asked. I squeezed her hand and smiled. Until then, the trip had been just a plan. Once we boarded the ship, it would be real. We'd sail away from land and try to find a whale. Grandma stood next to me like she understood that I needed to make the moment last. I wondered if she liked to put down a good book before turning to the last page too.

With one hand still holding Grandma's, I signed *"Ready"* with the other, then took a deep breath. Together we stepped from the metal ramp onto the plush carpet of the ship.

When we found our room on the fifth deck, a woman with dark brown skin, wearing black pants and a light blue shirt with gold buttons, smiled like it was the best news ever that we'd arrived. She shook our hands and said something to us. I guessed she was introducing herself. Her golden name tag read JOJO, CABIN STEWARD, GHANA. Grandma introduced us and let her know we were Deaf. Jojo took a business card from her pocket and wrote something on the back, then handed it to Grandma.

I leaned over to read it: *Customer relations can page me if you need anything.*

Jojo opened our door and handed us each a flyer with a map of the ship and a schedule for the rest of the day. She showed us around the cabin, which took two seconds since it was about the size of my bedroom at home.

After Jojo left, Grandma said she wanted to rest. Even after all the traveling and waiting in lines, I couldn't imagine sleeping any time soon. Grandma told me to go ahead and explore the ship.

First I found one of the swimming pools on the eighteenth deck. That wasn't even the highest point— there were two decks above that, with more pools and hot tubs and a game room. People gathered around the bars, holding bright pink and yellow drinks with little paper umbrellas perched on the edges of the glasses. The ship was like a floating city. It would be impossible to see everything, even with a week to explore. Still, I would try. I ran around like I had only a day to take it in.

A few more bars and restaurants were scattered

around the ship. On the same deck as customer service were gift shops, an internet café, and even a library.

A weird feeling that I couldn't place stirred in my stomach. I was restless, as if I were forgetting something. Maybe I'd been so busy working on my plan to meet 55, and there wasn't anything left to do but wait.

At the safety drill that afternoon, the crew herded everyone from our deck into one of the bars. They showed us how to put on life jackets and where the lifeboats were so if the ship hit an iceberg, we wouldn't end up like the passengers on the *Titanic*.

Afterward we stood on the deck and looked out at the water we'd be sailing across soon. The color wasn't the same as what I was used to. The water in the Gulf Coast always looked a little muddy. This was much bluer. Sea lions lounged on the wooden docks of the harbor.

More people with their fruity umbrella drinks mingled around us. The railing vibrated against my hands, and I looked around to see what was making noise. People around us clapped, with their mouths opened like they were laughing and cheering.

Grandma looked up and covered her ear that wore a hearing aid.

"What is that?" I asked.

"Foghorn." She lowered her hand to add, *"That means it's time to leave."*

The ship lurched as it pulled away from the dock. If anyone back home figured out where to look for Grandma and me, well ... they'd find that ship had sailed.

26

I hadn't seen any kids on the ship, which wasn't a surprise since school was still going on. But that evening at the "welcome aboard" party, a girl across the pool waved to me. She looked about my age and had straight black hair, light brown skin, and the kind of glasses I'd wear if I needed them—black frames that made you look smart. I waved back. It seemed like she might come talk to me. I was there for Blue 55, but I couldn't get to him any faster than the ship would go. Maybe it'd be nice to have someone else to talk to while I was on board. Most passengers looked older than Grandma.

Grandma tapped my shoulder. *"Dinner?"* She downed the last of her drink, then stuck the paper umbrella behind her ear. I nodded and looked back at the girl, then waved again as we left the deck. I'd look for her later.

Each table in the dining room was covered with a

white cloth and had a silver vase of flowers. Some people sat at big round tables; others sat at booths or tables for four. Grandma and I had our own table by a window. The waiter—CONSTANTIN, ROMANIA—unfurled the cloth napkins and placed them in our laps.

It was the nicest restaurant I'd ever been to. When I opened the menu, I got really worried.

"There aren't any prices," I signed to Grandma.

"Get whatever you want," she answered. *"It's all included in the price of the cruise."*

Of course. It seemed so much like a real restaurant that I'd forgotten we were on a ship.

"It's okay," she added. She could probably tell I was embarrassed. *"At some restaurants on board, you do pay at the end, but not in the dining rooms and the buffet."* She looked over the menu and said, *"Let's get two different things and share."*

When Constantin returned with a basket of rolls and a butter dish, Grandma told him she'd like the tilapia with rice and steamed vegetables. She signed at the same time she was talking to him so I'd know what she was ordering. Then Constantin turned to me, and I pointed to the salmon with mashed potatoes. He said something else, then flipped the menu over when

I didn't understand him. The dessert page. Everything looked so good, even the things I'd never heard of. Grandma signed, *"I'll get the cheesecake. Which one do you want?"*

I wanted to say *"One of each,"* but decided on the crème brûlée. *"Not sure what it is, but I'll find out."*

Grandma laughed and said *"Good choice"* as I pointed it out to Constantin.

It was nice to see Grandma laugh. I didn't expect her to ever stop missing Grandpa, but maybe this trip would help her get back to her normal self again. Ever since we'd started the planning, it seemed like that drizzly November in her was looking brighter.

The water outside the window looked flat and smooth, except for the white-capped wake the ship made as it sped through the ocean.

Grandma touched my shoulder and signed, *"Look!"*

I turned to see what had caught her attention. The dark gray triangles sticking out of the water reminded me of sharks' fins. But then the animals leaped in arches out of the water together, five of them diving down into the waves and then jumping back up again.

"Dolphins!"

Grandma clapped her hands. *"Yes! Looks like they're*

racing the boat." The pod of dolphins jumped and dived together next to the ship. It felt like a good sign, seeing them as our journey started.

I wondered if Grandma wished that Grandpa were there, watching the dolphins with her. They were supposed to take this cruise together. I wanted to ask her about him, but thinking of him might make her sad. She probably thought about him all the time, though. So maybe it wouldn't hurt to mention him.

"What was your favorite cruise?" I asked her after Constantin brought our plates.

She handed me a forkful of tilapia. *"Hard to choose. I liked them all. After so much time I can't remember which beach was which. But my favorite memory was when we found the karaoke bar."*

"Really?" Of all the entertainment they'd seen on their travels, watching people sing at a karaoke machine couldn't have been the most interesting.

"Yes. I think it was on our cruise to Jamaica. We were wandering the ship at night and felt loud music coming from one of the bars." Grandma covered her ear like she had when the foghorn sounded. Then both hands bounced and fluttered in front of her, showing me how the thumping bass of the music trembled the floor.

"The Calypso, the bar was called. We stopped in to get a

drink and see what was going on. That was the first time we saw a karaoke machine. We sat and watched for a few minutes, then put our names on the list to take a turn ourselves."

"You and Grandpa? At the karaoke machine?"

"Yes. The words to the songs were right there on the screen. That was really for the people who were singing, but it allowed us to enjoy the lyrics, too, instead of just watching people sing."

"So what did you do when it was your turn?"

"We signed one of our favorite songs! When we flipped through the big book of all the songs the club could play, we found one from a musical we had interpreted in college."

"And you got up and did the song together?" As hard as I tried, I couldn't imagine my grandparents standing in front of a crowd in a karaoke bar.

"We did! And Grandpa got the crowd to sing along as we signed the lyrics. He was always good at bringing other people in. You're like him in that way—able to communicate with people you don't know. I'm always in my own head too much to know what to say to other people."

Grandma must have been thinking about someone else. I didn't ask her what she meant because she looked so happy talking about Grandpa I didn't want to interrupt the memory.

"And when the song was over, we got a standing

ovation! We started to go back to our table, but the next couple asked if we'd sign while they sang. We kept it going the rest of the night. We didn't know many of the songs, but we did what we could on the spot with the lyrics in front of us." She shrugged. "*And so what if we did mess up? No one would know.*"

I couldn't believe I hadn't heard that story before. I'd have to ask Mom about it when I got home. Maybe she didn't know all that either. I found myself wondering then what my parents were thinking. After all the planning I'd done, I was there on the ship, right where I was supposed to be. At the same time, I wanted to be at home with my family at the dinner table, even if I didn't always catch everything they talked about. They must have been worried about us by now. Or angry. Maybe both. But if I called to tell them we were okay, I'd end up explaining more than I wanted to. "Let the cat out of the bag" was another expression I'd never understood. What does that have to do with telling a secret? And why would a cat be in a bag anyway?

I didn't realize I was smiling until Grandma brushed two fingertips along the end of her nose and then shrugged to ask, "*What's so funny?*"

"*Just thinking about Dad,*" I answered. "*Some of the things he says . . .*"

"Like when he says 'Let's hit the road' and looks like he's punching a street?"

"Yeah, that." When Dad showed me that humpback whale record he used to listen to, I should have shown him the website with all the different whale songs. Maybe he'd like to hear them again. I wondered when he'd stopped listening to them.

Grandma and I were both too full to finish our dinners, but we magically found more room when Constantin set our desserts in front of us. I still wasn't sure what crème brûlée was made of, other than sugar and some sort of cream. Whatever it was, it was my new favorite food.

When Constantin returned to clear our plates, he showed me a note that read *How do you sign "beautiful"?* It's a little hard for a new person to sign, but he practiced it a couple of times and did okay.

As we got up to leave, he signed to Grandma, *"Goodbye, Beautiful."*

I couldn't believe it. Grandma was actually blushing.

When we got back to the room, the clear plastic holder next to our door held two packets. I gave one to Grandma and flipped through the other as I sat on the edge of the bed.

I waved to get Grandma's attention, then when she looked up, I asked, *"What do you want to do tomorrow?"*

She turned a page of the schedule. *"I don't know. Try my luck at the casino, maybe."*

One thing caught my eye as I scanned the next day's events. An Alaskan wildlife presentation by Sura Kilabuk, the naturalist aboard the ship. Alaskan wildlife had to include whales. It'd be a few days before we got to the sanctuary, but until then I could learn more about Blue 55. Maybe Sura knew about him. Since Grandma didn't pay for Wi-Fi access, I wouldn't be able to check online to see where he was while we were at sea. I'd feel better if I at least knew which way to look.

27

He called out to anyone, to no one. Then stopped to listen. Noises filled the sea around him. Dolphins chattered as they leaped in arcs above the surface. Waves swelled and crashed. Water bubbles popped when a school of fish scrambled away. The low songs of whales traveled through the ocean. A sea full of sounds, with none for him.

He reached for those songs he couldn't sing, trying to grab a call when a wave of sound trembled the water.

If only he could catch it, he'd keep it with him until the sound became a part of him. Then he would answer back and make the tremor of his song float through the water like theirs, and they would know him and answer.

Was there anything out in the ocean like himself? He kept calling just in case his someone was there.

28

I've had breakfast buffets before, but nothing like what was on the ship. It was more like every breakfast buffet from every restaurant I'd ever been in, all shoved into one place. It'd be impossible to try everything. I'd never had French toast and waffles and pancakes in the same meal. We'd picked a good cruise, even though there hadn't been many choices left.

Grandma went to lie by the pool and look out at the ocean while I went to the wildlife lecture. I found my way to a big theater with hundreds of cushy red seats and a stage. It was too early for the presentation, so just a few people were scattered around the theater.

Sitting in the middle of the front row was the girl I'd seen by the pool the evening before. Maybe she liked whales too. I pulled my notepad and pen from my pocket as I took the seat next to her.

Two people stood on stage near the podium, fiddling

with the microphones and getting the slideshow ready. The one holding the microphone had the same straight black hair and light brown skin as the girl next to me.

I'm Iris. I'm Deaf, I wrote on the notepad.

I laughed when I read what she wrote back. *I'm Bennie. Not Deaf.* Good, so she wasn't afraid of me.

You like whales? I asked her. *Or other animals?*

Most animals. Especially sharks. I'm going to be a shark biologist.

Working with sharks? Maybe this girl wasn't afraid of anything.

I get to come here with my mom every summer when she's working on the ship, she added to the note.

I pointed to the woman at the podium, and Bennie nodded.

BRB, she wrote. At the front of the stage, she waved her mom over. Sura leaned over to talk to her and looked in my direction when Bennie pointed. Sura returned to the computer on the podium while Bennie ran back to her seat next to me.

People in the audience settled into their seats and turned toward the stage when Sura talked into the microphone. Since we were so close to the front of the theater, I could see her mouth and catch some of what she said. It seemed like Sura was looking at me while she talked, and she held the microphone low enough that it didn't hide her mouth. Bennie must have told her I was Deaf. That morning Grandma said that she should have requested sign language interpreters for us, but everything happened so fast that she didn't think of it until we left. I hadn't thought of it at all, since I didn't know interpreters ever worked on cruises.

Soon the lights dimmed for the PowerPoint presentation. A spotlight stayed on Sura as she narrated over the slideshow, but with all the pictures and video clips and text on the screen, I could follow along without watching her.

Alaska sure had a lot of wildlife. I thought we'd never get to the whales. It was interesting stuff, I had to admit. Black bears weren't as scary as I'd thought. They pretty much leave you alone. You just have to stay out of their way and make some noise when you're in their area so you won't startle them once they see you. Grizzly bears are a different story. You wouldn't want to come face to face with them whether or not they were expecting you.

After looking at pictures of bald eagles, mountain goats, seals, and sea lions, I nudged Bennie and wrote on the notepad: *Any whales?*

Whales are last, she answered.

Maybe that was Sura's way of getting everyone to stick around for the whole talk, saving the most interesting animal for last.

Finally we got to the whale part of the presentation.

On a slide with the heading "Bubble Net Feeding," Sura showed a pod of humpback whales feeding on a bunch of fish. She clicked over to a video titled "Whale Watchers Capture Bubble Net Feeding in Action."

The humpback pod worked as a team to hunt for their food. The whales zoomed in on a school of small fish. They circled and circled to drive the fish into a tighter and tighter group. Once all the fish were in a tight bundle, one whale blew bubbles from his blowhole while the rest continued to circle. That's why it was called bubble net feeding: the fish wouldn't swim through the bubbles, so it kept them in place like a net would. Then the loudest whale dove below the school of fish and bellowed a feeding call. The bellowing drove the fish into a tighter ball and up to the surface as they tried to escape the sound.

I wondered how the whales decided who was the loudest or who was the best bubbler. Did they have tryouts or something? I knew that whales were smart, from everything I'd read, but that took some serious planning. Maybe Sura would know. At the end of the presentation, I asked Bennie if she could introduce me. She nodded and pointed out to the hallway.

Sura sat behind a table stacked with books, and people were already lining up to talk to her. She signed the books for passengers who bought them. Bennie and I chatted back and forth using the notepad, with some gesturing and pointing thrown in. I got that she and her mom were from northern Canada, which was really cold.

The woman in line ahead of us was never going to stop talking. I shifted from one foot to the other while we waited for her to ask her thousand questions about every species of animal in Alaska or whatever she was doing. Finally she moved on, and Bennie introduced me to her mom. Sura held her hand out and said, "Nice to meet you." After shaking her hand, I showed her the question I'd written on the paper. *The bubble net feeding. How'd they figure that out?*

She wrote down an answer, then slid the paper over to me.

We're not sure. Amazing, aren't they?

Okay, yes, but what kind of answer was that?

But I want to know how they communicate, I wrote. *How'd they come up with that plan for catching fish?*

I'd worked with radios enough to know how each

part communicates with the next. Shouldn't scientists who study whales know all about how they talk to one another?

That's one fun thing about science, Sura wrote. *The wondering. If we knew all the answers, there wouldn't be anything to search for.*

Well, that didn't sound like much fun to me, leaving a bunch of questions unanswered.

Bennie said something to her mom, and Sura's answer looked like "Great idea!"

She turned a page in the notepad and wrote, *Tomorrow I'll be announcing whale sightings from the bridge. You're welcome to join us there if you'd like. You'll get the best views.*

Where is that? I wrote. When I explored the ship, I hadn't seen anything that looked like a bridge.

Deck eight. Bennie can show you.

That did sound good—getting the chance to see whales in the wild. Maybe Grandma would like that too.

What time?

I'll be up there by 5 a.m. You know what they say: the early bird gets the whale. No, I didn't know anyone who said that. Not even my dad.

Bennie took the notepad and wrote, *Meet for breakfast at 6?*

Okay, I'll ask my grandma.

Sura wrote, *She's welcome to come too.*

Grandma wouldn't want to wake up that early, but I'd ask anyway. I wasn't a morning person either, but if that was when the whales got up, I would too.

Do you know Blue 55? I asked Sura. *I'm wondering where he's swimming now.*

I was ready to tell her all about 55 and his song if she didn't know who he was, but she smiled and pulled her phone from her pocket. A blue icon on the phone screen was labeled "Track 55." The map that came up when she opened the app showed a black dotted line with a blinking blue dot at the end. It looked kind of like the map I'd seen online.

That's him? I wrote.

Yes. This app shows where his song was last picked up, but it's been a while since anyone's heard him. Sura zoomed in on the map, then pointed behind us and to the right. *Out that way, last anyone knew.*

After thanking Sura and Bennie and telling them goodbye, I took the elevator up to the top deck and stood at the railing. I looked in the direction Sura had pointed and felt closer to Blue 55.

29

Bennie waited for me outside the buffet entrance. I'd told Grandma the night before that she was invited to come with me to watch for whales from the bridge, but when I mentioned the time, she flopped over in bed like just the thought of waking up so early was enough to knock her out. *"I'll wait for whales that wake up at a more reasonable hour."*

Bennie led me through the dining area, and I shrugged as a way of asking "Where are we going?" She pointed toward the back of the room and gave a thumbs-up.

I'd felt like I was getting used to the ship, but it was full of surprises. Bennie led me past the lines of people, through one dining area to another, almost to the back of the deck, where there was another buffet line. It served the exact same stuff as the first one, but there wasn't a long wait. Most people stopped at the first food line they saw, like I had.

We took our salmon eggs Benedict and banana waffles to an outdoor table, with a view of the ocean around us. I set my notepad and pen between us, and Bennie handed me a rolled-up navy-blue scarf from her coat pocket.

I pointed to myself and mouthed, *For me?*

She nodded and pointed to me too, then rubbed her arms and pretended to shiver. True, I had been cold, but I didn't know it was that obvious. Even with my coat zipped all the way up last night, the wind chilled my neck and upper chest.

"Thanks," I signed. I tied the scarf around my neck, and Bennie stood up to show me how to tuck it under the collar of my coat. Big difference.

She wrote on the notepad, *I thought you might want to borrow a scarf since it didn't seem like you had one. You're out of school already?*

Bennie had told me the night before that her parents homeschooled her, then boat-schooled her when her mom worked on cruise ships. I thought about making up something to tell her why I was there but realized I didn't mind telling her the real story. Even though we'd just met, I felt like I'd known her for a long time.

I shook my head. *School's still going on. I had to come now because I want to meet Blue 55.*

Bennie's eyebrows rose, and her mouth dropped open as she read the note. "You're going to meet him? I mean, sorry, I forgot—"

I waved her off as she reached for the pen, since I understood what she'd said. It felt good to share my plan with someone who was as excited about the whale as I was.

I hope so, I wrote. *He's supposed to be in Appleton around the time we get there.* I hesitated before telling her about the song. She might think it was a dumb idea. But she knew more about whales than I did. Better to find out now if something was wrong with my plan. If she told me it wouldn't work out, I didn't know what I'd do.

I made a song for him. The sanctuary workers will play it from the boat when they go out to tag him. I looked down at my plate as I slid the notepad to her, then glanced up to see her expression.

She smiled while she scribbled on the page. *Can I hear it later?*

Sure. I took the last bite of my waffle and smiled back at her. Bennie knew more about whales than I did, and she liked my plan. Maybe it really would work.

After breakfast Bennie led me to the bridge of the

ship, which as it turned out was not like a bridge at all, so I wasn't sure how it had gotten that name. It was a giant room that took up the middle of deck eight. Floor-to-ceiling windows wrapped around the room, giving us a view in all directions. A long wooden counter topped with a dashboard of screens stretched across the bridge. So many dials, knobs, buttons, and joysticks filled the counter, I couldn't imagine how anyone ever learned what they were all for. A few overhead screens showed a radar, views of the ship, a map of our route, and rows of numbers that must have meant something to someone. A man dressed in black pants and a white shirt with gold stripes on the sleeves stood at the front of the bridge, looking out. I figured he was the captain. A couple of other crew members sat in black leather chairs at the controls.

For a few minutes we stood at our places near the front windows while Sura made announcements into a microphone. Nothing but still waters stretched out ahead of us. Maybe it was the wrong day to look for whales. I turned when Sura pointed to our right. At first I didn't see anything. Then a plume of spray shot into the air. Bennie glanced at me and motioned like she was writing with an invisible pen.

Humpbacks, she wrote after I handed her my notepad. I looked out at the water again. Even though Sura had binoculars, I didn't know how she could tell what kinds of whales were out there from so far away. Closer to the ship, a whale shot up out of the water, then crashed down with a giant splash. It almost didn't seem real. The whale was about the size of a school bus, and there he was flying out of the ocean. I turned to Bennie to ask, *Did that really happen?* The wonder on her face answered my question. She must have seen whales a thousand times, but she still looked thrilled at the sight of them.

Another whale breached, then left behind a wall of splashing water after it sank beneath the surface again. Seeing them in real life was nothing like looking at pictures or videos. I ran to the windows closest to the whale who had just leaped up from the water. Bennie tapped my shoulder and pointed to the other side of the ship. I looked in time to see another whale crashing down onto the ocean's surface.

I'd have to try to describe all this to Dad. I hoped I'd be able to get across how beautiful they were. These were the whales he listened to so much on that old record. The humpbacks, the symphony players.

After a while I got better at catching sight of the spray from the whales' blowholes, so I knew where they were. Sura estimated we were surrounded by about fifty whales. I wondered if Blue 55 ever swam with other whales, even though they didn't speak the same language. Andi had said he'd swim toward other whales, but then he'd go back to swimming alone again. Maybe he swam *near* those other whales but not really *with* them. Kind of like how I was at school.

When Bennie let me know that her mom was wrapping up the whale watch announcements for the morning, I looked at the time and realized we'd been on the bridge for more than two hours already. Hadn't I just gotten there?

Before we left I wrote a note for Sura. *How'd you know they were humpbacks from so far away?*

She waved me over to a table and pulled out a chair for me. From her messenger bag she removed a folder and flipped through some papers until she found the one she was looking for. The paper had a bunch of pictures of blow spouts from whales. The top of the page had the heading "There She Blows!"

Like in Moby-Dick, I wrote. Captain Ahab said that when he saw a spout from the white whale. I remembered some of the book from a kids' edition that Grandma had given me. I'd tried to finish it a few times because I wanted to find out if the whale got away from the people who were hunting him, but I always fell asleep before I got to the end.

Sura nodded and wrote, *Each kind of whale has its own spout shape. If I spot them before the wind blows away the spray, I can identify what kind it is.* She pointed to the picture of a humpback. The water that shot up from the whale's blowhole was shaped like an upside-down teardrop. Some other whales blew out water in almost the same shape, but in a taller, thinner teardrop than the humpback's. Gray and right whales blew double spouts of water in the shape of a heart.

Sura turned to another page in her notebook, which showed pictures of whale flukes. Those were all different shapes, too. If she was close enough to see a whale's tail, she'd know what kind of whale it belonged to.

On the back of the paper, I wrote, *What about Blue 55?* and slid it over to Sura.

At the bottom of the page, she drew a quick sketch. Blue 55 had a fin on his back like a fin whale, and the tail of a blue whale. Another way he was different from any other.

30

It would be easier if he could forget the others he'd sung to. But the memory of a whale is long and deep. A whale who swims in the ocean for a century still remembers the first whales he knew. Just as strongly, he remembers those he never knew, the ones who drifted past.

He dove below a wave. The deeper he swam, the more the water resisted, pushed him back up where he didn't want to be. At the ocean's surface the sunlight illuminated the whale families he couldn't belong to.

He pushed back, swimming harder, until the dark swallowed him. The depths were emptier, darker, quieter. Yet less lonely, because there was no one to answer his calls with silence.

What was a whale without a pod? What was a whale without a whale song?

He didn't try to create a song by sending air flowing through his body. He kept his breath still.

Air and space did not make music.

Air was only air.

Space was nothing more than space.

31

It was our third day on the ship already, but it felt like I'd just left home. At the same time the days somehow passed slowly. At lunch I'd think of a conversation I'd had that morning, and it felt like it had happened days ago. It wasn't going by slowly in a bad way. Not dragging like on a school day where you'd swear someone had glued the hands of the clock into place. Each night I wasn't ready for the day to end, even though it seemed it had started so long ago. I almost forgot why I was on the ship—to meet Blue 55. Almost. Each day on the ship brought me closer to him.

I didn't want to spend the day in the cabin, but I wasn't going to do anything until my stomach settled down. It churned every time I sat up. When Jojo came by to clean the room, I told her I wasn't feeling well.

She picked up a notepad from the nightstand and wrote, *Back in a minute.* When she returned she propped the door open and handed me a cold can of pineapple juice.

I slid the notepad across the nightstand while she made Grandma's bed. *Thanks. Guess I'm seasick.*

She took the pen from me and added, *Usually people don't get seasick when the sailing is this smooth.*

True, the boat hadn't been rocking at all. Whenever I looked out into the ocean, there was hardly a wave. I didn't know another explanation for how I felt, though.

Jojo handed me a new page she'd written on. *I haven't seen my family for six months. Sometimes I miss them so much I feel sick. Maybe you're homesick?*

I'd always thought "homesick" meant you just missed being away from home and wanted to go back. I never knew it could make you actually feel sick. Maybe that was what was wrong with me. It wasn't just that I missed home. Mixed in with that was everything I was worried about, like how mad my parents must be and whether or not I'd get to meet Blue 55. What if the sick feeling was my body trying to tell me that I shouldn't be here on this ship? If my plan didn't work, Blue 55 would swim through the ocean as lonely as always, and I'd go back home to face the trouble I was in, all for nothing.

The feeling was much worse than the emptiness

I felt in my stomach when I had to leave a radio sitting broken on the shelf. It was like an emptiness that was never going to go away.

Of course I couldn't tell Jojo any of that. I smiled and thanked her again for the juice.

When I caught up with Bennie later, she pulled a notebook from her pocket. She'd started carrying one like I did, to write messages to me. She was picking up a little sign language, too, so we communicated more and more with signs. She didn't pretend to know more than she did, and she didn't mind when I corrected her. She even laughed at her own mistakes, like when she signed *"bathroom"* instead of *"Tuesday."* Some signs were pretty close, but just moving the hand the wrong way made a big difference in meaning.

"Are you and your grandma getting off the ship in Juneau?" she asked.

"Yeah. Not sure what we'll do." That day would be the ship's first port stop. Some people would spend the day in Juneau and go sightseeing or on a small boat for a whale watch. We'd seen so many whales from the ship, but most passengers didn't have the view from the bridge like Bennie and I had.

"Think I'll look for someplace with internet so I can check in with my parents." I'd been thinking I should

send a message to my family. They had to be worried, even though Grandma said she was updating Mom to let her know we were okay. When I asked her what Mom had said, she just waved me off and told me, *"She'll get over it."*

Use the internet café here on the ship, Bennie wrote. *I can log you on as our guest.*

You can? Like for free? I didn't think Grandma would want to pay for internet time, but I hadn't thought about asking Bennie to help me get online.

Sure, I'll show you how.

That offer was too good to turn down. *Okay, great! Do you have something you can do too? I don't want you to be bored while I check email and stuff.*

Yeah, I'll watch shark videos.

The café was like a coffee shop, with a counter where people could order drinks and snacks. Some people sat at tables and chairs with their laptops. Mounted along each wall was a narrow table with desktop computers. Bennie pointed to the cups of gelato behind a glass case near the counter and gave me a thumbs-up. After we each got a dish—chocolate mint for her, red velvet for me—I sat at a computer near a window, all the way to the right. Starboard, I should say. Bennie had taught me some ship vocabulary. The right side of the ship was the starboard side, and the left was the port. The front was the bow, the back the stern. But some signs on the walls pointed out the fore and aft parts of the ship so I wasn't sure what the differences were.

Bennie pulled up a chair next to me and showed me how to log into the ship's Wi-Fi, then opened the computer's notepad. *The cruise line gives us some guest accounts, like for when my dad or a friend is visiting. You can use that login while you're here.*

Wow, thanks! First I checked on Blue 55. The map on the sanctuary's website showed a dotted line, not the solid one I'd hoped to see. A guess of where he was. He still wasn't singing.

I hadn't noticed that Bennie was looking at the map too until she squeezed my hand. She turned her screen so I could see it, and typed, *Sometimes I don't feel like talking to anyone either. Maybe he's like that.*

Since no one ever answered him back, I couldn't blame Blue 55 if he quit singing forever. I wished I could tell him how close I was and that I had a song for him. He couldn't give up just yet.

Bennie tapped my arm and signed, *"Song?"*

Right, I'd told her I'd play Blue 55's song for her. I brought up the sound file from my email, then hit play.

Bennie's mouth dropped open like she couldn't

believe what she was hearing. She turned to a man across the room and said sorry, then hit the volume down button on the keyboard.

She pointed at me like she was asking "You did this?"

I laughed at her surprise. *"Yes."*

"How?"

I signed *"school,"* then pretended I was playing each instrument one by one. *"And . . ."* I opened the tuner app on my phone, then turned the wheel to "Tuba" and invited Bennie to tap some of the notes. The hertz readout in the corner showed her how close the notes were to fifty-five hertz.

"Cool!" Bennie signed. After trying out a few more instruments on the tuner, she clicked to a screen I hadn't used before and said something into the phone. A line graph rose and fell as she talked. This screen had a hertz readout too, showing the frequency of Bennie's voice. Way too high for the whale—almost two hundred hertz—but it was interesting to see. She held the phone in front of me, inviting me to talk into it.

"Me?"

"Try it."

I glanced around to see if anyone else was looking at us, then leaned toward the phone. I'd do something quiet. The wavy blue line appeared on the graph when I hummed and then skipped higher when I giggled. Bennie and I took turns humming into the phone to see what the graph and hertz readout would do. If I hummed deeply enough to feel the vibrations in my chest, I could make the frequency lower. Interesting, but it still wasn't going to get anywhere near fifty-five hertz, no matter what I did.

That must be what it was like for Blue 55. He knew what sound he needed to make but just couldn't do it. I closed the app and typed a message to Bennie: *I wish I could make a sound like his. I'd add it to the song.*

Maybe that was what was bothering me about the song I'd made—all the notes that played at his frequency were made with instruments. Even though I'd added the sounds of other animals to it, there wasn't a living thing that sounded like him. Only Blue 55 himself.

Bennie signed *"Wait,"* then pulled her own phone from her pocket. She opened an app that showed a picture of a microphone in the center of the screen and a sliding bar marked "Lower" and "Higher" on either side.

Bennie touched the microphone, then talked into the phone. She pointed to my phone and drew a check mark in the air, asking me to check what she'd just recorded. I opened the tuner app and held the phones side by side while Bennie's recording played. One hundred hertz. A lot lower than her real voice.

The graph on my phone bounced as I laughed. *"Can you make it lower?"*

Bennie scrolled the bar on her voice modulator app until the readout on my screen told us we'd hit the magic number. Fifty-five. She held the phone toward me again and hit the record button. I hummed at the phone, then we adjusted the recording until it would sound like something Blue 55 might recognize. Bennie said she'd email the sound files to me so I could add them to the song. I wasn't sure how I'd do that without my computer software, but I searched on my phone for audio editing apps and found a free one that looked good. I'd be able to load the song onto it and then slide in the files from Bennie.

I slid the keyboard back to me and typed, *Can you show me that tracker your mom had for Blue 55?*

She held her hand out, then added the tracker for me after I gave her my phone. I'd be able to check on 55's progress without having to get on a computer.

Time to check email. I held my breath as I signed in. Just as I thought, the screen was full of unread messages. Besides my parents and Tristan, Wendell had emailed me. I scrolled down to the first one, sent the day I left.

Let me know when you get where you're going.

And two days later:

Did you get there? Where are you going to look for the whale? I'm getting worried.

For me the days were flying by, but they had to be crawling for everyone back home. I couldn't believe I hadn't thought of that. I was almost too embarrassed to answer Wendell.

Wendell,
Sorry I didn't get in touch before, but I haven't had internet service. I'm okay. After I find the whale, I'll tell you all about him.

The messages from my family were about the same, wanting me to let them know where I was and if I was all right. Mom added:

Grandma says you'll be gone a few days. Is that true? How are you going to make up all the work you're missing at school? I'll go by there and pick up your books, but I'd like to know what to tell them.

Don't worry about being in trouble. I'm sure this was your grandmother's idea. It's the kind of thing she'd do.

I could leave it at that and let Grandma take the blame. Maybe I wouldn't be grounded for life after we got back.

Mom,

Everything's okay. I'll catch up on my work when I get back. Please don't worry. I'm having a great time with Grandma. Yes, it'll be a few days before we get back. Sorry for taking off like we did without telling you first.

I guess it's the kind of thing I'd do too, because it wasn't Grandma's idea. Please don't be mad at her.

Love,

Iris

Houses and buildings added to the landscape of mountains and snow as we closed in on Juneau. Grandma would be ready to get off the ship. That morning she said she'd meet me back in our cabin so we could go into town together.

The cabin was empty when I got back. I found Jojo in the hall and asked if she'd seen Grandma. She didn't know where she was either.

Grandma wouldn't leave the ship without me. Would she? I sat on the edge of the bed to wait.

She'd been having so much fun on the cruise. This is what we'd all been wanting her to do at Oak Manor—join in on the activities and make some friends. But that wasn't the point of this trip. We were there to meet Blue 55.

Thinking of Oak Manor reminded me of why Grandma was living there. Maybe Mom was right about Grandma needing people to look out for her. I was having fun too, but I was ready to be on land again for a few hours. And I wouldn't take off somewhere and forget Grandma.

Just before I gave up to go look for her, the cabin door opened, and in walked Grandma.

"*Ready to go?*" she asked.

"Yeah, I'm ready. Where were you?"

"Origami class." She held up a red paper swan. Its long neck moved back and forth, and the wings flapped when she pulled gently on the swan's tail.

"You did that in your class?"

"Yes, with just one square of paper." Grandma showed me how she'd folded the square again and again to create the swan. "And I made something for you." She pulled another folded paper shape out of her purse and placed it into my hand. A blue whale.

"Like it?" she asked.

"You made this for me?" I moved a delicate fin up and down with my fingertip.

"With some help. I stayed after class to ask the teacher how to make a whale."

I couldn't let on I'd been annoyed with her or that I'd worried she'd left me. Even though Grandma had been at her own class and meeting other people, she was thinking of me. And the whale. She didn't forget the reason we were there.

I set the whale on the nightstand and thought about Grandpa's poems. Paper wasn't always flat. Sometimes it was folded into a shape that used the space around and above and below it to tell a story.

A brochure from our cabin showed what there was

to do and see in Juneau. One page pictured trails that were easy to walk.

"*Maybe a hike?*" I suggested.

"*I have another plan,*" Grandma answered.

"*Another plan?*" I hadn't noticed her looking at the Juneau information.

She pulled two tickets from her purse and handed one to me. Printed in black letters across the ticket were the words "Glacier Shuttle, All-Day Pass."

"*We'll see the glaciers up close?*"

"*And touch them.*"

Like Grandpa wanted to do.

We made our way to the shuttle stop near the cruise ship terminal and boarded along with a few other people who'd gathered at the corner. The driver waited until the bus was almost full before pulling away from the curb.

Near the end of the twenty-minute ride, the shuttle left the paved road and drove through bumpy tree-lined trails. The driver pulled up to a narrower trail, and we got out to follow wooden signs the rest of the way to the glaciers. I wanted to run up the path, but I walked slowly enough to keep pace with Grandma. Bennie's blue scarf tucked under my coat collar shielded my neck from the cold air. I'd have to thank her again for letting me borrow it.

We stopped to read a sign with a picture of a U-shape valley, covered with blue-and-white ice. The description beneath the picture said that glaciers carved the mountains there. For millions of years, the heavy ice crawled over the mountains like a slow bulldozer, knocking aside dirt and rocks as it reshaped the mountainside.

I looked ahead of us at the glaciers, trying to imagine them carving out the curves between mountain peaks. I'd always signed *"valley"* with my hands moving down to a V shape, but maybe that wasn't always right. So the glaciers would reshape my sign, too. From now on, whenever I described to anyone what the valleys here looked like, I'd soften the sign into more of a U shape.

After a few minutes we were close enough to touch the glassy, ice-covered mountains. We'd sailed by some glaciers on the way, but the view from the ship didn't show the reflections of blue in the ice. Other colors, too, ones I didn't have names for. Maybe they didn't have names because they didn't exist anywhere but in glaciers. Ignoring the cold, I removed a glove to run my hand along the ice. We were there to touch a glacier, and touching it with a glove probably wouldn't count. The wall of ice was smooth, but not flat like I'd thought it would be. Like frozen waves instead of the flat sheets they looked to be from a distance. In some areas the ice was so thick, it seemed the mountain was made of ice. Then, just a few feet away, brown rock showed through a hazy ice window.

This was the same stuff I got out of the freezer at home for my water glass, but it was so much more than that. This frozen water was powerful enough to carve mountains. It sculpted the landscape here, as if it decided there would be a peak, over there would be a valley, over there a ribbon of ice running down the mountain. Sure, I'd learned about glaciers in school, but it was kind of like the breaching humpbacks—seeing them up close made them more real.

A man who looked like a park ranger, dressed all in brown, talked to some of the people who'd been on our shuttle. I wondered how he could hear anything through the furry flaps of the hat that covered his ears.

In a spot where the ice gave way to bare rock, I ran my hands along some scars in the mountain. They were like claw marks from top to bottom. I took out my notebook and wrote a question for the park ranger.

What made those marks? I pointed to the grooves.

After reading that he wrote back, *Scrapes from glaciers.* He motioned for me to follow him, then picked up a chunk of ice from the ground. He held the ice against the side of the mountain and dragged it down the length of a groove. I shook my head, not because I thought the ranger was lying to me, but because it was so hard to picture that. It seemed like the ice would just drip off the mountain as it melted, not rake a path on its way down. The ranger nodded like he understood my disbelief.

The ice is so heavy, he wrote, *that when it slides off, it leaves these deep scratches.*

I placed my hand on the bare rock, still freezing to the touch, even though it was no longer covered with ice. Like the memory of the glaciers was so strong, the sunlight couldn't get through it.

Farther down the trail, a group had gathered on a small beach carved into the mountain, next to a waterfall. Some people held their hands out toward the waterfall, then laughed and pulled away. Grandma walked ahead of me. Before I got close to the waterfall, the spray that flew into the air chilled my face with dots of icy water. I stayed back while Grandma continued walking. The water from the fall rushed into the pool of turquoise water below. I knew without being able to hear anything that this water was noisy.

Grandma held out her hand to catch the spray of glacier water before the sea claimed it. She stood closer to the waterfall than anyone, but she didn't seem to notice the cold. When she saw me watching her, she signed, *"It's freezing!"* So she had noticed it, but hadn't backed away. I took a step toward her, then stopped. I'd leave her with this moment, face lifted before the rushing waterfall, drops of glacial water sliding down the lines on her face. I wondered if she felt like Grandpa was there next to her, feeling the cold water too.

Grandma laughed. A real laugh, one that shook her shoulders and deepened the lines around her eyes. When was the last time she'd done that? Since before Grandpa died, for sure. If it was possible that he could still be with us in some way, this is what I'd want him to see.

Even when the water is icy, the sea can melt away a drizzly November.

32

Our next stop, Skagway, was a pretty town, but it was hard to think about anything but Blue 55. Everything I'd worked for would be happening the next day. I'd gone through so much to make it happen, and then I couldn't believe it was time. At least, I hoped it would be—55 still wasn't singing. Maybe my song would work, and he'd start singing again when he heard it.

Grandma and I ate burgers and onion rings at a restaurant that used to be an old saloon. When it was time to pay, Grandma handed the waiter a fifty-dollar bill and left a big tip. *"Had some luck at the casino."*

"Nice! Keep winning, and you can live on the ship all the time."

Grandma laughed at that. *"I wish!"*

After lunch we did some sightseeing around town. A small crowd in a park watched lumberjacks with chainsaws carve upright logs into sculptures of bears and salmon. From there we wandered into the down-town area.

Grandma stopped at the door of a gift shop and asked, *"Want to look around in here?"* The shop took up most of the block and had everything from bum-per stickers to T-shirts to packaged salmon. Post-cards with Alaskan scenery filled a spinning rack. Right then it hit me how much I missed my family. I couldn't stand to think about how worried they were, so I'd been trying not to think about them at all. It wasn't working.

I shuffled through a few cards with animals on them, then settled on one with a picture of a breach-ing humpback and "Alaska" written in cursive letters in one corner.

At the cash register I paid for the postcard with change from my pocket and stepped aside. With a pen I borrowed from the counter, I filled out my home address on the three blank lines on the back of the postcard. Next to that was space for a short note.

Dear Mom, Dad, and Tristan,
   I wanted to let you know I'm thinking about you. Please don't worry about us. Sorry for leaving with-out telling you.

I just had to find the whale.

                                        Love,

                                        Iris

When the customer at the counter left with his bag, I showed the cashier the postcard and tapped the "Place stamp here" square in the corner. She pointed across the street and said, "Post office."

I found Grandma browsing through the T-shirts. *"Just going across the street to mail this,"* I told her. *"Be right back."*

She held up a green "I Brake for Moose" T-shirt to check the size. *"Okay, I'll stay here and look around."*

I hadn't been to many post offices—just the one near home sometimes when one of my parents had to mail a package—but this had to be the tiniest post office in the land. It looked more like a little cabin, with wood paneling all around the inside walls. Only one person worked at the counter, and a few people stood in line. I wanted to ask if I could go ahead of everyone since all I needed was one stamp, but that was probably against post office rules. Instead of hanging on to the card to send later, I gave it to the postal worker to mail for me right then. By the time it got to my house, our trip would be almost over. The important part, anyway. If

Blue 55 was in Appleton like he should be, I'd be meeting him soon. Nothing else would matter after that. My family would know I'd been thinking of them, and not just of myself.

I didn't see how I'd get any sleep that night, thinking about how close I was to Blue 55, about all I'd done and how far I'd come. We'd be sailing into the sanctuary's waters soon. We might even be sailing by Blue 55 right then. He needed to sing again so I'd know. I opened the sound file on my phone so I could feel his song against my hand, and wished he was out there joining in.

If I didn't get to sleep by six, I'd go out to the front of the ship to watch us pull into Appleton.

At some point I did fall asleep. When I woke up, Grandma's bed was empty.

I sat up in bed, wondering where she could be. Maybe she was just out for a walk. That was the kind of thing she would do. But in the middle of the night? I grabbed my coat and wandered into the hallway. Empty.

Maybe something came up, and she didn't want to bother me. Or could this be like the time she took off for the beach without telling anyone? But she couldn't have gone far—we literally were on the ocean. I couldn't think of where to look for her. It was too late for any classes to be going on. Usually if she wasn't in the cabin, she was out on deck reading or watching the water. It'd be too dark to see much, but I couldn't think of where else to check.

The ship was as busy in the middle of the night as it was during the day. People swam in the pools and mingled around the bars, carrying their umbrella drinks.

I had to try to think like Grandma. Where would she want to go?

The casino. Even though I wouldn't be allowed in, I'd have a good chance of spotting her from the wide doorways. A crew member kept his eye on me as I stood at the edge of the casino entrance. I guess to make sure I wasn't going to run in and try my luck at the slot machines. The place was packed, even in the middle of the night. As far as I could tell through the haze of cigarette smoke, Grandma wasn't there. Same thing on the opposite side, when I circled around to the other entrance. Some of the machines weren't visible from where I was, so I'd check back later if I had to.

It was impossible for one person to search the whole ship, but I looked everywhere I could think of. I even tried the internet café and the library. When I didn't find Grandma at the pool, out on deck, or in any of the diners, I went back to the cabin to see if she'd returned.

Still not there. She should've left me a note, at least. Nothing on the desk except the daily schedule and Jojo's business card. I turned to the back of the card, where Jojo had written *Customer relations can page me if you need anything.*

Did she mean at any time? Of course she would be asleep, but this was important. This wasn't a call for extra towels or a room cleaning. What if something had happened to Grandma?

I ran back to the elevator, clutching Jojo's card. Maybe the people at the customer service desk wouldn't need to call her, but they'd find Grandma somehow.

Surprisingly I wasn't the only one who needed customer service that time of night. Three people were in line ahead of me. They couldn't possibly have anything as important as a missing grandma. While I waited I tried to think of where else to look.

Finally it was my turn. When I stepped off the carpet onto the concrete floor in front of the counter, vibrations tickled my feet. I slipped out of my shoes and stood there in my socks. Music was playing somewhere nearby. Loud music, with those low bass sounds that really shook a radio speaker.

The man behind the counter waved to get my attention, saying something that looked like "Can I help you?" I shook my head and stepped aside to let the passenger behind me take his turn. The thread of a memory waited for me to grab on to it. Something about what Grandma had said that first night on the ship.

The carpet muffled some of the music, but there was enough of a vibration for me to follow. It grew stronger as I ran, shoes in hand, toward the stern.

In front of the Tipsy Marlin Bar, I stopped. During the day it was always empty. Not now. The bar was packed with people, dancing and laughing and holding drinks. At the front of that crowd, in the lights of the stage, hands flying, was Grandma. A banner hanging from the ceiling read "Tipsy Marlin Karaoke Night."

As far as I knew, there weren't any other Deaf people on board, but everyone was watching Grandma. This must have been going on for a long time, because she'd taught the audience some sign language. The words "Break it down" appeared on the lyrics screen, which Grandma signed. Then everyone did some weird dance and signed together, *"Stop, Hammer time!"*

It was like Grandma was signing a language everyone in the world understood. Mom wouldn't believe this. She'd been wanting Grandma to make friends, and now it looked like she'd made a whole roomful.

Watching Grandma reminded me of the humpback whales that leaped out of the ocean. The symphony players. If someone could write Grandma's signing on sheet music, every color would be splashed all the way up and down the musical scale, and off the page.

I was too amazed to be mad at her. As I stood there holding my shoes in one hand, I wondered if my own family would feel the same way about what I'd done. I'd wandered off too, much farther than Grandma ever had. But if they saw that this was where I was supposed to be, that I was doing exactly what I was supposed to be doing, maybe they'd understand just a little. The way Grandma looked then—that was how I'd feel when I met Blue 55.

She'd also taught the audience how to do Deaf applause. Instead of clapping when the song ended, everyone waved their raised hands. As Grandma stepped off the stage, she got a standing ovation.

I didn't care if I wasn't allowed in a bar. I ran to Grandma and hugged her, then stepped back. *"How . . . ?"* I couldn't even finish my sentence.

"I'm sorry to worry you. I didn't think I'd be gone for so long. I couldn't sleep, so I got up to take a walk around the ship, and stumbled upon karaoke night."

"*I mean . . .*" I pointed to the stage. "*That. How did you do that?*"

"*After I watched some of the performers, someone tried to get me to go up and sing. I told them I'm Deaf, and they asked me to sign the songs with them. Pretty soon I was doing my own performance and getting the crowd to join in. Looks like everyone had fun, right?*"

Yes, it did look like everyone had had fun. More importantly, Grandma had.

I'd wanted to make that trip by myself. For the first time I was happy that a plan of mine failed, so I could be right there with Grandma.

33

The chattering of dolphins filled the water as the pod raced past him. They'd played like this throughout the day, falling behind and darting ahead, then leaping in front of him.

He led them to a school of fish. They were too large for the whale to filter through his baleen and swallow, but they made a feast for the dolphins. While they ate, the whale circled the fish to keep them close.

The pod swam slowly, weighed down by the meal. The whale glided alongside a dolphin and lowered his head, an invitation to swim onto his back. This is how they communicated, soundlessly. The dolphin threw herself onto the whale. He sank down to keep her just below the surface, then propelled his body through the water, ahead of the pod.

This happened once in a great while, this meeting with dolphins. They would find him and spend the day leaping and racing alongside him, chattering. If only he knew what drew them to him, he would try to bring them closer more often. Was it a sound he'd made that was like theirs? If it was, he would sing that sound again and again. He wasn't like them—they didn't sing the same songs—but they understood each other in a way. He knew they had fun diving alongside him, jumping onto his back for a ride through the surf.

The whale dove down, then up to the surface, bursting out of the ocean. The water splashed high around him when he crashed down on his side. He rejoined the pod, notes of joy waving through his song.

If they could play like this every day, at least for a little while, he wouldn't be so lonely. But dolphins never stayed for long.

34

This was it. The day when everything I'd planned, all the work I'd done, would come together. It would be worth it because of what would happen in just a couple of hours.

Bennie joined Grandma and me for breakfast. After loading up my plate at the buffet, all I could do was stare out the window, too excited to eat.

It didn't feel like the boat was moving anymore. We were there.

"Ready?" Grandma signed.

I nodded but stayed in my seat, clutching my backpack. The whole reason for the trip was right ahead of me. Of course I'd have to leave the ship to get any closer to the sanctuary, but I couldn't make myself stand up. Until then I hadn't failed. Soon, that could change. Even if I did get to see the expedition, it might not work out. Maybe Blue 55 would swim away, like he had before, or avoid the boat altogether. He had no way of knowing what this meant to me. He might come and go without a glance, or not show up at all.

So many ways to fail, all right in front of me. But I had to try.

First I'd check to see how close 55 was to the sanctuary. I'd been avoiding the tracker app, since there was nothing I could do about where Blue 55 was. But now, it was worth finding out if we had to hurry off the ship right then or take our time. That was if he was singing at all.

Instead of the dotted line that had been on the screen the last time I'd looked, a solid black line traced 55's path. When I saw the blinking blue dot that showed where he was, I closed the tracker app and set my phone facedown on the table. That solid line I'd been so desperate to see had finally appeared. I just didn't expect it to be so far away.

I picked up the phone again, even though I didn't want to look. If I left it on the table, it didn't have to be true yet. Maybe the program just needed to refresh. But no, when I reopened it, there was the current time and date. Blue 55 was singing again, but from far away. One of the detours he sometimes took, for reasons no one knew. I tried to push away the thought that crept into my mind: I wasn't going to meet Blue 55.

Grandma and Bennie looked at me with questions on their faces, waiting for me to explain what was wrong. All I could do was hold the phone out for them to see.

"Washington?" Grandma signed.

The sanctuary had to know the news. What were they going to do? I opened up their website and found a new post: "Operation Tag 55—Headed South!"

Well, folks, nature is unpredictable! We're relieved to find out that Blue 55 is alive and singing, but the bad news is he's nowhere near Appleton as usual. For some reason he changed course, and is swimming off the Washington coast, heading toward Oregon. We will still go forward with the tagging, but it won't happen here. A couple of us will be flying to the marine mammal sanctuary in Lighthouse Bay, Oregon, where we expect Blue 55 will be in a few days. We'll work with the staff there to go out to tag 55 with a tracker.

No mention of the song that I'd made for him. When I opened my email to send Andi a message to ask about it, I found that she'd already written to me.

Dear Iris,

Well, we have good news and bad news, which you know if you're keeping up with Blue 55. Here's a link to our latest post in case you haven't seen it, and to Lighthouse Bay's sanctuary. It's a great place, one that I think would be good for 55 to hang out in for a while if he wants to, but we'll see what he does. Since they're in warmer waters, they take care of whales and dolphins year-round. It'll be interesting to see if Blue 55 interacts at all with the animals there. He'd have a captive audience, you could say.

I did pass along your song to them, and I'm sorry to say they don't want to play it. We'll have the hydrophone and speaker aboard the boat so we can listen for the whale, but the team wants to just get out there, tag him, and get back to the sanctuary without adding anything else to the plan. They're worried that playing the song over the boat's speaker would make it harder to hear Blue 55. I mentioned playing your song afterward, but they didn't think it was important, since the goal is to tag him with the tracker. I disagree with them and think it'd be interesting to find out if he responded to the recording. But since we'll be at their sanctuary now, it's really their call.

Sorry I don't have better news for you. We'll still broadcast the expedition online, so you'll be able to watch when and if we meet Blue 55. And whenever he does come to Appleton again, we'll play your song for him.

Andi

I wanted to throw my phone at the wall and watch Andi's dumb message shatter into a thousand pieces. Instead I pounded the table and shoved my chair back. I couldn't stand to think about what this meant. I handed my phone to Bennie so she and Grandma could read the update.

Before he changed course Blue 55 had finally been swimming toward a friend. I'd felt like we were in this together, both heading toward the place where we'd find each other. But it was just me, all along.

Bennie showed me the screen of her own phone, where she'd typed *Now what?*

I shrugged. There was nothing to do. This didn't make sense! Nothing in the world was singing back to this whale, except for one Deaf girl.

I'd check out the sanctuary Andi mentioned, at least

to see where Blue 55 would be. Maybe I'd watch the tagging expedition online after all. Which I could have done if I'd stayed home, with my family and Wendell and a bowl of popcorn.

After Grandma handed my phone back to me, I clicked on the Lighthouse Bay link from the message. The screen filled with a picture of a blue bay next to a tall white lighthouse topped with a red roof. A page labeled "The Residents" showed a picture of each animal at the sanctuary, along with a brief description. Some of them were free to come and go, as long as they were healthy. Part of the sanctuary was like a hospital for injured and sick animals, and they lived in either indoor pools or in sea pens until they were rehabilitated and ready to return to the open ocean. The bay was made from an underwater canyon, almost as big as the Grand Canyon. So even the water near the docks and the shore was miles deep, instead of sloping from shallow to deep water like at the beaches I was used to.

Some of the animals were retired performers from places like SeaWorld. They were too old or sick to continue doing shows, but they didn't know how to hunt for food in the wild. They lived in the large sea pens so they had plenty of room to swim around but still had people to toss fish to them. Without being asked, two of the dolphins there still performed their old show routine three times a day, right on schedule. A beluga whale whose tail had been injured by a propeller lived in another outdoor pen. There were also albino animals, such as a pink dolphin and a seal. Their color made them too obvious to hunt or avoid predators, and they'd been abandoned by their families.

It reminded me of the TV movie about Rudolph the Red-Nosed Reindeer that played every year at Christmastime. Here was the Island of Misfit Toys for ocean mammals.

Blue 55 wasn't injured or sick like any of those animals, but maybe he'd feel at home and stick around for a while if he heard a familiar song. I didn't understand what was so hard about playing the song after the tagging.

The news page on the site had an announcement— "The Return of Mara"—about a young whale they'd helped rescue two years earlier. She was found stranded on a nearby beach, and staff from the Lighthouse Bay sanctuary was able to return her to the ocean. They weren't sure she'd survive long after that, though— she was barely old enough to make it without her mother, who wasn't anywhere around. They named her Mara and tagged her so they could track how she was doing. She surprised everyone by making it on her own. Each summer since then, the sanctuary staff celebrated when Mara returned to Lighthouse Bay, where the people who'd rescued her could watch her swim. She was there at the bay right then, and was a blue whale, like 55's mother.

I wondered if Blue 55 and Mara would be able to communicate a little, if they spent enough time together. She hadn't interacted with other whales much. No telling how much language she had or didn't have. Maybe they could be like Bennie and me and become friends, even though they spoke different languages.

Yes, Lighthouse Bay would be the perfect place for Blue 55. And here I was, more than a thousand miles away. I couldn't believe it. If only I'd known earlier that this might happen, I could have flown to whatever airport was closest to the Oregon sanctuary and made my way from there. Instead I'd walked right onto the ship that was going to keep me from meeting Blue 55.

My plan was crumbling like the wire insulation in that radio I'd worked on at home. All the parts were in place, but with nothing to connect them. I traced the etched whale on the compass with my finger as I thought about what to do. No point in leaving the ship any longer. My whole reason for being there was swimming away.

"We'll think of something," Grandma told me. Bennie nodded in agreement.

I wanted to believe them, even though it was hopeless. All the new problems were wrapped up in my head in a tangled ball I couldn't unravel. If only Blue 55 had been singing lately, we'd have known where he was and in what direction he was headed, instead of getting hit with the news on the day I was supposed to meet him. Maybe it was a last-minute decision and he didn't feel like telling anyone, like Grandma when she took off for the beach that day.

Bennie tapped me and signed, *"Paper. I forgot mine."* I handed her my notepad. She set it in the middle of the table between her and Grandma.

"Phone, too," Grandma signed. *"Show me that sanctuary."*

Grandma scrolled through the Lighthouse Bay site, then opened a map on the phone and scribbled some dates on the notepad.

"If we rent a car and drive to the sanctuary after getting off the ship in San Francisco, we'll miss him." Grandma

scrolled up the map. *"Let's see how far it is from Cape Oliver."*

Before ending the cruise in San Francisco, the ship would stop at one port in Oregon. Bennie brought up a map on her own phone and found the distance to the sanctuary from that last stop, Cape Oliver.

Grandma jotted down more dates and a schedule. *"We'll have a chance if we drive there from Cape Oliver. Maybe we'll even be early. If that's the case, we'll stick around until he gets there."*

"What if we can't get back here on time?" Even if the ship stayed in port all day, we probably wouldn't make it back after driving all that way, meeting Blue 55, then driving back to the ship. I didn't know how we'd get all our things from the cabin and get back to San Francisco to fly home if we really did miss the boat. Plus, Grandma was enjoying the cruise. I didn't want her to miss out on the rest of it because of me.

Grandma shrugged. *"We'll figure it out. Meeting the whale is the important thing, right?"*

Maybe I wouldn't even get to meet the whale after all, but there wasn't a better plan. Then I thought of a way I could get to Lighthouse Bay on my own. There was no reason for Grandma to miss any of the cruise.

I spelled out *"b-u-s"* and pointed to Cape Oliver on the map. Then I wrote: *I could go by myself, and Grandma can stay here.*

Grandma leaned over to read my note. *"That's too far. I don't want you going all that way yourself."*

I tapped the thumb of a five handshape on my chest to argue back, *"I'll be fine."*

Before Grandma could answer back, Bennie touched my arm and signed, *"Kid,"* and pointed at me. I shrugged, wondering what she was getting at.

The ship won't leave a kid behind alone, she wrote on the notepad. *They'd have to wait for you. You can't leave the ship without your grandma anyway.*

So that wouldn't work. I really wanted Grandma to stay on board. She was happy here. She'd found fun things to do. And she was really trying to come up with a way to meet Blue 55. Maybe meeting him would make her happy too. *Okay,* I wrote, *we'll drive. But we might not make it back before the ship leaves.*

Bennie read my note, then flipped to a new page.

She smiled and wrote something down, then set the notepad on the table for us to see.

The train is faster.

35

Now that Blue 55 was singing again, I could keep better track of where he was. But there was nothing to do except let the ship bring us closer. Even if we did get to the sanctuary on time, I wouldn't get to see him. The expedition crew wasn't even willing to take a speaker on board to play the song, so they sure weren't going to pick up a stray girl. Maybe I'd at least get to see Blue 55 swimming, if he decided to hang around the sanctuary. Even from a distance, I could recognize his blow spout.

That would have to be enough, since he wasn't going to hear the song I'd made for him. He still wouldn't know anyone heard him. When I got back home, I'd send the song to more sanctuaries along his path. Maybe one of them would play it when he swam by. I wouldn't be there to meet him, but he'd know he wasn't alone.

The train that Bennie showed us was a scenic ride that a lot of cruise passengers took during the port stop at Cape Oliver. The round-trip ride took three hours, and it stopped at the halfway point for a break, so people could get out to take pictures and buy lunch. Instead of getting on the train to ride back to the ship, Grandma and I would catch a shuttle to Lighthouse Bay. If we got there before Blue 55 did, we'd hang around until he arrived, even if it meant missing the rest of the cruise.

I didn't want to think about the other thing that might happen: we could get to Lighthouse Bay to find that Blue 55 had already come and gone.

That afternoon I joined Bennie and Sura on the bridge for the fjord tour. Sura would make announcements about the scenery and wildlife around us as the ship sailed through a narrow passage with walls of glaciers on either side.

Bennie said a local pilot would get on board to help the captain. I'd thought pilots were only for flying planes, but it turned out that was also what they call people who steer ships. Anyway, this local pilot who knew the area a lot better than the captain would guide the ship around the ice so we wouldn't crash into anything.

The ship eased into the narrow passage of the fjord. Ice bobbed in the water, pushed aside by the waves created by the ship. Seals lounged at the base of the mountain and on ice floes. The ice reflected more shades of blue I didn't have names for. I never knew snow-cone-syrup blue was a color found in nature. I closed my eyes for a few seconds to see if I could still picture it. Maybe I'd never see another glacier again, so I wanted to hold on to that color.

Bennie tapped my arm, then pointed to the right after I opened my eyes. *"Watch,"* she signed. At first I didn't see what I was supposed to be looking at. Then blocks of ice tumbled into the water next to us, making waves that splashed onto the rocks.

I pointed and shrugged to ask Bennie how she knew that was going to happen. She pointed to her ear. So they'd heard it? Some kind of sound warned of the glacier breaking apart. More chunks of ice crashed into the water. Melting ice always looked so quiet, but this was noisy. The counter in front of us wasn't vibrating when I touched it, so it was a different kind of sound than the foghorn. Bennie pointed to a glacier next to us, then wrote *calving* on our notepad. I looked back at the glacier, still wondering what such a crashing and falling apart sounded like. She signed something that looked like *"break"* and then *"watch."*

A giant block of ice separated from the glacier and floated away from the mountain.

On the page where Bennie had written *calving,* I added *Like a baby glacier.*

Yep, a glacier calf! she wrote.

What does it sound like?

She covered her ears and said, "Loud."

What kind of loud? I wrote.

Really loud.

But there were all kinds of loud; I knew that much. Was it a scream? A crash? Maybe the opposite of a crash, whatever that was, since this was a ripping apart.

Bennie tapped the pen against her mouth like she was thinking. She could tell I wanted to know more, even without my asking her. Then she wrote, *Thunder.*

I never would have guessed that two totally different events could make the same sound.

She wrote more notes and used some signs to tell me what her mom was announcing. *Air bubbles have been trapped under the ice for hundreds of years. All that pressure squishes them out of shape. When the ice melts or breaks away, the bubbles make a loud pop.*

Like they were screaming out after being trapped for so long.

I pointed to the seals and wrote, *The noise doesn't bother them?*

She shook her head. *They hang out here on purpose. The glacier noise makes it hard for orcas to hear them.*

Like with the humpbacks' bubble net feeding, I wondered how the seals figured out that a noise could help them. Instead of using it to get food like the whales did, the seals used it to avoid *becoming* food.

The ship inched along through the fjord. Looking ahead, I didn't see how we'd be able to squeeze through the narrow space between the mountains. As we got closer I saw that there was plenty of water on either side of us. Still, the pilot had to drive slowly because of all the floating ice. Most looked like chunks that the ship could easily knock aside, but Bennie said we were just looking at the tops of those chunks and that most of the ice was below the surface.

We were only partway through the fjord when the ship stopped completely. The pilot talked to the captain while pointing at the water ahead of us, then shook her head. Then the captain picked up the microphone.

The engine jerked, and we started inching backward. The front of the ship turned bit by bit to the left.

I shrugged at Bennie, then pantomimed turning a big wheel, even though no one actually turned a wheel to steer the ship. *"We're turning around?"*

Bennie pointed to the floating ice in the water and signed, *"Dangerous."* Then she took the notepad and wrote what the captain had just announced. *Sometimes you have to know when it's time to give up and turn back.*

"Did you see the glacier calving?" I asked Grandma when I got back to the room.

"No, that must have been on the other side of the ship. I saw ice rolling off the side of the mountain, but nothing breaking apart like that. What was it like?"

"Beautiful and sad at the same time." That wasn't enough. How could I possibly describe what it was like to witness a glacier tearing apart?

I sat across from Grandma and said, *"Handshape poem?"*

She didn't hesitate or dismiss it as Grandpa's thing this time. *"What shape?"* she asked.

I held up my hands into fives, like in Grandpa's tree poem, but bent my fingers into claws. A good shape for frozen things and mountains and floating ice: spread-out fingers to show something big, and bent to show the jagged peaks. It was also the handshape for signing "frozen" and "rough," so it was perfect for a poem about the icy mountain of the breaking glacier.

First I signed *"frozen,"* then reached up to trace rising and falling curves of mountaintops. My hands showed Grandma the layers of ice that pressed down and trapped the pockets of air inside. With spinning hands I showed chunks of ice tumbling down and crashing into the ocean, making rough waves. Then I held them out for the bigger block of the glacier, breaking and drifting away.

"The glacier screams, watching a piece of itself float farther and farther from home."

Grandma joined in when she could see the glacier calving too. *"The new iceberg rides the rough waves in the sea."* Her hands outlined its shape, smaller and jagged with new breaks.

I showed her that what was left of the glacier clung to the mountainside. It looked rougher then, with sharp edges marking the missing ice.

She raked her hands, as if they were claws, on the glacier and then straightened her fingers a little to draw softer waves—the scars on the ice melting. The new iceberg drifted so far away it was a speck in the ocean. *"Time and distance smooth out the memory of what was lost."*

I didn't know anymore if we were still talking about the iceberg, or about 55 and me, or my family, or Grandma and Grandpa. Maybe it was all those things.

36

I woke up early and couldn't get back to sleep, so I went to the internet café to check on Blue 55's progress. My phone couldn't connect to the Wi-Fi from our cabin.

It was so early the gelato wasn't even out yet. I'd have to work without it. The sanctuary's website didn't have any updates, so I switched over to the map that showed where 55 was. He was making progress. Too much progress. A TV screen above me showed the cruise ship's route. With the stops we'd be making along the way, 55 was going to get to Oregon long before we did if he kept up his pace.

All along I was in such a hurry to meet him, and now I just wanted him to wait for me. *Please slow down.* I touched the blinking blue dot on the screen, as if I could hold him in place. I imagined myself chasing him across the ocean forever, never getting close enough to even catch sight of his breath.

I'd tried so hard to do everything right, to do what was best for Blue 55. He needed to hear that song; I was sure of that. It looked more and more like I'd have to go back home without having played it for him or seeing him at all. The more I tried to reach him, the farther he swam away.

Before leaving I checked my email, even though I cringed while opening it. If anyone at home was in a panic about us, I wanted to send a reply that would calm them down.

The first was from Tristan.

Iris,

I still can't believe y'all did this. I know you've both told Mom you're okay, but tell me for real. Is everything all right? I don't know what I can do from here if it isn't, but tell me where you are, and we'll help you if you need it.

Write back to Dad, too. Mom says he hasn't been sleeping since you left.

Love you even though you're totally ridiculous,

Tristan

I couldn't believe Dad was so worried that he wasn't sleeping. I opened his last email to me.

Iris,

You know that record I showed you, with the whale songs? I don't know if I told you that a copy of it is in space. The Voyager space capsule. It's true. It's carrying a lot of things from Earth, including the whale song record. If there's alien life out there somewhere, the items in the capsule will let them know what life is like on Earth. Maybe one day someone will figure out what the songs mean.

I know I told you I wanted to find those whales when I heard them. But even if I had, even if they were right in front of me, I wouldn't have known what to say.

Please let me know how you're doing. Better yet, tell me where you are. I'm worried sick. You can't imagine how much I miss you.

Love,

Dad

At the breakfast buffet I found a small table near a window. I never thought I'd miss the school cafeteria, but I wondered how everyone at school was doing and what they'd been talking about at lunch while I was gone. Most of the time I felt invisible, but they had to notice I was gone, right? Maybe Nina found someone new to bother by now. I laughed and took a bite of my cheese omelet. And what about Mr. Charles? A pang of guilt hit my stomach when I realized I hadn't even thought of him much. He'd told me before that whenever I was absent, he went to work at one of the schools with more Deaf kids, helping out in classrooms or filling in for interpreters who were absent.

People around me in the buffet area stopped eating and looked up like they were all listening to something. Some of them shoveled in a last bite of food as they stood up and ran out. I finished my mango juice and followed the stampede out to the deck.

On my notepad I wrote *What's going on?* and showed it to an old woman next to me.

After reading the question she cupped her hands around her mouth and yelled, "WHALES!" at my face.

There wasn't a whale sighting announcement on the schedule for the day, but obviously whales didn't always follow a schedule. Maybe Sura had spotted them and went to the bridge to announce the unplanned whale sighting.

Each time I saw a group of passengers pointing at something, they were always on the opposite side of the ship. Sometimes they laughed and clapped. The whales must have breached, putting on a show for whoever was watching. Then I'd switch sides to get a better view of the action, and the people on the side I'd just left would do the pointing-laughing-and-clapping thing. Whales were swimming right near the ship, and I missed out on every one of them. I stamped my foot on the deck, angry all over again about the sanctuary not using my idea. Blue 55 was going to be right there, and they weren't going to play the song I'd worked so hard to make for him.

After about an hour the crowd thinned out when there were no more leaping whales to see. Passengers returned to the pools and bars and dining rooms.

The breeze chilled my face as I leaned against the railing and watched the waves. I tucked my scarf under the front of my coat. My heart beating against my hand reminded me of Blue 55's song, so I kept it there.

Yes, things had turned out terribly, but I was on a ship sailing over the ocean. Not a bad place to remarkably fail. I'd made it that far, and I'd tried really hard to help out one whale. I stared out at the water that was so calm it had to be as quiet for everyone else as it was for me.

Then a plume of teardrop-shape spray erupted. And another spray, smaller than the first.

The shadows of two whale backs brushed the surface. Humpbacks, if I remembered right from what Sura and Bennie had taught me. One large and one small. A mother and a calf. I looked around at the other passengers. No one else seemed to have noticed. It was almost like it hadn't happened. Maybe I'd imagined the whole thing.

When I looked back, the Y shape of two whale flukes lifted up from the surface, then sank down.

"Thank you," I signed to them. Then I laughed. Those whales showed up right when I needed to see them. I wasn't mad anymore about missing the breaching humpbacks with the rest of the crowd.

The mother and calf sighting was mine alone.

"Gelato time?" Bennie asked when I caught up with her later. It did sound good, since I hadn't eaten for about two hours.

The ship was on its way to the next stop, Icy Harbor. We planned to stay aboard, since Bennie said there wasn't much to see there.

"What flavor?" I asked when we got to the café.

"Church," she signed.

I held back a giggle and wrote, *Not for me. Tastes like bricks.*

Bennie's forehead crinkled with confusion, then

she pointed to the "Chocolate" label behind the glass. I showed her how to draw circles with the letter *C* on the back of her hand, instead of tapping it for "church." She laughed at her mistake when she caught on. I wished Mr. Charles had been there to see it.

After we stopped giggling we picked up a chocolate and a pistachio and spooned some of each into the other's bowl until we each had a perfect chocolate-pistachio blend.

We settled into our seats by the window and checked out the map of 55's path. The blue dot seemed to be racing to Oregon. How could he have covered so many miles since I'd last checked?

Bennie looked worried too and checked the ship's route on the TV screen like I had. *"Maybe he'll slow down."*

"Yeah, hopefully," I answered. *"Nothing I can do from here."* I sighed and brought up my email to see what was new from home.

After asking me to reply back with more than "We're fine," Mom wrote:

I went to the school to collect your work for you to catch up on when you're back. I don't like you missing so much. I had to think of something to tell the office that didn't sound completely ridiculous, like that you and your grandmother took off on a trip to who knows where. I told them there'd been a family emergency, and you'd be back next week. That's all I knew from what you and Grandma have told me. Oh, and when I was in the office, I saw that girl Nina. Isn't that who you got in trouble for shoving? She seemed really nice. She says she hopes you're okay and that you inspired her to learn sign language.

Usually when people use a phrase like "fell over laughing," they mean it as a figure of speech. "I laughed really hard" is what they mean. But I actually fell over laughing at that. I sat on the floor next to the computer table and wiped tears from my eyes. Whenever I tried to explain to Bennie what was so funny, I'd start laughing all over again.

Finally I stood up and turned the computer screen to Bennie so she could read the email, then I pointed to the last line. *"She's terrible,"* I signed. On the computer's notepad, I added, *She's always signing and signing, but I never have any idea what she means. It's like she gets* worse every day instead of better. *Maybe that library book she checked out is for some other country's sign language, because it's nothing I know.*

Bennie shrugged, then typed, *It's nice that she wants to learn anyway.*

Not that nice if she won't even listen when I tell her I don't understand her. Anyway, not much point if it's that bad.

After reading my message Bennie wrote, *Probably no worse than you speaking whale, right?*

37

Bennie suggested we go swimming the day the ship was docking in Icy Harbor. The pools wouldn't be as crowded as they usually were, since a lot of people would be leaving the ship for a few hours. Luckily Grandma had told me to pack a swimsuit before we left home. It hadn't occurred to me I'd need one on a ship that would be sailing past glaciers, but the pools on board were heated. Grandma didn't want to swim, but she would sit out on deck and read, right after her Zumba class.

Bennie was right—the pool wasn't crowded at all. A few people sat around in the hot tub, and one man sat on a floating chair in the pool, a beer can in the chair's cup holder.

I jumped in and swam the length of the pool, then floated on my back. It had been so long since I'd been swimming. When we lived at the coast, we used to go out all the time. Tristan and I would bodysurf the waves or float in our inner tubes if the water was calm enough. The current would carry us so far down the beach our house was just a yellow speck in the distance. Tristan always kept change in the zippered pocket of his swim trunks so we could each buy a cone at the ice cream stand to eat while hiking back home.

A splash of water snapped my mind back to the cruise ship's pool. Bennie laughed and backed away. I tried to pretend I was mad, but a laugh escaped as I splashed her back. She ducked under the surface before the water could hit her, so I waited until she came up for air, then got her good. Before she could get me back, I took a deep breath and swam to the other side of the pool. I popped out of the water and held up my hand to signal Bennie to stop.

"Do you feel that?" I asked.

She shrugged. *"What?"* She backed up a little, as if she suspected my answer might be a splash to her face.

I placed my hand flat on the surface. Something other than our splashing or the ship's engines was moving the water, with the steady rhythm of music. It was still just us and the man on the float in the pool. Nothing I could see that could've been vibrating the water like a radio.

"*Music*," I signed. We'd talked so much about the whale song, that was a sign she'd picked up.

"Oh, that." She pointed to something on the other side of the floating chair. I swam to see what she was talking about. A blue-and-white cylinder floated in the water next to the man.

Bennie swam up next to me and pointed at the object again, then signed, "*Music.*"

A speaker. There weren't any wires connected to it, so it must have been Bluetooth. My parents had one stuck to their shower wall with suction cups.

The man's phone rested in a cup holder. The music that played from there was coming through the speaker.

I signed "*buy*" and "*here*" to Bennie, to ask if the gift shop on board sold the speakers. She shook her head.

The ship was still moving, sailing past mountains in the distance. But soon we'd stop in Icy Harbor. Bennie waved to get my attention, but I held up a hand to ask her to wait. I didn't want to let go of the plan that was forming in my head. I imagined throwing a speaker into the water to play 55's song for him. Maybe I could really do it. The song was with me all the time. Not just the memory of it, from when I'd held my hand on the speaker while it played. The sound file was on my phone. I could play it for him, if I just had a way to carry the sound to where he was swimming.

If I'd had any idea I might need a speaker, I'd have brought one from home. I could throw the Bluetooth into the water after connecting the signal to my phone. Or I would've salvaged parts from the radio in that Admiral set in my closet to make a speaker. Then I'd have to make it waterproof somehow. . . .

Bennie followed me when I climbed out of the pool to dry off and get my phone from my bag. I typed out a message and showed her my phone. *I want to get off in Icy Harbor after all. I need to get a few things.* As soon as she read the message, I started making a list.

She shook two O handshapes to remind me there was nothing there. No stores or good restaurants.

I looked out at the town we were approaching. *All I need is a junkyard.*

38

Sura wanted to stay on board but told the crew at the exit that Bennie could go with Grandma and me into Icy Harbor.

Bennie hadn't been to the junkyard before, but she knew it wasn't close to where the cruise ship stopped. Not much of a tourist attraction. It wasn't really a junkyard, but more of a dump, which was even better since I wouldn't have to pay for anything. But it could be messy since people dropped off trash there.

A couple of shuttles were parked near the harbor, ready to take passengers to whatever there was to see in town.

Bennie and I took a seat up front after boarding a shuttle, and Grandma asked the driver, "The dump, please," as if it were a totally normal request from a tourist.

I don't know what he said to her, but she handed

him some money from her purse, and it looked like she said, "It's important." She took a seat then, across from Bennie and me.

Bennie was right—there wasn't much in that town. A few people got out when the shuttle driver stopped at a bar, and more got out at an area that had some shops and a fishing pier. About ten minutes later, the driver pulled up to the Icy Harbor Dump.

Grandma signed at the same time she talked to the driver. *"We won't be long. Will you wait for us?"* He checked his watch and held up ten fingers, then waved a hand around like he was tracing a road. He had his route to get back to.

Whether or not this place had what I needed, ten minutes was enough time to figure it out.

The dump looked sort of like Moe's Junk Emporium, but with more things in piles. Maybe that was stuff no one wanted. Instead of a trailer for an office, there was an old school bus that was more rust-colored than yellow. Next to the bus stood a rickety wooden shed with the word PAINT in red letters over the entrance, and a dead appliance section like at Moe's.

A man with a bright red face and small eyes stepped off the bus-office. He looked like a lobster who had transformed into a human. Also, he looked like he

probably ate at restaurants like the Cattle Prod. He
and Moe would be good friends. As I ran up to him, he
started to say something, and I pointed to my ear and
showed him a list I'd written out. His blue work shirt
had "Giblet" embroidered on the pocket. Grandma and
Bennie came up after me. Giblet touched the first item
on the list—a radio—then pointed to a plywood struc-
ture with an "Electronics" sign. I asked Grandma to
look around for some kind of plastic container to hold
the speaker parts. A small cooler would work, if I could
seal the lid closed somehow. Something smaller that I
could carry in my backpack would be easier. A PVC
pipe would work, as long as it had the cap pieces to seal
off the ends. I'd have to drill a hole in it somehow for
the wires to poke through. Bennie ran with me to the
electronics shed. Before going in I pushed on the side
a little to make sure it wasn't going to topple over with
us in it.

Looking over all the scattered electronics made me
miss my room again. It didn't matter that I'd never
let my collection get so disorganized or that most of it
wasn't in my room anymore. Right then I missed it all.
I missed home. I wanted to see my parents and Tristan.
I wanted to visit the antique shop and see if my Philco
was still there. I wanted to see Mr. Gunnar. It hadn't

been that long since I'd been inside the store, but so much had happened since then, it was hard to imagine everything at home staying the same while so much had happened with me.

Bennie waved to snap me back to our time-limited shopping trip. The radios and stereos at the dump weren't nearly as old as what I usually repaired, but that was good. Tearing into a boom box from the 1980s wouldn't bother me like pulling a speaker out of an antique radio would. I turned a boom box around and twisted a finger to show Bennie I wanted to take out the screws. She gave me a thumbs-up and ran back to Giblet.

While I waited for Bennie, I looked around the piles of stuff for something smaller. The boom box speaker could work, but it was bigger than I wanted. Whatever I ended up making, I'd have to carry it with me to Lighthouse Bay, if we did get there on time. In the corner of the shed, I found the perfect thing—a handheld cassette player. People played music on them before CDs, and long before we could download music on computers and phones.

Bennie came back with Grandma and gave me the screwdriver. Grandma handed me a plastic thermos. It wasn't the kind you'd pour the drink out of into a mug, but the kind that was like a tall cup with a lid. A hinged spout lifted up for drinking. I'd check later to make sure no water would get in. It could be exactly what I needed. After removing the speaker from the cassette player, I slid it into the thermos. It fit, by a hair. The wires would thread through the drinking hole. I thanked Grandma and Bennie, then stuck the thermos in my backpack and signed, *"Headphones."* They glanced around the shed with me, until Bennie picked up a tangle of head-phones that was like a pile of thin snakes. I held my backpack open for her to throw in the whole bundle. I'd only need one set, but there wasn't time for untangling. And it was always good to have a spare.

From there I ran toward a pile of pipes and over-turned toilets. Next to a rusty pipe were a few tubes of leftover caulk. The ones without caps wouldn't be any good. The caulk inside would have dried up. I picked up the two that were still capped. Each one felt like it had more than I'd need. One was the white caulk that people used for the edges of sinks and bathtubs, and the other was the clear silicone kind. I uncapped the clear tube and squeezed out a bit to check that it hadn't dried out, then recapped it and threw it into my backpack.

Bennie turned toward the shuttle, then looked back at me and pantomimed honking a horn. Grandma waved to the driver and held up a finger, asking him to wait another minute for us. Happy as I was to find the dump, I didn't want to get abandoned there.

Giblet walked over to see how we were doing, and I pointed to the last item on my list. The wire I could salvage from the electronics there wouldn't be enough. I needed long strands of wire.

He waved for me to follow him. I told Grandma and Bennie to go ahead to the shuttle and that I'd meet them back there in a minute. Giblet led me to a section of big wooden spools. He tapped a wire-wrapped spool, then held a hand up to his ear as if it were a telephone. I knelt down and held the end of the wire, which was coated with black plastic for insulation. Perfect. The spool looked like it'd held hundreds of feet of wire when it was full. Not much was left, but it still had a lot more than I needed. I signed *"Thank you"* while mouthing the words to Giblet, then unrolled the wire from the spool. With the bundle of black wire wrapped around my hand, I ran and leaped onto the shuttle for the ride back to the cruise ship.

I had my waterproof speaker. Now I just had to put it together.

39

Bennie sat with me in our cabin to help with the speaker. Once we'd gotten back I realized I wouldn't be able to work without a screwdriver and something to strip the ends of the wire. Bennie came back with a small set of screwdrivers borrowed from the ship's electrician and some wire cutters—even better than the scissors I'd asked for. I assembled the speaker pretty quickly, then attached some of the long wires. While I worked, Bennie untangled a set of headphones. All I needed from them was a connector that would plug into my phone jack. After trimming down the headphone wires, I stripped off a little of the plastic coating, then twisted the ends together with the telephone wire. I plugged the speaker into my phone and brought up the sound file that held Blue 55's song. Bennie smiled at the song that played, made of musical instruments, the calls of ocean animals, and a bit of our own humming voices tuned to fifty-five hertz.

The bathroom sink was small, but it had enough room to test the thermos. I filled the sink with water and pushed the thermos down into it. The lid was good—when I removed it, the inside of the thermos was dry. The only part I'd have to seal would be the drinking hole, around the wires I'd pull through it.

Bennie held the thermos as I placed the assembled speaker inside and threaded the long wires through the spout. After twisting on the lid, I squeezed the clear caulk in the space around the wires. It didn't feel like it was heavy enough to sink underwater, just bob under the surface a bit. But just in case, the caulk would keep water from getting in.

The caulk wouldn't be totally dry until the next day, so I had to make sure the spout stayed out of the water until then. Now to test it in deeper water. *"Back to the pool."*

After changing back into our swimsuits and returning to the pool, Bennie got in while I sat on the edge with my phone. While the song played I checked the speaker to make sure it was working. The thermos in my hand hummed with Blue 55's song.

I placed the speaker into the pool and asked Bennie, *"Can you hear it?"*

She nodded. Other people who were swimming must have heard it too. Heads turned in our direction as the music played.

I pointed down, wondering if Bennie would hear it underwater. She ducked below the surface, then came back up a few seconds later and twisted a hand from side to side, like she was saying "Sort of." Maybe it wouldn't matter, since whales could hear better than we could, but I'd feel better knowing the song was traveling through water. Bennie pointed to the phone, then raised a thumbs-up a few times. As I pushed the volume's up button on the side of the phone, the song vibrated stronger and stronger in my hand. More people turned to look at us.

Bennie smiled and waved me into the pool. She took a deep breath and went underwater again, and I followed. The vibrations of the song for Blue 55 trembled in the water. The waves of the song rose and faded, following the pattern I'd made that I hoped was close to his.

I let the song continue to play as I swam beneath it, then floated on my back in the water. Here was a song that 55 might recognize. As long as we reached the bay on time, he would hear it in a few days.

Before the ship pulled away from Icy Harbor that

evening, I connected my phone to the Wi-Fi. Not to check Blue 55's tracker—I did wonder, but at the same time didn't want to know. Wherever he was swimming then, there wasn't anything I could do about it. Grandma and I would get to Lighthouse Bay, and *somehow* I'd play the song for him.

But I'd been thinking about adding more of myself to the song. I wished I could share my own language with him, but that wasn't possible. It would have to be enough that he could hear a little of my voice on the song I'd made, through the speaker I'd built.

I never liked talking out loud in front of people, but for some reason I didn't mind doing it for Blue 55. I downloaded a voice modulator like the app on Bennie's phone, then clicked record and spoke into the phone: "Hi, it's Iris. I'm here."

40

Since it might be our last night on the cruise, Grandma and I took our time standing out on deck before going to bed. We probably wouldn't be able to fall asleep for a while anyway, thinking about our side trip to Lighthouse Bay.

I'd never seen a night so dark. Wendell would have loved it. So many more stars than we could see at home. It looked like one of the glaciers had shattered onto the sky, dotting the blackness with shards of ice. I scanned for the unblinking brightness of Jupiter. It was harder to find in the star-crowded sky, and of course it wouldn't be in the same place as when Wendell showed me. Or maybe it was that I was in a different place. Too much had changed since then. Sometimes it felt like I'd just left home, but I'd been away long enough for planets to shift in the sky. At the same time things hadn't changed much at all. I was still so far away from the whale I'd set out to find.

If I'd been at home right then, I could have been on the Jacksons' balcony with Wendell, looking at Jupiter with him.

Then I spotted it, way off to the left, as clearly as if Wendell had been sitting there pointing it out to me. He was probably in bed asleep, but I liked the thought that maybe he was looking at Jupiter right then too.

I hadn't planned to get online again, but I decided to send one more email.

Dear Wendell,

Thinking of you because my odds of succeeding are astronomical. Ha-ha, get it?

About that planet you want to find—it was kicked out of the solar system millions of years ago, right? So how do you know about it? I don't mean just you, but how does anyone know about it since it happened that long ago?

Anyway, I was just thinking I'm kind of like that planet. I was on one path, and something knocked me onto a new one. I'm still going.

Iris

Bennie walked with us to the exit when the ship docked in Cape Oliver. None of us said anything along the way. Grandma and I each had a small bag packed. If we didn't make it back before the ship left that afternoon, we'd have a change of clothes and our toothbrushes with us. We did pack our suitcases, even though we weren't going to haul them with us. If we had to meet the ship in San Francisco to pick up the rest of our things, we wouldn't have to take time to pack. Before we'd left the room, I put the origami whale in the front pocket of my jeans for good luck.

Hopefully we would make it back, because I wasn't ready to say goodbye to Bennie. But I had to go. A whale was pulling me off that ship and down the Pacific coast. I signed *"Thank you"* to Bennie. As we hugged I realized I was still wearing the scarf she'd lent me. I reached to pull it off as I signed, *"Yours."*

She shook her head and placed a hand on mine to stop me. *"Yours."* Then she scribbled something on the notepad before handing it back to me. *Good luck. Whatever happens, you made a great song.*

I squeezed her hand; then Grandma and I walked through the exit and onto the gangplank.

Bennie had told us how to get to the train from the ship, and pretty soon we found signs, and a crowd, to follow—a lot of cruise passengers were headed to the railway tour.

After walking a few blocks, we saw a huge black train sitting on the tracks, steam billowing from the engine. It didn't look like trains I usually saw, but more old-fashioned, like something from a black-and-white movie. A man in a blue suit and a conductor's cap stood outside the train and waved everyone aboard.

Grandma handed him our tickets, and we found seats near the front. I couldn't believe we were almost there. This was it.

It seemed to take so long for the train to fill up and get going. I was ready to just go already and get to Blue 55 before he left the bay. Maybe he'd already been there. I was afraid to check, but I had to find out if there was even a reason to go anymore.

I reminded myself then that whales can hear from so far away. Even if 55 had left the bay, he wouldn't have gone far. I'd play his song for him anyway. He'd be close enough to hear it, and know that someone out there heard him and answered. So why didn't I feel better, knowing that one way or another I'd play the song I'd made and he'd hear it?

I thought back to what Tristan said, when he reminded me that Blue 55 wasn't one of my radios.

Maybe I wasn't doing this for 55. He thought I was trying to fix the whale, to make myself feel better.

No, that wasn't it. He did have a song that no one else could tune in to, but he didn't need fixing any more than I did. I pushed the doubts aside. Of course I was doing this for him.

When I took out my phone, I noticed there wasn't much of a charge left. The night before, I'd tested the speaker once more, and left the phone plugged into it instead of plugging it into the charger. If I went through all this just to have a dead phone ruin it, I'd never get over it.

I turned off my phone to save whatever battery life was left and asked Grandma if I could check the map on hers. The tracker showed a blue dot blinking right near Lighthouse Bay, and the time of his last recorded song: just an hour ago. He'd be there soon, if he kept swimming in the same direction. But would he stay? I was literally cutting my chances of meeting him down to the minute.

My leg jiggled as I switched over to the sanctuary's website to check for news. Not much of an update, just a "Today Is the Day!" post about how some of the staff was going out in a boat soon to catch up with 55 and try to tag him.

Before handing Grandma's phone back, I checked a new email that had come in. Wendell had replied to my message.

Dear Iris,

Scientists figured out that the other giant planet used to be there because of the effect it had on everything around it. The other planets and their moons would have different orbits if there hadn't been something else that size pulling on them. Our whole solar system would be different. We wouldn't have seen Jupiter that day you were at my house because it would be in another part of the sky. Even though that planet has been gone a long time and it's really far away now, it still affects the planets it used to share space with.

Come back soon, Iris. It's not the same here without you.

Wendell

The train shuddered and lurched forward, gradually picking up speed as we rolled down the tracks along the Oregon coast. I drummed my fingers on my thighs. This was it, almost the end of my journey. Later, when the train stopped at the halfway point, we'd be just a ten-minute shuttle ride from the sanctuary.

I tried to tell myself that Blue 55 would be there at the bay or he wouldn't. There wasn't anything else I could do except show up.

Still, I was nervous. I kept trying to get a view of the landscape ahead of us, hoping to see something that looked like a train stop. Grandma put a hand on my leg to stop its bouncing. I got up and moved to the passenger car closest to the engine to get a better view and to give my jittery legs something to do.

The train climbed a hill, and when we rounded over the top, a wooden building came into view. A man wearing a khaki shirt and pants waved from the front of the building as the train slowed to a stop.

After we got off the train, Grandma asked the man where to catch the shuttle; then we followed the path in the direction he pointed.

Finally, we were almost there. Grandma took my hand and even ran a little, laughing. I'd have to think of some way to thank her for bringing me on the trip. Without her, it couldn't have happened.

When we reached an area with shops and restaurants lining the streets, a blue sign on a pole pointed the way to the shuttle stop. We were back to walking, since Grandma was out of breath from the short run.

We turned the corner to see a shuttle stop ahead of us, and a shuttle rounding the corner, driving away. I ran ahead to the bench at the stop to read the sign next to it: SHUTTLE STOP, EVERY TWENTY MINUTES.

Twenty more minutes. Then a ten-minute ride. Blue 55 would probably be tagged by then, swimming away from the sanctuary. *Train gone.*

I glanced around frantically like a shuttle map was going to appear. Maybe one of the stores knew the route, and I could hurry to the next stop, wherever that was.

Grandma pointed ahead of us and to the right. *"You can make it."*

"How? Where?"

"I'll meet you at the sanctuary. Run to that whale."

41

I tore through downtown Cape Oliver, weaving between the shops and restaurants and tourists. At a small redbrick library, I leaned against the wall to catch my breath and check once more on Blue 55.

My phone screen showed the battery life with the tiniest sliver of red. Like that line from Ms. Conn's pen, this could ruin everything. Even if I somehow made it to the sanctuary before Blue 55 left, I might not be able to play the song. All that work I put into it and all the distance I'd traveled to get there could be worthless because I hadn't plugged in my phone overnight. I'd never forgive myself for that.

Nothing I could do about it now. I'd have to just get to the sanctuary and see what happened. Until then, I'd save whatever life the phone had left. I shoved it into my sweatshirt pocket and turned in a circle, trying to figure out which way to go. I'd run the way Grandma had pointed from the shuttle stop, but a straight shot wasn't possible with all the buildings in the way. The main street was on a diagonal, so I wasn't sure if I was heading the right way or running parallel to where I'd been.

I ran again in a direction that felt right, while picturing the map that Bennie had shown us. The sanctuary was farther down the coast, I knew that much. Finally I found the beach, but couldn't see the train tracks from here to help me figure out where I was. What if I ran in the wrong direction? By the time I figured it out, I'd be even farther away from Blue 55. I touched the compass on my necklace, tracing the outline of the whale, wishing 55 could somehow show me how to reach him.

Then I smacked myself on the forehead. What I needed was hanging right there around my neck. I laughed at myself as I unclasped the necklace and opened the compass. Mr. Gunnar was right—it still worked. I'd navigate like people did for centuries. The compass needle pointed north. I turned so that north was at my back, and ran.

When I got close to the sanctuary, I didn't need a map or compass to tell me I'd found the right place. I put the compass in my sweatshirt pocket next to my phone as I ran toward the red roof of a lighthouse.

If I got there before the boat left, maybe I could convince them to change their minds about the song. I'd play it for them and show them how easy it'd be to just toss the speaker into the water. It could wait until after they tagged him so it wouldn't interfere with his song as they listened for him. It was okay that I couldn't get on the boat. I'd wait inside the building and watch the tagging on the video screens. Or I could stand outside and maybe get a glimpse of him as he swam in the bay. The important thing was that Blue 55 would hear his song.

An orange boat that looked like the one in the video from last year when Andi tried to tag 55 was in the water. Ahead of me was a jetty, with large rocks on either side like ones I'd seen in Galveston. That would get me farther into the bay.

After a few steps along the jetty, I slowed my pace. Waves crashed over the rocks and splashed onto the surface, slippery with seawater and algae. Twice I fell on the way to the end. The orange boat was ahead of me on the left, heading toward the sanctuary building. Was Blue 55 somewhere nearby, or were they going back because the expedition had failed again? Or maybe they'd already tagged him. When they got close enough, I'd flag them down. I peeled off my sweatshirt and dropped it onto the jetty with my backpack. After the run, I needed to cool off.

I started to wave as the boat got closer to me; then I lowered my hand. Andi and the man behind the wheel were both smiling. Andi held the tagging pole, which no longer had a tracker at the end. The man took one hand off the wheel to give Andi a high-five.

They were celebrating. They'd tagged the whale. Blue 55, the reason I was standing there. I'd left home to fly and cruise and ride a train and run to him, and he was gone.

I tried to be happy for Andi and her team. They had set out to tag Blue 55, and they'd done it. But I couldn't feel happy, not yet. For the first time since I started the trip, I cried. It wasn't the kind of cry that was for one thing, but the kind that brings up everything sad or unfair that ever happened.

It was possible to miss someone you'd never met. I'd come all this way because I felt alone, and thought Blue 55 did too. Alone, even in a crowd. And now he was swimming away from me. There I was, completely alone, standing in cold wet clothes on a jetty. I thought back to what the captain had said during the fjord tour. *Sometimes you have to know when it's time to give up and turn back.*

I shook my head and wiped my face. No. This couldn't be the end. I wasn't ready to give up yet. Blue 55 hadn't given up, after all those decades of singing with no one answering him. If he had, I wouldn't know about him. I wouldn't have been on that cruise ship.

There had to be something more to do, some hope to grab on to.

Blue 55 wasn't so far away yet. I wouldn't see him up close, but wasn't I doing this for him? Maybe Tristan had been right all along, and I was really doing this for myself. I was the one who was lonely, and I'd wanted the whale to hear me. But right then, all I wanted was to let him know I heard him, that he'd connected to someone. The song I'd made wouldn't be exactly like his, but it was as close as I could get. Everything I'd done would be worth it if just a few notes of the song touched his heart. I'd show him that there was at least one place in the ocean where he could find music like his own.

Wherever he was he'd still be close enough to hear his song. I grabbed the waterproof speaker from my backpack and plugged the wire into my phone. The red line showing the battery life was thinner than a hair. I tossed the thermos into the water, for the song to play as long as it would.

If I could catch sight of Blue 55 for a second, I'd have that to hang on to. I'd come for so much more, but at least I'd have something. A glimpse of his back or tail or breath right then would be like the hum of radio static against my hand. Even if I didn't feel his music, I'd know I'd gotten really close.

I scanned the waters all around the bay, back and forth, frantic. Flat waters, with the kind of stillness that must have been quiet. *Just let me see you. Let me know this wasn't all for nothing.*

No, not nothing. I touched the origami whale in my jeans pocket. At least I'd brought Grandma to the sea, and it washed away the drizzly November in her soul. She'd navigated her way through her grief. My weird, funny grandma, never content to stay in one place, who knew from the start that I should have the name of a whale. She'd never be an ordinary grandma. She was the kind who would take your hand and join you on an adventure, who had to break free like those bubbles trapped under the glacial ice. Life would never be the same without Grandpa, but we'd be all right. Grandma knew that now too.

And I'd made a good friend. I hoped we'd make it back to the *Siren* before it left port so I'd have more time with Bennie.

I'd missed seeing the whale. This whale who I knew without even meeting him, from the time I first learned his name. He'll never know that someone out there felt that way about him. Maybe he wouldn't have understood anyway, but I would have liked to have told him.

I'm sorry. I did everything I could. I'm here now.

Then I saw it, out in the waters ahead. A gray-blue whale, swimming toward me. Maybe it was another whale. There was no way to tell from where I stood on the dock.

But then, after a column of spray from the blow spout, the whale's back arched. The crescent of the dorsal fin rose above the surface, followed by the broad fluke.

There she blows.

And there, I jumped.

42

Cold water knifed my face as I dove into the bay. For as long as possible, I stayed under the surface, pushing through the water while aiming for the spot where I'd seen 55's blow spout.

My lungs screamed for me to breathe. I lifted my head for just a second and inhaled like I'd never get another breath, then ducked below the surface again. With eyes wide I scanned the waters around me for Blue 55.

I kicked the water, reaching for a growing shadow ahead, not stopping until the whale was right in front of me.

This wasn't how I'd planned to meet him, but it was happening. No picture I'd ever seen could compare to seeing the whale up close. He didn't seem quite real before, when he was just an image on a screen or a photo on my wall. I floated in the bay, staring into the whale's dark eye, impossibly small for such a huge animal. No bigger than the palm of my hand. But when I gazed into its depths, it was like 55 was showing me everything he'd ever felt and everything he'd ever seen.

He stared back. Was there recognition there? A connection? Did he have any idea how far I'd come for him?

It didn't matter anymore. We were there, together. I'd found him. He'd never know what he meant to me, but that was okay. I didn't speak his language, and he didn't need to be fixed. He was the whale who sang his own song.

We circled, studying each other. I surfaced to take a breath. The orange boat from the tagging expedition was headed in our direction. I'd have to join them soon, but I wasn't ready to leave the whale I'd been chasing for so long.

Blue 55 wouldn't need to breathe again, maybe not for another twenty minutes. He waited, hovering beside me, each time I surfaced. We were almost close enough to touch, but maybe he'd want to keep some distance. He didn't swim away; just glided around me, keeping his eye on mine. I held out my hand. Those waters were his home, and I was a guest. I'd traveled more than four thousand miles to meet Blue 55. The last few feet would be up to him.

He drifted closer, closing the gap between us, until his face brushed my fingertips. I slid my open hand alongside his body, the dark gray-blue skin. His parents had given him their colors but neither could give him their language. So he made his own.

And I'd have just a moment to share mine with his. I rested my hand on his side, then tapped out his name.

55, 55, 55.

You're a poem, did you know that?

A new poem came to me then, just as easily as if Grandpa were there signing it with me. I kept my hands in the five handshape but closed the fingers together. A good shape for ocean waves and music.

Your music sailed through the ocean
and over the land
and carried me here.
Sing your song.

I will never write down the poem. It belonged to this whale, and I'll leave it here in the sea, where it will live in the space above and below and all around him.

43

He remembered a time, one he'd tried so hard to forget. A time before he knew the loneliness.

The song he'd ached for, had searched for in the world's seas, was here. Calls like his own filled the waters around him. He didn't know this place, but the feeling it gave him, one deep in his memory, told him he was home.

The whale dove down and rose up and reclaimed every song he'd ever created and abandoned on the waves. He sang them all, right then, in a bellow of music that ripped through the ocean.

And after all the years of calling and searching, after so much time and loneliness, so many calls left unheard and unanswered, the whale thought that maybe, finally, someone was listening.

44

Sound can move anything if it's strong enough.

The bellowing song of Blue 55 traveled through me so strongly that my body vibrated like one big radio speaker. Of all the sounds in the world, this one had to be the most beautiful. I knew that without ever having heard a thing. I'd made a song for him, and he gave me his own right back. I wished I could stay right there forever, where I'd always feel the waves of that music.

The cold and the need for air were the only things that could tear me away. I grabbed for the surface, while 55's music still rippled the water. He swam back to me, nudging my side like he was making sure I was okay.

We surfaced together, then swam toward the boat. I raised my hand to wave.

Andi stood up near the front. She pointed at me as she said something to the driver. Then she turned to me, and her mouth formed the question "Iris?"

I nodded and smiled, even though I was shivering. The man tossed me a life preserver. Before grabbing on for them to pull me aboard, I rested a palm on the side of the whale's face to tell him goodbye.

Keep singing, Blue 55.

As the boat drove us toward the sanctuary building, I was thinking the cold water must have frozen my brain. It looked like my parents were waiting for me on the dock.

Frozen as I was, I wasn't hallucinating. My parents stood there, arms around each other, on the dock in front of the sanctuary, along with Grandma. I braced myself for them to lecture me about the Serious Trouble I was in. But they didn't. Certainly it would come, but they were holding it for later. Dad was the first one to wrap me in a hug.

When he let go I stepped back so he could see me. With shivering hands I signed, *"I didn't miss the boat."*

"Or the train," he added. He put his coat around me and led me inside.

"Sorry for everything," I told him. *"Am I grounded for life?"*

He nodded. *"Maybe longer."*

Totally worth it.

"Make a splash" is another figure of speech I understand better now. Usually it means to make a strong impression and to get a lot of attention. Thankfully I did make a big splash when I jumped into the water, because it caught the attention of a man on a nearby dock. He flagged down Andi and pointed me out. I didn't remember screaming when I hit the water, but apparently I did that, too.

After my email to Mom asking her not to blame Grandma for our trip, my parents had guessed that I'd gone looking for the whale. My postcard from Alaska was a bigger clue. All they had to do then was search online for news about Blue 55. They got on a plane to Oregon and drove to Lighthouse Bay, where they met Andi.

My punishment would wait until we got home. For now, they just wanted to see me and know that I was all right. And I was. Grandma and I would head back to the ship to finish the cruise, then fly home together. We promised not to take any detours.

Mom didn't say much; she mostly just held me. Now and then she pulled away to brush back my damp hair and look at me like she was making sure I was really there, before holding me again like she'd never let go. I hugged her back to let her know that was okay with me.

Andi brought me another cup of hot chocolate. That helped to warm me up, along with Dad's coat and the blankets the staff gave me. While my clothes dried I'd changed into a sanctuary T-shirt and a pair of pajama pants I had packed, after we picked up my backpack from the jetty.

I did get that tour Andi had promised, even though we weren't at her sanctuary in Appleton. The staff let her show me around and introduce me to all those animals I'd seen on the website. Computer screens in one of the offices showed graphs with wavy lines that moved up and down. They looked like the graphs I'd seen in articles about whale songs. Andi pointed out the labels for each one, showing where the hydrophones were that picked up whale songs. A line on the last graph moved up and down close to the line labeled "55 Hertz." Blue 55's graph, showing that he was singing.

Andi slid a notepad between us and wrote, *Have you thought about what you'll be when you're older?*

I shrugged. I'd always figured I'd do something with electronics but wasn't sure what that would be, what I'd do every day for a job.

All of this—Andi pointed to the computer screens—

and what you did with the song is called acoustic biology. People in that field study sounds that animals make when communicating.

I could work with sound. And whales. Like those scientists I'd read about who studied whale songs to make migration maps. I learned the song of this whale, and I will learn it for others.

Andi added, *You'd be good at it,* then crossed it out. Beneath that she wrote *You're good at it.*

Before we left the sanctuary, Dad held my hand as we stood at the window to watch Blue 55 swim throughout the bay. He would stay, or he would move on. After swimming in warmer waters for the winter, maybe he'd come back here, to this place where he'd heard his song. And he'd remember a girl who swam with him when it first played.

He and Mara, the young blue whale, might learn to communicate with each other, just a little. As she grew older Mara would look and sound more like his mother. They didn't speak the same language, but once in a while, one of them might say the right thing. They'd have that much. And that would be worth coming back for.

45

The first thing I did when I got back to school was hurry to Sofia Alamilla's room. I had to make it quick so I wouldn't be late to Ms. Conn's class. Everyone kept waving and trying to talk to me in the halls, which slowed me down.

As soon as she saw me, she stopped writing on the board and grabbed me in a tight hug. Everything I'd thought to say to her disappeared. How could I explain what she'd done for me? If she hadn't shown the Blue 55 documentary, I wouldn't have known about him. We wouldn't have found each other. He'd still be out there on his own, not knowing anyone heard him. And I wouldn't know that anyone heard me.

Sorry for missing so much school, I wrote on the board. *I'll catch up. Thank you so much for teaching me about Blue 55.*

I'm so happy you're all right, she wrote. *I hope you found what you were looking for.*

I started to write that yes, I'd found the whale and played the song for him. But Ms. Alamilla knew that. By then, the news had spread about where I'd been. She must have meant something more than the whale.

Yes, I did. I gave her another quick hug before running off to Ms. Conn's class.

Nina signed *"Welcome back"* as I slid into the room, and it wasn't that horrible. At the last second I dropped into my chair, and Mr. Charles and I signed together *"By a hair."*

So much had happened in the time I'd been gone, but I could count on Ms. Conn and her pickle face to never change.

Ms. Conn gave us time to work on our reports during class. And I needed it, with all the catching up I had to do. Since I knew so much more about whales than I had just a week earlier, I thought the report would be easy to write. Then I found there was so much to say about them, it was hard to decide where to start. I took out my notes and added what I'd learned from Sura about bubble net feeding.

As I wrote about whale communication, I kept thinking about Grandpa and what he'd told me about the sei whale that day on the beach. *A whale can't find its way through a world without sound. . . . But it's different for us. . . .*

Mr. Charles tapped my desk. When I looked up he signed, *"Are you thinking about whales or something else?"*

"Both," I answered. *"Whales, and my grandpa."*

Mr. Charles smiled. *"What would he say about the trip you took with your grandma?"*

On the flight home Grandma had asked if I'd thought about talking to my mom about going to Bridgewood. I wondered what made her think of it then. The trip didn't have anything to do with that. Did it? I didn't like the way my stomach felt when I thought about going to a new school with new people, even though we'd share a language.

Grandpa had told me I would find my way, even though it might take time to figure things out. Maybe finding your way sometimes means you can't stay where you are.

"Grandpa would want me to do for myself what I did for the whale."

46

*"She is responsible. Think of all she did, all she figured out
on her own!"*

Grandma was in the living room talking to Mom. I'd
called her and told her I'd been thinking about what
we'd discussed on the plane. I did want to go to Bridgewood. From the upstairs game room, I had a view of
the conversation if I peeked through the railing.

*"Sure, she shouldn't have taken off like that. The
whale song moved her so much she couldn't help herself."*
Grandma didn't sign *"move"* as in moving from one
place to another, though the song did that too. She
touched her heart.

Mom wiped her eyes with a tissue Grandma handed
her. *"I always felt so left out, the way you and Dad could
talk to each other, the connection you had with your Deaf
friends. Like you have with Iris now."*

"I'm sorry," Grandma signed. *"We didn't mean to leave*

you out. And no one means to leave Iris out, either. But it's happening."

"I don't want to lose her if she's around other Deaf people all the time. She won't need me anymore."

"She'll always need her mom. She's already lost, spending every day with people she can't talk to. Don't you think Iris wishes she could see that whale every day? But she didn't try to drag him back here to live with her. She helped him feel more at home."

Mom didn't argue with that. It seemed like the conversation was winding down, so I backed away from the railing and went to my room, where Mom found me a few minutes later.

"Grandma thinks you want to go to Bridgewood." She looked like she was trying to laugh a little, as if she wanted to add, *"Isn't that ridiculous?"* She also looked nauseated.

There was my chance to back out, to pretend that it was some crazy idea of Grandma's. I'd already hurt Mom so much.

But then everything would go back to like it was before. All day, every school day, with no one but Mr. Charles to talk to. The thought of going to a school where I'd know hardly anyone was scary, but it was better than the dread I'd feel about spending my next years of school like the last ones. If Blue 55 could find happiness hanging out at the sanctuary with animals he'd never met, I could be happy at a new school.

I set aside the electronics parts I was pretending to organize, and sat on my bed next to Mom. The origami whale was perched on my nightstand, worse for the wear from the swim in the bay. Grandma had remade it for me on the plane after I'd unfolded it to let it dry. She offered to make a new one on paper that wasn't faded and blurred, but I wanted to keep the one she'd made on the ship, the one that was with me when I met Blue 55.

After a deep breath I told Mom, *"I do want to go. I want to be around other Deaf kids like Wendell. People who speak my language."*

"I speak your language," she answered.

"I know, and I'm really happy you do. And that Dad . . . sort of does. But you don't have to unless you decide to. You know it's different for Deaf people. I can't keep going through the school day all alone."

"I think it'll be hard for you, starting over with so many new people."

"Every day is hard."

Mom rested her head in her hands, and I leaned over to put my arm around her. I tapped her leg so she'd look at me again. Even though it might give away that I was watching the conversation downstairs, I told her, *"You'll never lose me. I'll always need my mom."*

47

I opened a chat window and found Wendell online.

Guess what? I typed.

You hitched a ride on an African safari and you've befriended a cheetah.

Close, I answered. *I'm going to Bridgewood next year.*

Wow, really? That's awesome! So you finally talked to your mom.

Yeah. She still doesn't like the idea, but she said okay. I'm going to be nervous, though. I'll hardly know anyone.

Yeah, unlike where you are now, most popular student, class president, and all that.

I sat back and laughed. If Wendell were there, I'd throw a pillow at his head.

So how grounded are you? he asked.

Forever.

See if your parents will let you stop by sometime, he added. *My mom said I could invite you over for dinner to welcome you home. I think she was worried while you were gone, so she wants to see you too.*

Okay, I'll try. Any cool planet sightings or eclipses to see?

Not this week. But I'm pretty cool, so you should come over anyway.

Good enough. I'll stop by whenever my parents let me out of their sight.

I was elbow-deep in a radio when Tristan came in. "Ready to go?"

"Almost," I signed with the leather gloves still on. Really, the radio would take a lot more time, and some parts I didn't have yet. I'd take it back to Mr. Gunnar after fixing it. Probably.

Tristan helped me straighten up my workbench and put things away. I let him, even though he didn't know where to put everything. He set the radio on an empty spot on a high shelf I pointed out for him. The repair would wait for another day. Time to take Grandma to the beach.

Grandma and I walked the dunes to pick wildflowers for the grave of Iris the sei whale. I filled her in on how Blue 55 was doing. His tracker app showed he was still hanging around the sanctuary, though he'd swim away some-times and return later. Andi had forwarded a record-ing of the song I'd made to the staff there, and talked to the acoustic biologists about how interesting it would be to find out how Blue 55 responded to it. Through an underwater speaker in the bay, they played his song sometimes. Other sanctuaries along his route would do the same, when he swam in their waters.

An update on the Lighthouse Bay website said that he'd visited all the sea pens. Sometimes he and Mara swam together. How long would he stay? Would he return to the sanctuary every year? It was impossible to know, but it'd be fun to find out what happened.

Grandma squeezed my hand. *"You did a good thing. Thank you so much for going on the adventure with me. It was exactly what I needed. Even though Grandpa wasn't around to enjoy it, I feel like he's with me again. I think when I was that sad, there wasn't any room for him. Now there is."*

Then she told me about her new home.

"What?" I replied. *"A cruise ship? Full-time? How?"* I didn't know people could do that. Apparently she'd been looking into it. Not many people lived on cruise ships year-round, but it was possible.

"You saw how happy I was. I'll be at sea all the time. It doesn't cost much more than Oak Manor. It's just for a year. Then I'll decide what to do."

A year. So many days without Grandma around.

"Do you know my favorite quote from Moby-Dick?" she asked. "It's not the one about the drizzly November in the soul, though I like that one too. 'It is not down on any map; true places never are.' Where we traveled together isn't on any map, and I'll get to keep it with me all the time."

The wildflowers we'd left on the whale's grave rolled across the sand when a gust of wind blew. I rearranged them and stuck the stems into the sand while I thought about what to say. Grandma couldn't leave. Yes, she'd been really happy on the cruise. But a whole year away from us?

She tapped me so I'd look at her again. "And this way your mother won't worry about me wandering off. Not far to go on a ship."

"Is this because of what I said in Skagway?" I asked. "About living on a ship if you had a big win at the casino? You know I was kidding, right?"

She nodded. "I know. But after what I've done, how could I stay? Think about what it'll be like." She held up a hand, two fingers pointed at her own face.

I lifted my hands to argue with her, then let them

drop to the sand. She was right. They'd never take their eyes off her.

A few days later an envelope from Bennie arrived in the mail. She'd emailed to ask how I was doing and to get my home address so she could send me something. Inside the envelope were some photos of the cruise. One was of Bennie and me sitting on deck together, in a photo I hadn't noticed the photographer taking. I looked happy. In another that was taken from the deck below, I was by myself looking out over the water. I'd probably been wondering where 55 was and if I'd find him.

I'd give Grandma the picture of the two of us, from our first day on the cruise. She could keep it with her while she sailed to wherever she'd be during the next year.

The last picture was of Grandma performing in the karaoke bar. I tacked it to my wall. Whenever I felt sad about Grandma being away, the photo would remind me that she was where she needed to be. Not a place on any map.

48

Ms. Jackson said I could ride with her and Wendell to school. I'd do that most days, but for my first day at Bridgewood Junior High, Mom wanted to drive me.

She parked at the curb and waited while I sat there looking out the window at all the students heading into the school. Was this what I wanted? I didn't know any of those people.

But I could. I hadn't known anyone at my old school either, not really. Here, I'd have a chance.

Mom touched my arm. *"You know you can always change your mind,"* she signed after I looked at her.

"I know," I signed, even though I wouldn't change my mind.

She smiled and pointed toward the front door of the school. I turned to see Wendell, wearing his "I Need My Space" Saturn shirt and waving to me from the top of the steps.

I laughed and leaned over to hug Mom. She held me like she didn't want to let go but would do it anyway. As soon as I sat back, I threw out an *"I love you,"* beating her to it.

"You're going to do great," she signed as I opened the door.

Across the street was the elementary school, where Mr. Charles would be working. Knowing he was nearby helped me miss him a little less.

Before walking up the steps, I turned back to wave goodbye to Mom. But she wasn't looking at me. She was watching a group of Deaf students standing under a tree. I wondered what she was thinking as they hugged and signed to one another. Maybe she was seeing what I'd be able to have, what I'd be a part of now. Even though she wouldn't see me, I waved goodbye to her, then started up the steps to my new school.

A sound can move anything if it's strong enough. It can shake walls or break glass. It can knock a whale onto a new path. It can pick someone up and carry her far from home where she doesn't know anyone. The vibration of the whale song would stay with me always.

Blue 55 had found a new home. Maybe some friends. I would too.

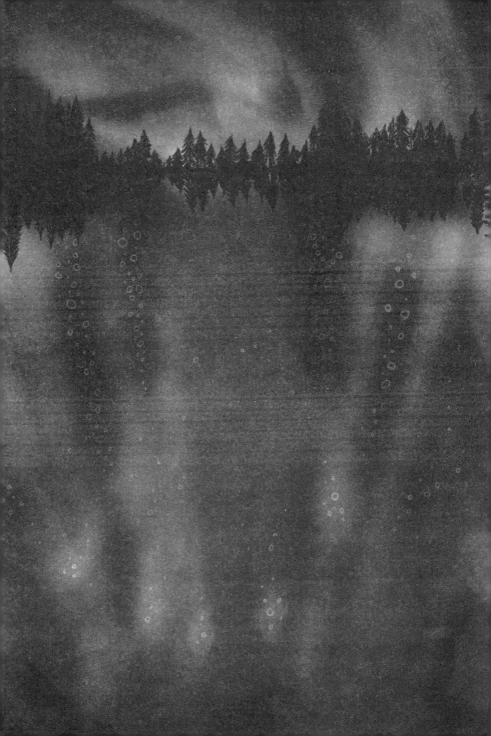

AUTHOR'S NOTE

Whale Communication and the 52-Hertz Whale

The whale in this novel is fictitious but is based on the real 52-hertz whale, also known as the Loneliest Whale in the World and 52 Blue. As of this writing, no one has met him and he does not wear a tracker. He's known only because of his unusual song. Some marine biologists hypothesize that he is either malformed in some way or is a hybrid of two species of whale. When I learned about the 52-hertz whale, I wondered about what life was like for a whale that sang like no other, and wished I could find out how he was doing.

Maybe one day someone will track down the 52-hertz whale, and we'll learn more about him and why he sings the way he does. For this story, the whale is made up of the few characteristics we know for certain about 52 Blue, plus my own imagination and what I learned from researching whales. But I also gave him a different identity. By fictionalizing the whale, I had the freedom to create his story, physical description, and song pattern. I chose the fifty-five-hertz frequency since it's close to the real whale's sound and because the repeated "five" in his name ties in with the sign language poetry in the story. Blue 55 is a hybrid of a blue and a fin whale, the world's two largest whale species. Though hybrid whales are rare, these two baleen whales are closely related enough to reproduce, and there have been a few known blue-fin hybrids.

We are able to hear the song of 52 Blue, and all whales, because of underwater microphones, or hydrophones. A hydrophone system originally used for the US military to detect enemy submarines was made available to marine biologists in the late 1980s. By using the equipment to listen to whale songs, scientists can identify and track species of whales in the oceans. In 1989, scientist William Watkins of Woods Hole Oceanographic Institution (WHOI) noticed one whale song in the North Pacific Ocean that didn't sound like any other. In some ways, the song sounded like those of blue and fin whales, with short and frequent calls. But the frequency was much higher: fifty-two hertz instead of the normal fifteen to twenty-five hertz. For humans, it's a low sound—like the lowest note a tuba can play—but it's a high one for blue and fin whales. The song would continue sometimes for hours before stopping as abruptly as it had started. For the next twelve years, Watkins and his team recorded the extraordinary song from fall to late winter, when the whale swam out of range of the hydrophones.

In addition to having a unique song, this whale has an unusual migration route. While most whales visit the same areas each year, the 52-hertz whale's path varies from one year to the next. Some years he travels much farther north or west than others, and at times he has meandering routes, wandering up and down the Pacific coast. He can swim up to forty-two miles a day, and the presence or absence of other whales doesn't seem to affect where he travels.

Of course, it's impossible to know whether or not 52 Blue is actually a "lonely whale." Another scientist who has recorded him, whale communication expert Christopher Clark of Cornell University, said in a 2015 BBC interview, "The animal's singing with a lot of the same features of a typical blue whale song. Blue whales, fin whales, and humpback whales: all these whales can hear this guy; they're not deaf. He's just odd." Dr. Clark also points out that other unusual whale calls have been recorded, and some whale populations have their own regional dialects.

Though the WHOI researchers found that the 52-hertz song was coming from only one source, more recent recordings suggest that there could be more than one whale calling at that frequency. Data from John Hildebrand of the Scripps Institution of

Oceanography shows similar calls off the California coast, in locations too far apart to have come from the same animal. Perhaps there is a small population of whales who sing at this high frequency.

The song of the 52-hertz whale has changed over the years, steadily growing lower. Whether from ocean noise or his own maturity or some other reason, he now sings at a frequency of about forty-seven hertz.

He isn't alone in changing his song. Some whale species, like humpbacks and bowheads, add new "verses" to their songs each season, sometimes picking up parts of songs from other groups of whales they encounter. Perhaps the musical complexity makes them more desirable to potential mates, or perhaps they just enjoy singing new songs. Some whale communication changes out of necessity. Noise pollution in the ocean has led some whales to change their songs over time. With constant ship traffic and oil drilling, the ocean is far noisier than it used to be. Much like people talking loudly to be heard in a noisy room, the whales have to adjust their sounds to hear one another over the other noise in the ocean.

We might never know what whales are saying, but we can keep listening.

DEAFNESS &
SIGN LANGUAGE

Around the time 52 Blue was discovered, I was discovering sign language. As a psychology major, I wasn't planning to get into the field of interpreting, but I took a sign language course as an elective. Then I took another. At the time, those two courses were all the college offered, but I wasn't finished. I started taking sign language courses taught by Deaf people, outside of school. At the end of each six-week course, I signed up for the next, and our small class would pick up where we'd left off last time. I continued that for about a year and a half, and started interpreting for some of the college's Deaf students during my last semester as a student. I moved out of state after graduating, but I knew I wasn't leaving sign language behind. What had started out as a fun elective would turn into a career and a never-ending education. My first interpreting jobs after college were in public schools, and I continued to learn more and more from sign language workshops and the Deaf people I met.

I was surprised to meet so many Deaf people whose families never learned sign language, or never learned it very well. Unlike Iris, most Deaf people do not have others like them in their families. Most deafness isn't hereditary, so about 90 percent of Deaf children are born to hearing parents, who are unlikely to know sign language. Especially in areas without a high deaf population, the sign language interpreter is often a student's only exposure to sign language and the only adult the student can communicate with.

The character of Iris came to me as the kind of person who'd be compelled to track down the lonely whale, since she's one of the many kids who go through every day feeling like she isn't heard. At the same time, it was important for me to write a character who would not wish to be "cured" but is comfortable with her deafness, and learns after her journey to advocate for herself about her own education and need for a community.

Like any group of people, the deaf population is a diverse one. The characters portrayed in this story communicate using American Sign Language, though not all deaf people do. Some prefer to speak and lip-read only, with the help of speech therapy sessions, and use hearing aids or cochlear implants to enhance the hearing they do have. Others, like Iris, prefer not to communicate orally, especially if their deafness is profound. Many Deaf people, like Iris's grandmother, may use their speaking and lip-reading skills when communicating with people who don't sign and use sign language with other Deaf people.

Giving Iris a set of Deaf grandparents allowed me to show the language and culture they share, and their connection to one another. Without those moments of joy, readers not familiar with deafness might assume that Iris wishes she could hear. The Deaf community is a strong one, and despite the isolation and frustration its members experience because of the language barrier, most wouldn't want to change their deafness, any more than the rest of us would be willing to give up our friends, language, and culture. Like everyone, Iris does wish to feel heard, and for a place she belongs.

The title of the book that Iris finds in Ms. Jackson's classroom is fictitious, but the information she reads about sign language is true. Thomas Hopkins Gallaudet traveled to France to learn about educating deaf students, then returned to the United States with Laurent Clerc, a teacher and former student of the French school. In 1817, they founded the American School for the Deaf in Hartford, Connecticut. Deaf students from all over the country attended the school, bringing with them the signs they used in their own homes and communities. These signs, combined with the French sign language used by Clerc and Gallaudet, eventually became American Sign Language. The largest population of the school's students came from Martha's Vineyard, Massachusetts, which had such a high rate of hereditary deafness that even the hearing residents regularly used sign language.

Later, more states built boarding schools for deaf students. In these residential schools, generations of students passed along sign language and Deaf culture. Though many deaf students still attend residential schools, most are now mainstreamed with hearing students in schools close to home. Ideally, they have other deaf students and teachers to interact with, but that opportunity doesn't always exist, especially in small communities.

American Sign Language is a natural language, with its own rules and grammar, rather than an invented system to represent English visually. Like spoken languages, signed languages are created by the people who use them, and they grow and change over time. They aren't modeled after a spoken language but develop independently, from interactions among a population of people. Because of this, signed languages vary from country to country and can have a very different grammar from a country's spoken language. The signed languages of England and the United States are not at all similar, even though those countries share the spoken language of English. American Sign Language has similarities to French Sign Language, though. There are even regional differences within a country, much like accents in spoken language. As with all languages, new vocabulary is added as needed, because of technological advances, for example.

Sign language involves more than just the hands. Facial expressions are an important part of ASL grammar and can compare to "tone of voice" in a spoken language. Raised eyebrows, for example, show that the sentence being signed is a yes or no question rather than a statement. Also, the space in front of the signer is important and makes sign language three-dimensional. Signs can indicate the direction someone traveled, map out the placement of buildings, or show how two cars crashed. Changing the movement or placement of a sign can completely change the meaning.

For those interested in learning sign language, it's easier than ever to find a class. Many high schools and colleges now offer sign language courses, and there are free online video courses. The best way to learn is from Deaf people who use sign language regularly, so looking for videos in which Deaf people are demonstrating the signs will provide the most accurate model of the language.

Look for an opportunity to learn this unique language—it's fun to do, it's a great skill to have, and you might meet some new friends.

Though I've interpreted in many different settings in the twenty-plus years since I started out, I still remember those first students I interpreted for. Iris and Wendell are made up of many of the funny and smart Deaf kids I've met and admired over the years who I've seen struggle to figure out where they belong. I hope I've done them, and the lonely whale, justice with this story.